RECKONING

SYN FRASER

RECKONING

ISBN: 979-8-9878556-3-8

Also By

Fallen Guardian Series:
Redemption
https://mybook.to/riLc

Solstier Chronicles:
Emerald Fire
https://www.amazon.com/Emerald-Fire-Solstier-Chronicles-Book-ebook/dp/B0CV1VK8R1

To my wonderful, and chaotic children!

Shelby, for being that amazing sounding board! You have a knack of corralling all my new ideas and inspirations.

Kiana, for the unconditional love. You're one of the best cheerleaders a mom could ask for.

Jonathon for the inspiration in which you tackle every day. Somehow you always manage to do so with a smile.

And lastly, Ethan. You've become one of the strongest supports in my life. Thank you for dragging me into the social media era!

CONTENTS

PROLOGUE

Silver moonlight illuminates the tree tops to cast deep and eerie shadows over the field. Around him, his soldiers crouch in the darkness, their breaths still. Fingers clamp against their weapons, ready for his order to advance.

Aric squints and scans the area as new lights flick on inside the old farmhouse. The tension builds until his limbs tremble and his muscles ache. Twice now, his hand drops to the familiar weight of the sword at his side.

Before he can give the command, his ears perk at a faint sound just out of sight. Peering into the shadows, he makes out Riordan's nod, drawing his attention to the back of the house. Sweat coats his skin as he lifts his hand to pat the air. The action causes his soldiers to sink lower.

Across the tall prairie grass, the screen door opens with a wail, screeching against its rusty hinges. Heavy footfalls rattle the dilapidated porch as he walks the small perimeter. *Julian.*

Aric's gaze lands on the familiar face, tanned skin, intense eyes, and stubborn jawline. The thought of their past leaves a bitter taste in his mouth. How many battles have they fought together? Now, chance brings them to opposing sides, yet he still holds fast to his orders.

Aric's heart thuds as the seconds tick by, stretching the mission into infinity. Fingers grip his sword as he holds his breath and listens for any sound that can give their position away. Riordan stays low within the grass, and Aric glances at him with a look of warning.

From inside the house, a woman's voice drifts out, humming a soothing lullaby. Once their target disappears inside, Aric exhales, his chest easing a bit.

"Careful, he will not make this easy for us," Aric hisses. Eyes track each member of the team to see who understands and responds with a nod. Together they move forward in perfect synchrony, their feet padding lightly through the field.

When they close the distance to a few yards, Aric raises a hand, signaling them to stop. Inhaling, his senses train on the house.

The cool night breeze whispers secrets through the windows. While the other members are still, he knows each one strains above the murmuring of life to identify the room they need.

Aric moves forward and gently sets his foot down on the splintering wooden porch. Under his weight, the boards moan like a sickly old man in the throes of death. There's a chance the creaking will give them away, which is why Aric sent his unskilled soldiers to the front.

Tilting his head, he listens to the surrounding sounds. The combination fills the air with a soft drone that harmonizes with the symphony of the night.

Sharpening his focus, he picks up the sound of animals hushing each other, like a whispered warning. A few disturbed leaves rustle in the bushes as the wind picks up. His body moves of its own accord, blinking once before he swings his sword free of its sheath with practiced ease. The hiss of steel is deafening in his ears.

His brothers take up positions on either side of him. Titus flexes his wings and Riordan lets a small smile slip as they take the stairs two at a time.

Kicking open the back door, the sight of Julian taking up a position in the tiny kitchen is its own reward.

"Aric?"

Even if he couldn't hear the shock in his voice, the emotions blatantly ripples over strong features. Shoulders square, wings shift as Aric takes the hilt of his sword in both hands. Riordan and Titus move to flank Julian, hands tightening on the hilts of their weapons. The motion snags Julian's burning eyes for a millisecond before he shoots Aric another stare.

"Why?"

A fresh wave of acid surges into Aric's throat as he stares at Julian. His mind scrambles for the most diplomatic response. From his position, Julian's glare is hot enough it almost sears the smirk off Riordan's face. They will discuss this moment for years, if not centuries. His heart races as he slowly and deliberately turns to Julian, holding his gaze before speaking. When he does, his voice is toneless, almost robotic. "It appears I have no choice."

Julian's response dies in his throat as the front door flies off its hinges and slams into the wall. Three tall figures in shining armor step over the threshold, weapons drawn. Julian jerks his sword free of its scabbard, the cold steel rasping as Riordan lunges. A shudder shoots through Aric's body as the clang of metal rattles off the walls.

Aric's soldiers move with precision, their muscles bunching and flexing as they advance with military-like order. A clash of metal against metal echoes through the room as Riordan fights with a viciousness that pushes Julian back. When a foot collides with Riordan's chest, it sends him toppling over the coffee table. Pushing to his feet, Riordan gives his head a shake and pins Aric with a fierce snarl. "Go! We've got him."

"No!"

Julian's desperate cry stabs through his heart like a hot poker as he tightens white knuckles on the hilt of his sword. His legs beg for him to turn around and help his friend. His mind batters at him to honor his duty. In the end, his head wins as he races up the narrow stairs leading to the second floor.

He's not fool enough to think there'll be forgiveness waiting for him once this night is over. The cold sweat that prickles his brow only confirms his suspicion.

Once his foot reaches the tiny landing, Aric tucks his wings in to maneuver the tight hall. Shoulders brush the plywood walls as his boots thump over worn hardwood floors. When his shoulder hits a doorframe on his left, he peeks inside.

The small bathroom, though clean, is free of any decoration. Ahead, not ten feet away, the only other door kicks his heart rate up.

Inside the bedroom, a metal frame on his left supports a sagging mattress. A skinny lamp decorated with butterflies casts a yellow glow on a vase of white moon flowers. Stepping through the door, Aric's size chews up the open space, causing a soft gasp from someone on his right.

Yanking his head in the general direction, he spies a wooden crib near the inner corner. Draped in creamy white fabric and simple yellow bows, the bundle inside consists of soft fleece blankets, and nothing else.

When Aric looks to the woman kneeling on the floor beside the crib, her crystal blue eyes steal the air from his lungs. Creamy, flawless skin the same shade as ivory shapes a round face and full lips. Various strands of bright russet hair fall free from the loose ponytail to frame a gentle jaw. In her arms, a small bundle sleeps, despite the events transpiring downstairs.

Though covered in a soft yellow blanket, curls similar to Julian's peek from beneath the edges. Her tiny features relax peacefully in sleep. Dark lashes rest against soft skin that radiates a serene light.

Aric's world shifts as he stares down into her cherub-like face. His breath still, he shifts from side to side as if the walls of the room close in on him.

"You're here to kill us."

Aric's eyes meet hers, and he takes in the depths of the desperation etching her face. His throat constricts at her words. Not a question, but a statement. His stomach sinks, his breathing labored. The weight of his sword is heavy in his hands, the metal cool against his skin. *You have your orders. Finish it.*

His arms shake as he struggles to lift his blade, his body revolting against his brain's commands. The reprieve he's searching for comes in the form of Julian bursting into the room.

Slamming into Aric's side, Julian knocks him back a step before gathering the woman in his arms. Pulling her to her feet, her grip on her sleeping child never falters as one arm snakes around Julian's waist. The scowl Julian stabs in his direction has the bile returning to Aric's throat.

Tucking the woman behind him, Julian steps in front of Aric, his eyes blazing. "This is wrong Aric. You know it is." The hoarseness of his voice easily reaches Aric's ears.

"I have orders."

"Fuck your orders. We were friends once. Does that mean anything to you?"

Aric heaves a heavy sigh and drags a hand through his hair. "You know it does."

"Then let us go."

From where he stands, Aric can hear his soldiers waking on the lower floor. They'll be barging into the room to finish what he can't any minute. Easing the death grip on his sword, Aric shakes his head. "They'll never stop looking for you."

"They will if they believe she's dead." Julian shoots a knowing smirk at the bundle of blankets inside the crib. His body is tight until Aric manages a nod. As if he'd sprung a leak, tension flows from him as he ushers his wife and baby toward the second-story window.

"Take her."

"Damara-"

"Julian, I'll be right behind you. I don't want her to get injured if I crash into the ground instead of landing on it." Her voice takes on a hint of desperation as she shoves the baby into Julian's chest.

Julian stares down at the bundle of blankets, his face a mask of conflicting emotions. The baby stretches with a soft grunt before she brings her knees to her stomach and settles in her father's arms. With a look that borders on gratitude and warning for Aric, he leaps out the open window. His wife follows immediately, her eyes tearful but determined.

Footfalls thunder on the stairs, matched by hurried, heavy breathing that shakes the thin walls. Aric arranges a believable lump in the blankets within the crib, then poses with his sword raised.

Killing the light with a flick of his wrist, he pins his eyes in the doorway. In the split second he spots Riordan near the threshold, Aric stabs his blade into the bundle. The manufactured light that explodes from the crib momentarily blinds all of them before it fades.

"Julian?"

"He jumped out the window with his human. I suppose the babe wasn't important enough to take with them."

"Probably knew we wouldn't stop if they took it." Riordan snickers as he leans out the window to search the field below. "Our orders are to kill him, Aric."

"*Your* orders are to kill him. Mine were to eliminate the Nephilim."

"Fair enough."

"Sir! We've spotted them a quarter mile to the North."

Aric's heart seizes as a cruel sneer blooms over Riordan's mouth and he spots the battle lust behind Titus's eyes. Schooling his features, he sheaths his sword and takes a step back. Each breath becomes painful as Riordan plans a quick but brutal strategy to intercept their target. With Julian's life at stake, Aric realizes it's time to pick a side.

"Aric?"

"Hmm?"

"I said we could use your help. Are you in?"

He turns his head towards the voice, a smile tugging at the corners of his mouth. His shoulders rise and fall in a shrug as he nods a confirmation. "Absolutely."

CHAPTER 1

Thirteen years later:

Inhale. Exhale. No one else is stopping, so just keep going. Aside from the chirp of a dozen sneakers on the gymnasium floor, the sound of her own labored breathing is the only thing Theia hears. *I'm going to die.*

Another inhale pulls in the scent of sweat and a faint trace of bleach. Her chest tightens as each step sends a stab of agony through already knotted calves. As if the Fates have bigger plans than a little adolescent humiliation, Coach Moore's whistle trills.

The ends of Theia's dark ponytail are slick with sweat as she breathes in ragged gasps. Every muscle is on fire and her heart bangs against her chest. Draining the last drops of her water bottle, she listens as the other girls collapse in a similar fashion.

When she presses her forehead against the cool rubber of the tatami wall-mat, a chill spreads through her body. After counting to ten, twice, the trembling in her legs ease. With a deep breath, she straightens and stretches. Beside her, Rhynne makes a big show of flopping to the ground in exhaustion.

"Who's idea was this again?"

"Yours," Theia pants through teeth, groaning when the muscle in her calf extends to a near-breaking point.

"That's right." Rhynne offers a lopsided grin as she shoves hair from her flushed face. "I didn't think it'd be this bad."

"They're called suicides, Rin. What did you expect?"

"I'm an idiot. Why do you listen to me?"

Theia lets out a faint laugh between deep breaths. "Isn't that what best friends do?"

"Did your legs die? I think mine are dead."

"Nope. Mine are too busy screaming to die."

When the boys ran their drill sometime earlier, Theia recalls thinking it looked fun. Now, as her legs shake and her lungs seize, she can't recall why.

A sharp whistle blast signals the end of the exercise and snaps Theia back to the present. Squealing sneakers come to a stop as the group in front of her takes a collective breath.

"Everyone warmed up?" Coach Moore bellows, a satisfied glint in his eyes betrays the punishment they're about to endure. "Take a breath. Shake it out. And head out to the track."

Looping arms, Theia and Rhynne follow the others through the side door. Every step she takes has her legs mounting a protest, but she stumbles forward. Around her, the air is alive with groans and grunts as they cross the open field.

"Ew! It's already sticky out here." Rhynne observes with a whine, her pretty face wrinkling.

Theia's chuckle, high and clear, cuts through the humid morning as she recounts the many advantages of living in the South. Towing her friend along, their feet crunch over gravel and dry grass until they reach the track.

Near the center of both groups, Coach Moore separates the girls from the boys. The whistle around his neck bounces between stern lips as he motions them to huddle closer.

"Boys are going to go first."

"Isn't that sexist, Coach?"

"No, Angela." After passing the clipboard to Assistant Coach Michelle, he pulls a black stopwatch from a pocket. "They've been sitting while you girls did your warm-up. Which means their muscles are more rested. Not everything needs to be a news article."

"That's not what my mom says."

Light brown eyes narrow under bushy brows as arms cross the bulk of his chest. "I can only imagine some things your mother might say."

"Okay girls." Coach Michelle cuts in, tucking a piece of mahogany hair behind an ear. "Take a seat."

Theia steps up on the metal bleachers, the steel already warm against her fingertips. Around her, the teenage girls' chatter, their conversations blurring together in a stream of mindless noise. After a look around, Theia takes a seat next to Rhynne and checks the time.

"How much longer is this thing?"

"Depends on how well everyone does. Why?"

"I have a biology test at nine and a German test at eleven."

The freckles on Rhynne's pert nose dance as she grins. "Some day they'll make a pill for what's wrong with you." Eyes twinkle as she gestures to the two dozen boys on the field below. "Can't you just enjoy the view like every other girl here?"

Theia's eyes track the flicking motion of her friend's hand and spots Joey Kinley. Easily the cutest boy in the entire school. His blonde curls are damp with sweat, his deep blue eyes set with determination. The arrogant smirk on his lips when he looks up to the bleachers tells Theia he's more than aware of his good looks.

"I think he has enough admirers."

"I heard my dad say he's a lock for the four-hundred again this season."

"Is that a big deal?"

"It's only the hardest race to run," Mercedes sneers over one shoulder before Rhynne can respond. "How do you not know that?"

Since the girl already faces forward, Theia swallows her retort and settles for an eye roll.

"She's extra bitchy 'cause she thinks Joey is going to ask her to homecoming this weekend." The glare Mercedes shoots back doesn't faze her friend. Then the first of five boys line up and Mercedes recovers her composure. "But seriously," Rhynne whispers, "Joey holds the time from last season."

As Coach Moore methodically calls out each boy's name, he times their laps on his stopwatch. Theia takes advantage of the temporary respite to massage her aching thigh muscles. However, the pounding in her head refuses to budge. Every raucous cheer or holler only makes it worse, as if an invisible hand tightens each nerve in her skull.

True to gossip, Joey wins the four-hundred run for their school. With a leap in the air and a pump of his arms, he incites a battle of cheers between Rhynne and Mercedes.

As Coach Michelle calls the girls forward, Theia follows with her head down and her hands shoved deep into the pockets of her shorts. Studying the grassy path beneath her feet, she tries to ignore the butterflies living in her stomach. The girls who ran for the team last season line up on the start line. Theia hangs back while searching for that spark of motivation everyone talks about.

At the line, Mercedes raises an eyebrow, her jade eyes twinkling as she flashes Joey a mischievous smile. A neon pink tank top and black shorts that hug her hips highlight her slender frame. Long, tan and tone legs appear to bunch beneath her. When the whistle blasts, she springs into action with powerful and graceful strides.

"Don't worry." Rhynne whispers with a nudge, "we won't be running against her."

"Why not?" Theia fidgets, her toe drawing patterns in the brown grass.

After a huff and an eye roll, Rhynne answers, her voice intentionally nasally. "Mercedes always runs the four-hundred. There are plenty of other races we can do, though."

Theia smooths a hand over her ponytail and checks the time again. "Fine by me. I'm only here 'cause you wouldn't stop asking."

"You're a good friend, T."

Theia grins. "I'll remind you of that when you bring up homecoming."

Laughing, Rhynne gives her a squeeze. It seems like centuries ago when the two started kindergarten. Shy and awkward, Theia stood out. Rhynne quickly took her under her wing and the two became fast friends. Nine years later, the two are inseparable.

"Well, it was this, or cheerleading."

"Even *I'm* not that good of a friend."

"You six, line up."

"Wish me luck. And if I make a fool out of myself, tell Granny to forward my mail to the all girls' home in Orlando." After glancing down the line of competitors, she opts for the far left. Every movement calculated, she tucks her body low and fills her lungs with a shallow breath.

At the whistle, Theia lunges off the line. Her muscles stretch and contract with each stride. For a moment, her senses go haywire. Beside her, girls fight for space within their narrow lanes, until Theia pushes ahead.

With every step, her breathing grows louder. Yet, in the silence, she hears nothing but her own feet hitting the asphalt. Sweat pools around her neck and runs down her back as she pushes herself harder. By the time she crosses the finish line, she's panting and deaf to the sound of anything else. Walking back to the start, Rhynne appears out of nowhere.

"Holy cow, T! How did you do that?"

"Do what?"

"T!" Rhynne cries, tugging on an arm. "You're fast."

Theia blinks, trying to recall moments of the race. Each step to the group takes an eternity as the sweat beads from her face. "I... am?" A strange numbness replaces the searing fatigue in her legs when Coach Moore claps her on the back.

"Nice time, Theia. You may be in the running for the four-hundred," Coach Michelle announces, jotting a time down on her clipboard.

"You did good, child." Coach Moore adds with another clap on the back, his eyes shining with pride before he orders the next group of girls to the line.

Shrugging off the praise with a soft "thank you", Theia attempts to blend in with the background. The daggers Mercedes aims at her and Joey's slow wink hold the prospect just out of reach. *What did I let Rhynne talk me into?*

In what seems awfully quick, the following groups finish and already walk back to join the group.

"Time to see who'll run the four-hundred this season." With a stern but encouraging expression, Coach Moore motions for Theia to step up to the line.

"That's *my* race," Mercedes snaps.

"Technically, it's mine." Coach Moore corrects his eyes hard. "Mercedes has a time of one minute and three seconds. Think you can beat her?"

"I d-don't know."

"She'd be better at the two-hundred." The voice comes from behind her as Mercedes stands at the line, stretching her long legs for a second run.

"You can do it, T!"

Theia ignores the piercing glare from Mercedes, but her stomach roils with dread as she musters a tight smile for Rhynne. *Don't puke. Do not puke.*

Taking her place at the start, she tries to swallow back the bile in her throat. Her heart pounds in her chest as she stands shoulder to shoulder with Mercedes.

Fingers dig into the hard asphalt, her legs quivering as she coils her muscles in preparation. The whistle sounds, signaling the start of the last race. Adrenaline surges through Theia's veins like a river bursting through its banks. Digging with her back foot, she pushes off with every ounce of strength, her heartbeat pulsing in her ears.

Clenching her jaw, she uses her thighs to push herself upright. Her legs wave the white flag, but the steady sound of Mercedes shoes on the track pushes her forward. Taking the lead, Theia creates a small gap as she focuses on the finish line.

Lifting her heavy feet, she trudges along. Lungs burn and muscles quake at the unfamiliar exercise. Teeth set against the pain, the heat of exertion under her skin increases until sweat trickles into the corner of her eyes. Every breath shallow and ragged, Theia fights the urge to collapse.

As she approaches the finish line, her fingers curl around her fists. Straining to keep each step even, the tightness in her legs tells her the slightest misstep will cause her to stumble. When she overshoots the finish line, she releases a silent whoop of relief. Giving up the tight rein on her body, she slows herself until she can manage a walk.

Then the cheers erupting behind her reach her ears. Turning, she observes boys and girls except for four, hoop and holler. Mercedes and her closest friends, the only somber faces in the group.

Using the tail of her shirt to wipe her face, she grins at Rhynne. Not even the icy hatred Mercedes carries can dull the thrill of beating her at something other than homework.

"Congratulations, Theia. You're running the four-hundred for Lincoln Memorial this season."

Even with the persistent drumming in her head, Theia enjoys the hurrays. *Is this why so many people fight for a moment in the spotlight? For the sensation expanding within my chest?*

"What was her time?" Mercedes steps forward, her shoulders shaking.

"Fifty-five seconds."

"How is that even possible? I want a do-over."

"Nuh-uh." Coach Moore clips tightly. "I gave you more than enough time to rest. No, do-overs. And I'll tell your mother the same thing when she calls."

"We can always use fast runners on the two-hundred."

"Oh, stuff it, Angela! I'd rather sit this season out." With a toss of her blonde ponytail, Mercedes heads for the school, friends in tow.

"Don't worry about her, T. She's just a sore loser." Rhynne mutters, pulling Theia in for a tight hug. "I'm proud of you."

CHAPTER 2

Rhynne bounces ahead of Theia, her backpack jostling with each jump. Slowing, she spins on her heel and throws Theia a mischievous smirk. "I can still see the look on her face! I swear it's seared into my brain."

Theia nods, her stomach twisting. "It was like looking in a mirror."

"I'm sure. Right before the envy sparked in her eyes. It's nice to see it on someone else's face."

"Rin."

Rhynne offers a grunt and resumes walking beside her. "But I mean... she had it coming, if you ask me."

Theia clutches the race schedule in her hand, the smooth paper crinkling. "Now, all I have to do is run like that every time." With a deep sigh, she nibbles the corner of her mouth, her heart dropping an inch.

"Coach wouldn't give it to you if he didn't believe you could."

"And you said nothing to him?"

"No way!" Rhynne shakes her head, her blonde curls bouncing in defiance. "We don't talk about the team at home. To us, he's just Dad."

"That works?"

"Must. Mom hasn't poisoned his food yet."

Theia chuckles and shakes her head, running fingers through her wild hair. She can't help but wonder what it would be like to grow up with parents. How different would her life be? Not that her grandma doesn't do her best, but sometimes the old-school mentality is hard for Theia to comprehend.

"I wonder what Granny will say," she muses aloud, folding the schedule into a tight rectangle before shoving it in a back pocket.

"Does she know you tried out?"

"I told her I had an early bio test." With a nonchalant shrug, she ambles across Mr. Randall's well-manicured lawn to round the corner for their street.

"T." Rhynne lets out a frustrated sigh, her eye roll dramatic.

"She understands nothing beyond schoolwork." Theia explains, tightening a hand on the strap for her backpack. "To her, sports are a waste of my time." As they pass a group of boys shooting hoops on the makeshift court set up in the street, the thump of the ball rings in her ears.

"Speaking for the team, I'm glad you came this morning."

"I'm sure. Now I get to watch you bat your lashes at Joey."

"Nuh-uh. I'm over him."

Theia's head spins so fast she dumps dark chocolate hair over her eyes. Shoving it back, she peers at her friend to determine what's changed. "You've been all about Joey since the first grade."

"He's a tool."

"Uh-huh. So, who's the new target?"

"His best friend, Abe." After a wink and a giggle, Rhynne steers the toddler's bicycle from the sidewalk to its yard.

"You coming over?"

"Afraid ol'granny is going to thrash you?"

"Nah. At worst, she'll ground me."

"Hm. What's today?"

"Um," Theia cants her head to one side, "Thursday."

"In that case, lead the way, oh fearless one." Rhynne hooks an arm within Theia's and steers them toward the cherry red house with apricot shutters.

While not nearly as extravagant as some of the other houses on the block, Ellie Martin keeps it tidy. Every Saturday, one of the Samuel boys cuts the lawn while her grandma works in one of the many flower beds. By the time she has a hefty pile of weeds on the ground beside her, she's located most of her gnomes and restores them to their rightful place.

Stopping at the hand painted mailbox with its bright monarch butterflies, Theia swipes up the small stack of letters before continuing up the drive to the white-trimmed porch. With summer weather starting early this year, it'll be time to touch up the chipping paint covering the sturdy wood banisters and planks. A chore entrusted to Theia for the last two years. No matter how she might try to get out of it.

Just inside, the smell of freshly baked bread greets the girls. When Rhynne's stomach grumbles in response, she offers a sheepish grin.

"So much for solidarity."

"Hey, I'm here aren't I?"

"Coming for the food doesn't quite carry the same weight." Theia laughs, kicking her shoes off at the door and setting them on the rickety wire rack.

Inside the kitchen, Granny pulls a pan of bread tins out of the hot oven. Afternoon sun streams through sheer curtains covering wide bay windows.

Under the sunlight, bright yellow walls gleam around counters full of fresh loaves of bread. Stuck to the walls about two feet from the ceiling are several plaques with cooking quotes. "Dishes taste better if you don't burn them" and "There's always room for vanilla pudding."

With her love of cooking and baking, Granny claims one half of the kitchen. The stove's four tall black legs stand in a square around the center of the room, like a gateway to another city. Beside it sits a double oven, with a myriad of small appliances littering the counters that Theia has no name for. Short spice racks rest beside the stove, two of them mussed from this week's round of bread.

In the space remaining stands a large square table covered in a white cloth with its eight matching chairs.

Stuck to the walls about two feet from the ceiling are several plaques with cooking quotes. "Dishes taste better if you don't burn them" and "There's always room for vanilla pudding." In the space remaining stands a large square table covered in a white cloth with its eight matching chairs.

As big around as she is tall, granny wipes her hands on the apron covering her clothes and takes a breath. Using the back of her hand to swipe across her forehead, she looks up with a smile to see Theia in the doorway.

"How was school?"

"Fine." Theia replies as she digs two bottles of water from the refrigerator. As her grandmother gives her a once over, she suppresses the urge to squirm. Something about Theia's appearance has her running a hand over her own white hair, features pinching.

"You look like something the cat dragged in."

"My Nan tells me the same thing," Rhynne laughs, accepting the bottle of water Theia offers. "I'm never sure if that's a compliment or not."

"Have you ever seen the sort of things a cat will drag into the house?" Granny asks as she turns to shear two thick slices from a fresh loaf of bread. "Trust me, dearie. It's *not* a compliment." Dropping the slices onto a couple of plates, she sets them on the table for the girls to enjoy. "Dig in."

"Outstanding." Scrambling to one of the empty chairs, Rhynne tackles the plate in front of her. After taking the time to lather on butter and strawberry jam, she bites off a chunk with an obnoxious groan. "Thanks Mrs. Martin."

"You're welcome," Granny murmurs as she resumes stuffing cooled loaves into empty bread bags. "How'd did your test go?"

"Pretty sure I passed." Setting her backpack next to a chair, Theia takes a seat and begins ripping pieces off her slice of bread. "The essay question was tricky."

Rhynne chokes and pours half her bottle of water down her throat before she's plants an elbow on the table. "What essay question?"

"The one about dominant and recessive genes."

"Kill me."

Theia grins. "I'm sure you'll pass just fine."

"I hope so. Otherwise, I'm off the team and you'll be on your own for track meets." As the words fall from her lips, Rhynne's face flushes. Catching Theia's glare, she averts her eyes and fidgets with the hem of her shirt. Meanwhile, the teapot whistles on the stove, sending up wisps of steam.

Granny lets out a loud sigh as she dunks her tea bag into the hot water, swirls it around and then plunks it onto a saucer. With a glance at Rhynne and Theia, her brow furrows as if to ask *what track meets*, before lifting one thin eyebrow in a silent inquiry.

Theia chokes down the bread, washing it away with a big gulp of water. Anxiously, she sits up in her chair, her ankles crossing beneath the seat. "I made the track team," she announces in a booming voice. Her grandmother blinks in surprise before pale blue eyes widen. Wrinkles around her lips deepen as if a cloud passes over them.

"Is that so?"

A chill brushes over her as she picks up on the coldness of her grandmother's curt reply. Her expression hasn't changed, but her voice drops slightly and it causes goosebumps to rise on her arms.

"Granny, I was amazing. I mean, really nervous at first, I thought for sure I was going to puke." Theia rambles, studying her grandmother for the slightest crack in her demeanor. "But then Coach told me I had a great time and they could use me to run the four-hundred meter!" Despite the hollow pit growing in her stomach, Theia's lips curve into a small smile.

"I see. So you lied this morning."

"N-no. I really had a bio test."

"So, you didn't leave early to try out for track?"

"No. I mean, yes, try-outs were before school."

"Rhynne, I believe it's time for you to head on home. Why don't you take some bread to your mother while you're at it?"

Flashing an apologetic look at Theia, Rhynne stands from the table. "Thank you, Mrs. Martin." After another look from the doorway, her friend skedaddles out the back door, leaving Theia to sit through yet another lecture.

As she waits, Theia's finger traces the lines and curves of the wood grain on the armrest. The creak of her grandmother's chair punctuates the second hand on the clock behind her. With a toothpick of anxiety inside her, Theia squirms as the tension builds like water filling a glass. Across the table, her grandmother sips her tea; the steam rising causes wrinkles to form on the old woman's face. Another shift in her chair breaks the silence with a loud squeak.

"Help me understand Theia. Am I awful to you and just don't realize it?"

"No!" The furious shake of her head sends dark curls over her eyes, forcing Theia to swipe them to one side.

"Do I appear a hostile dictator?"

"No."

"Then why on Earth would you lie to me?"

Theia shrugs a slender shoulder. "I don't know."

The force of a weathered hand hitting the table makes Theia jump. "Poppycock." The spit of her grandmother's version of a cuss word snaps her hard stare from the table, forcing her to meet her grandmother's glare. "You lied to avoid an argument. It makes your life easier, and it's the lazy way out."

"I didn't even say anything!"

"Am I wrong?"

The prospect of eating more bread when she already carries a ton of lead in her stomach has Theia shoving her plate toward the center of the table. "No."

"Okay. So what's the argument you *didn't* want to have this morning?"

"It doesn't matter. I already know what you're going to say."

"Do you? That's an interesting talent. Can you see the future as well? I'd love to win the lottery, just once before I die."

With a light scoff, Theia lifts her chin. "Sports are a waste of my time. Time I can better spend on the academics that will get me into a good college."

Ellie Martin gives her a slow to form grin before saluting her with her teacup. "Nicely done. So, if you know my opinion, what's the problem?" Setting her cup down with a clink, her grandmother folds her hands atop the table and levels a piercing stare in Theia's direction.

"There's more to life than school."

"And you think sports will fill the void you have inside you?"

Theia doesn't answer as she stares out the window into their backyard. The sunshine she walked home in dissipates as clouds roll in to bring some much needed rain. When she meets her grandmother's look, the sadness around her eyes drops Theia's heart into her stomach. "I'm sorry I lied."

"I know. But you're still calling Coach Moore and telling him you can't join the track team this year." When Theia opens her mouth to object, her grandmother lifts a small hand to silence her. "Not this year. Maybe next year."

"Next year I start highschool. Then you're going to be on me to work twice as hard."

"I'm not made of money, Theia. College is expensive. Which means scholarships."

"College is a long way off, Granny."

"Closer by the day."

With a long sigh, Theia leans back in her chair. "Fine. If I call the coach, can I go to the lock-in tonight?"

"What about school tomorrow?"

"We have the day off. Homecoming is this weekend."

"I see. If you hadn't lied, I might've said yes. As it stands, you're grounded for the next two weeks."

"Granny!"

Ellie's lips thin, her eyes taking on a serious, distant look, before she grumbles. "You think you can just waltz in here with them big blue eyes and get your way? You got another thing coming. Your mother spent her whole life trying to pull the wool over my eyes and now I'm immune."

"This isn't fair."

"Life isn't fair, little girl. It's high time you figured that out." Pushing herself away from the table, she dumps what remains of her tea down the sink and resumes stuffing loaves of bread into their bags.

Left at the table, Theia considers arguing her case, but her grandmother's set shoulders warn otherwise. Shooting to her feet before she can follow where the thought leads, she grabs her backpack and heads to the narrow stairs that lead to the second floor.

Inside her room, Theia slams the door behind her. Her breath aches around the tightness in her chest as if someone has wrapped barbed wire across it.

With a thud, her bag lands in a corner. Stumbling across the room, Theia collapses on her bed, eyes scouring until they reach the small wooden frame resting atop her nightstand. Grasping it delicately between trembling fingers, she studies the exquisite features of the woman within.

Bright red hair falls around a heart-shaped face. Soft lips form a serene smile for whomever holds the camera. Theia's own eyes hold the same deep shade of Egyptian blue, her lips the same curves. There is where the similarities end.

Damara, granny says, was renowned for her steadiness and her amiable spirit. Her heart was huge and blind enough that she fell for a man that didn't deserve her. Other than the mention of him as "that man", he lives in vague stories of him leaving before her mother passed.

She has no photos of him within her room, as if he never existed, and Theia is the result of immaculate conception.

On lonely nights when moonlight spills through her window in as a gentle caress, Theia would swear he's near; his presence a warm blanket draped across her shoulders. A flood of grief for what never was bursts from her chest like a broken dam; hopelessness lurking inside the tears that threaten to drown her.

CHAPTER 3

Tap, tap. Theia groans, her raw emotions taking up too much space in her chest as she lifts her head from the pillow. Through gritty eyes, she focuses on Rhynne's face in a window, a cheeky grin in place. In the distance, the rain clouds clear so the setting sun can paint the sky with ribbons of orange and soft pink.

With a sigh, she slides off the bed and shuffles to the window. The lead blocks her legs morph into slowing her progress. Wild hair hangs loose around her face and shoulders, so she gathers it into a ponytail and opens the window. A gentle whoosh escapes its casing as Theia pushes it high enough for Rhynne to climb through.

"Girl, what took you so long?"

Theia lowers herself to the bench under the window with a grimace. "My legs are revolting."

"Hm. Well..." with a bounce on the foot of the bed, Rhynne settles with a smile. "You'll get used to it."

"Granny says I have to quit the team."

"Why?"

"To be honest, it didn't seem like a great time to ask."

"That bites."

"I just wish I could understand why she hates sports so much. It's not like I'm going to fail my classes for a few practices and meets that happen on the weekend, anyway."

"My dad will understand, T." Rhynne nervously taps her fingers on the comforter. "We can still go to the lock-in tonight, if you want," she adds.

"Actually, I can't. Granny has grounded me for two weeks." Theia rises on stiff legs and drops across the bed beside her friend.

"I don't think Granny has ever grounded you."

The corners of her mouth twitch as memories fill her mind. "Once. When we tried hitch-hiking to Disney World after your parents canceled their trip."

"I forgot! What were we, ten?"

"Nine, I think."

Rhynne lets out a laugh, the sound echoing off the walls. "We were dumb."

Theia smiles, the memory offering a brief reprieve from her troubles. "Yeah, but it was fun."

"Do you want to talk about it?"

She shrugs a shoulder, picking at a loose thread on her blanket. "I don't know. It's just... it's hard to explain. Granny's always been strict, but it's like she's trying to control every aspect of my life."

"I get it. My mom's the same way sometimes."

"I feel like I'm not allowed to make my own choices."

"You are. You just have to deal with the consequences."

"Thanks, Rin. You're the best."

Rhynne leans closer, her voice dropping to a whisper. "And if you ever need to blow off steam and rebel a little, you know where to find me."

Theia can't contain her giggle as a spark of mischievousness ignites within her. "You mean go to the lock-in any way?"

"I was thinking more like sneaking into Mr. Stenler's pool again."

"Nah, the lock in will be more fun. And if I'm going to add to my grounding, I'm going to make it worth it."

"What's the chance she's going to come up here to check on you?"

"Slim." Theia chews on her lip as the thought builds. Checking the time bolster's her nerve. "Specially this time of night."

"So, we're really doing this?"

"Yep. Pack me a bag while I go change?"

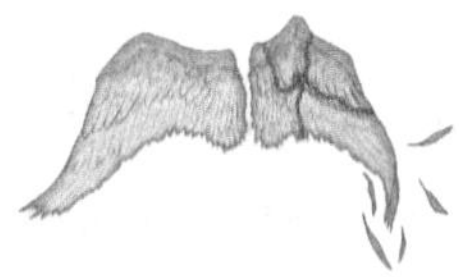

Twenty minutes later, the girls clamber down the wooden lattice, their feet muffled when they touch the dewy grass below. The sun had already sunk in the sky, painting the horizon with a warm, but twilight hue. A cool breeze sweeps past them and Theia zips up her hoodie to keep out the chill.

Rhynne takes the lead as they weave between backyards and side yards. Occasionally, they peek over fences before climbing them and step lightly to avoid crunching the gravel.

Neither speaks until they emerge on a sidewalk lining the street several houses down. After sharing a look with her friend, Theia glances back and notices an ache rising in her throat. Still, she pushes forward.

"I can't believe you came!" Marcy greets them with a bright smile as she skips down the school steps. Inside, the noise from over a hundred teens spills out onto the front lawn. "I wasn't sure someone like you did this kind of thing."

"I dragged her out for the night," Rhynne chimes in as Theia composes herself to offer a hesitant smile.

"Well, it was this or homework," Theia mumbles.

Marcy gives her a once-over and shoots her gum back into her mouth. "You're a real, like, smart kid, huh?"

"Not really. I just study."

"Gross." Marcy glances back at the school, tucking a strand of black hair behind an ear. "Are you coming in? Everyone's waiting for you."

Pausing, Theia lifts a brow. "Why?"

"There's a wager on whether you'd show after the performance you put on this morning," Marcy replies with a grin. "Thanks to Rhynne, I just won some cold hard cash."

"Don't mention it," Rhynne murmurs, giving Theia a curious look.

When Marcy hooks an arm through hers, Theia's gut tightens. There's something about the girl that unsettles her, she just can't narrow down why. Regardless, she has to physically restrain herself from shrinking away at the contact. A knowing smirk creeps on Marcy's face, as if sensing her unease.

"FYI," Marcy whispers, piercing her personal bubble when she leans closer. "Mercedes is going to blow her top when she sees you."

"Awesome." Theia grumbles, her eyes finding Rhynne a couple of steps behind them.

Rhynne's brow creases. "Because of this morning's tryouts?"

"That, and Joey's new obsession with Theia." Marcy declares with a wink as she pulls Theia through the doors.

Stepping inside the gymnasium sends Theia reeling. In a matter of hours, teens have transformed the bare room into a giant kingdom of sorts. Rows upon rows of tiny beds stand wall to wall. Surrounding them are colorful towers of pillows and blankets with an occasional stuffed animal. Frozen, Theia's heart sinks at the cramped space; her doubt growing with every second.

"Okay kids," Principal Adams begins, his business suit crisp, wingtip shoes gleaming under the bright lights of the gym. "Listen up." With the help of his trusty microphone, his raspy voice booms. After an obnoxious clearing in his throat, he tries once more to cut through the noise. "Kids, I need a moment of your time."

Despite his best efforts, the students continue to talk amongst themselves, paying him no heed. Coach Moore resorts to blowing his whistle ten times louder than any blast this morning. When the shrill shriek echoes around the room, Theia claps hands over her ears with a wince. As expected, teens freeze, turning to give Principal Adams a quick moment of attention.

Principal Adams coughs. "Thank you, Coach."

"My pleasure," the coach grunts before walking away.

Theia tenses as Marcy steers her toward a group of girls huddling around Joey Kinley. "This is my squad," she announces proudly. "Say hi girls."

One petite blonde shuffles forward with a friendly smile. "I'm Amber," she says, offering her hand.

Scrubbing a hand across the back of her neck, Theia forces a tight smile. "Hi."

"This is Nina, and that's Cara." Flashing another grin, Marcy gestures behind her. "I'm sure you already know, Joey."

"I saw you run this morning," Theia begins, flashing a shy smile. "You're pretty fast."

Light blue eyes twinkle, his smile producing dimples around his mouth. "I thought so too, 'til you ran."

Heat floods her face as Theia inspects her sneakers. One hand sweeps a dark curtain of her hair over an ear while the other adjusts the weight of her backpack.

"You have plans for homecoming?"

His question snaps her eyes back to his, barely registering his confident swagger. Swiping a damp hand along her denim-clad thigh, Theia scrambles to locate Rhynne. In the process, she catches sight of Mercedes.

As the queen bee of their eighth-grade class, she leans against a far wall, her friends close enough to bask in her glow. From where she stands, Theia spots her jade eyes narrowing at the sight of her proximity to Joey Kinley.

"There you are," Rhynne says happily, latching onto Theia's arm. "I lost you in the crowd."

Theia releases a soft sigh at Rhynne's arrival, not missing the cool, practiced smile Marcy aims at her. Though she plasters it on her face in welcome, there's a distinct tightness around her mouth that speaks nothing of friendship.

"This bag is getting heavy," Theia announces, giving Rhynne a pointed stare. "Why don't we find a place to settle down and grab something to drink?"

Cara's eyes glow a bright green when she motions to two unoccupied cots. Theia and Rhynne exchange a cautious look before setting their bags down. *This may not have been the best idea.*

While Coach Moore locks the double doors shut, trapping them inside, Theia searches for an excuse to flee back to the solitude of her bedroom. Suddenly, Joey strides forward. After he plows a hand through his hair, his tousled blonde curls as disheveled as ever, his eyes intense.

"So, what do you think?" His voice is low but sure. Theia stammers, not understanding what he's talking about until he adds, "I'm trying to ask you to go to homecoming with me."

She freezes in place, unable to comprehend the situation. After a few moments of silence, she finally manages a soft "Oh," before realizing that was supposed to be her answer. "I th-thought you'd be going with M-mercedes."

"Nah." With a soft chuckle, Joey lifts a shoulder, his eyes unwavering. "I thought I'd change it up this year."

With a million thoughts careening inside her brain, Theia struggles to latch onto one. Rhynne's helpless shrug behind him offers no clarity. Judging by the daggers Mercedes throws in her direction, going to homecoming with Joey Kinley will be the equivalent of falling into a nest of vipers. Her fingers twist in the hem of her t-shirt, as Theia tosses a glance at Joey. "I'm sorry, but I don't think I'm going this year." Her fingers tighten in the fabric of her shirt. "You should ask Mercedes."

Theia isn't sure if he'd heard her since he continues to stare at her with no sign of reaction.

Bit by bit, he comes to terms with the fact that she refused. Shoulders stiffen, his eyes glittering dangerously. She notes a small flicker of movement in his clenched fists after a twitch of his lips forms a firm line. Shifting ever so slightly, he straightens and tucks his chin in toward his chest.

"I'm thirsty," Rhynne declares lightly before taking Theia's hand and dragging her free from the situation. The two hadn't made it five steps when Theia allows her shoulders to sag.

"You're a godsend, Rin." Theia mumbles, running a hand along the kinks in her neck. "In case I don't tell you enough, I'm saying it now."

Rhynne wrinkles her nose and flashes a quick mischievous grin. "Are you kidding? I would've butchered the jig to watch someone smash that ginormous ego."

"Enormous?"

"Nuh-uh." As they approach the long table lined with finger food and drinks, Rhynne takes a moment to consider her options. "At least now I can sleep easy without worrying Mercedes is going to stab you with her nail file."

"Speak of the devil."

As Mercedes approaches with her trio of girlfriends, Theia could swear the temperature in the gym drops fifteen degrees. With a flick of her wrist, she tosses her hair over her shoulder, offering what appears to be a friendly feral smile.

"Theia, Rhynne."

"Mercedes."

"What do you want now?" After planting hands on slender hips, Rhynne studies the group of girls with a shrewd expression.

"Simply to call a truce. I was hoping we could talk and maybe clear the air." She addresses Theia without ever really looking at her. Instead, buffing bright pink nail polish on her manicured nails.

The tiny voice in the back of Theia's head warns her to keep her distance. Even Rhynne gives a quick shake of her head, but still, she agrees to accompany Mercedes out of the gym doors. They walk up the cement steps side by side until they reach the girls' bathroom. Metal stalls line the walls, like soldiers standing at attention prior to battle.

Pale green tiles form a splash of color with the harsh fluorescent light under which several sinks stand ready for the next patron. A vending machine selling feminine products rests on one wall, an anti-drug poster with an aggressive slogan beside it.

One of Mercedes's entourage, Becca, walks the length of the room, pushing doors open on each stall. Apparently satisfied, she offers a curt bob of her head. It's not until Theia and Rhynne step into the room fully that an uneasy sensation blooms in her stomach.

Assuming where this conversation is heading, Theia raises her hands and takes a step backward. "I'm not going to homecoming with Joey. I told him to ask you."

"Really?" Mercedes snarls, her face flushed. "I'm supposed to believe that?"

"It doesn't matter what you believe. It's what happened," Rhynne snaps. Before the two can slink back out the door, another of Mercedes' lackey's spins the lock into place.

"This doesn't concern you, *MoodyMoore*. Maybe you should take your *Barbie* and go home," Andrea seethes, crossing arms over her meager chest.

"Don't have to ask me twice." Rhynne answers sweetly, folding her hand within Theia's. "Let's go."

Mercedes approaches, steadily drawing closer until the two of them press against the unforgiving tiles of the wall. "Oh," she purrs. "She's not going."

CHAPTER 4

A long breath eases the lightheaded sensation growing between her ears, doing nothing for her suddenly dry mouth. "I h-have n-no," Theia swallows, "no interest in Joey." The two face off, eyes locking for a moment before Theia looks away.

Tension crackles in the air equal to heat lightning to thicken the atmosphere. The girls surround Theia and Rhynne, forming an unbreakable barrier. A spark of trepidation races across the room until beads of sweat trickle down her spine.

"I don't know where you're getting this idea that there's something between Joey and me, but I assure you, there isn't," Theia speaks with conviction, her voice ringing clear and strong through the tense silence.

One of the girls stepped forward, her expression hostile and suspicious. "Then why was Joey looking at you like that?" she challenges, crossing her arms over her chest.

The weight of their eyes on her burns through her skin, making her squirm. Clenching her fists, she lifts her chin a notch.

"Joey can look at me however he wants. It means nothing," she replied, her voice slightly higher in pitch.

"You're nothing but a liar."

"What's your problem Mercedes?" Rhynne shouts, her voice snapping.

"*She's* my problem."

Theia knows she's in trouble. She had always been shy and reserved, and the aggressive energy of the girls surrounding her is making her heart race. She can breathe in the anger and hostility radiating off of them.

"Yeah," Becca adds with a harsh nudge. "She needs to learn her place."

"Her place?" Rhynne glares. "What is this, 1950?"

"It's time someone teaches her just how *not-special* she really is," Mercedes spits, jabbing a finger in Theia's chest. She's close enough to almost stand on her toes, giving Theia a front-row seat to the stale nicotine on her breath.

"You've become a real bitch, Mercedes."

Nostrils flare as she moves to stab her finger in Rhynne's direction. "This has nothing to do with you."

Rhynne grins. "And yet, here I am."

Seconds tick by as Theia struggles to ignore her stammering heart and twitchy muscles. Teeth set, she snags another breath before releasing Rhynne's hand to raise hers in a placating gesture. "I'm not looking for trouble. And I'm not trying to take Joey away from you."

"You mean like you stole her spot on the team?" Rochelle taunts, shoving her.

Stumbling sideways, Theia's heart stops as heat pours through her body. She grits her teeth, her fingers curling into a tight ball. "I stole nothing," she whispers. "I earned that spot, fair and square."

Mercedes scoffs, taking another step forward. "Sure you did. And your little playmate being the coach's daughter had nothing to do with it."

The sight of Becca shoving Rhynne back against the wall tightens the nerves in her body. Theia blinks when an uncomfortable pressure builds within her core. As she steps between them and Rhynne, her chin notches higher and her vision narrows on the four of them.

"You don't have to believe me," Theia says, her voice dangerously quiet. "But you won't hurt Rhynne."

Her friend's hand on her back sends a wave of relief through her body. A rush of energy zips from her toes to her head, sending her pulse into triple time. Leveling a glare on Mercedes, Theia continues. "If you have a problem with losing your spot, you should've worked harder to keep it."

"Think you're tough, huh?" Mercedes snaps, her hands fisting.

Theia peers at Mercedes, the rancid breath hot on her skin. Jade eyes flare and suddenly, Mercedes's perfect skin is a mosaic of boils, splotches and red veins. She could swear even her teeth rot away in that instant, leaving a crooked-tooth grin in its place. Before Theia can fully register the sight, it's gone, and Mercedes' face is the epitome of beauty with nary a mark or blemish.

"Time for your first lesson."

Consumed by the sudden change in her appearance, Theia misses the movement in Mercedes' arm until it connects with her face. Fire erupts across her cheek and Theia battles the need to be sick on the floor. When another steps forward to shove her off her feet, her vision swims. Before she can react, blows rain down onto her unprotected body. Every punch and kick lands as white-hot lightning, searing her skin as she hugs her knees to protect her face.

Teeth clench as Theia rolls into a protective ball, her dizzy mind scrambling to process the barrage of pain. Focus is impossible against the barrage of punches and taunts.

"Stupid girl," one sneers, her and spittle spraying Theia's bare arms.

She can hear Rhynne pleading for them to stop in the background. The muffled sound reaching her ears, as if she's calling from underwater. Still, the frantic pitch of her tone fills Theia with an icy dread. Someone's foot strikes the outer shell of her ear before agony explodes in her head after crashing into the tile floor.

Growing dizzy and disoriented, Theia's shoulders throb with the spastic rhythm of her heart. Bile rises in her throat, but there's nothing left to bring up. Weight lands on her back, pinning Theia to the floor.

Extending one leg, Theia's foot catches someone's ankle to crash them into the ground beside her. In retaliation, another one yanks her up by the hair. A sharp tug dislodges the elastic holding her hair back, sending the thick mass to cascade along her shoulders.

She's helpless. Nauseated and on the brink of unconsciousness. She tries to fight, to push off the floor, but every movement flares a fresh wave of pain, making her cringe. Her body feels like it's on fire, every inch stinging and throbbing. Fighting for words in her foggy mind, Theia tries to scream for help. Thanks to the thick block clogging her throat, her voice is merely a grunt of air.

When Rhynne rushes forward to pierce their shield of bodies, someone shoves her backward, crashing her head against the metal frame of a bathroom stall. The image of her friend laying awkward and unmoving on the floor fills Theia with an uncontrollable shudder.

Even as every breath becomes a chore and she fights the temptation to curl up and hide, blood rushes in her ears. The room around her shrinks until she can see nothing but Mercedes' smug expression not three feet away.

Sweat breaks free from her pores, coating her skin as Theia forces herself to her feet. Though her legs wobble beneath her, she stands tall. An ache settles in her jaw from the pressure of her teeth clamped tight, while a strange sensation fills her chest.

Fingers twitch, and legs shake as the sensation builds. Wind whips around the interior of the bathroom despite the closed windows and serene night sky just beyond. Eyes widen in the four faces before her. Catching the blood draining from their perfect faces fills Theia with a sharp energy. Inside her, her organs vibrate and her senses center onto every detail.

Adrenaline surges into her arms and legs, bolstering the muscles until Theia's body thrums with barely contained power. Her eyes narrow as she takes in the fear and desperation etching into every feature. Each breath is a rush of air as the sensation in her chest morphs into something significant, something that's always been there but never unleashed.

Curling her fingers tightly within the palms of her hands, Theia catches the crackle of energy humming across nerve endings. The quick response in her muscles causes her to inhale sharply.

In a sudden rush of power, Theia's arms fling out to her side. A blinding white light fills the small bathroom to seep into every corner and crevice. Shielding their eyes, the four girls stumble backward to save themselves from the force radiating outward from her body. Rhynne climbs to her feet, her eyes wide, her mouth open.

After a deep breath, Theia lifts her gaze from her targets and spies Rhynne. While her expression softens minutely, the growl of her voice is inhuman, even to her own ears. "Run."

Rhynne manages a frantic nod before dashing for the locked door. Fumbling for the deadbolt with trembling hands, she shoots one last look over her slender shoulder. "What about you?"

"I'll catch up." Once the door clicks shut behind the only real friend she'd ever had, Theia laughs. A dark chuckle, full of frosty malice that causes a shiver within the girls huddling before her.

Theia fights the urge to sprint across the room as she fills her lungs with air. Bits of debris and forgotten scraps of toilet paper whip within the gale force winds tunneling around the room similar to lost feathers in a hurricane. She steps across the precipice between herself and Mercedes, her heart hammering into a furious rhythm. A pulsing pain lingers at her temples from their attack, her clothes hang in tatters, and there are clumps of hair missing from her scalp. Bristling, she approaches Mercedes, stopping when they're only inches apart. "You said something about a lesson?"

So focused on her adversary, she regards the tinkling sound of tiles falling from the wall to crash on the surrounding floor as trivial. Metal stalls that line one wall creak and groan as their frames bend and twist. Footfalls in the hall pull her focus long enough to spin the tumbler in the deadbolt, securing the door without ever touching it.

Square windows shatter within their casings, sending a barrage of broken glass into the room. As the tension grows in her stomach, a sneer curls against Theia's lips as she studies Mercedes, cowering on the floor.

"I think it's time for *your* lesson." With nothing but a flick of her wrist, Theia sends her flying into a wall with a sickening thud. When her friends rush to her side, Theia sends them in the opposite direction with another jerk of her wrist.

The furious pounding outside the door snags her gaze for a moment, the pleading tone of Rhynne's voice smothering the raging torrent within her veins.

Inhaling deeply, she wills her anger to subside. In the center of a swirling vortex of wind and debris, Mercedes stands to her feet, cradling an injured arm to her chest. When she meets Theia's hard glare, her face pales and her eyes widen in horror.

"You'll never bully another girl again," she promises, her voice deadly calm. Rolling her shoulders, she bounces from foot to foot as her chest tightens. The frenzy brewing in her gut magnifies until it rips the half-dozen mirrors from the wall. Torn pieces of the anti-drug poster float violently around her face.

Every time she narrows in on Mercedes and her clique, the squall inside her turns into a torrential storm. With little choice, Theia squeezes her eyes tightly shut.

Her chest heaves as tears prick the back of her eyes and her whole body trembles. Knuckles turn white as she clenches them into fists, her fingernails digging into the flesh of her palms. Every breath produces a shuddering sob as she grapples for control against the tidal wave of emotions that threaten to drown her. Raising one arm, she clutches frantically at the side of her head.

Powerful and scared shitless, every inch of her body tenses, as if bracing for an impact she can't see coming.

Her throat tightens until no sound can escape. Shoulders jump with the rapid movement of her breath. Emotions roll out of control inside her brain, making it impossible to home in on just one.

The realization she's lost control of the situation grips her heart with cold, dead fingers.

"Stop!"

The deep baritone of his voice serves as an icy blast. All at once, the tension leaves her body and the wind settles. Thanks to the carnage, the bathroom she's standing in is unrecognizable. On either side, tucked tight into the corners, Mercedes and her friends whimper. Behind her, a tall man steps around her to pin Theia with strange blue eyes. Speaking in a soothing and placating voice, his strange accent dances across her senses.

"You're going to hurt someone. I know you don't want that."

Wrapping her arms tight arround her waist, Theia takes a stumbling step backward. A fluttering and queasy sensation takes up residence in her stomach to contradict the sudden dryness in her mouth. Her breath hitches while lips tremble. With a gasp, she searches his face for an explanation. A furtive glance in Mercedes' direction makes her head spin. "She hurt me."

"I know." Lifting his hands, the strange man steps sideways to kneel over Mercedes' folded form. "But it's not entirely her fault." His breath hisses against teeth as Theia watches him reach in and pull an incorporeal figure from Mercedes' body.

Wriggling and squirming, it screeches with a sound sharp enough to force Theia to cover her ears. "Good evening, Aamon," he purrs, his fingers tightening on the wriggling form. When he turns his attention to her once more, his face softens visibly. "Go home, Theia. I'll take care of this." As if her hesitation is clear on her face, his voice becomes soothing. "Go on now. No one here will remember what happened."

Chewing her teeth along her lower lip, Theia rocks from side to side, her feet shuffling. Where moments before, emotions thundered within her head, a serious pounding is all that remains. Adjusting the torn pieces of her shirt, Theia runs the flat of her palm across the top of her head to smooth her hair back and nods. Speechless, she tiptoes across the littered floor to pull herself up high enough to creep through an open window frame and drop to the wet grass on the other side.

When a fresh breeze sweeps up the fat hill to draw goosebumps across heated flesh, she huddles deeper into her arms. Casting a quick look over her shoulder, Theia observes the strange man setting the room to rights, as if nothing ever happened. For the first time since she can remember, Theia can't squash the idea that something dark lives inside her.

CHAPTER 5

The effort it requires wiping away the results of Theia's meltdown drains most of his power. Teeth set, Adriel uses most of his reserves to restore the girls' minds to a more peaceful state, and steal every memory he finds involving Theia's actions.

Even as the wispy figure screams its rage, he digs deep to find the strength to finish the whitewashing. After he takes a long look from corner to corner, Adriel releases a loud exhale, spins the deadbolt to open the door, and leaves the room with a smile.

He'd done all he could do. Now it's time to move on. A sense of relief washes over him as shifts his form from the school and into the night.

The absence of stars in the sky makes the darkness even thicker as he slips into a small group of trees beyond the football field. The moment he felt the surge of power centered in the small town, Adriel acted. What he found far exceeds any of his expectations. He certainly hadn't expected to find one of his own kind at the crux of such chaos.

Melchom is going to enjoy this.

Inhaling the warm, early morning air, he searches for even a fraction of patience. Fingers flex and tighten his hold on the bodiless figure in his hand, his words short and to the point. "Where's your body?"

Empty eye sockets widen before renewing the struggle. Once Adriel tightens his fingers further to turn knuckles white, the form reconsiders its options and motions with an insubstantial arm.

With a growl, Adriel trudges through the undergrowth. Boots crunch over dead leaves and twigs for quite a while before he stumbles into a clearing. Following the direction towards a rotted tree trunk, Adriel releases his hold.

Freed, the bodiless figure flits across the night sky in a blur of motion. A chuckle falls from Adriel's lips as he closes the distance with little trouble. One knee presses into the damp earth as he reaches inside the hollow log to wrap his fingers around a solid leg. The demon's other leg kicks, his arms scrambling as Adriel drags him out of its hiding place.

Adriel's boot presses down on the demon's chest, eliciting a gasp. Desperate to get free, bony fingers claw at Adriel's jeans. Feet kicking over the ground to create small furrows in the peanut-colored soil. "Did you know?" He asks while maintaining constant pressure.

Dull blue eyes stare up at him with an arrogance he considers wiping away with the heel of his boot. Instead, he increases the weight of his foot. "Did you know what she was *before* you triggered her?"

There's a tremor in his whispers when he utters them, something incoherent and desperate. Something bobbles under the press of his boot before the demon strangles out a single word. "No."

"Did you harm her?"

"No," he croaks, spittle spraying over the smooth leather of Adriel's boot. Lips curl and he makes a mental note to toss them the moment he gets home.

"What do they call you?"

After another miserable attempt to free himself from Adriel's boot, the demon's body sags limp. "Aamon."

"How long have you been possessing that girl?" Seconds pass as the demon ponders an answer. After thirty, Adriel once more increases the pressure until it releases a high-pitch groan. "How long?"

Rattling a wheeze of air, the demon shrugs one shoulder in response.

"We'll see what Melchom has to say about all this." As if comprehending the full weight of his fuck up for the first time, its face drains of all color. Pus dribbles over his cheeks from the bursting boils on his face, tainting the fresh air around the two of them.

Latching onto one scrawny shoulder, Adriel shifts to send their forms across hundreds of miles to Melchom's condo. Pausing above the rooftop, he waits for permission before solidifying them within the pristine foyer.

Catching the sight of debris from the woods falling onto the white-oak floors, Adriel's jaw clenches. The hand he fists in the demon's shirt tightens the instant heavy footfalls approach from the next room.

The rage fuming off Melchom is tangible. Though lean, he'd be foolish to miss the traces of power rolling off him. Ink-black hair falls over a prominent brow while blue-violet eyes sharpen at the sight of Adriel.

"What is so urgent you couldn't wait for a more decent hour?"

His tone is flat as Melchom speaks in the very American dialect he'd grown accustomed to, erasing any trace of his birth. Flinging Aamon forward, Adriel takes a step back as the demon crashes onto the floor near Melchom's feet. "I found this one in Florida. A teenage girl there was under his influence for who knows how long."

Melchom lifts one dark eyebrow as he shifts his gaze to the sniveling demon before him. Clearly sensing the danger he is in, the demon shifts to his knees. More boils appear to pepper his face a moment before he sobs incoherently.

In an effort to request mercy, Aamon reaches for Melchom's feet, a mere three inches in front of him. The growl Melchom releases inspires Aamon to snatch his hand back.

Full lips curl with disgust before Melchom pins Adriel with another look. "Possession *isn't* an urgent matter."

"No, Sir. But while he was doing so, he triggered the powers of a Nephilim." Shock cascades over strong features until Melchom wipes it clean.

From where he stands, Adriel catches the sound of teeth grinding, as does the demon at Melchom's feet. With a whimper, it cowers, folding himself as tightly as possible to become small.

"Which Nephilim?"

"Theia St. James, Sir."

Melchom's roar thunders, bouncing off the glossy white walls surrounding them. The sound reverberates through Adriel's bones, his hands curling into enormous fists. Every stomp of Melchom's boots across the polished wooden floors sends tremors through the ground beneath them.

Charged with his power, the air crackles with intensity as it reaches a boiling point. When he turns to face Adriel again, flames dance around his pupils and lips thin against white-even teeth.

From his perspective, Melchom resembles every inch a beast ready to pounce. Muscles coil tight and his breath becomes ragged, as if he can barely restrain himself. It's only a matter of seconds before he unleashes his fury on the hapless victim kneeling on the floor before him.

Every inch of Melchom's tall frame visibly vibrates when he comes to a halt several feet away. Thumb and forefinger apply pressure to the bridge of his nose while he collects himself by some meager degree.

"I gave him my word. She's been under my protection for thirteen *fucking* years." Spinning on his heel, Melchom strides forward and plucks Aamon off the floor by the scruff of his neck. His body slams into the nearest wall with such force that tiny cracks appear in the plaster a heartbeat before several framed pieces of artwork crash to the floor.

"And just like that, some worthless demon in search of a joyride undoes all my work?" One large palm wraps around his scrawny neck, pinning Aamon in place under a cruel grip. Without so much as relaxing a finger, Melchom sends a sideways glare at Adriel's silent form. "Relocate her. *Now*."

"And him?"

"I'll take care of him." Melchom plows a hand through his hair, his features pinched. The air shifts around him as Adriel departs, leaving him alone with the low-ranking scum littering his floor. As messes go, he's cleaned up worse. It's the prospect of relaying his failure to Alexandria that has Melchom twitching like a crack addict in need of one good score. "Fuck!"

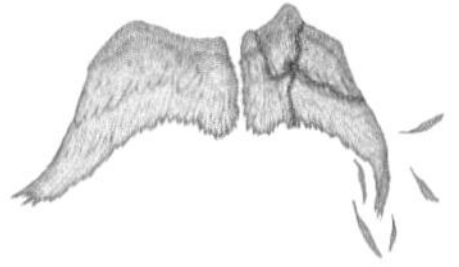

As Ellie lay in her bed, a slight breeze trickles through an open window to keep the room cool. With a groan, she rolls to her side and wills sleep to come. Closing her eyes tightly, she quiets her mind to focus on nothing but sleep, to no avail. Even if she could turn her brain off, the uneasiness in her chest demands attention.

For the hundredth time since this afternoon, Ellie considers talking with Theia. "What am I supposed to say?" She wonders aloud, as if the wind will have an answer. "It's okay to lie to me? I know you mean well?"

With another toss, Ellie settles with her back towards the window. "And what will she learn from that, exactly?" The discomfort in her chest grows until she abandons all hope of sleep. "Fine."

Throwing the covers back, she takes her time sitting up. Every joint protests with a creak as she hooks a leg to sit up on the edge of the bed. Fingers comb through the snarled knots of her white hair before she pulls the housecoat on over her nightgown.

With a shuffle of feet to the window, the cool breeze sends chills down her spine. She searches the night sky for the answers that will clear her mind. Not so much as a star twinkles back at her.

As the unease in her chest taunts her, Ellie admits there's only one person who can put her at ease. *Theia.*

It's been hours since the giggling in her room went quiet. *The poor girl is probably fast asleep in her ignorance of life's problems.* "Like I should be," she murmurs with a gentle scoff.

Against her will, Ellie's eyes shift until they land on the framed photograph gracing her dresser. Her frail hand trembles as she lifts it from its resting spot to trail a finger over the familiar lines, fondly smiling back at the image.

"She reminds me so much of you, Damara." Ellie whispers, unable to stifle a catch in her throat. "Theia is stubborn and kind. Smart as a whip, that one." The shaking in her hand jostles the frame as Ellie fights with the tears that struggle to break free. "But sometimes, I see something else in her. There's a fearlessness in her, Damara, that will be her catalyst."

Ellie heaves a sigh and with one last brush of her thumb, she returns the photo to its usual spot. Shaking the twinge from her hands, she walks from the room. She doesn't want to stop long enough to consider what she'd give to say these things to her daughter and not a colored snapshot of her face, afraid of what her answer would be. Instead, she pads barefoot out of the room and into the kitchen without looking back.

The room is dimly lit. However, Ellie maneuvers with ease as she prepares a pot of water for tea. While she waits for the water to boil, her gaze fixates on the large clay pot of forget-me-nots and moon flowers sitting in the window. After a little extra water to keep the plant happy and healthy, the teapot pierces the quiet with a shrill whistle.

Preparing a cup with sugar and a splash of honey, she fills it to the brim just as Theia bursts through the back door.

Ellie wheels around, clutching her chest. "What in Sam's hell do you think you're doing, child?"

Theia rushes into the room and slams the door behind her before collapsing to the floor, knees drawn to her chest. The prized violet t-shirt Ellie had bought last week is now almost unrecognizable, riddled with horrid tears and rips.

That Theia hides her face behind a thick curtain of hair instead of its usual neat ponytail, Ellie finds curious. Closer inspection reveals clumps of hair missing to expose patches of pale scalp underneath.

With a hand to her throat, Ellie rushes to her granddaughter's side, placing a shaky hand on Theia's quivering shoulder. "What happened, sweetheart?"

Theia responds with uncontrollable sobs that seem to erupt from a place deep within. When at last she lifts her face, Ellie inwardly flinches at the sight of such torment in her turbulent eyes. "I'm a m-m-monster!"

"What!" Ellie scans her granddaughter's face for any sort of clue why she'd think such a thing. Coming up empty, she does the next best thing. Kneeling on the floor beside her granddaughter, Ellie gathers her trembling frame close to her chest. "Hush now, Gran's got you."

She can't be sure how long the two of them sat there before Theia's sobs settle, but Ellie fears the crick in her back is now permanent. With a soft croon, she brushes hair away from the teen's face and searches her eyes. "Now, tell me what happened."

As Theia explains how she and Rhynne snuck out for the lock-in, Ellie clamps teeth over her tongue to hold the lecture at bay. When she tells how a couple of girls jumped her in the girls' bathroom, Ellie's blood boils. "I want their names. I'm calling Principal Adams first thing in the morning."

"No!" With a horrified gasp, Theia scrambles closer to the door. "You can't."

Undeterred, Ellie sits back on her heels. "I understand you think it'll make things worse, but you can't just sweep stuff like this under a carpet."

"Please, Granny." Fresh tears fill already red-rimmed eyes, threatening to spill forward. "You don't understand."

"I'm listening. Help me understand."

Other than an occasional hiccup, Theia sits quietly, lost in her thoughts. It takes more strength than Ellie could've imagined sitting there unmoving and silent until the teen's ready to talk. Somehow, she outlasts the stand off, inhaling deep as Theia lifts her chin.

"When they attacked me, I made myself small." Theia's voice is soft and tiny as she relays the rest of the events, forming another crack on Ellie's tired heart. "When they hurt Rhynne, I got hot all over."

"Theia, we've talked about this. You got angry."

"But there was this force. Inside me. Trying to get out." When Theia meets her gaze, Ellie's stomach twists from the torment staining her youthful features. "I wanted to hurt them."

The sharp dread that lands in Ellie's chest sucks the air from her lungs. She tries telling herself that force could literally mean anything, but the gnawing sensation in her gut says otherwise.

Ellie recalls when Theia came to her thirteen years ago. He'd mentioned being prepared for such things, but after so many years without so much as a blip, she relaxed. *Maybe too much.* On the off chance that she's assuming the worst, she prods gently. "What do you mean, force?"

Theia sighs and offers a meager shrug. "I don't know. I was just so hot. All I could think about was making Mercedes as helpless as I felt."

"So this force, was just you being angry?" Ellie's shoulders sag. Reaching out, she pats Theia's hand gently. "Honey, all people get angry. It doesn't make you a monster."

"Unfortunately, people like Theia can't get angry."

Ellie whirls on the floor to confront the strange voice in her kitchen. Eyes narrow on Adriel's familiar face and unique blue eyes.

Scrambling up from the floor, she pulls Theia to stand behind her. "What is that supposed to mean?"

Adriel sighs. "I warned you Mrs. Martin. I told you to monitor Theia's behavior. You promised me you would."

"It isn't her fault a bunch of girls beat the crap out of her." Ellie stiffens, her hand clutching onto one of Theia's.

"No," Adriel offers a slight shake of his head, "it's not." When he attempts to peek around Ellie's round figure, the teen shuffles further out of sight. "But if I hadn't intervened, she would've hurt those girls. Without breaking a sweat."

Ellie raises her chin. "She's not a monster."

"Of course not. I've done what I can to eliminate anyone remembering what happened. As far as school and your friends are concerned, you both moved away weeks ago."

"Moved? I've lived in this house my entire life." Ellie sputters, casting a furtive look around the kitchen. "I raised my daughter in this house."

"There are things that know Theia exists now. She won't be safe here." Adriel braces a hip against the ceramic basin of the deep sink beside him. "I'm sorry, but you have to move."

"Well, isn't that just dandy," Ellie snaps.

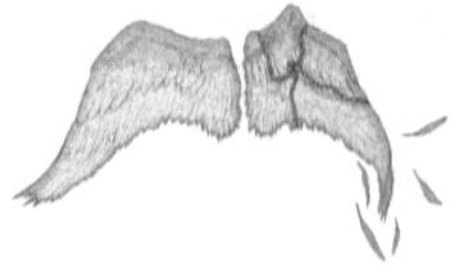

While her grandmother agonizes over what to bring with them, Theia wanders aimlessly within her bedroom. Tonight's events have upended both of their lives without so much as an apology and even after several glasses of water, she can't shake the pain in the back of her throat.

This is my fault. I did this. The sharp rap on the outside of her door stops Theia in her tracks. When it inches inward to reveal his arrogant face, Theia grinds her teeth together. "What?"

Raising an eyebrow, Adriel nudges the door open enough for him to lean against the doorjamb. "I thought you might have questions."

"Questions?" Theia scoffs. "Like who you're supposed to be? Or what episode of the Poltergeist am I living in? Do I need to steer clear of green soup in the near future?"

Despite a serious demeanor, he smiles. "They call me Adriel. The green soup thing is a myth, I'm afraid. Very cool movie effect, though, I'll admit."

"Great. I feel loads better now."

"Theia, you're not a monster. And you're not possessed."

"You mean like Mercedes was? I saw the thing you pulled out of her. That's a demon, right?" A cool breeze slides through an open window to draw goosebumps on her arms.

"You saw it?" Shock skids across a superb poker-face before he tucks it away. "Did you always see it?"

"No," with a shake of her head, Theia plops on the foot of her bed. "There was a moment this evening when I got a glimpse of something horrid, but it was only for a second."

"Interesting."

"So, if I'm not a monster and I'm not possessed, what am I?" As her grandmother laments over whether to bring her plants or her mother's china, Adriel continues to watch her with open curiosity. "You must know something."

"I know a little about a lot of things." He grins when Theia's unable to suppress her eye-roll. "I know you're special. I know while you have a lot of your mother in you, you also have a lot of your father in there, too."

The last part snaps Theia's attention back to where he stands nonchalantly in the doorway. "You know my father?"

"Only in passing. What has your grandmother told you?"

"Just that he walked out before my mother died of heartbreak. And now he's dead." Theia picks a fingernail over the pad of her thumb. When one dark eyebrow climbs higher on his forehead, Theia senses his skepticism, even as he remains steadfast in his silence. "There's more to it, isn't there?"

"A lot more. Unfortunately, we don't have the time to take a stroll down memory lane."

"Why not?"

"Because before too long, the disturbance you caused tonight is going to attract attention."

"From more demons?"

"Worse, I'm afraid."

Theia's laugh comes out as a dry sound. "What's worse than demons?"

"Angels."

If Theia had a mirror in her hand, she'd wager her expression is nothing short of comical. Sitting there, she searches for a sign he's kidding but only finds a more solemn stature than usual.

The only time Granny speaks of angels is to retell the bible versus showcasing their mercy and fierce protection. Theia can't recall her ever mentioning they'd be worse than demons. *If so, why does she continue to attend Sunday service every week at the small church in town?*

"Alright, child, I think I have everything we're going to need," Ellie announces, her eyes narrowing at the sight of Adriel in the door to her bedroom. After tossing her gaze left and right, her round frame bounces in a huff. "You haven't packed a thing."

Theia mumbles an apology and shoves herself to her feet. On autopilot, she dumps the contents of her backpack across her bed and begins shoving random items inside.

The slight frame with her mother's photo, along with several pictures she'd pinned to the wall of her and Rhynne. Next, she jams in the ragged bunny she's had for as long as she can remember. After filling it the rest of the way with several articles of clothing, she leaves just enough room for the jewelry box her mother used as a teenager. Cinching the ties tight, she slings it over one shoulder.

"You'll be safe here. When you get to town, look up this woman." Adriel says before passing her grandmother a small piece of paper. "She can help with Theia's anger. It won't be much, I'm afraid, but it should help keep her in hiding."

Ellie gives him a curt nod. After adjusting the pots of flowers in her arms, she jams the paper within the depths of her purse. "Time to go."

Theia shuffles to the door and cants her head as Adriel continues to block her passage.

"This should be enough to get you all settled. My boss is setting up a new account for you under the name I just gave you."

"Thank you," Ellie clips before reaching past him to drag Theia through the threshold. The two of them trudge through the quiet house without a word between them.

In the car, Theia squeezes her frame amongst a car heavy with items her grandmother deems too important to leave behind and sets her backpack on the floor at her feet.

From the door to the kitchen, Adriel stands silently, watching as her grandmother hurries to the driver's side of the compact car. Before she can think better of it, Theia lifts her hand in a small wave just as the car's engine sputters to life. When he responds with a brief salute, Theia averts her gaze.

Her grandmother sets the cherished plant on the armrest between them before clicking her seatbelt. Eyes trained ahead, she shifts the car into gear.

The nausea over what her grandmother is leaving behind spoils inside Theia's stomach. Tapping a finger over the hard plastic on her door, she searches for something to say. After several seconds of agonizing uncertainty, she settles on simplicity.

"I'm sorry Granny."

When pale blue eyes eventually meet hers across the dark interior of the car, the lack of blame on her tired features only adds to the nausea Theia already battles. "I know, child. It'll be alright."

CHAPTER 6

Fifteen years later:

Theia jots down her notes for the hour amidst the beeping monitors. After the scare the Thompson baby gave her department, she takes extra care to record his current state.

Once she's done initialing the records, an alarm from an isolette three units away sounds off. Before her colleague can even get up, Theia silences it and adjusts the Cooper baby.

"She dislodged the sensor again, didn't she?"

Theia grins as she fits the heart rate sensor back into place and resets the monitor. "She just likes to keep us on our toes." A glance at the clock gives her fresh energy. "Well, my shift's almost over, sweetie. Be sure you give Mary twice your effort now."

Brenda stifles her giggles with the back of her hand before picking up her notes. "She said three of them kept her shift hopping most of the night."

"They tell me it makes the shift go by faster," Theia replies with a smile.

"Hm. I'm not convinced." Brenda takes a step back and looks over Theia's shoulder. "Heads up."

Theia's nose wrinkles as she turns. The sight of baby Thompson's parents hovering just inside the unit steals a good share of the vigor she'd just located. Still, she approaches them with a friendly smile.

"We just got your little guy settled a few minutes ago." Since the father looks the most uncomfortable, Theia addresses the mother. "You're welcome to come sit with him."

"How is he?"

"He's doing good. He gave our Dr. Sinclair a test run, but all his numbers are looking very well." The news drains the stiffness from the young mother as she sags into her husband's embrace.

"I know this place can be a little intimidating." Theia leads the way to their baby's isolette one small step at a time. "We have the room dark to keep them comfortable, but there are small lights near every station should you need it."

As the parents approach the small bed for their baby, Theia spots a familiar expression of fear and apprehension she's seen a hundred times. "I don't know if the doctor spoke to you, but his bilirubin numbers are slightly elevated, so we have him under this light to bring them back down. But otherwise, he's doing very well."

"There's so many wires," Mrs. Thompson murmurs behind the hand she brings to her mouth.

"Most of them are standard. Heart rate and oxygen. We also monitor the temperature to make sure he's retaining body heat as well. Do you want to hold him?"

The brown eyes she lifts to Theia's widen into saucers. "Can I?"

"Of course you can. You're his mother." Stepping sideways, Theia gestures to the padded glider rocker near the corner of their area. "Have a seat and I'll bring him to you."

A soft tremor shoots through the mother's slight frame as she lowers herself into the rocker. His expression frozen, her husband takes position off her left shoulder, his hands in his pockets.

As Theia bundles the baby into a soft comforter, she explains the wires and their purpose. After placing the baby in his mother's arms, she takes a few steps away from their bonding moment.

"Babies know the sound of your voice. Yours too, Dad. So feel free to talk to him." While Mrs. Thompson brushes her lips across the small head of hair, her husband sinks to his knees beside her. No longer impassive, his face is a roadmap of emotions as he wiggles one finger within a tiny fist.

After a glance at the clock shows her shift all but over, Theia hovers on the border of their family time. "My shift is over, but if you need anything, Mary and Vanessa will be here all night. Stay as long as you like."

Oblivious to anything but the baby in her arms, Mrs. Thompson makes no acknowledgement. Mr. Thompson, however, rips his eyes away long enough to give her a shaky but polite smile. "Thank you."

On an exhale, Theia retreats quietly back to the nurses' station to see Brenda finishing up her notes as Marcy scrubs in near the doorway.

Gathering her things, she can't shake the image of the Thompson family from her mind. For every successful outcome, there are countless more heartbreaks, but she hopes this one has a happy ending. Something in the way Mr. Thompson looks at his son. A protectiveness that tugs at her heartstrings.

Theia exits the neonatal unit and steps into the hallway when Brenda comes up behind her.

"So, want to grab some dinner?" Brenda offers with a warm smile. "I know Billy has made a mess of the kitchen by now, and I'm dreading going home to clean it."

"I would, but I have a blind date tonight."

"Ooh? Do tell."

Theia shrugs as they round the corner to see a familiar face at the bank of elevators. As an intern, Jared spends more time here than she does, and that's saying a lot. Realizing Brenda is still waiting for juicy details, she pushes the button for the elevator and offers a sheepish grin. "Not much to tell. His name is Steven, and he works in the city. That's all I know."

"What?" Brenda frowns. "Who set this date up?"

"Vanessa."

As the elevator doors slide open, Jared laughs. "Be careful. She set me up with her cousin last week. Longest night of my life."

Wrinkles grow on Brenda's forehead. "You just had an eighteen-hour surgery two days ago."

"I know."

Theia laughs and offers a small shake of her head. "You two are dorks. I'm sure it'll be fine. If it's not, I'll bid him a goodnight."

"Uh-huh." Brenda digs in her bag for the bright pink umbrella just as the elevator reaches the ground floor and says, "Don't follow my example; take my word for it. You cannot expect one-night stands to endure the test of time."

"You love Billy."

"Yeah, but sometimes I have a hard time remembering why." When the trio reach the large glass doors, Brenda gives Theia another once over. "Where's your umbrella?"

Theia looks out at the soft rain pattering the large parking lot. "I'm just parked over there. It'll be fine."

"Okay. Don't call in sick next week. I know where you live." Brenda threatens with a friendly smile before popping her umbrella open and dashing out into the rain.

Tugging the collar up on her coat, Theia dips her head and trudges a short distance to her *has-seen-better-days* Captiva.

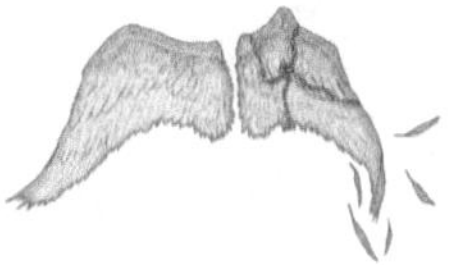

"I can't believe Vanessa didn't tell me about you sooner."

Theia stops mid-motion of pushing her cheesecake across her plate to offer a wane smile. "Vanessa is good people." *I'm going to kill her, with my bare hands.*

White table cloths cover the tables attached to booths upholstered in fine leather and smooth wood. Crystal glasses and polished silverware catch the occasional glow from fat candles to twinkle in the otherwise dim dining area. High-back chairs line a marble slab bar on her left, complete with more candles and small bowls of bar snacks.

The waitstaff dresses in dark blue uniforms with thin black ties and creased black slacks. Every male server wears their hair neatly trimmed while the ladies sport chic buns at the nape of their necks.

Around her, the patrons chatter quietly amongst themselves, their forks near silent on the square chinaware. While it's certainly out of her price range, Theia can't find fault with the establishment. If only she could say the same for her date.

"She is," Craig agrees around a bite of his triple chocolate cake. When bits of crumbs shoot out from between his lips to scatter across the tabletop, Theia struggles to keep her face impassive. "She's great people. I'm adding her to my Christmas list after tonight."

After another attempt at a polite smile, Theia nods and resumes to toying with her dessert.

"So, how long have you been a nurse, again?"

"Three years." Theia's answered the same question for him three times since dinner started, so her reply is automatic.

"That's right!" Craig's hand slaps the table, drawing several glares from the surrounding patrons. "You know, if you'd gone to school a little longer, you could've been a doctor."

Theia's smile fractures. "I actually enjoy being a nurse."

"Why? Us doctors have way more perks. Last week, I had to take my..." As he drones on with another story, Theia's mind wanders.

Next week it'll be fifteen years to the day since Granny drove them to Retirement Town, USA. Otherwise known as Northern Michigan. Theia shifts her grip on her fork to disguise the tremble in her fingers. *Fifteen years.* Most of the time, it seems like another life. Others, not so much.

Theia can still picture them clearly in her grandmother's house, still see the wraparound porch and her beautiful flower gardens. The way the sunlight danced off the windows and how the grass glistened with the morning dew in the early hours. Just like every other time, thoughts of home come with memories of Rhynne.

"Can I get you two anything else from our menu?"

Theia blinks rapidly at the sudden interruption and represses the urge to hug their server for disrupting an unhappy trip down memory lane. While Craig takes his time pondering over an answer, Theia shakes her head frantically.

Their server flashes a sympathetic smile before producing a black leather case. "I'll just leave this here," she replies with another smile before slipping away to tend to another table.

For a moment, Craig stares at the smooth black case as if it's prone to vicious attacks. Her smile brittle, Theia pulls it across the table. "How 'bout we go dutch?"

Relief cascades over otherwise mundane features. "Most women aren't so practical."

Teeth set, Theia counts to ten as she digs around in her wallet for enough cash to cover her portion of the bill. While she loved her job, it doesn't exactly leave her much for frivolous spending. As it is, her portion alone is going to cut into her grocery money for the week. "Are you okay with leaving a tip?"

"Sure."

Shoving aside her plate for the busboy, Theia stands and shrugs into her coat. Craig's voice prattles on and on as he talks about his plans for the week, giving a hint where the conversation will go next.

"Thank you for dinner. It was nice."

"I thought I'd see you get home safely."

Codeword; booty call.

After she tucks a strand of hair behind one ear, Theia loops her purse around one shoulder. "I have an early morning tomorrow."

"I see." After he tosses a couple of small bills on the table, Craig jams his wallet into the back pocket of his pants. "In that case, I'm glad we split the cost of dinner."

Her smile falters as Theia spins on her heel. While the days are still warm, the night's carry a bitter wind that whips around the corner of the building as Theia approaches her car. When the chill creeps under the tail of her coat, she digs her hands deeper into her pockets as she makes her way over to the driver's side. The hand he places on the doorframe prevents her from opening it enough to slip inside.

"I didn't mean to offend you."

Theia raises an eyebrow. "I never said you did."

Craig scrubs a hand across the back of his neck. "I didn't mean to come across as trying to get into your pants."

"I think you did."

He looks away, his smile sheepish. "Kind of failed, huh?"

"Kind of. Sometimes you need to know when to fold 'em."

"I like you Theia." After removing his hand from the door, he drags it along the back of her arm. "I think you'll be good for me, and…"

"I'm sorry, Craig. I'm not interested." Theia interrupts, then slips into her driver's seat and pulls the door shut behind her. As an afterthought, she engages the locks before starting the engine. Craig spends another minute hovering outside the door to coat her soul in crud before he wanders off to his own Bentley.

After taking a moment to replay one of Granny's lectures on manners, Theia puts the car in drive and makes the quick jaunt to the superstore closer to home.

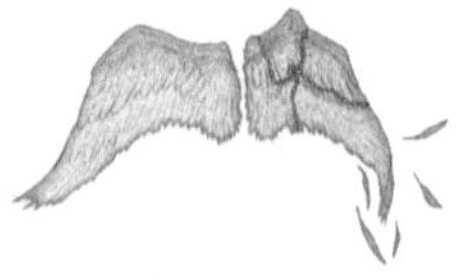

Twenty minutes and a lot of prioritizing over what she can do without this week, Theia stands in the one open line waiting to check out. Just yesterday, Brenda had been on a rant about the self-service checkouts the chain store plans to put in and the prospect of leaving people without jobs. Normally, Theia can sympathize with the little guy, but standing in line as her neighbor checks out in front of her has her reconsidering her stance.

"Please, Mom!"

"No, Simon. You don't need it."

"Jessica got new shoes," the boy whines, clutching the small frail box containing a stuffed blue dog.

"You sister needed the shoes. You don't need another toy." His mother, Theia recalls as Rachel, reminds in a patient tone as the cashier continues to scan her items.

"I'll clean my room for an entire week!" The child bargains, clutching the toy tight to his chest.

"Mom said no." Jessica declares as she leans against the side of an already full shopping cart.

"No one's asking you, snotface," her brother sneers.

"Mom! Simon just called me a snotface!"

As the second whine joins in with the first, Theia presses a thumb to her growing headache. She shifts the basket of items on her arm, her mind full of reminders of why she works with babies. The children continue to bicker in front of her as their mother trains her focus on the total ringing up on the small screen attached to the checkout lane. As the minutes tick by at an alarming rate, Theia's thumb picks over the zipper on her wallet.

"Is that everything?" With a pointed look at the small boy, the cashier's finger hovers over the total button.

Rachel sighs before perusing her cart load. "That's everything."

"Mom!" Simon wails, adding a stomp of his foot.

"I said no, Simon. Go put it back."

Simon continues to stare at his mother with a look of annoyance clouding his features. Wearing an expression she'd seen on her grandmother a hundred times, Rachel conveys a warning.

Accepting defeat, Simon crosses his arms over his scrawny chest. As if sensing Theia's gaze, he looks back with a dark scowl before poking his tongue out rudely.

"Mom!" Jessica moans as she jerks on her mother's coat before pointing a finger in her brother's direction. "Simon just stuck his tongue out at the neighbor!"

Rachel blinks once, as if seeing Theia for the first time. After a shaky smile in her direction, she bends down to chastise Simon for his lack of manners, then offers a plastic card to the cashier. Once the cart inches forward, Theia sets her small basket down on the belt.

"Kids right?" The cashier grins as he scans the first of her items.

Theia smiles a reply. Unwilling to voice the opinion blaring in her brain as her neighbor wrestles kids into their coats not ten feet from her.

A peek at the time shows Theia it's already past her usual bedtime, increasing her impatience to finish up her shopping and go home. When the cashier reads back the total, Theia scowls at the meager amount of food she goes home with. Counting out the bills, she passes them over and waits for her change.

"I'm not talking to you," Simon declares.

"Simon. Put on your coat so we can go home," his mother reasons while his older sister stamps a foot impatiently beside the cart.

"No!"

As the scene continues to unfold, Theia rubs another thumb against her skull and the headache barely contained within.

"Have a good night. Thanks for shopping with us," the cashier declares with a practiced smile as he hands her the receipt and her change.

Theia once again responds with a smile and drops her wallet in her open purse before gathering her bags and moving for the double doors near the front of the store. No sooner does she pass beyond the tall security devices when a loud blare shatters what remains of her patience.

As the alarm continues to wail, the round security guard posted to the left shoots to his feet. Hands hitch the heavy belt falling from his hips as he puffs his chest out to approach her.

"Cheese and biscuits," Theia grumbles under her breath, setting her bags down at her feet to produce the small receipt.

"I'm going to need to check your bags, miss."

With a curt nod, Theia waves a hand. "Be my guest."

The security guard, Randy, according to the blue stitching across the front of his uniform, heaves a sigh and begins rifling through her purchases.

Bushy eyebrows pinch together as he jostles the items left and right before moving onto the next bag. When he finishes with the last one, he rests thick hands on his hips and peers down at her over the bridge of his bent nose. "I'm going to need to see inside your purse as well," he declares.

One eyebrow creeps up her forehead as Theia considers his request. Already she can feel the aggravation rise to the surface like a wave until her fingers tingle with the extra sensation. *Calm down. Please calm down.*

After a deep breath, Theia opens her shoulder bag wide enough for him to search and her stomach drops when she spots the small box containing a big blue dog. *Brat!* Theia clenches her teeth and closes her eyes until the darkness around her vision disappears.

"You're going to have to pay for that."

"It's not mine."

"It's in *your* purse," he adds plainly.

Teeth grind as Theia digs out her wallet and hands him her last ten-dollar bill to cover the cost of the toy plus tax. "Keep the change," she clips, gathers her bags and exits the store.

Once she's outside in the cool night air, her pulse settles to normal. Instead of rushing the short distance to her car, Theia takes a seat on the metal bench.

Dropping the bags at her feet, she pulls the toy from her purse. After witnessing the display the neighbor kid gave, it's clear how the toy ended up in her things. Ripping the top of the box open, Theia withdraws the stuffed dog.

When the neighbor and her children finally move through the exit, Theia makes an exaggerated show of *walking* the dog along the thick slats of metal that make up the bench beneath her. Simon's initial surprise changes to murderous intent as he goes by, but his mother clasps a hand over his around the cart's handlebar.

"Serves you right," Theia mumbles, then gathers her bags and heads for her car. A small piece inside her twinges over the petty display she made, her brain already replaying one of Granny's lessons as she dumps the bags in her trunk. The rest of her dismisses it as a valuable lesson.

CHAPTER 7

Aamon creeps forward through the passageway, despite the challenge of navigating in darkness. The further he travels, the stronger the stench of sulfur and burnt hair becomes. Each inhale lodges the stink deeper within his nose until his eyes water. When screams of torment careen around the stone walls, a shiver rushes across his spine.

Not too long ago, such screams belonged to him. Never again, he vows and continues towards freedom. Rounding the next corner drops the bottom out of his stomach.

Less than twenty feet ahead, Aamon slinks deep within the nearest shadow to study the pair of demons loitering outside a narrow doorway. While one scrubs a bloody hand down the front of his pants, the other dips his head to light a cigarette.

"I thought he would've talked by now," grumbles the one on the left as he stares at his bloody hands with a murderous glare.

Beside him, his buddy takes a long drag from his cigarette. When the familiar scent of nicotine reaches Aamon's hiding place, his fingers curl in response. *How long has it been?* "Melchom said this one would be tough to crack. It's only a matter of time."

"I don't know, man." After another failed attempt to wipe the blood from his hands, the demon gives up and jams his hands into the deep pockets of his jeans. "After all that, he's given us nothing actionable."

"They all crack, Jorah." Aamon flinches with the twisted smile spreading across the other demon's face and sinks deeper against the wall.

"Yeah? Is that the reason they sent him to us?

"Unless you want to be the one to tell Melchom the incubus won't talk, we keep going."

"Why does he have such a hard-on for Eli, anyway?"

"Rumor around the upper pit is he seduced a human, and she's in hiding with his child."

Aamon covers his gasp with one grimy hand. He'd heard his own guards whisper the same thing. *Which means I've been listening to Eli's screams as I make my escape.* That realization adds a tremble to the hand clutching his mouth. He'd only met the incubus a handful of times, but Eli had been cordial every time.

"I thought Shax banned him from the human realm."

"He did," smoke curls out with the demon's reply. "But when he staged a coup with Rome, he let Eli off his leash. Got caught up with the Brennan girl."

Jorah's brow wrinkles. "I thought she sided with the angels."

"The *other* one," the demon snaps tightly. "Now she's running around with a Eli's child."

"What? Melchom doesn't have enough demons under his command?" Jorah asks tightly, casting a look behind him into the small chamber where their subject waits and recovers.

Crushing out his cigarette with the toe of his boot, the other demon offers a twisted snarl of a smile. "It isn't just another demon. It'd be a

Cambion. Those are few and far between. With one of those, Melchom would be almost unstoppable."

"Unstoppable for what?"

"Doesn't matter. Break time's over."

"Fine. This time you handle the knife and I'll ask the questions."

Once the demons disappear inside the small chamber, Aamon crawls forward. The shrill scream that pierces the air, freezes his limbs. Hands ball into small fists as he leans against the stone for balance until his breathing can settle.

"I didn't even ask him anything yet," Jorah grumbles from within.

"Just reminding him what's at stake. I won't be reporting that we failed."

Aamon chases the shudder from his legs before he inches a few feet. Someone needs to give Melchom a taste of his own medicine.

In the time it takes for Aamon to reach cool night air, he emerges with a plan. Regardless of how much time he's wasted around in Melchom's pit, he can easily recall the scent of the Nephilim's power.

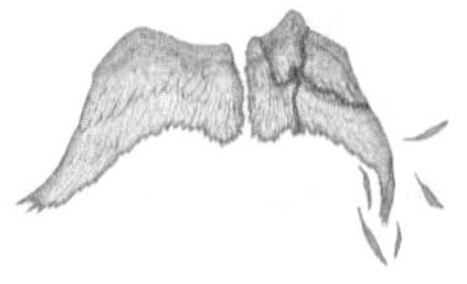

After two dead-ends, Aamon sits outside a modest house in a quiet neighborhood. Like most of the others on this street, this house is a mixture of brick and wood siding. The pale shade of sea-foam green attracts little attention nestled between houses of brighter colors. Two squares of glass jut out from two of the end walls to form barn-style windows. Inside, white blinds in every window nearly reach the bottom windowsills to prevent anyone from seeing in.

When he creeps closer, he's assaulted by the sweet stench of honeysuckle and roses coming from small flowerbeds. While her lawn is neat and manicured, it makes the untidy mess from the yard beside hers appear worse. Overgrown with both grass and weeds, it camouflages the various toys left outside by children, despite the recent deluge of rain that leaves the ground soft beneath his feet.

Inside, the Nephilim wanders from room to room, busy with what Aamon assumes is her nightly ritual. The years have added so many layers of maturity to her face and figure, Aamon fears he's stumbled across the wrong one. Then he glimpses familiar deep blue eyes to squash the doubt. He'd spent a long time in Melchom's care. It's obvious in her now adult appearance.

Still weak from countless nights of torture, Aamon doesn't entertain the idea he's strong enough to subdue her himself for long. No, he's going to need help. *That poses a dilemma.*

Unless he wants to end up like Rome, he can't risk trusting another demon with his plan. While he can't fault the demon for wanting out from under Melchom's thumb, Rome now serves as a glaring reminder of just how wrong things can go.

He won't believe me. As the tiny voice in his head needles, the words thin Aamon's lips. He's going to need proof. Any thought of an alliance rests on the credibility of his find.

Hiding within the one bush without thorns, Aamon loses track of the time until a slight breeze disturbs a small wind chime. Soft, tinkling sounds fill the quiet night, jerking him back to the present.

Inching from the bush, Aamon creeps along the shadows around the house until he finds a window not quite latched. After easing the small pane upwards, Aamon slithers through the opening to settle soundlessly on the living room carpet.

Devoid of clutter and chaos, the only piece of furniture is an overstuffed couch facing a small television. A mirror hangs on one wall, propped up by a nicked wooden stand. Jagged scratches, however, mar both mirror and stand.

Around him, the crisp scent of cleanliness lingers in the air. The effect of her power wasn't as strong while he hid outside, but inside, Aamon registers it like a punch to the gut.

Sweat gathers over dry skin as his breathing becomes labored. Swallowing beyond a parched throat, Aamon resorts to licking his lips repeatedly as he stands motionless. Rubbing a finger across his right cheek, confirms his suspicion of a fresh boil. Every survival instinct he's relied on tells him to get the hell out of here. Find a dark hole to hide for a few hundred years and hope Melchom forgets all about him.

Before Aamon can finish the thought, his pulse races and his muscles quiver. Heat rushes from head to toe as his vision swims. When he registers a slight flare of pain in his palms, Aamon relaxes the fists. The swelling within his chest pushes him to take each step across the living room towards the hall leading deeper into the house.

Aamon pauses at the first door on his right and peeks through the narrow slit of the unlatched door. His breath stills as his eyes sweep across the dark interior to the foot of the bed.

In the time he stands fixed, she tosses left and right restlessly before settling with a sigh too big for the room. One foot sticks out from the thick comforter to draw his attention to the silky smooth skin of her calf. Teeth set, Aamon shoves down the urge boiling within his stomach. Just another reminder of the time he's lost at Melchom's hands.

Withdrawing from the doorway before temptation becomes too great, Aamon looks over his shoulder to see the bathroom behind him. Changing directions, he steps into the tiny room.

Like the rest of her house, her bathroom is tidy and devoid of personal touches. White walls drown against smooth white tiles and a stark white vanity. Behind him, a clear shower curtain hangs inches shy of the floor.

Even the lace curtains hanging in front of a small window high off the floor are bare of any color.

Humans are intricate creatures, he muses. Aamon marvels over the one-of-a-kind qualities of each one. During his search, he finds nothing that offers a clue as to her personality. Hell, he couldn't even discern her favorite color unless that color is white.

"Get this over with," he mutters under his breath. Stumbling toward the sink, Aamon catches sight of himself in the flat mirror inches above the sink. Lips thin against crooked teeth as he observes his sickly complexion.

The only evidence he still lives lay in the fresh boils peppering his skin. His usual dishwater blonde hair he usually wears neat, now reaches his shoulders in dull strands. Even the tattoo's he'd decorated himself with appear aged and lackluster. The rise in his blood pressure causes several of the boils to rupture while others weep a mustard-like pus. The stench of sulfur that follows, spurs Aamon into action. Swiping the heavy brush from the vanity, Aamon jams it into his pocket and slinks out the way he came.

Outside, Aamon allows the soft drizzling rain to soothe his raw skin before he sends his form hundred of miles to the east.

Night, black like a filthy blanket covers the city below him. After he appears in an alley behind a dumpster, Aamon uses the thick shadows to make his way from street to street. The noise of passing cars, the raised voices of a couple arguing and an occasional bark of a dog slam against ears no longer accustomed to their chaos.

More than once, he senses the gaze of a human before he scurries out of sight. With any luck, if one notices his putrid appearance, they'll assume him plague-ridden and offer a wide berth. Still, the unpredictability of human nature is enough to unsettle Aamon's stomach.

His journey painstaking and hindered by shadows, Aamon reaches the designated alley and settles in a dark corner. Empty save for a few large dumpsters and several overflowing trash cans, the alley reeks of wet, moldy garbage. The intermittent whiff of blood and rotting meat reminds Aamon of his prison cell.

The filth of the city stains the walls of the surrounding buildings and sidewalk, cracked in various places. Overhead, the whoosh of cars prevents the silence from ever settling.

While he waits, his gaze lands on a young man ten feet away. One hand braces his weight against the brick building while he relieves himself. Aamon's nose curls when the rank odor of alcohol and urine reaches him.

"Hmph. I didn't think you'd hang around for me."

The amused tone comes from the narrow space behind him causing Aamon to spin and take a reflexive step backwards. His reaction produces an odd sneer across thin features. Reluctantly, Aamon tips his chin upwards to meet murky brown eyes. "W-we had a deal, Riordan."

"No. We have a meeting. Maybe that meeting will help us strike a deal," Riordan pauses while he runs a hand through hair as yellow as the field of daffodils that grew beside Aamon's house as a child. "Maybe not. I'm curious why you would offer to meet with me knowing full well my opinion of your kind."

Aamon licks his lips. "I don't trust any of my kind not to run back to Melchom."

"Ah, Melchom." Riordan releases a bored sigh. "He's a worse blight on humanity than the rest of you."

"Which is I why I came to you. We can both get rid of him with your help.

"Help? Why would I help you?"

One hand rests on the brush in his pocket. For a hot second, he considers his options. Run and hide, or stage a coup. If it's the latter, he'll need the weight of Riordan behind him. Any doubt he still harbors, vanishes with the notch of his chin. "I've located a Nephilim."

Riordan's head rears back as if Aamon had struck him. Like a bug under a microscope, he remains motionless so the angel can study him for any sign of deception. As if finding none, Riordan's jaw sets and his lips flatten, preparing Aamon for his next question. "And you expect me to believe anything you say?" One thin eyebrow lifts, his sarcasm blatant.

"No." Withdrawing the hair brush from his pocket, Aamon leans enough to offer it without having to take another step. "I brought proof."

Even as his eyes narrow, Riordan accepts the brush. Lips purse in thought as he brings it to his nose. After several deep inhales, his features pinch and crease lines appear on his forehead. "I can't smell anything but this cesspool of human waste," Riordan grumbles. Teeth snap impatiently before he produces a soft glow within the palm of his hand to illuminate their dark corner. When the dark strands trapped amongst the bristles absorb the light and multiply it to illuminate the entire alley, Riordan quickly snuffs it out.

Aamon's head stutters. "I stumbled across her years ago. Come to find out, Melchom is hiding her from you."

"Why would he do that? He has no more hope of controlling them then we do."

"I don't know." Aamon refuses to consider the hours he's wasted contemplating that very thing.

"Her name?"

"Something St. James."

Riordan stills. While he licks his lips greedily, a spark explodes inside his muddy brown eyes. "Are you sure?" Aamon's unsteady nod encourages another odd sneer from Riordan. "Where is she?"

"Do we have a deal?"

"I'm sorry, Sir. They're in a meeting."

Riordan doesn't take the time to give the angel a passing glance as he plows towards the Council's chambers. The rush of adrenaline he'd experienced after meeting the demon hasn't lost its shine. If anything, it intensifies. *They can't ignore this.*

After several failed attempts to open their eyes, Riordan shoves through the immense double doors with a grin on his face. Three similar expressions of shock greet his unexpected arrival.

Pushing himself from his chair in the center, Councilor Gregory settles the bulk of his weight with a huff. "What is the meaning of this?"

"My apologies," Riordan murmurs with a quick dip of his head. "This couldn't wait."

Councilor Rebecca eyes him around the bridge of her perfect nose, her reply cool and sharp. "This is Damien's time, Riordan. You have no right to interrupt."

When Riordan turns to scan the room, he blinks to see Damien standing not three feet away. "My apologies, brother. I'm afraid this is an emergency." Although ice-blue eyes narrow, Damien retreats from the podium. With a sweep of his arm, he motions for Riordan to take his place.

"Hmph," Councilor Gregory grunts and takes his seat once more. Seconds pass as he arranges each precise fold of his robe before resting his clasped hands atop the massive table that runs inches shy of the length of the room. "You have two minutes. Exact." He nods at the timekeeper before waving for Riordan to continue.

"I have the location of a Nephilim hiding amongst the humans," Riordan declares. The effect of his words on the three councilors vary. Rebecca's eyes squint, bunching at the corners. Gregory shoves his chair back from the table and Samuel covers his gasp with a hand.

Out of the three, Councilor Rebecca recovers first. "Are you certain? There can't be too many left."

Instead of searching for the words he needs to convince them, Riordan produces the hairbrush. Three long strides carries him close enough to drop it on their table with a thud. "See for yourself."

No longer muted by the odor of the human city, the Nephilim's scent fills the large room. At first, Riordan marvels at the clean scent of something citrus.

Then he registers a taste of what she's capable of. Though inconsequential to some, the immense power within the strands of hair trapped amongst the bristles rattles their very foundations.

Tremors cascade from wall to wall, riddling their pristine surface with minor cracks. Candle flames flicker against an invisible force only to burn brighter when it passes. The air itself pulses with furious energy to skim across his exposed skin. Scorching at first, it subsides into a soft hum of force. When the potency of her energy shifts to gush across the floor, even Riordan takes a reflexive step backwards.

"I don't understand," Councilor Rebecca begins, smoothing a finger over the small wrinkle in her forehead. "It's been centuries, how are they still so powerful?"

"This can't be the product from one of the Fallen," Councilor Samuel adds. Before Riordan can advise against it, the man sends a soft fissure of energy toward the brush. When it ricochets tenfold to blast the wall behind him, Councilor Samuel drops to the floor. "By the grace," he whispers, reclaiming his seat.

With two fingers, Councilor Rebecca removes the hairbrush, tucking it out of sight beneath the table, then pins Riordan with a hard stare. "Do we know which one it is?"

"It's the offspring of Julian St. James." Riordan allows his grin to linger a moment before he scrubs it away with the back of his hand.

"Impossible," Councilor Gregory roars, red splotches mottling his face.

Councilor Samuel leans forward to direct his attention around Gregory to Councilor Rebecca. "How can that be?"

Instead of answering her fellow Councilor, Rebecca schools her features behind a stout façade. "Someone has misled you, Riordan. Our archivist's have recorded otherwise."

"They have been misled," says Riordan, calming his heart and keeping his tone neutral. "The St. James girl is alive and under Melchom's protection."

Councilor Gregory directs his slack jaw response to the angel standing silent near the back. "Damien?"

"This is the first I've heard of it, Sir." After a shake of his dark head, Damien continues in a weary tone. "None of my spies report Melchom's involvement with something so catastrophic."

"Even if they did, you think Damien would tell you?" Riordan counters. "He's still carries loyalty for Aric."

"As do most of us." While her words are short, Rebecca's implication is clear. *Tread careful.*

"The why of it doesn't matter," Riordan insists. "It's alive."

"How have you come by such information?" Tipping forward in his chair, Councilor Gregory rests his considerable weight on the table.

Riordan's eyes flicker to the groaning supports underneath. *Wait*, his brain pleads.

"Riordan?"

"Hm?"

"I asked you how you came by this information, when we haven't heard so much as a whisper of it's existence," Councilor Gregory gripes.

Riordan swallows to buy himself a second. In his head, he saw this meeting playing out differently. While they're not dismissing his claims, they aren't lining up behind him either. When he attempts to locate his confidence from earlier, all he finds is an uneasy stomach. "A demon," he admits, expecting the chorus of scoffs he receives in response.

Councilor Gregory's lips tremble, his brown eyes wide. "You're asking us to take the word of a demon over our most respected Seraph?"

"Aric isn't the angel you believe him to be," Riordan insists. The raised pitch of his voice causes him to wince. After a cough to clear his throat, he stumbles over his next words. "Time has changed him."

"That may be," Councilor Samuel concedes. "However, that doesn't mean he blatantly defied our orders. And you lack the proof you've been searching for to say otherwise."

Riordan quiets and shifts his weight from foot to foot. *Time to change tactics.* "Regardless of who it is, it's running loose down there. We should at least attempt to bring it in."

"I agree with that much," Councilor Gregory nods, pulling a nod from Samuel as well. With an expectant look for Rebecca, Riordan spots a tightening in her shoulders.

"Fine," she snaps. "Take a team. I want it unharmed, Riordan." Her smile cools. "You have a habit of sending them to the ether before judgement. I want this one alive."

"You can't be serious!" Riordan's head spins with this recent development. "I could lose a hundred men trying to accomplish such a mission."

"Then I suggest you choose your team wisely," Rebecca all but purrs with a brief smirk. "I won't have this one silenced before we have judged it."

"Of course, you'll have our gratitude as well," Councilor Gregory adds smoothly.

"And what's that worth to me?" Hands flex into fists at his sides before he remembers to relax them. *Might as well be a suicide run*, Riordan muses.

"A promotion," Councilor Samuel answers, raising a hand against Rebecca's objection. "You've been angling for Senior Seraph for quite some time."

"Aric is our Senior," Rebecca reminds through clenched teeth.

"Aric isn't here." Councilor Gregory replies. "I know you respect him. We all do. He's served us well, but Riordan is right. We need someone that will do the job."

Graceful lines in Rebecca's face pinch, but she holds her tongue. When she aims her lavender eyes at him, Riordan struggles not to fidget. "Agreed," she mutters. "But it better be breathing when it reaches this chamber."

Riordan dips his head once more before he takes his leave. Once in the hall, he has to resist the urge to give in to his laugh. Settling for rubbing his hands together, Riordan allows himself to imagine his new title.

Regardless if it's Julian's offspring, or not, it just became his golden ticket. The promise of a future he's fought for adds a bounce to his step as he proceeds toward the barracks.

CHAPTER 8

Humming along to an Ed Sheeran song, Theia tidies up her kitchen. Even though it's smaller than the one she grew up in, it meets her needs.

Renovated by a previous tenant, the peacock blue walls compliments the stark white cabinets and maple butcher block countertops.

Though clean, the rolled white linoleum floors show their wear with cracks and tears. The small round table in the far corner has four chairs tucked around it, although only one gets any use. A small pot of moon flowers for her mother's memory sits in the rectangle window behind the sink and Granny's apron drapes over the handle of the oven to serve as Theia's only additions.

When the song on the radio changes to something more upbeat, she dances at the sink as she rinses dishes. Leaving them to dry in the rack, Theia takes a step back and inhales the yeasty fragrance of home-made bread. The mixture in the air stirs long-forgotten memories.

She was six when she helped Granny for the first time. Eleven, when she thought she could deviate from the recipe. The result was more anvil than bread. Unwillingly, her mind carries her to the last time Granny made bread in their old house. With it, comes an onslaught of emotions Theia hasn't dwelled on in years floods her system.

Mercedes. The emotions spread like venom, constricting her chest until it's difficult to draw a full breath. Each one blossoms with such a force, Theia swallows against the bitter aftertaste. With a jolt, her muscles tighten and sparks dance across her fingertips as Rhynne's face flickers to the surface.

Memories of the carefree days they spent together act as a balm against the tumultuous storm raging within. Forced to focus on something else, Theia reaches for the bread and slides two of the three loaves into bags.

Minutes later, when the emotions are still strong enough to consume her thoughts, Theia admits defeat. Sweat covers her skin in the time she takes to find the plastic bottle at the bottom of her purse. The lack of rattle when she pulls it out drops the bottom out of her stomach. *Empty? How long has it been empty?*

Spinning it over in her hand, she notes her number of refills remaining and dials the automated number to begin the process of refilling her medication. Until then, she'll need to keep a tighter rein on things. *Yeah, sure.*

Theia spends the next few minutes pushing both the memory and the emotion it inspires to the back of her mind. Dragging a hand through her dark curls, she scoops up their length into her usual ponytail. Once each breath becomes a little easier, she picks up two of the three loaves of bread, retrieves her coat, and slips out the front door. The chilly morning air that greets her saps some toxins from the negative emotions to ease the pressure in her chest.

Thankfully, the drive to Brent Haven is short enough to keep any other dark memories from surprising her. After steering her car into the near empty parking lot, she kills the engine with a sigh. Pocketing the keys, Theia walks to the front entrance, armed with fresh bread. The guard in the front office flashes a warm smile as he buzzes her in.

"Wondered if we'd see you today."

"It's Sunday, Jerry. I've been here every Sunday for over a year now."

Jerry gives her a solemn nod as he passes a clipboard under the thick pane of glass. "Sadly, we see a lot of visits wane. People get busy with their lives, you know?"

Theia returns a smile as she scrawls her name into the visitor's log. "I'm never too busy for Granny." After a wave of her hand, Theia leaves one loaf of bread for Jerry and his team before pushing through thick steel doors.

"Good morning, Theia."

Theia returns the greeting with a smile as she passes the nurses' station and turns right at the first wide hall. A chorus of random noises assault her ears the further she ventures. Families talking, machines beeping, shrill ring of phones. Theia closes her eyes and takes a long breath until, one by one, the chaos ebbs. Pressing on, the distinct stench of antiseptic becomes stronger with every step. Each inhale leaves a little more of the pungent scent in her nose.

When she spots the bright red decorations on the wall outside the next door, Thea slows her steps and moves lightly on the balls of her feet. Though the door is partially open, hope blooms in her chest when she almost clears it.

"Theia Michaels!"

Breath stills as Theia closes her eyes for a second. When a deep inhale leaves yet more antiseptic inside her nose, Theia carefully spins on her heel and peeks her head through the open door. Her smile, though tight, carries a measure of warmth for the older woman nestled in the wide recliner with a mound of blankets in her lap. "Good Morning Gladys."

"You weren't trying to sneak by me, were you?"

Nudging the door the rest of the way open, Theia hovers just inside the threshold. Fingers tap against the warm bread in her arm as she gives her head a quick shake. "Of course not. I just don't want to disturb your rest."

Gladys Munson sits a little straighter in her chair before smoothing a hand over her silver-blue curls. "Nonsense child. All we do here is rest." After taking a minute to locate the large plastic remote in her blankets, Gladys mutes the small television. "Come to see your grandma?"

"Yeah. I brought her bread."

"Well, bless your little pea-picking heart," Gladys croons. "I know your visits mean a lot to her. Pretty sure I just saw them escort her back to her room after their Sunday sermon, too."

"Sounds like I'm right on time." Theia shifts to slip back into the hall when Gladys coughs obnoxiously.

"You know, dearie, my Matthew is still single. He's about your age."

Teeth clench as Theia tamps down the roll of her stomach. "I'm not really looking for anything serious right now."

"Well, I'll have him call you in case you change your mind."

Christ. "That'd be great, Gladys. You take care," Theia adds as she jumps back into the hallway. With a metered sigh, she pulls Gladys' door shut and continues to the next one. After a soft knock, she pokes her head into the room.

A mirror opposite to Gladys' room, Granny's is big enough for a single bed, one small nightstand, a tall dresser and a wide recliner.

This week, a bright red afghan drapes over her bed in place of the yellow and orange one from last week. Setting her bundle down on the dressers' top, Theia folds the rose pink and lilac shawl draped over the back of the recliner and hangs it over the footboard of the hospital bed. Instead of the usual framed photographs that consume Gladys' room, Ellie decorates with plants.

Moon flowers blooming up from a bright purple pot, grace the night-stand while a long planter of lavender sits on the thick window sill. A round planter of ivy hangs in one corner above a new one with wide green leaves and tiny pink buds.

"Theia."

With a smile full of warmth, she turns to see Granny inch her way out of the bathroom she shares with Gladys. The red fuzzy robe with blue and green butterflies hanging on the back of the door prevents her from opening it wide enough to maneuver the walker through, so Theia rushes forward to give it a shove. "Morning, Granny. I brought you some more bread."

"You did? I thought maybe you got lost on your way to something else," Ellie says with a laugh as she makes her way to the edge of the recliner.

"You say that every week."

"Hm. Might be time to invest in a good map then, child."

Theia chuckles and takes a seat on the foot of granny's bed. "You look good this week. How's your new medication?" Despite the obvious weight loss, Granny does in fact look more rested than she had last week.

"It makes me go to the damn bathroom every five minutes!" Ellie huffs and adjusts the small green crocheted blanket across her lap. "Can't get nothing done when I spend most of my day on the damn toilet, child."

"I'll talk to your doctor," Theia replies, careful to keep her grin from staying too long. "Gladys said you went to their church service this morning."

"Gladys is a nosey old goat."

"Granny!"

"What? Can't fault me for speaking the truth." Ellie makes a show of attending to her hair in order to avoid Theia's frown. "How are you? Work keeping you busy?"

"Mostly. We have a couple of new babies in the unit."

"See?" Granny's smile tips the corner of her lips to place wrinkles in the corner of her eyes. "I told you she's a good girl."

Theia's brow furrows. "Granny, who're you talking to?"

"Hm?" Ellie casts a look around. The confusion in her eyes lands like a knife in Theia's heart. "He's an angel, dearie. Come to keep me company."

"An angel?"

"Don't you go looking at me like I'm a few cards shy of a full deck." As Ellie pins her gaze to Theia, it takes an effort not to push to her feet and run out the door. Pale blue eyes roam from the top of her head to her raggedy canvas shoes. As if sensing the turmoil still brewing in her stomach, Granny's eyes narrow. "You still taking your medication?"

"I ran out," Theia answers stiffly. "Don't worry, I'll pick up the refill tomorrow on my way to work." Even with the change in conversation, Theia makes a mental note to speak to Dr. Winter about her grandmother's advancing dementia.

"You know what Dr. Burg told you."

"I know."

"You need that medication to regulate your emotions, Theia."

"I know." Theia contemplates rolling her eyes. Since Granny would take that as a show of disrespect, she settles for a soft huff.

"Do you? How in the world did you forget to have it refilled then?"

"I just forgot. Work is crazy," Theia begins as she rushes through a series of lame excuses. "I'm fine though," she assures. "I even went on a date last night."

One thin eyebrow lifts as Granny's hands form a tight fold in her lap. "How'd that go?"

"Meh. I think dating is overrated.

"Theia."

"Granny, I'm fine. I promise. Don't worry so much. You have enough gray hair."

"Pfft." Granny grumbles. "You realize I had none before you came along?"

"Yeah," Theia grins and gives her clasped hands a soft squeeze, "so you keep telling me."

The two talk quietly for the rest of Theia's visit. By the time she's ready to head out, she notes a bit more clarity in her grandmother's eyes. Seizing the opportunity, she tries again to convince her to come back home.

"No, dear," Ellie answers with a tired voice. "I'm good here. Besides, my angel tells me you're going to have a lot on your plate soon. Don't need to add taking care of me to it."

"Your angel, huh?" *How can she seem clear one minute, and then foggy the next?* Everything she'd read on dementia said it was progressive, not erratic. *Could it be something else?* Alzheimer's would fit better and it's similar to dementia in some people. *I'll have to have another conversation with Dr. Winters.*

"Don't get snide," Ellie clips. "He's here to keep me company."

"Granny, if you come home, *I* can keep you company."

"He says I should stay here."

"And you'd rather listen to this angel than me?"

Ellie pauses for a moment, her head tilting as if straining to hear something over a crowded room. "He says I'm doing this *for* you. Not *to* you."

The sense of helplessness sinks into her bones until it drains Theia's energy to argue. She'd rather have Granny home, but she couldn't force her. As much as she'd like to, Granny is still lucid enough to make her own decisions. *Doesn't mean I have to like them.* "Uh-huh." Theia shoves herself to her feet and retrieves her purse. "I better get going. Sundays are chore day, after all."

"Before you go, can you bring me my purse? I have something for you."

After stepping around the bed, Theia retrieves the giant handbag from beside the nightstand. Her grandmother digs around in its contents for a moment, grumbling to herself before she produces a shiny purple bank card.

"This is yours. I set up an account for you to help with bills and anything else you might need."

"Granny," Theia gripes, "I don't want your money."

"It isn't my money. It's your money," Ellie insists, shoving the bank card between Theia's hands. "My angel says they can't track it either. It'll help with what you have to do."

"Help with what? Who can't track it?"

"I don't know, dear, he won't tell me that part." Shadows descend across Ellie's face, adding wrinkles to the years she's seen. "Just that it will help you."

"Granny,"

"Theia. Please take it. I'll sleep better at night knowing you have it."

"Fine." Leaning down, she brushes a kiss to her grandmother's cheek. "I'll be back next week. Call me if you need anything."

"Don't worry about me. I'm doing well right where I'm at."

Later that night, as Theia lays in bed, her mind drifts back to her conversation with Granny. When they'd first gotten a diagnosis of dementia, Theia had done a deep dive into all the different types, but none of them really fit that well.

While Granny had difficulty recalling recent things, she can recite her past with the sharpness of a tack. She never misplaced money, or became confused about the present. Despite this recent sign of an imaginary friend, Theia still is unconvinced that what her grandmother suffers from is, in fact, dementia.

Huffing out a puff of air, Theia flops onto her back. The faint glow of a waning moon creates an ethereal battle with the shadows of night. As her toe brushes against the cool, smooth sheets, she wills sleep to come. The fingertip she traces along the blue flowers intricately stitched into her pillowcase does nothing to slow her breathing. Orange glowing numbers on her bedside clock show the time to be well after midnight. If she doesn't get some sleep, she'll never make it through her next shift.

When Theia turns her head and squeezes her eyes shut, memories flood her mind of the baby they'd just gotten in the NICU. The parents' fear and apprehension at the sight of their fragile son hit a nerve in her. *Is that how her mother felt when Theia was born? Had her father ever felt that way about her?*

Granny never said how long he actually stuck around, but since Theia's been with her since she was a few months old, she figures it wasn't very long. Exchanging the air in her lungs, she attempts to push those nagging thoughts aside, but sleep remains elusive.

With a groan, she kicks off the blue and purple quilt and pads along the dark hall to her small kitchen. After putting the kettle on the stove to boil, she grabs a mug and rummages through her tea collection. Chamomile, lavender, peppermint. None of them seem to fit her mood. After finally settling on a raspberry blend, Theia stares out her kitchen window while she waits for the water to boil.

The city, though small compared to some, is never truly quiet. At this hour, however, it's at least manageable. The lights of buildings flicker in the distance while she watches the silhouettes of people move about their lives. She wonders what their stories are and what struggles they face. It's a welcome distraction from her own thoughts.

When the kettle whistles, Theia pours hot water over the tea bag and lets it steep for an extra kick. Instantly, the sweet aroma fills the kitchen, and she takes a deep breath.

Walking carefully, she settles in one of the mismatched chairs at the round table. Steam rises from the mug, warming her hands as she takes a sip. Seconds tick by as the tension in her body eases. While the baby in the NICU still weighs on her mind, Theia knows she needs to let it go. "It'll consume you if you let it," she whispers, recalling the conversation she'd had while still in nursing school.

Finishing her tea, Theia heads back to her bedroom. As she climbs under the heavy quilt, the warmth from her tea leaves her sleepy. Focusing on the rise and fall of her chest, Theia sinks under the weight of sleep. Just as her breathing slows, a trickle of awareness skips across her skin.

CHAPTER 9

Theia's muscles tense as she attempts to pinpoint the cause of her racing heart. Her fingers curl within her quilt as she listens for any noise in her home. There's nothing: no jarring sound of a lock being picked, nor the uneasy creak of a door opening or window breaking. However, rather than calming down with the silence, it only heightens her nerves.

A shiver runs down her back as she silently creeps out of bed and tiptoes through the modest house, her heart pounding in her chest. Her eyes scan each room for any sign of an intruder, but everything appears to be in place. She breathes a small sigh of relief, figuring she's probably just being paranoid.

But then, a faint rustling sound from the direction of the living room catches her attention, and she freezes. Could it be the wind knocking something over, or something more sinister?

Gingerly, she approaches the window, peering out into the darkness beyond. The streetlights cast long shadows, and for a moment she spots something moving, just beyond the reach of the light. She squints, trying to make out the shape, but it's too far away.

Suddenly, a loud bang echoes through the room, causing Theia to jump back. She whips around, searching frantically for the source of the noise, blinking to register the broken remnants of her door. The tall figure that strides into her living room comes armed with weapons and wings. *Wings?*

"Hello, Theia," a low voice growls. "I've been waiting to meet you." As he dwarfs her living room, two more men cross the shattered threshold to flank him.

Theia's back hits a wall as she retreats, her lungs seizing. "Who... who are you?" She stammers, her voice never reaching beyond a whisper.

After a quick smirk, the man in the center executes a deep bow. "I'm Riordan. They sent me to bring you in."

"Who's they," she asks as she skirts to her left to put the couch between her and her intruders. Damp spring air trickles along the floor to brush over bare skin.

"Heaven," Riordan replies with a sneer, his tone edging on boredom. "I'm sure if you give up your father's location, the Council will show you mercy."

"M-my father?" Fingers twist in the loose tail of her oversized t-shirt as Theia's mind races with questions. "He's dead." From her position, she has a front-row seat to view all pretense of cordiality drain from his face. Murky eyes narrow a fraction before he launches himself across the gap to wrap a hand around her throat.

With a gasp, Theia's eyes round as her fingers claw against his grip. When he slams her hard enough into a wall to crack plaster, her struggle for air increases tenfold. Her feet kick at the air as she fights for purchase against the smooth wall behind her. "P-please," she wheezes, the fear in her voice twisting his lips into a cruel smirk.

"Tell me where he's hiding and I won't kill you here and now," Riordan purrs.

"Sir," ten steps back and to the right, one man steps forward, indecision warring in amber eyes. "Our orders are,"

"Stop speaking, Matthew," Riordan snaps, spraying spittle across Theia's cheek. "I want Julian."

"He's dead," Theia insists, her fingers working to pry his hand loose from her throat. When that doesn't work, she resorts to using her fingernails. While short and blunt for work, she catches a flare of pain in his eyes as she gouges at the underside of his wrist.

"No," Riordan grunts, tightening his hold. His fingers dig brutally into the soft flesh of her neck, cutting off her air supply. Theia's vision tunnels as he blurs into a hazy figure. The pressure on her throat forces bubbles of air between her lips. "Tell me where to find him."

Everything in her peripheral vision darkens before fading from view. The pressure in her skull increases with the need for air until it leaves her temples throbbing. Whether from the threat of passing out, or survival instinct, energy blooms within her. Theia allows the sensation to grow until her muscles quiver to contain it all. Heat spreads from her stomach to trickle down into her legs and up into her chest. Suddenly, oxygen doesn't seem so important.

Theia rotates her wrists to wrap her fingers around his forearm, nails piercing layers of flesh as she narrows her focus. Sweat beads across her upper lip and the agony in her head multiplies, but Theia pushes everything she has into surviving the night.

When the bone in his arm shatters, Riordan stumbles back with a cry sure to wake the entire neighborhood. Jumping at the opportunity, Theia propels herself forward until they both crash into the floor.

The two tumble for a moment in a mess of limbs and groans before they settle with Riordan beneath her. When his grip relaxes enough for the air to return to her lungs, Theia grunts but her vision clears to allow her to focus on his face less than an inch from hers.

"Bitch," he vents beneath her, gripping her upper arm with his good hand. With a grunt, Theia shoves against him to send him rolling sideways. With more force than she thought possible, she punctuates her escape by kicking him in the head before scrambling to her feet.

Shoving at the mess of hair, Theia misses the sharp kick he delivers to her right knee to drop her back to the floor in a swift swoop. The crack of her head against the coffee table echoes between her ears as bright lights dance within her vision. The next thing she feels is a hard kick to her stomach that lands her on her back. Theia blinks to see Riordan's face inches from hers, anger and confusion hemorrhaging from his eyes. Ducking her head, Theia closes her eyes and attempts to breathe through the dizziness consuming her.

"You're going to die here if you aren't careful," a smooth voice whispers in her ear. The instant effect it has on her frazzled nerves allows her to pull a long, steady breath. "Stop holding back."

Theia cants her head left, then right to locate the source of the voice. Since the two men Riordan brought are busy helping him to his feet, she assumes it wasn't one of them and she's quite certain Riordan's voice could soothe no one. *Does it matter? Get your ass up!*

Climbing to her feet, Theia lifts two fingers to the pounding in her skull, wincing when they come away wet with blood. As Riordan gathers himself, she takes several careful steps backward.

"I want her head on a spike," he directs to the men at his sides.

Again, the one he called Matthew looks hesitant. "Those are not our orders, Sir."

"Who is your commanding officer?" Riordan snaps.

"Damien, Sir."

Riordan nods. "And who is Damien's superior?"

When there's a long pause from Matthew, his comrade on the left speaks up. "You are, Sir."

"Precisely." Theia's blood runs cold as Riordan grins in her direction. "I want the Nephilim's head."

Theia gasps when the men square off against her, unsheathing swords with a deadly sharpness. "I don't want to hurt you," she stammers.

"Don't you worry about that, child." Riordan assures her as he takes several steps in her direction. "It'll be over soon."

Theia screams when the men charge, wings carrying them with ease across any distance she'd put between them. Liquid heat slithers over her skin when the tip of a sword catches her upper arm, just below the shoulder. For the first time in years, she allows her emotions to build without restraint.

The cool air filling the living room swells until it whips from wall to wall. Windows shatter in their casings to send shards of glass at her attackers. When a large piece slices Riordan's cheek, he exhales a sharp hiss.

"You're a fool if you think a little wind will stop me," he threatens, raising his sword.

Theia scurries backward toward the kitchen as her walls shake to contain the rage of the wind within her living room. When the one whose name she didn't catch stumbles through the doorway behind her, she sends a chair at his head. After a soft grunt, he crashes to the floor, unmoving. The medical professional in her tempts Theia to check for a pulse, but the sight of Riordan closing in outweighs her training.

With a lunge of his wings, he narrows the gap as his sword swings a wide arc toward her midsection. Theia whimpers and drops to the floor with her hands over her head as a chair flies from the table to intercept his blow. Splinters of wood rain down across the floor as the storm from the living room moves to the kitchen in a frenzy.

Matthew rushes into the room, sword raised, his hand up to shield his face from the debris the wind kicks up. As he reaches for her, Theia sends him crashing into a wall. Riordan's hand catches her ankle and yanks her across the smooth floor.

With a yelp, Theia's fingers scramble for purchase as she tosses her body sideways. Nothing to anchor herself with, she opts for a large piece of the chair and swings it with her good arm. Eyes round in Riordan's face just as the wood explodes against the side of his head.

While it doesn't knock him unconscious, it loosens his grip on her foot long enough for her to put more space between them. Since they block the only other exit, she slips into the narrow hallway.

While the corridor is wide enough for her to maneuver with ease, it challenges Riordan. With a snarl, he tucks his wings in at his sides before chasing after her.

Theia's chest aches as several emotions build uncontrollably. The fierce pounding in her head increases from the constant flow of energy surging out from her center. Scrubbing a hand across her face, she uses the wall to brace herself as she staggers toward her bedroom. The weight of Riordan's body slamming into her from behind sends them both falling to the floor.

Sharp shards of pain sting her palms as Theia attempts to break her fall. Bones rattle from the impact as he straddles her hips to trap her beneath him. White-hot pain explodes in her scalp as he wrenches her head back to expose her throat.

"We could've done this the easy way," his voice slithers in her ear.

The heat of his breath fills her with an icy dread, her stomach muscles convulsing with the need to puke. Her arms and legs tremble as she attempts to throw his weight off. With a bone-chilling chuckle, Riordan abandons his sword in the tight enclosure and withdraws a long, silver dagger from his boot.

Eyes wide, her lips tremble over the wordless prayer as she fights to dislodge him. In a blink, the pressure of his weight subsides as he slams into the ceiling with a sickening thud. After he lands in a heap, Theia staggers to her feet.

Just then, Matthew stumbles out of the kitchen. A trail of blood spans the left side of his face, but his voice is steady when he tries to talk her down. "I'm not here to kill you."

Theia scoffs. "Could've fooled me."

"Our orders are to bring you in. Alive." Matthew stands over Riordan's body. The tension that he exhales tells her that Riordan still lives. "Let me do that for you. Please."

Theia considers his request for all of two quick seconds. The furious shake of her head restores the tension in his shoulders. "I think I'll pass. Thanks."

With a deep sigh, Matthew lifts his sword and advances. Scrambling, Theia picks up Riordan's sword in time to deflect his attack. The vibrations that careen up her arm are enough to nearly rip her fingers from the hilt.

Since the walls prevent him from getting a full swing, Theia continues to deflect as she creeps toward her bedroom. Just as she crosses the threshold, Matthew lunges once more, only to slam into an invisible wall with a strained grunt.

Theia blinks once, closes the door, and engages the lock. She collapses against the smooth wood between her and her attackers and allows herself a moment to still her racing heart.

The moment gone, she races from corner to corner, cramming items into her backpack. Tugging on a clean pair of jeans, she stuffs her green hoodie into her bag, followed by the framed photograph of her mother.

Scanning the room, her eyes snag on the flash of bright neon pink. Diving under the bed, she retrieves the pair of sneakers with a heavy sigh. Normally, Granny would be livid to learn she'd left shoes in her room.

This time, Theia brushes off the lecture, playing on a loop inside her ears with a smile. "Sorry Granny." She retrieves her purse from the closet just as the door to her bedroom shatters into tiny pieces.

Falling backward, Theia scoots across the floor to avoid Riordan's advance. Up and over the bed, she chucks the alarm clock at his head before rolling across the other side. Stumbling to her feet, she gasps when Matthew's sword pierces her abdomen. Pain radiates within her stomach as bile rises in her throat.

Snarling, Theia jerks the sword from his hands and sends both men into the far wall. The foundation of her house gives a shudder from the force before her fingers give life to the first few flames that ignite curtains. With the raging wind still whipping throughout the house, it isn't long before a tiny fire becomes a raging inferno.

Her sights set on the front door, Theia grabs her bags and stumbles along the hall, separating the main part of the house.

Thick, black smoke builds as the heat from the fire scorches her bare arms. Shielding her eyes and covering her mouth with a piece of her shirt, Theia stumbles forward. Riordan's roar from her bedroom quickens her pace as she escapes out to the front lawn.

Lungs burn as each gulp of fresh air swaps out the smoke she'd ingested. Slipping on the damp grass, Theia staggers to her feet, an arm clutching her side as she all but falls into the front seat of her car.

Putting the car in gear, she's out of the driveway and down the street by the time her house explodes with a series of tremors she can feel in the steering wheel.

CHAPTER 10

Colin leans on his chair's back legs as he nurses the last of his beer. Though dimly lit and reeking with the stench of alcohol, cigarette smoke, and sweat, bright neon signs attract a bar's worth of patrons. Its usual sounds pulse around him with a mixture of laughter, pathetic pickup lines, and eighties hits blaring from the jukebox.

Every so often, the sharp clack of pool balls from the back corner adds a change to the monotony. When the record changes to fill the bar with the steady bass of a guitar, Colin's lips tilt into a smile. "Way better than karaoke night," he muses to himself.

"How can you listen to this," Jess asks as he pulls up the chair closest to Colin.

"Better than another rendition of whatever song the kids today deem popular." A wave of his hand snags the server's attention long enough for Colin to gesture at his beer bottle and then hold up two fingers.

"I dunno, bud. This stuff is decades old."

"Like us?"

Jess chuckles. "Good point." After tossing a look left, then right, he grins. "You get Kegan in this place?"

"Occasionally."

"I'm impressed." Once the server sets two cold bottles of beer on their table, Jess sits back in his chair and flashes a lazy smile. "Thanks, Cat," he purrs after glancing at her name tag.

Instead of the typical flutter of eyelashes Colin usually sees when Jess flirts with someone, Cat narrows her hazel eyes and takes a step back with a terse nod. The air around them cools slightly, despite her polite response.

"Must be losing your touch," he remarks when she moves away to tend to a table full of rowdy drinkers.

"Nah." Jess pulls a drink from his bottle and exhales loudly. "Some just require more effort."

"Uh-huh."

"You're telling me women just fall into your bed with no effort on your part?"

Colin shrugs. He'd never been big on the kiss-and-tell part since it's no one's business but his own.

"You need to write a book, man. Host a seminar or something."

Colin raises a brow as Jess dangles a bottle of beer from his fingertips. "I don't think so. If you like, I can get a t-shirt made up for you."

"Not really my thing." Jess chuckles. "So what are we drinking to this time?"

"Why do we have to drink to anything?"

"Um, makes it seem more appropriate?"

It's Colin's turn to chuckle. The deep sound vibrates in his chest before it trickles off to leave a grin on his lips. "Appropriate isn't really my thing. Pick something if it makes you feel better."

Behind them, a young couple breaks into a ruckus of laughter. Jess peeks over his shoulder. "I'm just happy to be alive."

"Alive is good," Colin replies, pulling a deep swallow from his beer. "Me too."

"Why are you always so negative, man?"

One dark brow lifts as wrinkles pucker Colin's forehead. "I just agreed with you. How is that negative?"

"It's like saying, hey man, good to see you. And someone replies, you too." After a shake of his head, Jess drains his beer and leaves the empty bottle on the table. "It's a little underwhelming. We just fought a badass demon! We should celebrate!"

"Keep your voice down," Colin hisses. After scanning the room, his spine relaxes. Thankfully, people are too busy in their own conversations or enjoying their alcohol to catch Jess's remark.

"All I'm saying is that we should live large and feel damn good about ourselves right now. Especially with Kegan back home where he belongs."

That last part Colin can get behind. The months he'd spent believing he'd never see the ugly mug again had been harder than he's willing to admit to anyone. Least of all, himself. If any of them deserve a happily ever after, it's Kegan. "How's he coping with his new limits?"

"Oh you mean the," Jess lowers his voice to a level below a whisper, "mortal part?" Colin nods and Jess's shoulders dance up and down in a half-assed shrug. "He says he can still kick ass with the best of us. But I'm not sure he was ever really that good."

"Yeah, right?" Colin chuckles and drains his beer, waving off the server when she appears ready to bring fresh bottles. "Took a round out of you more than once."

"Yeah, well, I was smaller back then."

"What do you mean, then?"

"Fuck off."

"I'm glad he's happy." The warmth that spreads within his chest only adds weight to Colin's statement.

"Any problems since you've taken over as Guardian?"

"Nope. I think most of the uglies got the message loud and clear." Just then, a tremor of power sweeps through the room to wipe the cocky grin off Colin's face. The front legs of his chair land on the floor with a crack as he sits up straight.

Shock ripples across Jess's face, no doubt mirroring his own. When the hair on his arms and the back of his neck stand on end, the bottom drops out of his stomach. "What the hell?"

"Are your symphony's skipping?"

Colin's teeth set. "No. Yours?"

"Nope."

"Which means it's not a demon," Colin surmises, but scans every corner of the crowded bar, anyway.

"So, what is it?"

Seconds creep by as the power swells and fills the small establishment. Despite its sweet smell, Colin's stomach rolls in response. Sweat gathers under his shirt as he plows a hand through his hair to hide the fact it trembles. "I have to check this out."

"Colin, man," Jess interrupts, his hand shooting across the table to stop Colin from taking off by himself. "I don't think you should go alone."

"We don't even know what it is." *Liar.* "I'll just scout it out. If I need you, I'll call you." *No, I won't.* Dropping several crumpled bills on the table to more than cover his tab, Colin waits until he's outside and halfway down the adjoining alley before he flashes in the direction the power originates.

Appearing on the edge of a dark parking lot, Colin walks the half-block toward the red and blue lights and the acrid taste of smoke. The commotion dragged neighbors from their beds, wrapped in an assortment of bathrobes or heavy jackets to ward off the dampness in the air.

Even though the chill is insignificant, Colin wraps his arms around his middle and trudges through the streets flooded with black water. Just ahead, the small house on the corner still smolders. All that remains of its structure are broken studs and charred beams.

On the street, firefighters work to clean up the debris on the front lawn while two of their three trucks pull away from the curb. Next door, a young woman stands on the porch telling her story to a police officer.

"Can you believe it?" Too loud to be considered a whisper, the lady gives a shake of her head. "Poor Theia."

Colin inches closer to the conversation as a man with thinning hair huffs hard enough to shake his slender frame. "No survivors, they said."

Pressing a hand to her throat as if to stop a sob from trying to escape, the lady gives her head a long, somber shake. "I'd hate to be the one to tell Ellie."

"It's by the grace of God she wasn't in there when this happened." Clasping his coat tighter around his slender frame, the male neighbor continues. "One firefighter said it looked like the gas line ruptured."

"Such a shame."

Once the conversation appears to die off, Colin moves closer to the house. When he inhales, his eyes water from the bitter stench of smoke and burned debris. Coughing to clear his lungs, he pulls a deeper breath, his brain catching on the slight trace of sweetness. Angelic.

He peers into the group of onlookers, his jaw tightening when he spots a familiar pair of dull brown eyes. *Riordan.* Which makes the angel that lived here, a Nephilim. Interesting.

Crouching, Colin scans the ruined structure. Slowly, his gaze moves from one giant mess to the next until a hand grips his shoulder. Shoving himself to his feet, Colin squares off with the owner of the hand.

The firefighter yanks his arm back and adjusts his helmet with a light cough. "Excuse me, sir. You can't be this close."

"Sorry." Colin backtracks the way he came until he reaches the dark parking lot. Digging his phone out of his pocket, he punches in a few numbers and waits for someone to answer the other end.

When the muffled ringing is silenced, Colin cuts off whatever blowoff he's about to receive. "We need to talk. I just came from the charred remains of a house. It still carries traces of a Nephilim. One that smells an awful lot like... you."

The deep baritone that fills Colin's ear raises the meter attached to his concern. "Give me fifteen minutes."

The dashboard clock shows half-past noon before Theia rolls into a vacant parking lot of a small gas station. Turning off the engine, she allows herself to slump in the seat.

Coupled with the exhaustion that leeches its way into her bones, the pounding in her head only increases with every passing minute. The silence in the car is overwhelming after hours of driving with only her thoughts for company.

At first, she'd listened to the local radio station report on the house fire she'd left in her review mirror. After a while, either she'd driven too far, or they'd simply found a juicier story.

Lungs squeeze. Glancing out the window, she stares blindly as the leaves rustle from a gentle breeze. It's peaceful here, away from the bustle of the city. *You can't stay here forever, Theia.* Her sigh grows. The situation she finds herself in is far from the realm of understanding. The only fact she can be sure of is that it has something to do with her father. "Seems like a great place to start," Theia clips. *How do we do that?*

After taking a deep breath, she reaches for the pill bottle in her purse. Tiny white pills rattle softly to provide a strange sort of comfort from the quiet. Popping two into her mouth, she gulps them down with a swig of lukewarm water from the water bottle she kept in her car.

"I just need to close my eyes for a minute." Resting her head on the back of her seat, Theia listens to the birds in the trees until the tension leaves her body. Her first instinct after reaching her car had been to pick up her grandmother and split town.

Operating on auto-pilot, Theia realized she was driving in the care-homes direction before taking a series of turns to head in the opposite way. She may not understand everything that's happening, but her grandmother is safer where she's at.

Sitting there with the spring breeze sweeping through the front seat of her car, Theia recalls her last conversation with her. *He says I should stay here. I'm doing this for you.*

"Dementia or not, Granny has more clue what's going on than I do."

Opening her eyes, Theia takes in the gravel parking lot and the run-down gas station. Having seen better days, the building is old and faded with peeling paint and a rusted sign above the door. The set of gas pumps is ancient. Their cracked hoses and fading numbers plant a seed of doubt about their function. She can't be sure how far she'd driven already, but eventually, she's going to need fuel. *Soon.*

A lone attendant sits in front of a rectangle window reading a magazine, barely glancing up when Theia exits the car and heads inside. The chime of a bell above the door inspires him to lift his bent head long enough to give her a quick perusal. "Can I help you with anything?"

"Do your pumps work?"

"For now." Closing the magazine, he sits straighter on his stool. "Owner talking about taking them out soon."

"Well, it's my lucky day then. I'll just be a minute."

Retrieving his magazine, the attendant resumes slouching. "Take your time."

Breathing beyond the smell of gasoline and cheap cigarettes, Theia walks the stubby aisles. Heading toward first-aid supplies, Theia throws several items into the plastic basket she hooks over one arm.

Gauze pads, ointment, rubbing alcohol. Tweezers and a small sewing kit for good measure. Turning left, she stops at the end of one aisle to grab a bag of chips and a bottle of water before snagging a cold bottle of soda from the cooler. The attendant is already sitting straight once more when she sets the basket down on the dinged counter.

"Is this it?"

"I'd like to prepay forty on the closest pump as well."

After peering out the dirty window, he gives her a nod. "That'd be pump two."

"Great." When he reads back the total, a knot forms in Theia's stomach. She'd never carried that much cash at once. Fingers knot around the strap of her purse as sweat gathers between her and her shirt. "Do you, um, have an atm?"

"Nope. The owner said it isn't worth the fees."

"Right." Fumbling around within her purse, hoping to stumble across a couple of large bills, Theia's fingers brush smooth plastic. Granny never told her how much was even in the account. *Either swipe it and hope for the best or we hitchhike.*

Gripping the card between thumb and forefinger, she swipes it through the magnetic reader. Her teeth chew on the inside of her cheek as she watches the screen change from processing to approved. Gathering up her bags, she bids the attendant a good day and hurries back to her car. Dumping the bags in the back seat, she fills her gas tank and is back on the road.

Theia drives until the sun sinks on the horizon and she spies a vacant motel on her left. Like much of the area, the motel has certainly seen better days. *It's this or the car*, the tiny voice in her head warns, so Theia pulls into the parking lot.

The neon sign near the road flashes vacant to reflect off the asphalt, creating a horror-movie-type effect. Reaching the small window at the front of the building, Theia rings the bell. A gentleman in his fifties with greasy hair and a stained shirt appears from the back, wiping his hands on a small towel.

"Evening," tossing the towel over his shoulder, the man gives Theia a quick glance.

"How much are your rooms for the night?"

"Seventeen for the night or eighty-five for the week."

"Just tonight, please."

"Sure thing. Cash or credit."

"Cash, please," Theia plucks her last twenty-dollar bill from her small purple wallet and slides it under the plexiglass window.

"Room eight," he says, sliding a small brass key attached to a large plastic keychain under the window. "All the way down, last room on the left."

"Appreciate it, thanks." Returning to her car, Theia creeps along the length of the narrow parking lot and parks outside the gaudy red door with a brass number eight on the front. Gathering her bags, she locks the car, sets her alarm, and slips inside the dark motel room.

Small and dingy with a single bed and an ancient television, it at least smells clean. Engaging the locks, she drops her bags on the bed and heads to the bathroom for a much-needed shower.

Between the blood sticking to her side pulling with every step and the pungent aroma of smoke clinging to her hair, the prospect of hot water and cheap bar soap becomes her own private version of heaven.

On her way, she turns the knob on the television, searches for a local news channel, and turns up the volume. Cracking the door to the bathroom, she steps under the hot spray of water as the news anchor drones on about current events.

CHAPTER II

Colin jams his phone into his back pocket and watches officers and firefighters sift through the charred remnants of the house from a distance. All Eleni could find on the paperwork was the name Ellie Michaels, an eighty-three-year-old widow who lives at a local care home. How this connects, Colin isn't sure, but the knot in his gut says it does. *Somehow.*

Even with the crisp air and the scent of a brewing storm on the horizon, the Nephilim's essence clings to his nose. Something dangerous ferments just out of his reach. The lack of information encourages his sense of bewilderment until he's itching to punch someone. Hard.

As he waits for his contact to arrive, he listens in as the officer in charge of the scene reports one fatality. Initial eyewitness statements believe her to be the granddaughter of the tenant on record. *Interesting.* The soft echo of footsteps behind him focuses Colin's attention away from the chaotic scene down the road before he can get more information. "You're late, Julian," he mutters as he shifts in time to see the angel emerge from the shadows behind the vacant carwash.

Muscles twitch in a stubborn jaw. "I had to make sure the scene was clear."

"What do you know?"

"I know a little about a lot of things, Colin. You'll have to be more specific."

He'd forgotten how much of an asshole Julian could be. The fresh reminder stirs countless memories that make him question how on earth he'd forgotten in the first place. "The fire left the house down the street in rubble, yet none of the surrounding houses were affected." Colin's jaw hardens and his hands clench when Julian takes a few steps to survey the damage for himself.

"Seems that way." Turning around, Julian regards Colin with a blank stare. "What's your point?"

"My point is, the explosion that turned this house into a pile of pickup sticks didn't so much as singe a shingle on the other houses. That takes an enormous amount of power."

"I agree." Arms cross his wide chest as Julian rocks back and forth on his heels. "What does that have to do with me?"

"Cut the shit," Colin snarls. "I spotted Riordan earlier trying to blend in with the looky-loos. That tells me the power is Nephilim. Who is she to you?"

Minutes tick by at a rapid pace before Julian manages any sort of reply. "We can't discuss this here. It isn't safe."

"Fine. Lead the way."

The men shift within the night air and glide the thousands of miles to a cabin built amidst a vast forest of snow-covered trees. When Julian materializes a few steps shy of the narrow porch that tips away from the foundation, Colin follows suit.

Small, the cabin contains two main rooms, what he hopes to be a bathroom, and a rickety ladder that leads to a loft. A wood-burning stove stands in the center of an outside wall, warming the tight spaces considerably compared to the freezing temperatures outside. In the air, Colin picks up the scent of honey and pine. Though unlevel, the wood floor stretches from room to room, worn smooth in spots from years of traffic. Very little in the way of furniture, Colin spots a square table under a large window with wooden shutters on the inside, and two roughly carved chairs. The complete lack of personal touch makes the photos and newspaper articles spanning the entire width of the far wall appear obsessive.

Stepping closer, Colin takes in the first several photographs. A chubby cherub face complete with dark, chocolate curls and eyes so deep a blue they hurt for him to look at too long. As he moves sideways, the subject in the pictures ages. From a stumbling toddler to a lanky little girl. While the years shed away a good portion of baby fat, the sadness in her eyes remains the same. Between the next set of pictures, Colin reads a local news article about a girl with incredible speed, landing the top spot on her school's track team. The next article comments on the sudden disappearance of the girl and her family, with no clue where they'd gone or why. Skipping ahead to the farthest row of photographs, Colin studies the classic lines of a stunning woman.

In the snapshot pinned to the wall, she's smiling. Though slightly crooked, her lips tip at the corners to reveal a set of dimples in each cheek. Long, dark lashes frame remarkable eyes as a flash of light he assumes came from the camera reflects brilliantly in their depths. Her hair, scooped into the same ponytail he'd seen in several of the other pictures, exposes a stubborn jaw and a graceful neck. She's wearing nurse's scrubs in the photo and while he can see she'd grown into a beautiful woman, she's nowhere near what today's society would deem perfect. "Who is she?"

"My daughter."

Julian's short answer steals the air from his lungs. Spinning on one foot, Colin searches his friend's face for any sign of deception. Shadows engulf hazel-green eyes, as a tic pulses in Julian's left cheek. As if sensing Colin's scrutiny, he meets it head-on with a lift of his chin. "You told me she died," Colin reminds him in a tense voice.

"I had to. Otherwise, they'd keep looking for her."

"How have you kept her hidden all this time?"

"I didn't." Julian inhales, the action bouncing a wide pair of shoulders. "Melchom did."

"Fuck, Julian."

"I know."

"Why didn't you come to me? After what you and Aric did for me and my regiment, I was in your debt. Will always be. I would've helped you."

Julian scrubs a hand across his jaw. "We spoke on your behalf because it was the right thing to do. Not because I was keeping score."

"Yeah and if you hadn't, we'd be existing in the ether instead of on earth." Colin paces the few steps it takes to cross the bare kitchen. He can't fathom knowing your kid is out there, hunted, and there's nothing you can do about it as a parent. Suddenly, so many questions he'd harbored for so long make perfect sense. Angels alike carried respect for Julian before he fell. Some questioned why he'd make such a choice with skepticism, while others accepted the council's explanation of treason. Colin himself hadn't fully swallowed the story until he caught rumors of Julian working with Melchom. "You made a deal, didn't you?"

"When Riordan found us, I lost my wife that night. I would not lose my daughter, too." Julian mumbled as he tosses another log on the fire. Bright red sparks sputter up from the coals to flutter soundlessly before fading. "Melchom kept her safe for almost thirty years, Colin."

"Yeah, well that doesn't mean you can trust him. Besides, Riordan sniffing around should tell you she's not safe anymore."

"I know."

"Does she know what she is? What she's capable of?"

"I don't know. I have kept my distance. The last thing I wanted to do was to lead them right to her."

"So, you've never met her?" Colin gives his head a shake. "How do you have all these pictures?"

"Her grandmother sends them to a P.O. box Melchom used to use as a dead drop."

"Okay, so her grandmother knows what she is? Will she have told, um?"

"Theia." Julian's lips curve into a smile for the first time that night and Colin would need to be blind not to recognize the same crookedness in the smile his daughter carries. "Damara loved that name." Raw emotion assaults him as it emanates off of Julian. Teeth set, Colin resorts to physically shaking it loose before it infects his logic.

"Does she know what she is, Julian? Can she control it?"

"I don't know. But I'm not going to just sit here while Riordan acts out some twisted perversion of a hunt."

"You know him better than I do, but if it were me? I'd draw you out just so you could take me right to her."

"That's a chance I'll have to take." The tight line along Julian's jaw tells Colin he'd decided.

As an idea springs to life, Colin's head quirks slightly. "What if there's a better way?"

When Theia blinks her eyes open, she stares at the broken bedside clock. The hands remain stuck at 3:42, the numbers blurry and faded with age. Theia blinks and rubs her eyes, trying to shake off the grogginess. It takes a moment for the memories to come back to her. *The fire. Riordan.*

Groaning, she sits up and winces at the soreness along her side. She'd stopped the bleeding and applied a few rookie-level stitches, but the sharp pain serves as a grim reminder. Regardless of who Riordan is or what he wants with her father, he'll kill her to get it. Despite her resolve, she shudders when a chill runs down her spine.

With a sigh, Theia swings her legs out of bed and rummages in her bag for clean clothes. Settling on a pair of black jeans, a clean t-shirt, and an oversized hoodie, she balls up her dirty laundry and shoves them to the bottom of the bag. Before leaving, she uses the phone beside the bed to check the balance remaining on the card Granny gave her. When the automated voice drones out a number, Theia punches the star key to hear it again. Wow! *Worry about what bank Granny robbed later. Get your ass back on the road.* "Right."

Slipping on her flip-flops, Theia shoves the card deep inside her purse and jams the purse into the little space remaining within her backpack. After giving the room another passing glance, she leaves.

At this time of night, the parking lot is empty, save for her car. After a recent rain, the bright neon lights glitter in small puddles across the long parking lot. Despite the spring coolness, Theia came to expect from the north, the air is calm. Not so much as a rustle across the field behind her. To calm the rolling of her stomach, Theia's head rocks slightly as she listens. Between the sound of the crickets and the soft buzz of mosquitoes, nothing strikes her as out of place. "You need to calm down," Theia mutters and pauses for a moment to consider her options before making her way to her car. As she slides into the driver's seat, keys poised at the ignition, the passenger side window explodes.

"Hello again, Theia," Riordan snarls as he tears her door open. Rough hands grip her arms to pull her kicking and screaming from the seat. Theia thrashes against his grip which only incites him to increase the pressure until she yelps in pain. With a grunt, Riordan slams her against the hood of the car and pins her with his body weight. Leaning in, his face contorts with anger until it twists his plain features viciously. This close, Theia picks up the familiar smell of smoke, a reminder of her house.

"How did you find me?"

"It isn't that hard Theia. See, all Nephilim have a unique scent." Brown eyes flash. "Makes tracking you, child's play."

"I'll keep that in mind," Theia grinds between her teeth as she brings up her heel with as much force as she can muster. When her foot connects with his crotch, his weight falls away from her in an instant. Breathing heavily, she scrambles to her feet, snatching her backpack off the ground and looping her arms through the straps. Riordan is already on his feet, his expression murderous as he cups himself.

"You're making a mistake, Theia," he growls. "You can't hide forever."

"I can try," she retorts, her eyes searching for an escape route.

The dense brick buildings or the freshly planted field serve as her only options. Theia opts for the buildings and makes a run for it. Riordan is quick to follow. His massive wings have him spanning the gap with little effort. Theia ducks and weaves, attempting to avoid his grasp when his hand buries itself in her hair. Yanking backwards, he slams her into the brick wall of a nearby building. Agony burst inside her skull and Theia blinks against the stars filling her vision. Around the sharp ringing in her ears, she barely makes out his next words.

"You're not as clever as you think you are."

"M-maybe not," she gasps. "But I'll go down swinging." Raking her nails down his face, Theia rejoices at the sight of blood before he jerks back with a howl.

Pressure builds in her stomach as she kicks at his legs. Teeth pin her lip between them as she brings down the small wooden tool shed on top of him. The effort coats her skin with sweat before she spins on her heel and runs the other way. The sound of debris hitting the buildings encourages Theia to run faster.

"I'm going to enjoy taking your head," Riordan snarls several steps behind her.

Theia pauses at several doors to the motel rooms lining the parking lot until she finds one loose enough for her to shove open with a shoulder. "Not tonight," she promises and latches the door behind her. Eyes peer through the darkness as she considers the bathroom window or the door adjoining the next room. The sound of his body slamming into the door behind her propels her across the room to shove open the door to the next room. Shoving one door open, latching it behind her, she scrambles to the next. She continues on that path with Riordan in quick, merciless pursuit. Theia has no idea how many rooms she's cleared when his hand snags her pack and jerks her sideways.

Rolling across the lumpy mattress, Theia puts herself between the bed and the wall. Muscles poised, she waits to see what his next move will be when it dawns on her, he's alone. "Where's your backup, Riordan? Didn't want to take part in your sadistic side-games?"

"Don't you worry. Heaven will be sending their replacements any minute now."

"I'll have to move fast then," Theia grins taunting Riordan into making his move. Leaping across the bed, Riordan slams a knee into the wall where she'd been standing not seconds before. Scurrying around the end of the bed, she picks up the table lamp and swings it like a weapon.

Riordan ducks, but the lamp still connects with the side of his head to send him reeling. Taking advantage of the opening, Theia grabs a nearby chair and smashes it across his back. When he falls to the ground with a groan, she springs forward to deliver a swift kick to his ribs.

Even as he grunts in pain, his hand snakes out to grab Theia's ankle and pull her off balance. With a cry in her throat, Theia falls to the ground. Riordan's eyes flash with fury as he straddles her hips. "I'm done playing games with you," he seethes. Rage mottles his face as blood trickles down his right cheek from under his hairline.

Fighting with desperation, Theia pummels his chest with her hands. When capturing her wrists proves unsuccessful, Riordan bounces her head off the floor beneath them. A heavy fog of darkness looms just out of sight, spreading through Theia's mind like a rampant disease. Vaguely. she computes the sight of Riordan withdrawing a new sword from its sheath only to raise it above his head. Panic unfurls in her chest as her hands search the floor for a weapon. When they land on a skinny piece of wood that made up the chair, she stabs it into his side.

With a shriek to make her ears bleed, Riordan staggers backward. Her hands shaking, Theia climbs to her feet and runs into the next room. "Back where I started," she grumbles and heads for the parking lot.

Instead of escaping in her car, Theia pauses outside the door. Wild emotions fuel the power building inside of her, heating her blood and quickening her heart. Theia's fingers twitch and tingle with the restraint of holding it back long enough until the right moment. As he stumbles in from the adjoining room, Theia braces herself and releases her hold on the swell of power.

Her hands shake as the sound of glass shattering and bricks snapping fills the air. The motel room shakes and groans under the force of her rage before collapsing around her. Hard tremors travel under the wet pavement of the parking lot to vibrate under her feet.

As fragments of wood and plaster rain down, it becomes clear Theia underestimates her power. While the objective had been the room Riordan is in, the sight of half the building buckling adds a tightness to her chest. Each fracture of the framework and crumple of the roofs sends up a plume of white dust as it settles within the walls. Unable to ignore the pinch against her heart, Theia braces her hands on her knees and gasps for breath.

The sound of bricks and debris shifting draws her attention to her intended target. Even from some distance away, Riordan's moans rise up from beneath the pile.

"We should go."

Whirling, Theia confronts the strange man with a charming accent. "And you are?"

"Colin. I'm a friend of your dad's."

"Good for you," Theia clips. "Why would I go anywhere with you?"

"Because I promised your dad I'd get you out of here."

"Sorry." Squaring her shoulders, Theia limps the short distance to her car.

"He's right you know. They won't stop." Eyes the same color as whiskey darken slightly as he studies what's left of the motel. "While your power is impressive. You need help."

"You're here to help me?" Yeah, right. *This is a new tactic from someone just like Riordan.* Anything to bring her in. But if she's honest with herself, she'll admit to the pure exhaustion riding around on her shoulders.

"I'm here to take you to someone who can."

"Who might that be?"

CHAPTER 12

Adjusting to the pain in his side, Riordan crosses the large foyer in a matter of seconds. After a glance over his shoulder, he slips into his quarters and locks the door. The pounding in his head rivals Heaven's choir as he takes a seat gingerly on the long couch. His features pinch as he lifts his shirt to examine the wound, hissing when his prodding results in a fresh stab of agony.

It's not the first time they have injured him tracking a Nephilim, but it's certainly the worst. Although unskilled, Theia evaded him twice now. If he hopes to secure the promotion, he'll need to wrap things up.

Muttering under his breath, Riordan rests his head on the back of the couch and steadies his breathing. Sleep is the only thing that'll heal such a serious wound, and it's the one thing he can't afford. Lips thin as he resorts to cleaning and dressing his wound the way a mere mortal might. Brushing the dust off the first aid kit, Riordan searches through what remains of his supplies when there's a soft rap on the door.

"What," he growls, inhaling as he presses a clean bandage against his side. Flinching, he secures it with several pieces of white tap before pulling his shirt down.

"Excuse me, Sir," a soft voice mumbles through the thick door. "Councilor Rebecca is asking for you."

Bitch. Biting back his initial response, Riordan clears his throat. "I'll be right there." As the footsteps recede, he sits there, contemplating his next move.

He needs to find Theia again, and quickly. However, the prospect of Councilor Rebecca breathing down his neck complicates matters. Making her wait too long for an update will do more damage to his promotion than if he can't bring Theia in alive.

Not that he has any intention of doing such a thing. At first, he'll admit he was open to the idea. But five minutes after meeting the monstrosity, cleared away any doubts the Council planted. Rotating his shoulders, Riordan nearly rolls the dice when his eyes land on the leather-bound dossier. Curious, he picks it up and begins thumbing through the pages.

This is everything Heaven has on Theia St. James. It isn't much. Other than a childhood friend she hasn't talked to in fifteen years, Theia only has one thing anchoring her amongst the humans. And she's living amongst a group of human elders, ripe for the picking.

Intrigue gives way to a slow grin as a plan takes shape. Dropping the file on the smooth table, he stands and adjusts his shirt to better hide the bandage underneath. Grabbing his phone, he dials a number. The other end rings three times before Aamon picks up.

"I need you to do something for me."

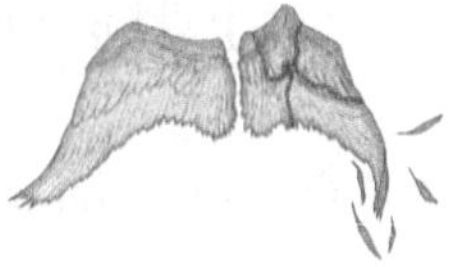

When the squeak of a squirrel overhead pierces his quiet, Aric looks up from his book with a scowl. What starts out as a subtle disruption grows until he's serenading Aric with sharp grunt-like sounds.

Peeking over his shoulder, Aric studies the platform his neighbor put up for the family of squirrels living in the white oak tree the two properties share. By the looks of it, the food started running low a few days ago.

"I have nothing for you," he informs the squirrel before scanning the book's page to find where he left off. Once he finds the spot, the soft chatter from the squirrel increases in pitch as he perches on a branch just inches shy of Aric's deck. "Go bug Nathan if you're hungry. He has the food."

Instead of scurrying off the way he came, the squirrel balances precariously on a thin branch to continue his squawking. A full minute passes before Aric slides his bookmark in place and leaves it laying on the hammock with a grumble. "Fine."

Opening the sliding glass door, he steps into the adjoining kitchen and digs through the produce at the bottom of the refrigerator. After selecting several pieces of fruits and vegetables, Aric washes them in warm water before cutting them into manageable pieces. Dumping the mixture into a bowl, he adds a handful of shelled peanuts and steps outside.

As if spying the treats, the squirrel races up several branches in the platform's direction as Aric lopes across the lawn. Leaving the bowl on the platform, he takes several steps back as the squirrel family descends in a flurry of activity. Most snatch what they can before retreating into the safety of the tree. One remains, picking over the offering with a light chatter of teeth.

"You're welcome." Aric makes a mental note to get the bowl back from Nathan later when a small burgundy car pulls into his driveway. In bold, blue letters that splash across the front of the license plate, Aric's nose wrinkles as he reads *Pure Michigan*. The sight of Colin unfolding himself from the driver's seat replaces his initial confusion with a rise in his blood pressure.

Jaw set, Aric circles around the front of the house. "Not interested," he clips, shooing Colin back towards the car before he can set one foot on the walkway.

Colin sighs. "Hear me out."

"No." Once Aric closes the distance, he spins Colin around and marches him back to the car. "I don't care why you're here or what you want. I'm retired."

"Even for her?"

Brows knit as Aric directs his attention to the passenger side of the car. Just as a tall brunette climbs out, the bottom drops out of his stomach. *Theia.*

While it's been almost thirty years since Aric last saw her, he remembers that moment vividly. Radiant blue eyes. Similar to the pigment used to decorate tombs. They are her mother's eyes, the same ones that have plagued his dreams for more years than he cares to count. Seeing them again lands like a sucker punch. Breathing becomes difficult and his hands tremble so hard Aric resorts to stuffing them in the pocket of his jeans. To distract himself with something else, he catalogs her disheveled appearance.

A messy ponytail secures most of the dark chocolate hair off her neck, but several strands slip free to frame a heart-shaped face. Fresh bruises and cuts pepper her cheek and jaw and she sports a couple of tears in a hoodie big enough for him to wear.

Tentatively, Aric inhales. At first, the sweet mixture of lemon and something else overpowers the soft stench of smoke and the metallic scent of fresh blood. No doubt she carries more severe injuries than Aric can note on the surface. From her position, she places the car between them while she studies him with the same scrutiny.

"Theia, this is Aric."

"What happened," Aric demands, ripping his eyes from her long enough to give Colin a fierce glare.

"She went and put herself on Heaven's radar."

"Of all the dumbass things to do," Aric gripes before giving his head a shake. "We were so damn careful."

"While I'm enjoying being discussed in the third person," Theia snaps with a frown that wrinkles her brow, "maybe we should get inside." The furtive glance she casts over her shoulders tells Aric she's expecting another attack. When she meets his eye again, the fear he spots in hers tenses his jaw. Before he can calm her, however, Colin takes matters into his own hands.

"They won't follow us here. At least not yet."

A dark, sculpted brow inches upward toward her forehead. "Not that I'm not grateful, but why?"

Aric shoots Colin a murderous glare should his friend think to offer any more information. "That's a long story." Stepping to his left, he sweeps his arm in the direction of his front door. "Come inside and we'll see what we can figure out."

"Just like that," Theia challenges.

The open speculation she aims in Colin's direction rattles his nerves. Nothing to be upset about. She trusts him. *Like hell!* "Or you can continue on your way and we never have to see each other again."

"He can help you, Theia," Colin soothes. Aric can sense his lip curling as Colin's lilting accent invades his ears. *Fucking leprechaun.*

After appearing to weigh her options, Theia steps around the car door, grabs a plump backpack from the back seat, and slams the door shut with a bump of her hip. "Lead the way Yoda."

With a brittle smile, Aric hopes his expression conveys just how fucked Colin is for even thinking of bringing this problem to his doorstep before he leads the way up the short stone pathway.

The moment Julian solidifies, crud clutters his essence. With a mental shake and a tightening of his jaw, he continues toward the three-story condo. Extravagant, the building boasts dark gray stone and white trim. Thick panes of glass make up three of the four walls to give one an unobstructed view of the Pacific Ocean.

To settle his nerves, Julian admires the salt and seaweed that floats along a breeze heavy with sand, coffee, and donuts. The moment he passes the threshold into the marbled foyer, George is there with a somber expression on a serious face.

"He's expecting you."

"Thanks, George," Julian replies, his eyes closing as the smell of wet dog replaces the fresh air he just filled his lungs with.

As extravagant on the inside as the outside, Julian strolls through the generous kitchen fitted with stainless steel appliances and granite countertops. Climbing the floating staircase, he moves to the second floor with practiced ease.

Down the wide hall lined with expensive pieces of art and sculptures, his boots thump across the polished wood floors before several antique Persian rugs muffle his approach. Poised in the doorway, he waits for Melchom to recognize his arrival before setting foot inside his study.

"I expected you to be here yesterday."

Julian keeps his face impassive as Melchom ushers him forward and gestures to one of the empty chairs across his desk. Lowering his frame into the one closest to him, he offers a non-committal shrug of his shoulders. "I wasn't aware it was anything urgent."

"If I call you, assume it's urgent." Violet eyes narrow slightly as Melchom pushes his paperwork aside.

"Got it." Resting his arm on the chair to his left, Julian concentrates on the slow, steady rhythm of his pulse. "What's the problem?"

"It's come to my attention that one of my prisons has allowed a demon to escape."

Julian blinks. "Wait, what?" His mind races as he struggles to piece together what Melchom is saying. "Which prison?"

"The one in Florida." Pushing himself up from his chair, Melchom paces within the space behind his desk, his voice tight with frustration.

Despite his determination to remain calm, Julian's stomach twists into knots. The prison in Florida is one of Melchom's largest and most secure. How exactly, did a demon escape from there? "Do we know how this happened?"

Melchom shakes his head. "Not yet. But soon."

Julian's stomach lurches as he considers all the ways Melchom has of getting information from someone. *They're demons. They don't deserve your pity.* As much as he'd like to agree with the small voice in his head, his heart pulls him in another direction. "What do you need me to do?"

"I need you tracking this demon," Melchom instructs as he drops a thin folder in Julian's lap. "He shouldn't be too hard to track. Keep it quiet. I don't need unnecessary attention from the humans."

"Understood." *Not after last year*, Julian muses as he thumbs through the file's contents. A demon with such a physical deformity won't be difficult to locate. Standing, his eyes meet Melchom's. "Consider it done." As he turns to leave, Melchom's voice stops him in his tracks.

"One more thing, Julian."

"Yes?"

"This is the demon that stumbled across your daughter all those years ago." Melchom's chin lifts as his nostrils flare. "I don't need to explain to you how important it is that he's brought back under lock and key, do I?"

His mouth dry, Julian swallows. "Absolutely not."

"Good. Let me know as soon as you have something." Taking his seat once more, Melchom waves at the closed door. "George will see you out."

Julian turns, rocking back on his heels as George appears in the doorway with his usual deadpan expression. Tipping the file in his direction, Julian lumbers ahead. Sweat appears on his forehead by the time he makes it back to the front door. It isn't until he flashes himself a few hundred miles away that he takes a deep breath.

Part of him reasons Melchom deserves to know about Theia's situation. What Melchom would want in return for his help is something to ponder. Colin may have been naïve in his youth, but he's right about one thing. He shouldn't trust Melchom.

His only hope now is that Colin can convince Aric to keep his daughter safe until Julian can wrangle this demon and figure out a way to protect her without putting her in Melchom's debt right alongside him.

"What's that saying about the best-laid plans," Julian wonders aloud.

CHAPTER 13

With a grumble, Aamon scratches an itch just under his right arm. Sweat pools at the small of his back as he checks his reflection in the rearview mirror. The first couple of times he'd possessed someone, his reflection unnerved him. Now, it's like changing clothes, or at least how he chooses to think of it.

Smoothing a hand over his sleek ponytail, Aamon allows the pale blonde tendrils to sift through his fingers. He tilts his chin slightly to the left and brushes the back of his knuckles across smooth, porcelain skin. As if suddenly aware of what he'd been doing, Aamon drops his hand into his lap with a sneer. *Pathetic. I am immortal.* This human with her perfect skin will be lucky to survive the night, he reminds himself before gathering his bags and climbing out of the ridiculously compact truck.

The human's poor eyesight is his greatest challenge so far. Twice, on the way over here, he nearly caused a car accident because of the serious visual impairment. Had Aamon known this would be such a significant issue, he would've worked harder to prevent her glasses from breaking during the possession. As it stands now, he has to take short steps and keep his gaze fixed on the wet pavement ahead of him.

Behind him, the sound of hurried footsteps force him to spin around, his fists clenching. Squinting, he recognizes the same blue scrubs his host is wearing and allows his hands to relax. With one hand clutching a crocheted shoulder bag, the woman rushes past him with a quick smile. It takes Aamon an extra moment to continue toward the adult care home.

While small for a demon, Aamon relied on his strengths. Not so much as physical but logical. Stuck in this form, he's even more vulnerable than usual. His mind cites all the ways humans can die as he absently scratches the same itch under his right arm. When he draws close to the front entrance, Aamon takes a breath to settle himself and gives the smooth metal handle a tug.

"Evening, Sophie."

Aamon manages a shaky smile as the guard behind the pane of glass with a nametag that reads Jeremiah slides a clipboard underneath. Closing his eyes, he relies on muscle memory to sign her name across the page before giving it a push under the glass. (Edit)

"Badge?"

"Hm?"

Jeremiah's head cocks as confusion draws his brows together. "You need to scan your badge."

"Oh. Right." His pulse quickens as he yanks on the straps of his purse. The sharp snap of one ripping adds another layer of sweat to the small of his back. "I keep telling myself I'll get a new one," he mumbles, adding a peek under his lashes at the guard. "It's one of those things you never get to, you know?"

"Yep. Been telling myself the same thing when my wallet fell apart."

As Aamon digs through the contents of the purse, he struggles to keep his tone light. "Haven't done it yet, have you?"

"No ma'am."

"Ah, here it is!" Flashing his bleached teeth, Aamon holds the plastic badge up to the card reader. "Have a good night Jeremiah." Clipping the badge to the front of his shirt, Aamon shoves through the metal doors, oblivious to Jeremiah's reaction.

Avoiding the nurse's station straight ahead, Aamon maneuvers quietly through the dimly lit hallways. At this hour, the residents are sleeping, so the staff is the only thing he concerns himself with. Just ahead, one nurse is leaving a room before something catches her attention. Setting her armload down on the small table in the hall, she slips into the room she just left with a sigh. Keeping his steps light, Aamon creeps forward and scans the name on the sheet until he finds the one he's looking for. *Ellie Michaels, room 3218.*

Backtracking, Aamon strolls through the maze of corridors until he finds the correct one. His grip on the purse tightens as he moves towards the gleaming door handle, only for it to open before he can grab it. Eyes wide, Aamon steps back as the nurse glides into the hall. Even with the lighting overhead, he resorts to squinting to make out her name tag, *Dee.*

"Evening, Sophie." Dee flashes him a tired smile as she swipes a hand across her brow. "Are you in this wing tonight?"

"I'm filling in for," Aamon's mind blanks as he grapples for the name lost in the vast amounts of useless information cluttering his hosts' mind. *Who cares how long it takes to boil a damn egg? Or the standard psi for a seventeen-inch tire? Why would a human waste what little time they have holding on to silly facts?*

"Andrea," Dee supplies.

"That's right."

"Alright." Dee caps the pen in her hand and stuffs it into a deep pocket on the front of her scrubs. "Just come find me at the desk when you're done putting your stuff away and we can go over everything I did for my shift."

"Sounds great." Aamon shifts from foot to foot when Dee makes no effort to move from the doorway. "I thought I'd peek in on Ellie first. I heard she's had a rough day."

"Mhm," Dee pulls the door shut behind her with a soft click. "She's taking it pretty hard."

"Understandable," Aamon murmurs and offers what he hopes is an emphatic sigh.

"Theia was the only family she had left. I'm not sure how she's going to cope long term."

"Odds are she won't," he states. "I'll be shocked if she makes it through the night."

Dee bristles. From where he stands, he can see her gentle face harden and her soft blue eyes sparkle with an emotion. "That's highly inappropriate and unprofessional."

Quickly, he realizes his mistake and, with a dip of his head, tries to salvage the situation. "My apologies. I didn't mean for that to sound so insensitive. I've just seen many humans pass on, and that grief can be overwhelming. Please accept my apology." Aamon struggles to sound sincere, but the stern set of her jaw tells him Dee isn't buying it.

She eventually nods her head. "Just be more careful in the future. These people have been through enough. They deserve a little empathy for the time they have left."

"Absolutely."

With that, Dee nods and heads down the hallway, leaving Aamon alone in front of Ellie's door. He takes a deep breath and pushes it open, steeling himself for what he might find inside. Tucked on the far wall, Aamon makes out the single hospital bed, flanked by a side table. The only source of light is from a small blue lamp with brightly colored butterflies in the sheer lamp-shade. Beneath the thick covers, he can make out a still figure. The steady rhythm of her breathing sends a shiver of apprehension through him.

Slipping past the wide recliner, Aamon moves silently towards the bed. A permanent chill gathers in his bones when he stops less than a foot away. As if possessing a sixth sense, Ellie's eyes open. Apparently familiar with his host, she relaxes with a sigh big enough to ripple in the air. The faux leather straps of his purse squeak as his fingers tighten around them. After a peek over his shoulder, Aamon acts.

His hands wrap around her throat to silence her sharp gasp of fear. Her eyes grow big, as if fully comprehending his intention, before her nails begin to claw at him. When her legs thrash to create a ruckus, Aamon leaps across her body to impede her movement as his grip tightens. In this moment, a surge of something foreign explodes in his gut as she struggles helplessly beneath him. Something twisted in him had always drawn him to death. How it strips away all pretense to leave behind a raw essence. As sure as he breathes, Aamon knows he'll seek more like her in the future.

In the present, his grip on her throat tightens even further until her face flushes with an alarming shade of red. His heart pounds at the rush of blood pumping through his veins as she fights back. The sight of her eyes darting back and forth searching for a means of escape brings a vicious smile to his lips. Beneath his finger, her pulse throbs angrily before it begins to grow faint. Eyes bulge in her face as her lips stammer soundlessly for air. Just before her body goes limp beneath him, light bursts within the room, bright enough to bring tears to his eyes. At the same time, a figure fills the doorway.

"What in the hell is going on in here?"

Aamon recognizes that the voice belongs to Dee as the light continues to multiply until its heat sears his skin. With a horrified gasp, he scrambles off his target and tucks himself into a corner as a large presence swallows the space in the small room. Golden hair and striking blue eyes send a quake of fear into Aamon's legs. With a trembling hand, Aamon covers his eyes and drops to his knees. From under the veil of his lashes, he watches as Michael strides over to Ellie's bedside. Inspecting the damage Aamon had already done, tightens his broad shoulders before he turns to address him with a voice that shudders to contain his fury.

"This woman is under my protection," Michael declares and while his voice never raises beyond a whisper, Aamon shudders with the force of it. "Who are you to think you can cause this woman harm?"

Aamon stutters. Since his voice is suddenly absent, he gives his head a quick shake.

Unsatisfied with his answer, Michael moves forward until his feet are inches from Aamon's face pressed to the cold tile floor. "I demand your name, demon."

"A-am. A-amon," he stammers.

"I know why you've attacked this woman," Michael says simply. "What I want to know is who sent you."

Aamon battles with the desire to keep his mouth shut. True, he'd made an alliance with Riordan, but so far all he's gotten from it is a confrontation with one of Heaven's mightiest. *Not exactly doing me any favors.* A full second passes before he's spilling his guts. "Riordan."

"I should've suspected as much."

"Are you going to send me back to hell?"

"No."

The unexpected answer prompts Aamon to lift his head an inch to peek up at Michael's imposing form. "You're not?"

"No." His head turns towards the woman frozen in the room's doorway before he regards Aamon once more. "Hell is too good for the likes of you."

Realization hits him square in the chest. *He's going to erase me altogether!* His mind scrambling, Michael leaves Aamon with no option but to release his hold on his host. Air whooshes around his incorporeal form as he scurries back to his own body. Buried under a pile of dead and rotten leaves, Aamon takes his first gasp of air and shifts once more to put as much distance between himself and Michael as he can. Once he's safe, he'll let Riordan know how badly he'd underestimated how smooth tonight was going to go. Then, it's time he gets a little gratitude for the alliance he made, Aamon muses. If Riordan wants any more help, he'll need to pay his debts first.

Bolstered, Aamon moves quickly within the wind coming off Lake Michigan, a smile already in place.

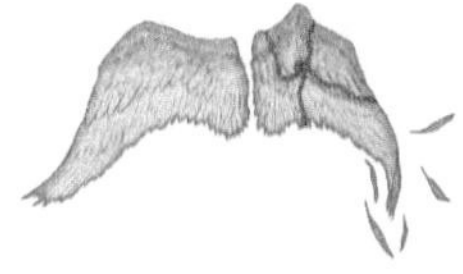

Theia battles with indecision as she follows Colin into the cozy house. The front door opens into a living room full and inviting with over-stuffed furniture. Books and old newspapers cover the hardwood coffee table that stands in front of the couch. Despite her nerves, Theia's initial instinct is to curl up with a good book.

On the far side of the room stands a fireplace made from gray stones. On its mantle, Theia notes a small collection of antique daggers and fat white candles. A vast collection of novels fill the shelves of the book shelf in the corner.

"Have a seat."

Theia turns to see Aric hovering just inside the room as if unwilling to get too close in fear of her bad luck rubbing off on him.

Taking a deep breath to steady her nerves, Theia sinks into the nearest armchair. She can feel the weight of Aric's gaze on her, but she refuses to meet it. Instead, she focuses on the crackling fire and the warmth it spreads throughout the room.

"So, what brings you here?" Aric's voice is calm and calculated, but Theia detects a hint of curiosity underlying his words.

"Colin says you can help me," she says, finally meeting his intense gaze.

Aric raises an eyebrow, clearly surprised by her revelation. "And why would I do that?"

"Because if you don't, she's as good as dead," Colin announces in a deadpan tone.

Theia turns to face Colin, a sense of unease creeping up on her. She hadn't expected him to be so blunt about her situation. She clears her throat before speaking up. "I need help finding a way to control this curse."

"You're not cursed." Amusement laces Aric's voice, and Theia can't help but tap her fingers against her thighs at his casual attitude. "You're a Nephilim."

"And what is that, exactly?"

Colin coughs into his hand just before the dull painting over his shoulder suddenly becomes a work of art for all the interest he shows it. Aric, on the other hand, just nudges one shoulder lazily.

"The offspring of human and angel."

Theia's mouth falls open at the revelation. She had never heard of such a thing before. "That's impossible."

"Unfortunately not," Aric says, crossing his arms over his chest. "And it would explain your...gifts."

Theia's head spins with the new information. She had always known she was different, but she could never explain the strange things that happened around her. The sudden gusts of wind, the flickering of lights, the way people seemed to be drawn to her. It all made sense now. "So, what does this mean for me? How can I control my... abilities?"

"It will not be easy," Aric warns her. "But I can help you."

"How can you help?"

"I'm a Seraph."

Theia frowns, her teeth chewing along the corner of her mouth. "What the hell is a seraph."

"We are soldiers for Heaven. Training those under my command to combat human emotions was my specialty."

Theia leans forward, her interest piqued by Aric's words. "You can teach me how to control my emotions?"

"More than that," Aric says, a glint in his eyes. "I can train you to use your abilities to your advantage."

"How did this happen to me?" Theia winces before blushing hotly. "I mean, I'm a nurse. I know the *how,* but why?"

"What does your father say?"

She blinks and cocks her head to one side. Doesn't he know? "My father is dead," she answers unsteadily, her voice whisper soft as if to lessen the blow.

Aric leans a shoulder against the threshold to the living room, studying her quietly. "How did you find out he's dead?"

"My grandmother," fingernails pick over the pad of her thumb as she searches for anything in the room more interesting than him.

"What else did she tell you?"

"I don't know anything specific about him," Theia admits. "Just that he took off when I was a baby. The devastation was enough to put my mother in the ground soon after."

Aric's nostrils flare, but he says nothing as he shares a quiet look with Colin. When he finally answers her, she'd have to be dumb, blind and stupid to not pick up on the tightly controlled anger in his voice. "Julian is guilty of a lot of things. But for the record, he never ran out on your mother. Not even when it would've saved his own neck in the long run."

"But, Granny said-"

"Then your grandmother was lying or misinformed," Aric clips tightly to cut off what she'd been about to say.

The idea of her grandmother fabricating a story to color her view of Julian raises Theia's pulse. She'd held her share of secrets over the years, true, but who doesn't? Meanwhile, she's just met this man. *Can she really believe anything he has to say?*

Aric seems to sense her hesitation and takes a step closer to her. "Look, Theia, I understand this is a lot to process, but I promise you, if I can help you, I will."

Theia's eyes flicker to Colin, who nods encouragingly. Slowly, she nods in return. "Okay, then. What's the first step?"

Aric's lips curl into a small smile, and for a moment, Theia can see the genuine desire to help her in his hazel-green eyes. "First, you need to sleep."

Theia blinks. "What?"

"Sleep. You look like shit. Tomorrow we can start assessing the extent of your ability and how much control do you have over it."

Theia nods slowly, her mind still mulling over the revelation about her father. She stands up from the armchair, the weight of her exhaustion settling heavily on her shoulders. "Okay," she says quietly. "Sleep sounds good."

Aric leads her to a cozy guest room at the back of the house, complete with a large, comfortable-looking bed and soft, fluffy pillows. He hands her a set of pajamas and a toothbrush, gesturing to the en-suite bathroom at the far end of the room. "Get some rest," he says kindly. "We'll talk more in the morning."

Theia nods again, feeling a sense of relief wash over her. For the first time in weeks, she feels like she's in capable hands. Dropping her bag near the bed, she perches on the edge. The weight of the day's events finally catches up with her and she sags back onto the mattress. She's asleep before her head hits the mattress.

CHAPTER 14

Riordan's heart thumps as he checks his phone for the fifth time since they escorted him to Councilor Rebecca's private chambers. His steps fall heavily as he paces the length of the room like a restless animal. *Aamon should've checked in by now.* That he hadn't, opens a realm of possibilities Riordan can't stop to contemplate right now. *Now,* he needs to focus on placating the councilors. "A feat easier said than done," he mutters.

Left to his own devices, Riordan's first instinct is to sink into the plump couch, put his feet up and grab a quick nap. After considering the struggle he faced standing up from his own couch, he squashes the urge and continues pacing. While the promise of a nap nearly slips through his resolve, he can't risk calling attention to his injuries.

He swallows hard when he reaches the end of his last walk around the couch. For a heartbeat, he entertains giving into the risk to take a seat. Instead, he sinks to one knee beside it and studies his reflection in the floor to ceiling windows dominating the open room.

Sunlight streams through them to illuminate every nook, leaving little space for shadows to hide. These are beautiful decorations, he muses, not walls.

Too grand to be private quarters, Riordan can't ignore a level of serenity that pulls him deeper. White marble floors flow, smooth like the water that likes just beyond. Rich purple curtains drape from ceiling to floor; a stark contrast to the panes of glass and pure whiteness of the floor. Just beyond the nearest wall, the soft chatter of a brook fills the quiet as it races over a riverbed of shiny stones.

Still monitoring his phone, which now shows nothing but black frosted glass where a missed call should be, he entertains himself with thousands of ledgers, stacked on entire walls of shelves. Red and black, the leather is worn where several silver rings clasp across the spine. Upon closer inspection, Riordan can't find anything to tell one apart from the other aside from the order she put them in. *Interesting*.

Like most angels, Rebecca's room is devoid of personality, save for one item. Hanging prominently in the center of the far wall, Riordan studies a simple oil painting.

The canvas depicts a gathering of people on a crisp fall day against a backdrop of tall mountains. So colorful, for a moment, Riordans imagines the birds singing and the wind rustling bright autumn leaves ready to fall. Children hang and dangle from a low branch of an oak tree while the rest lounge and chatter through the rest of their picnic. The reason she'd have to hang this painting sparks his curiosity.

Before he can ponder over it too long, the sweet scent of green apples mixed with salt alerts him to her arrival. Riordan turns just in time to see her slip into the room, adjusting the crisp folds of her robes.

"My apologies," Rebecca murmurs. "I didn't intend to keep you waiting."

"It's hard enough to bring the Nephilim in alive," Riordan replies, his tone cool. "Standing here idly only makes it harder."

Lavender eyes snap with a quick fury before she squashes it with a slow breath. "I was cleaning up your mess, Riordan. If you don't wish to stand around idly, waiting for me, perhaps you should show more restraint in your endeavors."

"The Nephilim destroyed that motel. Not me."

"Ah." Rebecca offers a slow nod, her voice adapting a measured tone. "Why did she collapse the motel, Riordan? Are you telling me it was sheer boredom on her part and had nothing what-so-ever to do with you?"

Riordan swallows around a tight throat. "No Councilor."

"I didn't think so."

A sharp reply flits across his tongue before he bites it back. "Understood," he grumbles lightly. "Is that why you asked to see me?"

"Among other things." She settles herself on the arm of the couch, studying him for a quiet moment. "One of your warriors brought a concern to my attention. Something about not capturing the Nephilim, alive."

Schooling his features, he begins smoothly. "I have every intention of bringing her to you still breathing, Councilor. But after witnessing the devastation she can cause, that may not be entirely possible."

"Yes. Thankfully, my archivist's report no casualties at either scene." Rebecca dips her blonde head for a moment, but not before Riordan spies a dark level of confusion in her eyes. "Why do you think that is? Has she had training?"

"I doubt it. Everything I've seen tells me she reacts off emotion. The stronger the emotion, the stronger the power."

"And yet, it's hurt no one."

"I wouldn't say that." Riordan snaps and stops his hand mid-motion from going to his side.

"No humans," she concedes.

"For now. It's only a matter of time."

"That's the reason our council sanctioned their imprisonment in the first place, Riordan." Rebecca's back straightens as she drops folded hands into her lap. "Humans are supposed to be their own rulers. We can't have Nephilim running amok threatening dominance."

"Agreed."

"Have you located any evidence to say it is who you believe?"

"You mean Julian?" Riordan pauses. Now's his chance to get the full weight of heaven behind him. The temptation to lie is heavy enough it leaves a bead of sweat on his forehead. "No. It claims to have never met the father."

"I see."

Unless he's mistaken, his answer relaxes the tension from Rebecca's shoulders. "It's only a matter of time, Councilor. Either it isn't who I think, which changes nothing. Or it is. Which changes everything."

"The council cannot, *will not*, charge Aric with treason without proof Riordan."

His jaw tightens. "Then I'll get you proof. One way or the other."

"That'll be all. You're dismissed." Rebecca murmurs as she crosses the room to pull one of her ledgers from the shelf. When he makes no move to leave, she lifts her head. Brows arch across her smooth forehead as her eyes narrow at him. "Is there something else?"

Giving himself a shake, Riordan pulls himself from his wonderings. "No, Councilor," he purrs and slips from the room while he wonders just what those ledgers entail. There isn't enough of them to be for humans, and too many for angels. *Right?*

Moving away from the door, he can't help but store his questions regarding Rebecca's ledgers away for a later date. As he readies himself to flash from the realm, a heavy hand drops on his shoulder.

Spinning to confront the blatant level of disrespect, his eyes widen to see archangel Michael less than one step behind him. While his ego has always been strong, the urge to lower his eyes is stronger. As he contemplates the sight of clunky boots on marble floors, Riordan waits for Michael to explain his arrival. He doesn't have to wait long.

"I came across a demon prowling an elderly care home tonight," smooth words shift across Riordan's skin as Michael speaks with a level of calm most are incapable of. "He was trying to take the life of Ellie Martin."

Riordan's gut twists painfully. *Now I know why Aamon never checked in.* Fingers press against damp palms as he distracts himself with tracing the laces of Michaels boots. Only once a level of calm blooms in his chest does he lift his eyes. While Michael's square jaw remains tight, his blue eyes glitter with questions.

"A demon," Riordan asks, cursing the way the words stutter over his lips before leaving.

"Indeed." Removing his hand from Riordan's shoulder, he catches Michael scrubbing his palm over the soft cotton of his blue t-shirt. "He told me he was running an errand, for you."

"Me?" Riordan allows his jaw to go slack and his murky eyes widen with shock. "Why would I send a demon to kill a human?"

"I wondered the same thing myself. The only thing I can figure is that it has something to do with the Nephilim you're tracking."

"I've been here," Riordan defends hotly. "You can ask Councilor Rebecca."

"Hmm, I may do that." Michael nods but strong features betray his level of disbelief over Riordan's answers. "Regardless as to the why. I've placed Ellie Martin under my protection. Should any demon or *angel* seek to harm her again, they will face my sword."

"Un-under," Riordan coughs. "Under-stood," he stumbles, inwardly cursing the vast amounts of sweats coating his skin. The stick of his clothes forces him to shift awkwardly.

As if satisfied with his response, Michael leaves, as silent as he arrived. Just how far off the rails this mission is, sparks a moment of panic within him. If the sensation wasn't so foreign to him, Riordan might give it the wide berth it deserves but the gripping weight against his heart is too distracting.

The first rays of dawn trickle through bare windows to cast a soft glow inside the room as the fog of sleep shifts. Theia releases a deep breath and stretches her limbs, testing the softness of the massive bed she occupies. The most comfortable bed she's ever slept in, allowing Theia a full night's rest tempts her to close her eyes and fall back to sleep until the sudden flood of prior events invade her brain. With a gasp, she uses an elbow to push herself upright while her heart carries a rhythm hard enough to crack ribs. *Aric.*

One by one, Theia tracks the memory of Colin bringing her to Aric for help. Instead, he offered an explosive revelation about her father. One that makes every story Granny told her about him, a lie. Like then, her stomach clenches at the possibility.

Could she? Definitely. Would she? No. Theia tosses her head side to side as if to cement that belief into her bones. "He's wrong," she mutters then shifts her focus to her surroundings instead of the nauseousness threatening to overtake her.

Even with the giant-sized bed dominating the bedroom, there's plenty of space left over. Painted in a soft white, the walls emit a gentle calming glow. Sewn with various shades of deep reds, golden yellows and sultry orange tones, the patchwork quilt beneath her breathes life into an otherwise sterile environment. A vast canopy of sheer ivory cloth hangs above her, draping over the sides to offer a thin veil of privacy.

To her left, a row of tall, elegant windows fill the entire wall, offering her a stunning view of rolling hills and a small copse of trees surrounding an enchanting lake. Aside from the bed, a hefty dresser graces one wall, an extensive bookcase, the other. *Far from the dingy motel room I slept in the night before*, she muses and throws her legs over the side of the bed.

The quick knock on the door has Theia swallowing her squeak of alarm. "Who is it?" *Really? I'm an idiot.*

"It's me, Aric."

Theia freezes as the smooth baritone of his voice slips beyond the closed door and wraps her arms around herself. *Stop it. He's not only a stranger, he's a liar.* When her stomach flips in response, Theia rolls her eyes. *I just need to refill my medication. Then, everything will be the way it was before this whole mess started.*

Crossing the room, she shakes the tremble from her hands long enough to crack open the door. At the soft protest of hinges, Aric turns around to peer through the meager opening she allows. Piercing eyes, a prominent nose and a strong, stubbled jawline invade her line of sight, forcing her back a step. "What is it?"

"I thought you might be hungry?"

Food. Before Theia can come up with an excuse that will have him walking away, her stomach grumbles. As heat flood's her face, Aric offers a tiny smile of understanding.

"This way," spinning on a bare foot, Aric retreats towards the other end of the house, leaving Theia little option but to follow.

The unmistakable fragrance of sizzling bacon and brewing coffee teases her as Aric leads her into a cozy kitchen with light wooden cabinets and granite countertops. Steam rises from a plate of eggs left on the counter while the bacon continues to crackle in a frying pan. With a soft grunt, Aric gestures towards one of the barstools before he moves to pull the bacon from the pan.

"I hope you like eggs and bacon."

"Anything is fine," Theia replies as she lowers herself gently onto the padded stool. When he shoots her a look of impatience, Theia forces a smile. "Is there anyone who eats meat that doesn't like bacon?" After a curt nod, he sets a full plate of scrambled eggs, bacon and toast in front of her. While Theia takes a bite of her eggs with a strained sigh, Aric sets a cup of coffee next to her plate.

"Not sure how you take your coffee, but I have sugar and milk."

"Sugar is fine," she mumbles around a mouthful of food then offers a sheepish smile. *He must think me half-starved.* In truth, it's been a long time since Theia sat down for a proper meal.

Between Granny living in the care home and her crazy work hours, she usually settles for whatever can be heated in a microwave. *Nothing wrong with enjoying a home-cooked meal*, Theia reasons as she savors each bite, basking in the moment of normalcy amidst the chaos overrunning her life.

Once she finishes, Aric swoops up her plate to wash in a deep sink before using a hand towel to dry them off. He's in the process of putting the dishes in their respective places when something occurs to her.

"Where's Colin?"

"He had to take care of some things."

"What things? He seemed hell bent on getting me here."

Aric gives her a quiet, long look. "Something about a motel?"

"Oh." Theia squirms in her seat as Aric continues to stare at her. "Was anyone hurt?"

"Not according to the internet."

"You have internet?"

"Why do you sound so surprised?"

"I don't know," Theia answers, mulling it over in her head before continuing.

"Really?" Aric drapes the hand towel in front of the stove then turns to give her his full attention. The way he leans a hip against the counter-top and crosses his arms in front of his chest leaves her mouth dry.

Don't look at his shoulders. Or his incredibly long legs! Focus on something less likely to make you stutter.

"Were you really a soldier?"

"Again with the surprise. Should I be offended?"

"No." Theia avoids his direct approach. "You just don't seem the type."

"Why not?"

Theia takes a deep breath to wrangle her thoughts. Strong and silent? Check. Physically capable? Check, check. If she tables the quiet sophistication of his house, Theia could picture him as a soldier, if not for one thing. "It's the hair." When Aric frowns, she tries not to notice how the action puckers his forehead or tightens his jaw.

"My hair?"

"Mhmm," Theia murmurs around a sip of coffee. "Most soldiers wear their hair much shorter." *Not that I'm complaining*, she adds silently. In her opinion, his pale blonde hair pulled back into a loose bun adds the perfect accent to his face. *Not that I should be noticing in the first place.*

"Hmm," Aric steps around the kitchen to add coffee to a large blue ceramic mug. "Do you know the history of long hair?"

"It has a history?"

"Traditionally, long hair symbolized masculinity. Think of Vikings, or your American Indians. Don't see many depicted with short hair, do you?"

As she watches him add way too many spoonfuls of sugar to his coffee, Theia's nose wrinkles with the epiphany. "I suppose not."

Aric takes a sip of his coffee, his eyes never wavering from hers. "To cut my hair is a sign of disrespect. A symbol of shame to the other Seraph's."

"You said you're a soldier. For who?" Even as her head spins with new information, Theia can't ignore the way his fingers flex around the mug in his hands.

"Seraphs are an order of warriors overseen by the Council. Think of them as the Council's right hand."

"That sounds ominous."

"As far as you're concerned Theia, the Council is very ominous."

"If you're a Seraph, why do you say *they* and not *we*?"

The expression in his hazel-green eyes hardens. "I retired." As if those two words should satisfy her, he takes another sip of his coffee.

From the corner of her eye, she studies the way his muscles move beneath his shirt. Before she realizes it, a shiver skitters down her spine. *What is wrong with me? I've never been this attracted to anyone before.*

She tries to convince herself that her sudden and intense emotions are a side effect of not taking her medications. But the growing flutter in her stomach says otherwise. Regardless, there's something unique about Aric that draws her. Whatever it is, it's best to steer clear of it altogether.

Pushing those feelings deep, deep under the rubble of everything else, she returns to their conversation. "I didn't realize one could *retire* from Heaven."

The smile he responds with is quick and brilliant. "Guess you learned two new things today." Setting his cup on the counter, he closes the gap between them until he's less than three feet away. The thorough once over her gives her leaves Theia's lungs tight. "Let's see this wound."

Busy trying to ignore the way her heart pounds and her skin prickles over his close proximity, Theia struggles to process what she was supposed to hear. "Wound?"

"You're injured." Aric tilts his head and studies her intently. "Let's see it."

"H-how do you know that?"

"I can read your mind," he states flatly.

Theia sputters as heat floods her from hairline to her toes. *Dear Lord! I've been sitting here like a horny teenager and he has a front-row seat.* As she struggles to center her breathing, her fingers grip the counter.

"I'm kidding, Theia."

After a sharp gasp of alarm, Theia whirls on the stool to face him, her eyes searching for anything that'll prove he's lying. The small twitch in the left corner of his mouth could go either way. Narrowing her eyes, Theia lifts her chin. "Then how did you know?"

"I can smell it."

Theia's lips purse. "Smell it?"

"Some angels have a unique scent. The stench of blood taints yours."

"Mine?"

Aric heaves a sigh that rocks his shoulders before he jams his hands into the front pocket of his jeans. "Yes, Theia. Lemon and mint." His lips thin. "And blood."

Now that he mentions it, Theia inhales deep and picks up the distinct smell of vanilla and cedar around him. She recalls the same fragrance on the bed she surrendered her exhaustion to the day before. Her eyes widen slightly. "I didn't know."

After another sigh fills the room as Aric frowns. "I'm not surprised. I understand why your family felt the need to shelter you, but it did you no favors. Now, let's see it."

Bristling over the jab against her family, Theia shoves herself to her feet and lifts her shirt high enough to expose the large bandage taped to her stomach. When he moves closer, her ability to breathe ceases. Heat slithers across her skin as he lifts two corners back to study the wound underneath. When he brushes a finger over the area, Theia counts the strands of hair in his bent head until the sudden rush of awareness passes. Despite what she tells herself, she can't argue with the sense of longing that explodes in her gut when he adjusts the bandage and steps away.

"It's healing fairly well." His voice is a low rasp, like a chainsaw coming to life. "Might explain why you were so tired when you arrived."

Theia opens her mouth to ask what he meant when footsteps echo through the kitchen. A second later, Colin appears with a frown marring his classically handsome features. "We have a problem," he announces, his gaze flickering between Aric and Theia.

CHAPTER 15

Aric's teeth set as Colin's arrival ramps up the tension in the air. Taking a breath, he folds his arms across his chest and speaks in a measured tone. "What's the problem, Colin?" Even as he voices the question, he mentally kicks himself. *Do I really want to know?* So far, Colin shows up with bad news and chaos he's been avoiding for nearly thirty years. Case in point, Theia.

A short time before, he noticed her body relax as she ate her breakfast with more enthusiasm than the simple food warranted. Now, she's drumming her fingers against the side of her leg and gnawing at her bottom lip. When Colin finally clues them both in, the blood drains from her face so quickly, Aric takes a step closer in case she faints.

"My informant just told me a demon attacked her grandmother," Colin says simply.

Theia's whispers. "What?"

"She's okay," Colin rushes to add, deflating the tension from Theia's shoulders. "Apparently, Michael has taken an interest in the human."

Brows knit as Theia's gaze bounces from him to Colin. "Michael?"

"The archangel," Aric and Colin respond in unison.

Their answer drops Theia's butt back onto her stool. One hand rubs methodically at her forehead as she stares off into the distance. "I thought she was losing her mind," she mumbles quietly. "I didn't believe her."

Crouching, Aric lowers himself until he's eye level with Theia. After she spends a moment avoiding him, her eyes lock on his and the effect acts as a bulldozer on Aric's lungs. The first time he'd stared into her eyes, he'd felt a peaceful sense of happiness unfurl in his chest. Now, the fear and worry darkening their vibrant color makes his skin feel two sizes too small. Swallowing beyond the tightness in his throat, Aric inserts a measure of kindness into his voice. "What did she say?"

Theia gives her head a rough shake. "Just that she had an angel visiting her. I thought it was a symptom of her illness."

Reacting on instinct, Aric folds one of her small hands within his. Teeth clench on his gasp as her cold hand lays unmoving in his. Using both of his, Aric vigorously rubs warmth into one hand and then the other. "You couldn't have known, Theia," he assures her in an attempt to retrieve her from the emotions she's drowning herself in. While she meets his eyes, the sense of vacancy he gets from her expression adds a new level to his worry. "Theia," he tries again, his voice slightly harder the second time. When that doesn't work, Aric tamps down on his own emotions to bark her name roughly.

Blinking, Theia focuses on his face. Her jaw flexes for a brief moment before her stubborn chin lifts defiantly. "I should've known."

Seeing her firmly rooted in the present, Aric drops her hands and pushes himself to his feet. "I don't like the coincidence of this." Fingers curl into large fists to ward off the sudden wash of desolation without Theia's hands in his.

Colin nods, "I agree. It doesn't feel random at all, but why would a demon target her grandmother?"

Theia lets out a shaky breath before responding. "Because of me."

Aric's head snaps in her direction. "How would they know about you?"

Theia releases a humorless laugh. "That's part of a longer story."

"One we don't have the time for," Colin chimes in. "My source also says Riordan is recruiting new soldiers to stop Theia. I give it a few hours at most, then they'll be here."

"She's not ready," Aric counters. "Without the proper training, all those emotions might as well be raw and exposed nerves."

"So train her, Aric." Colin plants his hands on a narrow set of hips. "It's your damn job."

"Correction, was my job." Rubbing a hand across the back of his neck, Aric begins to pace to burn off the restlessness growing in his stomach. "I retired, remember."

Undeterred, Colin pushes. "Is that what you'd like me to tell Julian? After everything that's happened?"

Aric's lip curls, his response a snarl of sounds. "Fuck you."

"Careful, Buddy," Colin soothes, retreating several steps towards the nearest exit. "We don't need you losing your temper right now."

The air in the room cools considerably as Aric battles with his inner demons and memories he'd rather forget. *Much like that night, his vision darkens until all he can make out in the sliver of moonlight is a vast cornfield. Knuckles tighten as the scene begins with Julian's cry of outrage. Panting, Aric struggles to reach the altercation in time. With the help of his wings, he stops the blade from descending on Julian's neck with hardly an inch to spare. The shriek of alarm sends him backtracking. His head throbs as he arrives just in time to watch her crumple to the ground. Pain twists like a knife in Aric's heart, dropping him to his knees. Under the layers of armor, he shivers as the cold breeze kisses over skin damp with sweat. As if still rooted in the past, he watches her warm blood coat his armor before seeping through his fingers.*

"Aric!" This cry of alarm is closer, snapping Aric's eyes open with a flutter. Blinking, he stares into Theia's face inches from his own. Just outside the window, thick, black clouds blot out the morning sun a moment before rain batters the soft ground. Theia jumps and squeaks at the snap of lightning and the crack of thunder right overhead. Framing his face with her hands, she forces him to meet her eyes, her desperation obvious. "Snap out of it!"

As a hard rain pelts the windows, Aric locks his eyes on Theia's. The memory is so vivid, his arms ache with the weight of her body and the scent of blood overwhelms his sharp senses until his stomach rolls. Once the initial shock passes, the bitter taste of failure clings to his tongue. With a stuttered shake of his head, Aric pulls in a breath as the skies clear. It's not the first time his past crept up on him, but he knows it won't be the last. *I can't afford to lose control like that, not with Theia's safety at stake.*

"I'm sorry," he utters, his voice rough. "I just... I got lost in my thoughts."

Theia's face softens as she lays a hand against his arm. "It's okay," she croons. "What happened?"

Aric hesitates. *Can't keep it from her forever. No,* he muses. *Just a little while lo*nger. "We can't stay here. I need to get you somewhere safe."

"What do you need me to do?"

The question reminds Aric of Colin's presence in the archway leading towards the living room. "Stick with Julian. Make sure he does nothing stupid." He registers Colin's quick nod although he makes no attempt to carry out the request. Instead, he rocks back on his heels anxiously, his amber eyes dark with concern. "What?"

"Are you prepared to do what needs to be done?"

Aric's gaze drifts over Theia standing quietly at the end of the counter. There's still time to walk away. Wash his hands of the whole situation and find some place quieter to spend eternity. *You'll go batshit crazy* within a century. Hell, there were times over the last thirty years they had tempted him to dust off his weapons and get back in the fight. The only thing stopping him is the dilemma of which side he should fight on. Now that Theia's neck is on the line, he finds that dilemma isn't nearly as complicated as it'd been before.

Meeting Colin's shrewd speculation, Aric gives his head a dip. "Don't have a choice. Do I?" Flicking the flat red button on the coffee pot to turn off the hotplate underneath, he starts for the basement. "Help her get ready to go. I'll be right back."

Theia isn't sure how long they've been driving, but the sun had sunk into the horizon a while ago. Overruled by Aric and Colin, she'd left her car in his driveway and climbed into the passenger seat of Aric's sleek, black Lexus.

As they drive, she can't help but notice the tension radiating off Aric. His grip on the steering wheel is knuckle white, his jaw set so tightly, she's certain he'll crack a tooth. After a deep breath, Theia attempts to pull him from his thoughts.

"Are you okay?"

"I'm fine." Aric's response is a growl that sends a shiver across the nape of her neck. Absently, she runs a hand over the goosebumps peppering her arms.

"Where are we going?"

"Someplace you can train without hurting anyone."

"And if I don't want to train?"

Aric scoffs, his eyes never wavering from the endless stretch of road in front of them. "Then you'd be better off letting Riordan put you down."

Theia gapes. "You make me sound like a rabid dog."

"Without control, that's what you'll be."

"I had control," she defends hotly. "For years I was fine. No flare-ups, no accidents."

His eyes leave the road long enough to send her a skeptical glance. "How did you manage that?"

"My grandmother took me to a therapist. After finding the right medication and dosage, I've been taking it ever since." Theia didn't think it was possible for his jaw to harden any further, but he proves her wrong.

"What changed?"

"I forgot to refill my medication."

Aric's grip tightens on the steering wheel until the leather groans under the pressure. "You forgot? How does someone forget something so important?"

Theia shrugs and turns her attention to her window. "I just did," she admits, swallowing beyond the ache in the back of her throat. "I didn't feel any different, so I thought I had more time."

"You didn't feel any different?" Aric repeats incredulously. "You're a bomb, Theia."

"I know that now," she grumbles pressing a hand to her flushed cheeks. "I'm sorry."

"Sorry won't cut it."

Theia flinches from his matter-of-fact tone and heaves a sigh. "I know."

"Do you have any idea what could've happened? You could've killed innocent people."

"But I didn't."

"You got lucky. Your grandmother should've had you learn control, not pump you with medication to numb the emotions."

"She probably didn't understand any more than I did."

"That's one theory."

Her pulse racing, Theia peers across the now dark interior of the car. "What's that supposed to mean?" Under the dim lights from the dashboard, Aric's nostrils flare, yet he remains silent.

Soon, they're pulling off the main road and onto an overgrown two track leading deep into the woods. The tension between them thickens as he stops the car in front of a quaint cabin with a wide porch built from two-by-fours.

"We're here."

Theia hesitates, her hand hovering over the door handle. Once she steps out of this car, there's no going back. The training Aric has in store for her will no doubt be intense. *Am I ready for that?* As Aric moves to climb out of his side of the car, she asks the question nagging at the back of her mind. "What if I go back on the medication? And promise to never forget refilling it again?"

Aric stills for a moment before swinging his shoulders around in the seat to face her. "Riordan has your scent Theia. And trust me when I tell you, he'll never stop looking." Earlier where his expression had been carved from stone, she spots a softening around his mouth and a subtle light in his eyes. "If you go back now, the only thing that medication will do, is get you killed."

The knot in her stomach twists painfully as Theia considers the truth of what he says. Either path she chooses will have their own share of risks. *Would you rather learn control and possibly live? Or go back to the zombie life until Riordan finds you?* It only takes a moment for her to nod her head and open the car door. Aric follows her out and walks around to the trunk to retrieve their bags.

Just ahead, the cabin stands on a thicket of weeds and fallen leaves. Warm, yellow light shines through small windows to chase the away the ominous darkness. In the distance, Theia picks up the faint sound of a dog barking along with the soft chittering of insects hiding within the tall grass on her left. When she breathes in, the pungent scent of pine, wood and rotting leaves fills her lungs. Dust coats the handmade porch, green with moss as neglected ivy strangles the wood siding and air plants sprawl down the walls.

"Certainly isn't the city," Theia breathes, her legs locked in place. She can't recall a time she'd spent so much as a night in the wilderness. When she was fifteen, she'd been invited to go camping with her classmates, but one look at the cluster of tents had been enough to chase her back into the humming bustle of familiarity.

"Come on," Aric prods.

As they approach the cabin, the front door swings open and a man steps out onto the porch. He's tall and muscular with short, dark hair and a thick beard. Prominent scars line his arms and face. *Wonder who he trained with.*

"You're all set Aric. I stocked the cupboards, and the woodshed out back. Should keep you set for a couple of weeks, at least."

"Thank you, Jericho." Aric replies, taking the steps of the porch two at a time. "This is Theia. Theia, this is Jericho."

"Nice to meet you," she murmurs politely, her smile faltering as she takes in the ugly scars marring what might've been a handsome face.

As if aware of her discomfort, Jericho looks away. "You too, Theia."

"Will, um," she pauses while trying to nail down a coherent thought. "Will you be training me as well?"

"No ma'am. I leave that stuff to Aric." Once Aric sets the bags down inside the front door, he turns and shakes Jericho's impressive hand. "I'm not far away so if either of you two need anything else, feel free to call me."

"Will do. Thanks again."

Jericho dips his dark head after flashing a genuine smile that peels the years from his face. "My pleasure." As he lumbers towards the beat up truck near the road, Aric ushers Theia into the cabin.

The inside of the cabin is cozy and rustic, with wooden walls and a stone fireplace. Something cooks on the stove, filling the room with a mouth-watering aroma that inspires a low, rumbling growl from her stomach.

Amusement flickers in Aric's eyes before an eyebrow quirks. "Hungry?"

With a sheepish smile, Theia jerks a nod. "Yeah, sorry."

"Don't apologize. It's been a long day," he says. "You should've said something earlier. I would've stopped."

"I didn't realize how hungry I am until I smelled that."

Aric chuckles, "Fair enough." Armed with a couple bowls, he crosses to the stove and lifts the lid on the pot, revealing a hearty stew. He fills both bowls with a shocking amount of food before passing one to Theia. "Dig in."

Her smile genuine, she pulls one of the two chairs away from the fat, square table and takes a tentative bite. Flavor explodes along her tongue, each one complimenting the next until she's nearly moaning in response. When she opens her eyes, the smile twitching along Aric's lips makes her wonder if she'd moaned aloud or just thought about it.

"Good, huh?"

"This is amazing." Theia grins and shovels two more spoonfuls into her mouth.

"Over the countless years Jericho has been cooking, I've yet to try something I don't like." Aric's spoon circles the inside of the bowl. "This is my favorite though."

As they eat, recent events preoccupy her mind. She's in a cabin in the middle of nowhere with a man she barely knows, because a stranger said she could trust him. This is how some of those, I shouldn't be alive stories start out. Theia battles with a flare of apprehension as Aric uses the edge of his spoon to scrape his bowl clean.

His eyes never stray from the bowl in his hands, so when he speaks, the sudden burst of sound causes Theia to jump slightly. "I didn't bring you out here to kill you, Theia."

Staring at him with wide eyes, Theia's mouth open and closes several times before sound emerges. "H-how'd you know?"

Wide-set shoulders shift up, holding a moment, then drop with a sigh that's too big for the small cabin to contain. His eyes shift slightly to meet her gaze with a directness she comes to associate with Aric. "Emotions were meant for human. Not us. At least, that's what the Council tells us. Some believe it's all part of a grand plan."

"You're talking about, if God doesn't make mistakes, then he made it so I would feel this way?"

"Kind of. Regardless of where a person stands on the debate, a lot of angels over the centuries have fallen victim to their emotions. Others, avoid the sentiment altogether."

"And you?"

"I've never mastered cutting myself off from the emotion, however, I don't telegraph it quite as loud as you do." With a small smile, Aric sweeps a hand around her face. "Your emotions color the surrounding air."

"Like magic?" Wouldn't that be cool! What kid wasn't obsessed with magic at one point or another. Theia is in the midst of exploring those possibilities when Aric's light chuckle squashes all those childhood dreams in one fell swoop.

"More like your aura reacts to your emotions. Not every angel can see them, of course, it's a talent much like your fire bending. Your food is getting cold."

"So, what exactly is the plan, here?" she asks between bites. Theia can't help but feel a sense of unease. She's in a strange place with a man she barely knows, about to train in a power she can hardly control. But the thought of hurting someone, of losing control and causing destruction, is even more terrifying.

The chair whines as Aric leans back. "We'll start with the basics. Breathing, meditation and visualization. Once you master those, we'll move on to more advanced techniques like defense, offense and energy manipulation."

"How long will all that take?"

"Depends on how fast you learn, Theia. We won't be able to hide you forever, so it's best to get started first thing in the morning."

Once she finishes her supper, Aric sweeps up the bowls and carries them to the sink. "There's a bedroom just off the living room, and a bathroom down this hall. Might be a good idea to call it a night. You're going to need your rest for tomorrow."

"Where will you sleep?"

"I don't sleep much. On the off chance I doze off, the couch will be fine." Aric states simply, retrieving her backpack and passing it to her over the table.

Fingers tighten on the thick straps as Theia rises from the table. "Okay. Night Aric."

"Goodnight Theia."

CHAPTER 16

The moment the air shifts around him, Aamon is on alert. "Any news?" he asks as Riordan appears less than ten feet away.

The angel takes a moment to search his surroundings, his lips curling from the stench of the alley. "Why do we always meet in places like this?"

Aamon offers a smooth shrug. The long, dark alley reeks of urine and trash bins. With an angry buzzing sound, a single, meager light-bulb on the corner barely illuminates where he stands. The rough concrete building covered in graffiti and grime behind him is cold, the heat of the day having cooled rapidly with the setting sun. A mixture of scurrying rats, the moaning of derelicts struggling to find sleep exposed to the elements, and the steady thrum of club music fills his ears. When he breathes in, a blend of trash, rotten food and the stench of decay clings to his nose. *Better than sulfur and rotting flesh.* Realizing Riordan still waits for an answer, Aamon offers a smile of jagged teeth. "I blend in here."

Riordan scoffs and situates himself near the center of the alley in a way Aamon assumes is to keep from touching anything that won't wash off. "I'm busy, Aamon. I can't keep running every time you call."

"I need an update. It's been months and Melchom still sits on his throne."

"I have bigger problems than Melchom."

"You might. I don't," Aamon insists in a tight voice. "You promised me the power to usurp him."

"In return for the Nephilim's head. Last I checked, I don't have that yet."

"That's your problem. I pointed her out." When a homeless person shifts restlessly in a damp box a short distance away, Aamon lowers his voice to a stern whisper. "I've done everything you've asked. Almost lost *my* head too. It's time to hold up your end of the deal."

"Ah, yes. Michael." Riordan's lips thin. "Thanks for the heads up on that, by the way."

"I was going to call you the moment I was safe. I didn't know he'd rush to confront you."

"This discussion is pointless. I can give you Melchom's power, but you'll never take him down by yourself," Riordan reasons, a sneer across his face when a particular rat ventures too close. As if noticing the flux in power, the rodent stands on his back legs and sniffs the air. Whatever he senses has him skittering off in the other direction with a rattle of metal trash cans.

A flutter grows in Aamon's stomach as he leans closer. "I have a plan. I just need what you promised."

"Melchom has an army of demons at his disposal."

"I've found a lot of allies while you chase your tail, trying to find one untrained Nephilim."

Riordan's nostrils flare. "You'll really betray your own kind?"

"I'm a demon. Betrayal is in my nature." Aamon flicks a tongue against his teeth, hissing when the copper taste of blood splashes over his tastebuds. "Besides, once they see this is *for* them, they'll settle. Eventually."

With a scathing glance, Riordan nods. "Fine. I'll give you the power of Melchom, but then you're on your own. I have better things to do than cater to your every whim."

Before Aamon can utter an agreement, bright light floods the alley. Shielding his eyes, his body jerks when a flash of heat sears across his skin before he falls to the ground. Muscles twitch with electric stimulation. Shaking uncontrollably, an unexpected surge of energy slams into his body. Screaming in agony as he lies on the dirty pavement and breaks out in a cold sweat. Even amidst the pain that threatens to overwhelm him, a power grows. Swelling within his chest, it coalesces and strengthens to pour into his arms and legs. Once the pain subsides, Aamon marvels at the sensation of superiority leaking from his pores. Gasping for air, he staggers to his feet, his legs trembling with a newfound strength.

With a smirk on his pinched features, Riordan stands off to one side. "There," he says, his arms folding across his chest. "You have power to rival Melchom."

Aamon nods, fighting to catch his breath. Blinking several times, his eyes burn with an infernal light as energy crackles around him. Reaching up to touch his face, the absence of boils over his skin nearly brings a tear to his eye. "This is incredible," he breathes as dominance hums alongside his organs. *I've never felt so alive!*

"Use it wisely."

Aamon's heart skips a beat as a grin tilts his lips. "I will."

"Don't forget our deal," Riordan warns, his eyes narrowing slightly. "Whether it's you or Melchom on that throne, the Nephilim is mine."

"You have my word."

"I hope so. Otherwise, Melchom will be the least of your problems," Riordan swears before disappearing in a burst of light.

Aamon spends the next few minutes plotting his revenge. Once he adjusts to the constant flow of energy, he leaves to gather his allies.

Stepping out from the shadows, Julian's form solidifies. So far, the demon is unaware of his tail as he flits from one city to the next. The erratic pattern of his movements makes predicting his next stop near impossible, leaving Julian no choice to but follow and wait for an opportunity. *Until now.*

That Riordan would make a deal with the likes of Aamon speaks volumes about his level of insanity. While Julian had a million reasons not to trust the Seraph, this new development tops most of them. *Most.* Figuring he's given Aamon enough of a headstart, Julian trails along behind him, waiting for his moment to strike.

A flash of pain erupts in her right hip as Theia crashes to the floor. *Chalk that up to yet another bruise,* her brain whispers as she climbs back to her feet. Adjusting her grip on the sword's hilt, she widens her stance and prepares for another round of humiliation. They'd been at it for months now. While Aric promised to teach her control, he failed to mention the hard-knock tactics.

Her day begins at four a.m. with a light breakfast and an hour of meditation. Then she runs headfirst into hand to hand combat and self defense training. After breaking for yet another light meal, Aric starts sword training. The day ends with emotional control and a hearty dinner. It isn't long after that Theia falls into her bed, exhausted and sore. They've been stuck on sword training so long today, she wonders if they'll even reach the emotional stuff before Aric calls a halt to the day. *You knew this was going to be grueling.*

"Again," Aric barks, to snap her back to the present. He's a formidable opponent, tall and broad-shouldered, with sharp hazel eyes that pierce through to her very soul. He's pushing her hard, but as much as she wants to scream at him and give up, there's a part of her that revels in the challenge.

Tightening her grip, she launches herself at him. The surrounding forest swallows up the sound of metal clashing as the two dance around each other. Even as the knots in her muscles add to the weight of her sword, she pushes forward. *You've come too far to let a little pain stop you.* Lunging forward, she aims her sword at Aric's chest.

After a shift of his feet, Aric parries and knocks her sword aside. Stuck in the momentum, Theia stumbles. Legs quiver as she remains upright this time, turning just in time to see Aric's sword coming straight for her head. Ducking, her ears pick up on the soft whistle the blade makes in the air as it clears her head by a few inches at most. Seizing the moment, she strikes. After her sword connects with Aric's, she forces her way past his defenses only to have him block her blow at the last second. Instead of the counter she's ready for, Aric uses his foot to sweep her legs out from under her.

"Come on, Theia," he taunts, a small smirk on his lips. "You're not even trying."

Theia grits her teeth to bite back her retort as a sharp wave of pain explodes across her butt. *He's right.* She's holding back, afraid of hurting him or herself. *Nothing to do but push through it,* as Granny would say. Muscles prime as her jaw clenches before she charges with renewed determination. Her movements quick and precise, she blocks his strike and counters with a swing of her own. Tiny sparks fly from the blades as they battle until sweat drips down her forehead and her muscles scream for parlay. By the time Aric is satisfied with her display, sweat pours off both of them.

After a step back, Aric's eyes scan over her for a moment. "You're improving," he remarks with a jerking nod. "But you're still too slow. You need to anticipate your opponent's moves," he adds tossing her a towel before wiping his face with the other.

"I don't see why I have to learn this. It's not the dark ages any more."

"True, but this is only way to stop an angel." With an arc of his arm, Aric brings his sword towards his front. As blade passes along the hard angles of his face, it threatens to take a swath of stubble from his chin. "Otherwise, Theia, you allow him to live only to fight him again later."

Theia's pert nose wrinkles as she scrubs a thick layer of sweat from her forehead.. "I'm not interested in taking a life. Not even Riordan's."

"What if it comes down to you or him? Will you hesitate?"

"I don't know."

Aric's lips thin slightly over her answer before he takes her sword and marches in the cabin's direction.

With a grumble, Theia jogs along to catch up. "What's that look for?"

"Riordan will not hesitate to kill you, Theia. Not for a moment. If you continue to doubt yourself, you're giving him the opportunity to accomplish his goal."

"Sounds like you two have history."

Vibrations flutter in the air around them as Aric bristles. Avoiding her gaze, he slips in through the back door and hangs the swords on steel placards nailed to the wall. Following him inside, Theia adjusts to the thick tension between them. Stopping at the sink, Aric fills two glasses with water before passing one to her without so much as a glance in her direction.

"Aric?"

"He was under my command for quite some time," Aric admits. "We have very different ideas on how to finish a job. Leave it at that."

Theia nods and stares at her reflection in the glass. Every now and then, she catches a glimpse of herself that makes her stop and do a doubletake. While she'll always have those few extra pounds, Theia's face is more lean, her eyes brighter. Her long, dark hair she wears in a sloppy bun instead of a ponytail after Aric used it to his advantage their first training session. Training has changed her, not just physically, but mentally. *Is this what it takes to become a warrior?*

"Aric," Theia says, breaking the silence. "Can I ask you something?"

Lifting his eyes from the glass, Theia tracks the shadows descent into his normally crisp, clear eyes. "Depends."

"Did you ever hesitate?"

His gaze heats as he continues to stare at her in weighted silence. Fingers tighten around the tall glass in his hand as his breathing hitches just enough to draw her attention. "Once."

"What happened?"

"That's a long story."

Theia flashes an imp-like smile. "I don't think we're going anywhere anytime soon."

"Really? In that case, why don't you tell me why that demon targeted your grandmother?"

Theia gasps for air as if he'd pulled her lungs from her chest. Everywhere she looks, the room shrinks and the available oxygen thins. It's almost as if an outside force presses down on her, making it impossible to draw breath.

Without warning, Mercedes' face rips through her conscious with brutal memories. As if back in the moment, Theia reacts to every punch and kick, hissing when someone rips a handful of hair from her head.

With a moan, she recalls the precise moment Rhynne is injured. The sickening thud her head makes against the bathroom stall chases away Theia's fear to allow blind rage to bloom in her stomach.

Like then, heat floods her arms and legs, unfurling from her chest. Absently, her fingers tighten on the glass in her hand until it shatters. The splash of water and bite of pain work together to snap her back to the present.

Blinking, she catches a sharp curse from Aric as he drags her to the kitchen sink. Rough hands cradle hers as he turns on the cold water to stem the blood flow.

"What happened?" Aric demands, his tone hard.

"I don't know," she stammers. "It was like being back there."

"You need to control your emotions Theia," Aric grits out as he uses a towel to apply pressure to her hands. "How are you going to face Riordan if you can't get through a simple question?"

"I don't know."

"You say that a lot. If you don't master these emotions, the power alone will cost you. I've seen Nephilim's push too far and never recover from the power surge."

"I'm sorry, must be nice to be all knowing," she snaps, jerking her hands from his grasp.

"I have experience you could learn from."

"I'm trying. It's not like this is easy for me."

"It's not supposed to be easy," he counters while digging through several cupboards. When he turns around with a first aid kit in hand, he motions for her to sit. "You've had easy for twenty-eight years, what did that get you?"

"Like you'd know what this feels like." When he again motions for her to sit, Theia plops her butt into a kitchen chair. "When have you ever struggled with anything?"

"I've struggled, Theia. We all have at one time or another."

"Somehow I doubt it's the same."

"Why? Because you're a Nephilim? You think your fight is harder than the rest of ours?" One brow lifts on his forehead as he swabs the cuts with antibiotic before applying several bandages.

"Since you ran away into retirement, I don't think you have the room to judge me."

Instead of the flare of reaction Theia was hoping for, Aric sits back in his chair with an expression of extreme patience. She'd hoped to get a rile out of him, something other than the cold aloofness he's shown her the last few months. What she gets however, is a look of condescending disapproval. Sitting there, Theia has a flashback to one of Granny's lectures for doing something foolish. Instead of cooling her temper, it fuels it.

"You have a lot of nerve to criticize me for taking the easy path," she snaps before pushing herself from her chair. "You shut yourself off to everything and everyone. I wouldn't call that courage." Depsite her rising temper, Theia can't miss a soft flare of emotion in his eyes as she marches past. Crossing the kitchen, she disappears down the hall to the one bedroom. Only after the door slams shut behind her does she take a full breath.

Frozen, she rests her head against the door adjusting to the sound of her blood pumping ringing in her ears. *Shouldn't have lashed out at Aric.* "While he's not so great for my emotions, he's done wonders with my defensive skills," she reasons quietly.

No doubt his solitary lifestyle left a thick layer of crud on his social etiquette. Not that Theia would ever claim to be a social butterfly, she at least has an inkling of what *not* to say. As she stands there unmoving, an image of Aric flashes behind her eyes. His wounded expression stains handsome features for all of one heartbeat before it disappears.

He hadn't flinched or offered an arguement as she blew by him. Lost in whatever thoughts pinball inside his thick skull. "Probably something along the lines of me acting like a spoiled child," she grumbles. Her outburst causes her insides to twist but the idea of apologizing makes her stomach pitch. Instead, she flops face down on the lumpy mattress and wills sleep to come.

The next time she opens her eyes, darkness envelopes the room. She has no idea how long she dozed but her full and aching bladder holds going back to sleep hostage until it's relieved. Rolling out of bed, she adjusts to the sore muscles protesting the movement and stumbles toward the door.

When she opens the door, her breath stills at the sight of a bowl just beyond the threshold. The fragrance of onions, carrots and some sort of meat waft off the stew in a merciless assault until her mouth waters. Recalling how little she'd had to eat that day, her stomach gives a hard rumble. Unfortunately, the pressure in her bladder increases to overrule her stomach so Theia steps carefully around the bowl and hurries to the bathroom.

No sooner does her hand land on the handle when it swings open from the inside. Just beyond, Theia gulps at the sight of Aric, wet from the shower with nothing but a thin towel spanning his lean waist. Suddenly starved for a different reason, Theia consumes every inch he leaves bare and even some he doesn't.

Taller than the average woman, Theia has never met a man that makes her feel petite. Aric accomplishes the impossible task, and adds a touch of vulnerability for good measure. Eyes devour the hard cords of muscles in his arms. The wet hair he slung over one shoulder drops tiny rivulets of water across the wide expanse of his chest. Her skin heats as she traces the path the droplet takes just shy of one nipple and further over leanly sculpted abs. Forcing her gaze north, she flushes to find him studying her silently.

As if sensing her arousal, Aric quirks a brow, his eyes dark and intense. Her heart slams into her ribs as Theia remains rooted in place. Reading her unease, Aric takes a step forward. Theia's pulse runs rampant as he approaches, the heat from his body leaves her contemplating running. When his hand lifts, her lungs fail as he tucks a stray piece of hair behind her ear. The simple gesture is enough to send shivers down her spine.

"Are you okay?" he asks, his voice low and gentle. Quite the opposite from his usual tone of indifference and cold judgement.

Theia's chin bobs unevenly. "I'm fine," she replies, unable to tear her eyes away from him. Drawn like a moth to a flame, she struggles with the urge in her fingertips to touch him. Nerves stretch and tighten as the tension between them becomes palpable. *Judging by the heat he's giving off, he wants me as much as I do him.* For some reason, that realization inspires a new rash of fear and more than a little excitement.

New to the sudden rush of liquid fire in her stomach and the clenching of her core, Theia's tongue darts out to wet her lips. The action causes Aric's eyes to darken further, his expression searing away her defenses. When he brushes a thumb across her bottom lip, they part at his touch, inviting him closer. With a growl to make her stomach flip, Aric pulls her flush against him and she gasps at the overwhelming sensations. The heat of his skin, the smooth muscles just under her palms and the scent of vanilla. When his lips crash down on hers, fierce and demanding, all she can do is hold on for the ride.

He tastes of the soap he used in the shower. Drowning in the touch of soft lips against hers, she groans aloud when his tongue darts past to sample her tongue. Hands grip his broad shoulders as Theia melts into him. *Is this what they meant?* All those books she's read spouting desire and lust had always been just a cluster of words until she reaches the end of the story. Now, Theia's unsure how to adjust to the emotions he gives birth to. All at once her skin is too tight, her breasts heavy. A hard throbbing near her center forces Theia's thighs to clench. When Aric dips and a hand in her hair to take the kiss deeper, the gnawing ache intensifies until it's stealing the breath from her body.

Whether he comes to his senses or picks up on her sudden bout of fear, Aric breaks the kiss and takes a step back.

Theia's eyes flutter open slowly, her chest heaving with each ragged breath. Without the heat from his body, a tendril of cool air causes goosebumps on her skin. She stares at him, wide-eyed and presses a finger to her swollen lips. Aric stares at her, his eyes dark and unreadable as if he's waiting for her to say something. Unsure of where to start, Theia fumbles for a coherent thought until he beats her to the punch.

"I'm sorry," he says, his voice low and husky. "That was inappropriate."

Her heart sinks at his words. She'd been so caught up in the moment, all memory of their arguement fled. Now that it's brought back to the forefront, she flushes. The voice in her head screams for her to retreat until she dies of old age. Her body refuses to budge. With a tip of her chin, she meets his heavy gaze with a bravado she's no where close to feeling. "No, I wanted that," she says her voice barely above a whisper.

Though his eyes widen in surprise, his jaw flexes until a small tic pulses in his right cheek. "Go to bed, Theia."

Theia nods, the heat in her cheeks multiplying as she turns and all but runs to the safety of the bedroom. As the door closes behind her, she experiences a painful revelation. *I never went pee!*

CHAPTER 17

With a harsh sigh, Aric flops over. Beneath him, the hard, lumpy couch cushions dig in against his back to rob him of any comfort. Hiking up one leg, he rests his knee against the back cushions and squeezes his eyes shut. The dense blanket of silence lying over the cabin makes it clear to him he's the only one still awake.

Down the hall, Theia's breathing evened out hours ago as she finds peaceful slumber. Since they've been cooped up together, Aric catches a glimpse of her being roused from sleep more than once. Her long hair a mess of tangles to frame rosy cheeks and heavy-lidded eyes. It didn't take long for that to become his most favorite sight in the world. And every other.

Her voice is quite distinct in the morning. Thick and husky. Unlike the gentle melody that accompanies her words once she's fully awake and ready to take on the day. As he lay there, Aric can't help but think she'll sound the same during sex, much like when he accidentally kissed her.

The heavy blow of that memory racks his body as he plays it on repeat inside his head.

Her response had surprised him. Aric half-expected to be slapped for the advance. Her outrage scathing until he found another to train her. Instead, she'd opened up and met his desire with a ferocity he'd never experienced before.

The amount of control it had taken to step away from her that night, still shocks him. Along with the fact that he'd nearly failed to do so. Groaning, he rolls to his side and jams an arm under the meager pillow. While sleep isn't vital to his health, it usually offers his mind a reprieve. *Usually*.

Lately, if he isn't obsessing over Theia during the daylight hours, she's invading his dreams. Hunger burning in her deep blue eyes as she beckons him closer. Her touch will sends shards of electricity through him as all that long, silky hair drapes across his skin in an innocent caress. The image his mind produces sends a wave of heat over him as all the blood rushes to his lower half. With a growl, Aric makes an adjustment in his pajama pants and grits his teeth.

"She's going to be the death of me," he grumbles harshly and shoves himself upright. Forgoing his battle for sleep, Aric slips out the front door into the darkness.

A chilly breeze caresses his burning skin, relieving a bit of the heat. Shoving a hand into his loose hair, he starts down the dirt path that leads to a small pond.

As he walks, the soft chitter of crickets distracts thoughts of Theia. Animals hiding in the tall grass scurry as the occasional hoot of an owl fills the air. Every inhale fills him with the sweet fragrance of wild flowers, the scent of coming rain and the richness of the black soil beneath him. *Anything is better than her intoxicating scent*! Of their own accord, his thoughts turn to the woman whose scent corrupts his senses.

A shudder creeps across his back as he imagines her pressing those soft curves against him, her thighs wrapping around his waist while he... "Dammit," Aric hisses sharply and stomps the remaining distance to the pond.

"What is wrong with me?" Fingers flex and dig into his palms as Aric berates himself for his traitorous thoughts. "Old enough to be her father," he seethes. *Or an ancestor.* If Julian knew the thoughts and feelings Aric's having towards his daughter, no way he'd deliver her to him without question. "He'd stomp my ass," he reasons, scrubbing a hand along his face. "Hell, I deserve it."

"You need to get over this." Aric crouches down and scoops up a handful of water from the pond. Tossing it back over his head, he groans as the cold droplets land on bare skin. Doing it again, he grits his teeth and pinches the bridge of his nose.

"Find your control," he mutters and waits for his heart to slow. Annoyed with his body's response, Aric bickers internally with himself. *Theia's innocent. She needs my protection. Nothing else.*

Unfortunately, his body doesn't seem to care what his head is ordering it to do, or *not do* in this case. Instead of calming the raging inferno pooling in his stomach, his body unleashes it to flow downward into his lower half. Jaw tight, he counts to one hundred. By the time he reaches fifty the carnal desires fade and his blood pressure steadies itself. Still, he continues to count for good measure.

Perhaps the counting keeps his mind sharp, or his body is an exposed nerve but when the sensation flutters over him with an icy dread, Aric's eyes snap open. Hands form fists at his sides as he listens to the soft ringing noise surrounding him. Someone is trying to establish a link. The bile rising at the back of his throat gives Aric a pretty good idea of just who is reaching out to him.

"What," he growls as he hones his senses in on his surroundings. The lack of power fluctuation eases some of the tension from his spine.

With the next trickle of wind, Riordan's voice invades his quiet. "We need to talk."

"So talk," Aric snaps as he retraces his steps to the cabin. *Never should've strayed so far from Theia. Stupid, stupid thing to do.* All because he can't seem to get a grip on his hormones and keep it.

"I know she's with you, Aric. I can sense you in the faint trails of her."

"Good for you, Riordan. Maybe one of my lessons stuck."

A heavy sigh infects the air before Riordan responds. "Hand her over Aric, and I promise you can go back to your quiet existence."

"And if I don't?" His heart races as he glimpses the cabin's porch. While the moon still high in the sky illuminates every rough inch, he trains his senses on anything out of the ordinary.

"I'll bring you before the Council as the traitor you are."

"That's funny coming from you. I'll bet you haven't been completely forthcoming about your actions. Careful, your wings might get singed right along with mine."

"You've allowed a Nephilim to grow into an adult, Aric," Riordan sneers, his voice laced with disgust. "Nothing I've done compares to that."

"In that we can agree," Aric creeps up the creaky porch steps and ducks inside the cabin. He studies the interior intently, before he allows himself to relax. Despite the air of confidence Riordan speaks with, he finds no threat to Theia anywhere in their immediate vicinity. "You should know, Theia is picking up our training like she was born for it. I'd be more hesitant if I were you."

"I'll take her head Aric," Riordan warns, his voice low and reeking with danger. "If you're with her, I make no promises about your survival."

Aric clenches his jaw, his fingers pressing deeper into the palms of his hands. Despite the level of control, a sharp spike of anger explodes within his chest at the threat. Just the idea of someone causing Theia harm ignites a raging fire inside his blood.

A long moment passes until he's sure when he answers, his voice doesn't betray the violent emotions that swarm through him. "Careful, Riordan. Unless you've improved immensely in my absence, which we both know is *highly unlikely*, you're no match for me."

There's a flush of silence in the air to enhance the ragged sound of Riordan's breathing. When he answers, anger and frustration color his words to bring a small smirk to Aric's lips. "We'll see about that."

Once the intruding essence fades from the room, Aric turns and spies Theia hovering on the other side of the kitchen.

Dressed only in a long t-shirt, the thin material stops an inch or two shy of her knees. The loose material hides nothing as it slides over soft breasts and wide hips. Long hair falls freely to frame her face before it drops off just below her waist. The sight of her is enough to stop Aric in his tracks.

Studying her quietly, a flash of panic dances across her soft features before a spark ignites in her dark blue eyes. Teeth chew across the corner of her mouth as her chin lifts in a defiant nature that's becoming familiar.

When she speaks, her roughened voice sends a cluster of shivers along his skin. "I need to train harder."

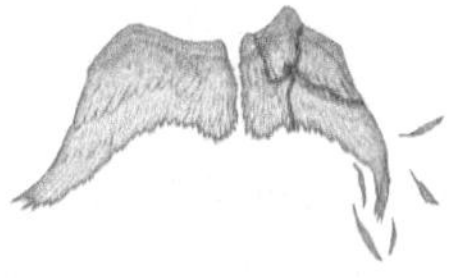

"Good evening, Sir," George says warmly as he accepts the stack of papers from Melchom.

"Evening George." Plowing a hand through his hair, Melchom crosses the foyer and pours himself a generous serving of brandy. "Has Julian checked in yet?"

"Yes, Sir. He said he located the demon, but that he doesn't stay in one place for longer than a night or two. Setting up an ambush may not be easy."

Filling the thick glass tumbler once more, Melchom downs the drink with a sharp hiss of air. "I don't care about easy as long as it gets done."

"I'll tell him, Sir. If there's nothing else?"

"No, that's all George. Thank you."

"Goodnight, Sir."

With a heavy sigh, Melchom steps out onto the balcony to get lost in his stunning view. The moon still hangs low on the horizon to throw splashes of white and silver across an otherwise dark ocean like paint thrown by a ghostly hand.

Laughter drifts up from the beach below as a group of friends sit around a small campfire made in the sand. The breeze carries faint sounds of music to tease his ears. While heaven isn't in the cards for him, a part of Melchom considers this place to be close enough.

When a hard pounding at the front door shatters his small piece of serenity, Melchom's lips twist as he marches across the room to answer it before it rouses George.

Swinging the heavy door inward, he has enough time to register Aamon on the other side before searing pain explodes in his side. Stumbling backward, Melchom clutches a hand against the pain as his head spins with possibilities. None of them explain Aamon's newfound power.

Another flash of agony sears his back as Aamon steps over the threshold. Melchom's sneer is immediate as he adjusts to the discomfort before absorbing it with a long, drawn-out hiss. Tipping his head left then right results in sharp pops as he plants his feet and counters.

His first wave of energy catches Aamon off guard to send the demon flying into a far wall. When his body crashes into one of George's favorite paintings, Melchom makes a note to make it up to him before focusing on the half-dozen demons accompanying Aamon. Extending one hand, he tightens the skin around their bones until a chorus of howls fills the room. Melchom's voice takes on an inhuman tone as he spits the warning. Once.

"I don't know what you thought was going to happen here. But if you don't go home now, I'll have to assign another to raise your children in your absence."

One by one, the demons recoil at the mention of their children, eyes wide with fear. Melchom recognizes it as a cheap shot but he has no plans to let Aamon unseat him without a fight.

"You're a fool, Melchom," Aamon snarls as he staggers to his feet. "You can't stop what's already in motion."

"Is that so?"

Aamon's eyes blaze with barely contained fury. "Even if you kill them, I'll just find others willing to move against you."

Melchom's arms cross his chest as he diverts his attention to the biggest threat. Raking his eyes over Aamon, Melchom utters his words with a level of deadly calm, it causes the demon to suppress a shiver. "Then I suppose I'll have to make sure you don't survive." Despite Aamon's newfound confidence, Melchom spots a flicker of uncertainty in his eyes.

"You've become weak," Aamon recovers, his voice dripping with disdain. "We all see it."

Melchom's grinding teeth bare in a wolfish grin. "You're about to learn just how weak I am," he sends a scathing glance at the group of demons hanging back. "The hard way."

Aamon steps forward. "You don't scare me."

Violet eyes narrow as he beckons Aamon closer with a flick of his wrist. "Prove it." As soon as he made the invitation, chaos ensues.

Descending like a pack of rabid dogs, Aamon and his lackeys attack. While Melchom's reflexes are on point, they have the advantage of numbers. Twice a blow slips past his defenses to make his ears ring before a set of claws tear across his back.

Aamon's stiff uppercut drops Melchom to one knee before he can shake off the stun. Warding off the raining blows, his eyes glow with an other-wordly light as a wave of energy sends the lesser demons backwards.

The distraction costs him as Aamon unleashes his own blast of energy. At the last second, Melchom avoids it by crashing into the long table in front of the couch. With a grunt, he stumbles to his feet, his muscles already protesting the impact. His attackers are on him in an instant. Amidst their snarls and grunts, Melchom deflects most of their wild punches and kicks. Blood trickles down his cheek from a cut on his forehead and after a vicious blow to his temple, his vision blurs.

"I told you. You're weak," Aamon growls, his eyes glittering with malevolence.

"Let's even the odds, shall we?"

The sound of Julian's retort unleashes a flare of relief in Melchom's chest. The demons turn and stare open-mouthed as the angel descends upon them, sword drawn.

Melchom catches his breath and push the waves of agony aside as Julian dispatches the lesser demons with ease. His movements are fluid and precise, like a well-oiled machine.

Demons scatter to avoid the deadly strikes of his sword to no avail. He calculates each swing and purposefully takes every step to cut them down before they can fight back. After the last one becomes a pile of sulfur reeking ash on once immaculate floors, Julia sheaths his sword.

The only one left standing, Aamon's eyes dart between Melchom and Julian. As if to emphasize his intentions, Julian raises his hands and steps back to a far corner. Melchom can smell the fear rolling off the minor demon as he realizes the grave mistake he'd made. It only lasts a second before his face twists with rage.

"You can't defeat me," Aamon sneers.

Melchom's lips curl into a malicious smile. "Watch me," he growls and lunges forward.

Aamon and Melchom battle it out in a vicious brawl, constantly pummeling each other. Sound of impact ripples through the air like thunder, echoing through the walls of the condo until it spreads outward into eternity.

Both sides are equally matched, and neither of them gain an advantage. Blood spatters from wounds inflicted upon both sides, but still neither demon gives an inch. Every punch and kick is met with equal force, while surges of energy emerge in an unrelenting dance of violence until sweat rains down their exhausted bodies.

Like Aamon, Melchom gasps for air. The torment flooding his body impedes his ability to draw a full breath and his muscles burn with exhaustion. Narrowing his focus, Melchom pulls in every stab of pain and the drained adrenaline until it fills him. Holding it there for a moment, Melchom releases it to fuel his waning power. A tremor cascades through the room as it multiplies inside him. When the ripples reach Aamon doubled over and fighting for breath, his voice trembles for the first time tonight.

"Please," he gasps.

Stepping forward, Melchom watches as Aamon sinks to his knees, his eyes lowering to the floor between them. "Who gave you this power?"

"Riordan."

Julian's audible gasp behind him draws Melchom's attention for a fraction of a second. "In exchange for what?"

After a loud gulp, Aamon's eyes flicker upward and down again. "The Nephilim's head." Despite the power coursing through his veins, Aamon's voice takes on a whine as he searches for survival. "Have mercy. I'll do whatever you ask."

"It's too late for mercy," Melchom answers quickly, his voice low and dangerous. "You never should've moved against me."

With a flick of his wrist, Melchom sends a shard from a shattered vase towards Aamon. Lodging itself in his neck, Aamon's beady eyes widen with surprise, his lips fluttering soundlessly. Blood creates a dark pool on the floor around him before he collapses in a heap. Without a word, Julian steps forward to issue the killing blow.

Nursing his wounded side, Melchom brushes away broken glass and littered debris to fill his tumbler with brandy. Dumping it down his throat, he casts Julian a sidelong glance. "Do I need to ask which Nephilim he was referring to?"

"It's Theia."

"And you were going to tell me, when?"

Julian shrugs one shoulder, his face unreadable. "I'm telling you now."

"She's the one causing the fluxes in power?"

"I believe so."

Heat fills Melchom as his vision narrows. Fingers clench against damp palms as he struggles to contain the rage teasing over exposed nerves. "What do you suggest we do about it?"

Julian's voice remains steady despite the fact that Melchom's temper is no doubt fluctuating within the walls of the room. "She'll learn to control her powers."

"And you're certain of this?"

"I am."

Melchom's teeth set as he refills his glass and drains it once more. Briefly, the welcome burn in his throat blots out the rest of the torment twisting his body into knots. "We had a deal, Julian."

"We did." Julian's gaze dances around the disheveled state of his living room, his lips quirking softly. "Now we're even."

"So, what's your plan?"

"I'm going to find my daughter."

Melchom contemplates lodging an argument against his decision. Aside from the fact Theia is a ticking time bomb, other Seraphs still hunt Julian. Even if he manages to locate her, he could either lead them straight to her, or lose his own head in the process.

His eyes shift out across the balcony as he weighs his options. In the end, it's the hard set of Julian's jaw and the glint in his eye that forces Melchom to nod quietly. "Be careful."

Julian says nothing, allowing the slow tip of his head to serve as acknowledgement before he flashes from the room.

Again, alone with only his thoughts, Melchom lowers himself carefully onto the couch. He leans his head back against the cushions and closes his eyes. For the moment, he allows himself to just be, to exist simply in this one moment of stillness.

These are the times he wishes he could just stay here, in this small slice of peace and forget about the battles he's constantly fighting. Unfortunately, that option was taken from him centuries ago. A wave of anguish sears across his skin as his aches and pains reminds him of the battle he just fought.

Lifting his lashes, he stares out at the ocean just beyond smooth panes of glass. His eyes trace the trickle from the soft glow from the moon over the horizon until he's breathing more evenly. Waves crash against the shore in a hypnotic rhythm to soothe his senses, but it's not enough to quiet the storm inside him.

With a growl, he sits up and allows his eyes to drift across his living room, taking stock of the damage.

The once pristine room is now a mess of broken glass, overturned furniture and scattered debris. Several of George's favorite paintings are ruined beyond repair. Shards of the vase George had toted around for hundreds of years cover the wood floors, one particular piece still dripping in Aamon's blood. A harsh reek of sulfur and smoke hangs heavily in the air from several ash piles Julian left behind. Not to mention streaks and splatters of blood staining stark white walls and expensive furniture.

Melchom shoves himself to his feet with a rueful shake of his head. "George is going to kill me."

CHAPTER 18

Over the next few weeks, Theia trains diligently under Aric's guidance. After several stumbles and close calls, eventually, she uncovers the grace in sword fighting. Hand to hand combat and self defense require less effort and Theia even locates solace in her meditation practice as well. Controlling her emotions, however, is another matter.

Regardless of the technique or strategy, Theia learns that mastering the sudden surge of emotions isn't as simple as Aric makes it seem. More than once he stares unflinching into her volatile reactions with a level of calm she struggles to acheive. At first his demeanor only served to strengthen the rampant feelings, now, she marvels over his hold. Even when she baits him with harsh words, Aric simply regards her like one would a spoiled child. Just as Theia figures she's got a handle on it all, Aric, like a barb says something to provoke her fiery temper which ends with a literal raging inferno or a torrential rainstorm.

"Theia," Aric snaps. "Focus."

With a soft shake of her head, Theia centers herself, giving Aric her full attention. Something in the way he moves inspires warmth in her belly. Smooth and graceful, Aric focuses on the task ahead of him and nothing else. Under the heat of the summer sun, he'd stripped out of his sweat-soaked t-shirt, giving her an eyeful of roping muscles and hard planes. His gym shorts ride low along a narrow set of hips, falling just shy of his knees to expose impressive calves.

Theia gulps down a lump of desire as she watches him explain a new technique. It had taken her all of five minutes the first day to learn Aric speaks with his hands. As he lays out the steps required, she can't help but track the way his muscles flex and strain with every motion. Like a freight train, she recalls their slip up a few weeks prior and the way those muscles felt under her hands. Bands of steel wrapped in velvet quivering under her touch, begging for more.

For a moment, Theia thought maybe he'd been fighting the same flare of hunger she had and her body responded with a hard thrum that still plagues her insides. It didn't take him long to squash that hope under a cool command to go back to bed. *Yeah. Right.* Standing with her body pressed against the bedroom door, Theia couldn't say how long she'd stood there, a mess of wild desire before she sneaked out to actually achieve the task that sent her from her room in the first place.

Once her bladder ceased it's torment, she crawled back into bed with a groan and lay unmoving until the sun began to rise. If she thought there'd be a discussion about the kiss they had shared, Aric was quick to fix that as well. He'd said nothing about anything beyond their training schedule for the day. And every day since. While Theia establishes a firm grip on her attention to the task at hand, the small voice in her head whispers through her head every time Aric's gaze lingers on her for a moment longer then necessary.

"Theia?"

"I'm sorry," Theia mumbles thickly, her nails picking a path across the side of her thumb.

With a quizzical expression etched on his features, Aric stops mid-motion. "Is everything alright?" he asks. When the gentle purr of his voice slides across her exposed skin, Theia finds herself wishing for the cool and aloof personality she's come to expect.

Her throat suddenly dry, Theia settles for a nod. "I just got lost in thought for a moment." Since her first taste of his firm lips, it's been a battle to keep those thoughts from infringing on her training. She needs to learn how to protect herself, and with a great deal of luck, survive her next encounter with Riordan. *Ogling my trainer doesn't help with any of that.* Once she believes she has her wayward mind properly chastised into submission, she'll catch a glimpse of him that speeds up her heart rate and she's back to where she started.

As if unconvinced, Aric studies her face for a moment longer. His gaze heats her skin as she struggles to maintain eye-contact. *Focus on the training*, she muses. Aric standing so close threatens her resolve. Especially when the wind kicks up and carries the scent of his skin to tease her.

"You can't let your thoughts wander, Theia," Aric explains in his best mentor voice. "You're supposed to be centering on one emotion and letting it build."

That's what I'm doing, her mind rails. *It's just not the one you instructed.* Heaving a sigh, Theia shoves aside her desire to be more present in today's training. "You're right. Can we start again?"

An arms length away, a flare of heat ignites in Aric's eyes. When his jaw tightens, Theia spots the familiar tick in his cheek a second before he's scrubbing a hand across his face. "Think of a time when you were frustrated. Not *angry*, Theia. Anger is not good for you right now, so we will take baby steps."

"Frustrated?"

"Yeah," he continues. "Maybe a bad date, or bad day at work?"

Theia situates herself on the large rock and offers a casual shrug. "None of that really bothers me." Teeth grip her lip as she considers quietly. "Or used to."

"What about relationships? A crush that wasn't mutual?"

"Hmm. The only relationship I have is with Granny." Theia swings her legs back and forth as she searches through memories to locate a feeling Aric describes. Her brows knit when she finds nothing. "I don't think I've ever had a crush."

Aric raises an eyebrow over her admission. "Never?"

Theia shakes her head, a smile tugging at the corners of her lips. "No."

"You're telling me you've never been attracted to someone before?"

Again, Theia shakes her head. "I've had friends. People I was drawn to, but never in the way you're implying."

"So, you've never.." Aric's voice trails off as if unable to finish his question.

Theia's cheeks flush as she clasps her hands together tightly. "No."

"I'm not sure what to do with that," Aric murmurs quietly. The heat in his gaze intensifies until like every time before it produces a pool of heat near her center. Instead of latching onto the warm sensation, Theia's brain sticks on the air of confusion in his words.

"I'm not broken Aric," she hisses. "I just never felt that pull so many people gush about."

"Never?" With a crook of his head, Aric steps closer until his thighs brush across the front of her knees. "You've never felt the knot in your stomach that says you need to possess someone? Taste their lips or the salt from their skin?"

Theia's breath catches when his words send a shiver across her spine an instant before her fingers form a tight grip around her hands. No one has ever spoken to her with such raw desire and intensity. Inches apart, the heat radiates off his body to send a wave of need coursing through her veins before infecting the surrounding tissue. What would it be like to experience such things with him? To feel his lips and hands on her? The shudder her body responds with pulls a hoarse groan from Aric.

"I...I don't know," she stammers, her face heating until the tips of her ears sting. "I've never really thought about it before."

"Maybe it's time you started," Aric whispers softly, his voice heavy with desire. Unable to look away from the electric heat in his eyes, her skin tightens when he brushes a thumb across her cheek. "Because, I have to admit, I've been thinking about it a lot lately."

Theia swallows hard, her pulse skyrocketing. Her head spins with the thoughts his words create as fire spreads outward from her center. Fingers twitch and curl with the sudden desire to bury themselves in his thick hair. Clenching her thighs together keeps her from wrapping them around his waist and pulling him tight against her until they both lay sated. Amidst all the heat, and need Theia also uncovers a level of uncertainty. Teeth chew against the inside of her cheek as she contemplates what happens after. Once the adventure is over and Aric realizes she's not exaggerating her level of inexperience? Can she endure the heartbreak that's sure to follow? Without condemning the world to an apocalyptic reaction?

The hunger in his eyes makes breathing impossible. Her lungs take a vacation as her internal regulator splurges on a hiatus. Sweat gathers at the small of her back as her body hums, craving his every touch. Closing her eyes, Theia finds her center amongst the turmoil. *You can't*, her mind harasses, *not until you have a handle on everything that will follow.*

Aric's expression hardens as he picks up on her hesitation. "I'm sorry," he whispers, stepping away from her. "I don't know what came over me."

Theia's heart twists as regret replaces the heat in his eyes. Her hands tremble with the need to reach for him as the explanation sticks in her throat. Regardless of her feelings, the unchartered waters leave her nauseous and unsure.

"I think we should take a break," Aric states flatly, turning away from her. "I need a minute to clear my head."

Even though a hush fell over the cabin hours ago, Aric holds no hope of actually falling to sleep. The couch creaks when he changes position, the ancient springs cringing under his weight. The musty smell his movements kick up is a far cry from the fresh lemon scent that tickles his nose whenever Theia is near.

As the rough fabric scratches across his back, his mind drifts. It's impossible to miss the heat and tension building between him and Theia. On cue, his brain calls up an image of her training. When he recalls the way her skin glows under the scorching sun, his gut tightens. The sight of her lip caught between teeth in concentration sends an electrical surge of need through him.

Laying there, staring up at the same water-stained ceiling, Aric chastises himself. He's supposed to be in control of his emotions and teaching Theia. Yet, he's unable to stop himself from wanting her. *What the hell am I doing? I'm her trainer, her mentor.* It'd be reckless to get caught up in the desire plaguing him. While his mind rails every reason he should keep his distance, his tall frame practically vibrates from suppressing the impulse. With a groan, Aric presses the heels of his hands against his eyes until the moment passes.

Theia.

Her name rolls off his tongue like a prayer and his body answers with an ache he can't shake free. The pull between them is undeniable and gets stronger with each passing day. Every time they touch, or an unfiltered look passes between them, energy crackles like a live wire searching for a conductor.

Releasing his breath, Aric scratches at the stubble on his chin as the full weight of the situation bears down on him. He's tried to ignore it, smother the need and focus on their training, but the more time he spends with her, he realizes he needs her more than he's ever needed anyone. Despite the harsh realities of their circumstances, with her around, Aric discovers a sense of serenity that grounds him. The moment she'd stumbled back into his life, Aric stopped agonizing over his past. His choices and sacrifices are no longer important amongst the soothing air of peacefulness Theia inspires.

You don't deserve peace. In an instant, his brain floods him with images from that night and the part he played. When the heavy scent of blood fills his nose, Aric's breath catches in a gasp. Running a hand through his hair, he attempts to focus on something else.

The sharp crack of a twig snapping outside causes him to bolt upright. Frozen, he hones every sense to detect anything unusual. Though he can't pinpoint anything specific, he slips off the couch. Bare feet move soundlessly across the worn floor as he approaches the front door. His hand settles on the handle when her soft voice behind him awakens every nerve under his skin.

"Aric," Theia whispers from the archway of the hall, "did you hear that?"

Pressing a finger to his lips, Aric creeps close enough to reply in an octave just low enough for her to hear. "Stay here. I'm going to check it out." He waits for her to nod before easing out the front door into the night.

While his mind races over the possibilities, adrenaline floods his system as he studies his surroundings. The full moon hands like a beacon in the black sky to cast deep shadows across the forest floor before illuminating much of the area around the cabin. The yapping of a small dog mixes with the low hoot of an owl in a tree nearby. Unseen animals shuffle through the underbrush to rustle leaves and fallen tree limbs. His ribs squeeze when he picks up the sound of something moving within the trees. Something heavy and weighed down. Crickets drag their legs along dry leaves as the breeze carries a hint of pine, earth and a faint trace of saffron. The hair on the back of Aric's neck stands on end as the air around him thickens like the tattered remains of a spider web.

Returning to the cabin, Aric bolds the door behind him. The simple mechanism won't do much to slow them down, but it might be enough to buy Theia a little time. Crouching, he passes below the large window to where she huddles just inside the hall, her eyes wide. "Get dressed. We need to go."

"Is it Riordan?"

Aric's lips thin at the tinge of fear he picks up in her voice. "I'd stake my life on it."

Theia freezes for all of a heartbeat before she moves quickly to the bedroom she claimed when they first arrived.

CHAPTER 19

Theia clamps her lip between teeth as she sneaks in step behind Aric out the back door. As they move cautiously, the moonlight overhead helps them gain some distance before she hears Riordan storm into the cabin. Finding it empty, he releases a fierce howl that shoots across the distance. Just like the wild animals, frozen in fear, Theia forgets to place one foot in front of the other.

Sensing her dilemma, Aric doubles back to clamp a hand around her wrist. His eyes, usually warm and comforting are hard and focused. Gesturing for her to keep low with a sharp nod, he guides her toward the cover of trees.

Theia matches his pace, keeping her movements small and steady as they navigate the maze of trees and underbrush. This close to him, her brain stutters on the scent of pine and damp earth mingling with his unique mixture of cedar and vanilla. Closing her eyes, she pulls a slow breath as the sound of heavy footfalls gets closer.

Not yet visible to their pursuers, Theia realizes it's only a matter of time. Soon the moonlight they used to escape will be a disadvantage.

As if coming to the same conclusion, Aric changes direction, pulling her right from the original path. When she stumbles over an exposed root, his grip tightens on her arm until she finds her footing again.

They move quickly and quietly down a dirt path that delves deeper into the woods despite the forest being shrouded in gloom. Aric's strong fingers intertwine with hers as they venture down a dirt path that delves deeper into the woods.

She can't determine how long they've been creeping around but by the time they stumble upon a wide clearing, the implication of dawn threatens their escape. Leaning against an enormous tree, Aric observes their surroundings with a blank expression.

Slipping in beside him, Theia ignores the sweat dripping down her back. "What do we do now?"

"We're losing the cover of darkness," Aric says tightly, before giving her hand a squeeze. "He can't track us so easily if we stay downwind, so our best bet is to slip around him and keep him behind us."

Theia nods, her body relaxing at the sound of any plan that doesn't rely on her meager experience. Her fight-or-flight response increases her heart rate and tightens her senses on everything around her until it's sharper and more defined. Instead of calming her frantic nerves, seeing and hearing everything leaves her muscles tight and achey.

A sudden rustle of leaves behind them spurs Aric into action, tugging her to the other side. Swiftly, they skirt around the clearing, careful to keep their steps silent while treading over a thick layer of dead leaves. The presence of dawn lightening the night sky complicates any forward progress.

Theia blinks when a flood of coppery liquid splashes across her tongue and she realizes too late the severe pressure of her teeth on her bottom lip. Easing their grip with a flexing of her jaw, she eases the pain with a brush of her tongue.

Inhaling sharply, she then trains her focus on Aric's strong back as he twists and winds them closer to freedom. A flare of hope sparks within her chest at the sight of a dark building shrouded in trees a hundred yards ahead when Riordan's arrogant voice forces them to take cover behind a large boulder.

"Come out, Aric."

Instead of rising to the bait, Aric gives her hand another squeeze. Peeking around the opposite side has dread dropping into her stomach like a rusty anchor. Part of her fears Riordan can hear the pained screech of metal giving way as the chain runs rampant within her.

Less than thirty feet away, Riordan poses in the open clearing, his hands folded behind his back. An expression of barely contained patience pinches his narrow features as he scans the trees. Similar to the four angels flanking him, his silver armor glints under the last traces of moonlight. "I'm not playing this game," he presses.

Another squeeze from Aric's hand draws her attention to his quiet gaze. Reading the gesture from his other hand, Theia nods and follows him toward the building on their left.

Behind them, Riordan's impatience is palpable in his deep grumble. "Fan out, they're here somewhere. I can feel it."

Theia's heart hammers against her chest as Aric leads them toward the building. Emerging from the tree line, they creep forward, the thick grass muffling their footsteps.

Once they're close enough, Aric presses a finger to his lips and leads her around the front of the small shack.

Behind them, a flurry of activity fills the silence as the angels call to each other in hushed tones. Glancing over her shoulder, Theia spies the angels spreading out in different directions, searching the woods frantically. The infection of Riordan's urgency taints what should've been a precise search.

Crouching next to the shack, Aric pulls her down next to him. The warmth he radiates draws her closer until his breath falls hot on her cheek. Beside her, he surveys the area, expressionless, until the sight of a beat-up old truck puts a twinkle in his eyes.

Aric nods towards the truck, his lips curling upward. "I think we just found our way out of here."

Theia's throat tightens. "You're going to steal a truck?"

"I'll bring it back when this is all over," he answers, already pulling a small leather pouch from his pocket.

The scrape of metal vibrates between her ears as she trains her gaze behind them. A minute later, Aric is pulling the driver's door open. "Get in," he whispers urgently against her ear, inspiring a rash of goosebumps.

Theia shrugs off her reaction and hops into the truck, sliding across the bench seat to the passenger side. Before Aric can climb up behind the wheel, someone stumbles over the wooden crates stacked precariously next to the shack. Theia waits, her breath stale in her lungs as the angel calls back to the others.

"Just me!"

"Be quiet," Riordan hisses, his arrogant voice now thin and frantic.

When the angel turns back, his eyes widen in surprise at the sight of Aric less than ten feet away. Without missing a beat, Aric reacts, his movements smooth and graceful as he keeps the angel from alerting the others. It's over as soon as it began.

With a quick strike of his elbow, Aric knocks the angel unconscious and disarms him before allowing him to fall in a heap. Stepping over the crumpled form, Aric climbs into the truck at the same time the engine rolls to life. A dance of his hand on the stick shift has him peeling out in reverse from the overgrown driveway and along the two-track dirt road.

Neither of them speak for the several minutes it takes to put some distance between them and Riordan. When Aric shatters the quiet, the noise it so sudden, Theia nearly leaps out of her skin.

"We need to lay low."

"That's what we *were* doing, Aric."

"We're better off in the city. All those people and smells will make us harder to pinpoint."

Theia rests her head against the headrest and wills her heart to slow. Aric's plan makes sense, but it also puts more people in danger. Riordan's lack of concern about appearing on the human's radar makes him unpredictable. Turning to face Aric, she searches for any sign of doubt. "What if we get caught?"

"We won't." His jaw tenses as he trades the dirt road for rough asphalt.

"But if we do-"

"I won't let him touch you Theia," Aric growls, reaching over to tuck her hand within his. "You have my word."

Despite the chill worming its way inside her bones, Theia finds comfort in his touch. Lacing her fingers through his, she rests her head against the passenger side window and closes her eyes.

When she next opens them, Theia struggles to pinpoint the reason for the ache in her chest.

Casting a glance left, she notes Aric's white knuckles on the steering wheel. Tension etches into every line of his body but he keeps his eyes trained on the cityscape just beyond the freeway. When she releases her death grip, the hand she held onto joins the other on the steering wheel.

"What's wrong?"

A tic pulses in his cheek as he spares a look in the rear-view mirror. "Riordan," he clips tightly.

The moment that name passes his lips, Theia's heart seizes. "What do-" Her lips thin and her nose scrunches at the tremble in her voice.

Forcing herself to breathe, she chases the tremor from her lungs and tries again. "What do we do?"

"We just have to make it to the city. If we can lose them, we'll blend in."

Theia stares out her window at the countless vehicles full of morning commuters. Clueless to what's going on around them, they continue along in real danger of becoming innocent casualties.

The loud flap of enormous wings alert them to Riordan's approach a second before his weight crashes into the roof. Cars around them honk and swerve as Aric weaves in and out through the thick traffic. "Hold on!" Sweat beading on her forehead, Theia latches onto the handle just above her window as Aric darts between cars with reckless abandon.

Metal creaks and groans when something heavy slams into the driver's side to send the truck sideways into a bright yellow hummer. After a quick exchange of paint, Aric steadies the truck back into their own lane. From where she sits, Theia watches dark rage bloom on the other driver's face as he shakes a meaty fist in their direction.

The extra weight on top tumbles sideways as Aric avoids a slow moving semi and cuts through a narrow gap to continue their escape. His voice is low and urgent the moment he chances a peek in her direction. "Do not lose control."

Theia gives a shake of her head. "I won't." While her stomach rolls and her heart races, her voice is surprisingly steady. The closer they get to the city limits, the denser and more chaotic the traffic becomes. She watches Aric's jaw clench as he maneuvers through the labyrinth of cars between them and sanctuary.

When a sword descends into the cab through the roof, Theia huddles against her door with a sharp gasp. The gash it leaves behind gives her an unhindered view of Riordan's feral eyes before he stabs downward again. This time, Aric's harsh scream bellows loud enough to rattle the windows.

Blood flows from where the sword pierces between shoulder and neck, running in thick rivulets when Riordan pulls it free for another attempt. Ropes of muscles in his forearms twitch as Aric struggles to maintain control of the truck.

Smothering her own screams, Theia scooches across the bench seat and stems the rampant blood flow with her hands at the same time someone slams into the truck's passenger side. Her eyes wide, Theia can do nothing but watch helplessly as the truck careens into a concrete barrier that separates lanes of traffic. Bracing herself, she tucks her face into Aric's shoulder as the crunch of metal and the shattering of glass assaults her ears.

The force of the impact sends Theia crashing into the unforgiving dashboard, her breath escaping on a whoosh of air, as pain erupts within her ribs and shoulder. Slumped over the steering wheel, Aric sports a fresh gash in his forehead while Riordan struggles to stand amongst the rubble ten feet away.

"Aric!" Giving his shoulder a hard shake, Theia's chest relaxes the second his thick lashes flutter open. "We have to get out of here!" Scooching towards the passenger side of the truck, Theia drags Aric's tall frame with her. Tucking her hands under his arms, she pulls his dead weight with every ounce of strength she has until they both tumble out the door and onto the hot asphalt.

A fresh stab of agony explodes in her hip as Theia scrambles to her feet. Barely conscious and losing blood quickly, there's little hope of Aric getting them to safety, leaving Theia with one option. Teeth clench as she bends over, wraps his arm around her shoulders and heaves Aric unsteadily to his feet. His pained groan stabs mercilessly at her heart as she drags him through oncoming traffic.

Behind her, slabs of concrete and chunks of metal land hard on the road as Riordan finds his feet. Peeking over her shoulder, Theia stumbles at the sight of apparent madness flooding his eyes. "Theia," he rages tossing what remains of the trunks front bumper from his path.

Fingers tighten on Aric's good arm as she hauls him towards the dam on the far side of the freeway. Tires squeal, filling her nose with the stench of burning rubber as vehicles careen around them. Horns blare and voices shout as they clear the first lane. With Riordan hot on their heels, Theia dashes into the next, her brain processing the oncoming semi-truck a second later.

Metal and chrome fill Theia's field of vision as the truck speeds towards them. In the square window, she can see the driver's eyes widen in panic as he slams on the brakes with a loud screech. His trailer swerves from side to side as he struggles to stop before running them over.

When it's clear, he won't be able to stop in time, Theia reacts. Wrapping her arm around Aric's waist, she extends the other toward the semi, concentrating so intently that it screeches to a sudden stop.

She's close enough for the heat from the grill to almost burn her skin. Shutting her eyes, Theia struggles to drown out the sound of crumpling tires and breaking metal as car's slam into the truck from behind. Dragging Aric across the lane, she uses a concrete pylon to steady herself before launching them both over the guardrail.

After what feels like an eternity of free-falling, they crash into the freezing water below. Her breath catches in her lungs as she gasps for air while still keeping Aric's head above the surface.

Her hands numb, she fastens a steel-like grip under his arms, her legs kicking against the current. Riordan's roar would've made her blood run cold if the water didn't already sap the heat from her body. Her chin lifts as her eyes meet Riordan's savage ones over the railing of the bridge.

Theia turns her attention to keeping them afloat as long as possible. Pushing off the bottom with her toes, she propels them further downstream. Her head snaps when his body grows lax against her. "No, Aric. Stay with me!"

Tears blur her vision as she rips him closer to her chest. "I have you. Just hold on. Hold on." Striking out again, she prays for something, anything, to slow their descent towards the raging dam. Desperation forces her to search the water for anything that will help, her body sagging when she spies a large tree protruding from the sandy shore.

Grasping at the branches, she uses the tree's weight to keep them from drifting downstream. Bouncing off the tips of her toes, Theia crosses the rocky bottom, her grip never wavering on Aric's lifeless form.

After painstakingly slow movement, she works her way until the water recedes to just above her knees. With a frantic look over her shoulder, she searches the bridge for any sign of Riordan, but finds nothing. Coughing to expel the water from her lungs, she drags Aric to shore, dropping his weight onto the wet sand before collapsing beside him.

CHAPTER 20

Aric's lashes flutter against the pounding inside his skull. Biting back the groan, he opens one eye and then the other to take in the dark and dingy motel room.

The walls are rough, covered in an ugly beige paint and exposing plaster in various places. Thick curtains on the one window hang unevenly, their once-white fabric now grey. When he inhales, the overwhelming odor of cigarette smoke and the stale stench of mold and mildew turns his stomach. The bedspread beneath him is rough, the sheets scratchy against his skin doing nothing for the hard mattress underneath.

Forcing himself to sit up, Aric blinks as the room spins around him. The pain that accompanies every slight movement is a sharp reminder of the injuries he'd sustained. Thick bandages wrap around his chest climbing upward around the opposite side of his neck. Testing the movement in his right arm, he gasps aloud with the memory of Riordan's blade piercing his flesh.

The television on the far wall drones on over the news muffling the constant pelting of the rain hitting the windowpanes outside. The iron tang of blood coats his tongue along with the remnants of bile in the back of his throat. Gritting his teeth, Aric searches for any memory that will clue him in on where he is. The last image he pulls up is the sheer terror on Theia's graceful features before everything fades to black.

Theia.

Scanning the dim interior of the room, Aric searches for any sign of her. Scraping a hand over his face, he grimaces at the sight of dried blood caked beneath his fingernails. Eyes dart to the only other door he assumes leads to the bathroom before he throws off the covers.

Dizziness and nausea threaten to send him back to bed, but he pushes it down and stumbles across the dingy green carpet under his bare feet. Easing the door open, his head spins as he notes her discarded clothes on the bathroom floor, but no Theia. Hands form into fists as he scrambles to put the pieces together.

The sight of her slipping inside from the rain leaves Aric to close his eyes and sag against the bathroom door. Her hands shake as she takes in the empty bed before her, plastic rustling against her fingers as her eyes swing to where he fights the urge to collapse.

"You should be in bed," her voice barely a whisper in the stillness, she steps forward to set her small bags down next to the television. "You've lost a lot of blood."

"Where are we?"

Theia's gaze pins him, the whites of her eyes glistening with unshed tears before she turns her attention to the floor. "Some fleabag motel."

"What happened?" Even as he asks, Aric sways on his feet. He's not sure how long he's been out but the cuts and bruises on her face tell him it was a while. "Are you alright?"

Her chin wobbles but she nods and swipes at a lone tear. "I'm okay." After brushing away the heavy mass of wet hair, Theia crosses the room and helps him back to bed. "You're not. You need rest."

Tipping his head just enough, Aric fills his nose with her fresh lemon scent as she leads him back to bed. Once he sinks into the rough sheets, she returns to the plastic bags she'd brought back. While she rummages, he notes the tremble in her hands as she produces small bags of chips, snacks and bottles of water. The added distance allows the tightness in his chest to ease and his brain to continue to function logically. "What happened?"

She hesitates, her eyes flickering with uncertainty when she finally meets his probing gaze. "Riordan caught up to us on the bridge," she begins, her voice barely above a whisper. "I stopped a semi-truck from hitting us, but it caused a pile-up. I've been listening to the news all day but so far they aren't reporting fatalities."

"Then?"

"Considering the options, I thought it best to throw us over the bridge and into the water. I dragged you to shore, and we spent the night in the woods before finding this place." Twisting the cap on a bottle of water, she passes it to him along with a plain granola bar.

His mind reels at the thought of what could have happened. "And Riordan?" he asks after dumping half the water down his throat.

"I don't know," Theia admits, her voice quivering. "I haven't seen him since we fell."

Aric tries to sit up, but a wave of dizziness overcomes him, and he falls back onto the bed. "We have to keep moving," he says, his voice straining.

Perching on the edge of the bed, Theia's chin notches slightly. "You need rest."

"We can't stay here. He'll find us."

"Maybe." Her voice is soft as she brushes a hand against his stubbled cheek. The immediate response tightens his gut and makes breathing even more difficult. "But we need to rest and recover. We can't keep going like this."

Kiss her! The thought rips through Aric's mind quickly to catch him off-guard and tempt him with its allure. As if aware of where his thoughts went, Theia's gaze drops to his lips. When she lifts her eyes to his once more, the sight of unabashed hunger tears through his tenuous control.

Wrapping a hand on the back of her neck, Aric pulls her close enough for his lips to brush gently against hers. This is not the time nor the place, but his body doesn't seem to care. The need to feel her close, to know she's safe, is overwhelming. "Theia," he breathes against her lips. "I'm sorry. I shouldn't have dragged you into this."

Her eyes soften as she leans into his touch. "I think it's the other way around," a half-smile tilts one corner of her mouth. "Pretty sure you'd still be flying under the radar if it wasn't for me."

"But you didn't know the danger, I did." Aric counters, his thumb tracing the curve of her jaw. "They could have killed you tonight."

"You too," she answers, her voice firm.

In the span of a heartbeat, Aric recites every reason this is a bad idea. In order to keep her alive, he needs to remain focused and clear but the tightness in his chest doesn't lift. Instead, his heart twists at the thought of waiting another moment to drown himself in the peace she promises. When she doesn't pull away, he dips his head to drink from her lips one more time.

What starts off as gentle turns primal at the first hint of her soft moan. Angling his head for better access, Aric devours her lips like a man seeking air. One hand skims over her back as Theia's fingers tangle behind his neck to pull him closer.

Reading her response, Aric deepens the kiss until it turns desperate. The soft nip of her teeth lights his body on fire and steals the breath from his chest. Shifting sends a swift stab of pain through him forcing Aric to break the kiss and rest his forehead against hers.

With a shudder, he closes his eyes and locates the control he needs to pump the brakes. "The choice is yours Theia," he murmurs, their heavy breaths mingling. Inhaling the scent of her skin and tasting her lips dissolves any hope he harbors for restraint. If they ride any closer to this edge, he may not be able to keep the train on the tracks, as much as he may want to. Alone for so long, Aric can't ignore how her simple touch brings him back to life in a way nothing else ever has.

"I need to feel you, Aric." A breath above a whisper, her response lands like a freight train. His stomach flips as Aric rolls onto his side, taking her with him.

The bed creaks under their weight as he props himself on his good arm and searches her face for the slightest hint of uncertainty. Instead, her eyes are bright with a fierce determination that makes his heart race.

With a smile, Aric leans in to capture her lips in a searing kiss. Her response is immediate as her hands glide over his chest and down his side. Under her touch, his body responds instantly. Heat floods his veins and he deepens the kiss, his tongue exploring her mouth with a hunger he hasn't felt in centuries.

Pulling back slightly, he dips his face into the crook of her neck to kiss and nip at the sensitive skin there until she's gasping for air. His free hand drifts down her ribs and into the tail of her wet shirt. Peeling it upwards an inch or two, Aric freezes, his body vibrating with the desire she's unleashed. When she makes no move to stop him, his hand slips under the cool material to dance his fingers over the hot skin underneath.

Hissing, Theia's back arches in order to get more of his touch. Grazing her neck with his teeth, his hand drifts over her ribs. Soft skin under his calloused fingertips kicks a shiver up his spine. The small voice in the back of his head reminds him to take his time and make this experience memorable for her while she drags blunt nails across his back.

Her soft moans become sharp gasps when he cups one breast, the ridge of his thumb brushing against her nipple until it hardens under his touch. When he takes it between his fingers and tweaks it gently, Theia nearly leaps out of her skin with a heavy moan.

His mouth on hers again, Aric memorizes every detail as Theia peels her wet shirt over her head before dropping it to the floor beside the bed. Any prayer he still clings to about coming to his senses vanishes as he pulls back to devour the sight of her bare from the waist up.

The sight of her creamy pale skin and the swell of her breasts sends a fresh wave of need through his body. The strength in her arms, and the power in her legs calls to him on a level he's not sure he can explain. Yet the way her eyes catch his and the flush on her cheeks for how he's looking at her, he's certain she knows full well what she does to him. The demand in his hands to touch her is overwhelming. The moment he does, Aric's harbors no delusions he'll ever be able to let go.

Reaching out to trace a finger along the curve of her waist, Aric relishes the whimper that escapes her lips. "You're so beautiful," he whispers, his knuckle grazing the underside of her breast.

"So are you," she breathes, her voice weak with longing as she trails a finger up the hard ridge of his chest. The light touch, coupled with the scrape of her nails, has his breath hitching.

A soft kiss turns to a heated tangle of limbs as Aric explores each breast thoroughly. Once he's learned all he can with his fingers, he ducks his head just enough to pull the hard nub between his lips. A hard growl rips from her throat to chase the light yelp of surprise. Pulling the elastic band from his bun, she sinks her hands into his hair.

When he chuckles against her skin, she responds with a hard shudder that rocks him. Sitting up, Aric peels her wet jeans from her legs. Nails scoring her skin softly as he drags the sheer scrap of material serving as the last barrier from her limbs. Standing at the edge of the bed, Aric makes quick work of his remaining clothes before re-settling beside her.

Heated flesh meets heated flesh and Aric groans when her soft curves press against his harder planes. *She's intoxicating.* Her scent, a heady mix of desire and arousal, lures him to dip his head to kiss along her collarbone until he forces back the urge to just take her.

Once he has a hold on the beast raging inside his gut, Aric takes his time mapping her body with his hands and his mouth. Her moans become louder by the moment as she writhes beneath him. The sight of her reaction to his every touch threatens to unleash the beast he just pent-up seconds ago.

"Aric."

The sound of his name on her lips nearly costs him. A soft gasp, followed by her nails pressing into his back, drives him closer to the edge. Pulling back to gaze into her face, Aric's breath hitches at the sight of her eyes, dark with lust and desire, and her lips parting with every breath.

Half afraid Theia will change her mind, he memorizes every inch of her and locks the image away into an impenetrable vault. Something to keep him warm on the nights that will follow.

Aric's heart thunders in his chest as he stares at her, his mind racing with the possibilities. Unwilling to consider them now, he tucks them away for another day and claims her mouth once more. At the same time his hand drifts down her back, he shivers as her fingers smooth over every scar he carries.

Dipping a hand between them, he groans aloud to find her wet and ready. Velvet folds slick against his fingers drive her hips off the bed with a sharp hiss. Grinding his teeth together, Aric forces himself to remain where he is. Since the moment he'd kissed her, he'd given up any hope of breathing right. Now, his lungs threaten to stage a revolt until he pulls in a breath deep enough to inflate them fully.

Before him, Theia watches him intently. Her skin flushed from the scrape of his teeth, the brush of his lips or the rasp of the stubble on his jaw only increases her beauty in his eyes. Lips swollen from his attention disappear between the pinch of her teeth. Like every other time, the sight she makes is a physical blow that leaves him gasping for more air.

When she turns her flushed face up to him, Aric leans down to capture her lips again. She tastes of desire and something deeper, something that calls to his very being. When nails grip his shoulders hard enough to break the skin, Aric slips a hand between them to find the bundle of nerves that has her writhing under his touch. Her breath hitches as he circles the hardened nub, his body holding steady with a shudder as she moans into his mouth. The slow slide of his erection over her sweet tissues has her muscles beginning to tighten forcing Aric to pull away from her mouth.

"Aric!"

Her cry of his name cuts through his restraint as her hips rock against the firm pressure of his hand, trying to find release. Aric's blood pumps hard in his ears, drowning out every sound in the world except for the animalistic growl in his chest and her sweet sounds of pleasure.

His vision narrows on the sight of Theia tossing her head back against the pillow as her legs shake. Nails bite into his arms as she rides out her release with a bucking of hips. Once the moment passes, she melts into the mattress with a low groan,

"Please, Aric."

No longer, sweet and clear, her desire roughens her voice to a level that forces his body to hum with hunger. Poised at her core, Aric leans down to trail kisses across her collarbone and up the graceful slope of her neck. Gasping, she drags his lips to hers and wraps her legs around his hips as he sinks deep into her body. His growl rips free from his throat as her heat surrounds him.

Leaning forward, Aric nips her lip before kissing the sting away. Every muscle convulses as he holds himself steady, giving her a moment to grow accustomed to their fit. When she shifts impatiently beneath him, Aric nearly comes undone.

Every breath, every word, every touch feels a little like heaven and a lot like a rollercoaster. When she tightens around him, his hips jerk in response. Another growl rumbles from him and he leans in to bite her shoulder. Theia's breath hiccups as he pulls his hips back and thrusts into her again. The heavy, rhythmic pounding stoking her desire until she responds with a shiver of pleasure. The change in his pace sends a spasm through her as she gasps his name.

"I have you," he promises, his voice thick with desire.

Theia's only reply is a soft moan as she move to grasp the headboard to hold herself steady with one hand. Each moan that falls from her lips has him hardening even more.

Arching into the pressure, Theia's nails dig into the headboard the moment an arm wraps around her waist to anchor her in place. Staring down into her face, Aric stills when he sees her eyes locking on his. Each breath, each pulse, he loses himself in her until he can do nothing but move. Theia whimpers in encouragement as his thrusts become harder and faster.

Fast and deep, Aric loves her until the heat in her blood reaches a fevered pitch. Fingernails score his back while Theia gasps for air around the raw desire tearing through her. The scent of her arousal thickens around them as the pleasure rises to a shattering peak. Her nub against the base of him sends a fresh wave of heat roaring through his body.

Burying himself so deep inside her nothing could ever pry him free overrides any other thought as he's consumed with the sounds of their bodies moving together. Theia's every whimper, moan, and breath fans the flames to a roaring inferno. Each tuck of her hips and grind of her body rocks him to the core of his being. Holding onto him tightly, she pulls him deeper. The tight throb of her core around him drives him off the edge as she explodes around him.

Aric's body stiffens with the force of her orgasm, her soft gasps and breathless moans holding his body to a rhythm until he can barely manage one last thrust. Burying his face into the crook of her neck,

Aric breathes in the scent that is Theia as he rides every spasm shooting through him.

White light dances in his peripheral as shards of pain overwhelm the remnants of pleasure to leave him collapsing next to her on the bed. Wrapping an arm around her hip, Aric tucks her into the fold of his body and buries his face in the soft tresses of her hair.

"Sleep now," he soothes gently, placing a kiss on her forehead.

Bracing her head with his good shoulder, Aric's hand rubs gently along the arch of her back until her heavy breaths slow and become even. Sleeping peacefully with her head under his chin, Aric lay awake contemplating how he'll ever let her go after today. The ache in his heart at the thought makes sleep elusive.

CHAPTER 21

"Sir, I'm sorry but they're in a meeting."

"Back off!" Snarling at the angel on the far side of the mammoth desk, Riordan pushes past her toward the conference hall.

"I believe the young woman told you already. They're occupied." Michael cuts in as he steps between Riordan and his intended target. "Take a seat. I'm sure they'll get to you when they can."

Plowing a hand through his hair, Riordan regards the tiny row of chairs on the far wall with a curl of his lip. "I don't have time for this."

"I suggest you make time," although Michael's voice is warm, Riordan locates the warning floating just beneath the surface.

He'd had her! Pacing back and forth, Riordan eyes the chair closest to him and fights the urge to smash it with one well-placed fist. He recalls the look of terror on her face floating down river, nothing stopping him from bringing an end to this whole sordid tale. Only to have his leashed yank. "This is a waste of time," he fumes. The receptionist gasps audibly at the venom in his voice while Michael simply resorts to lifting an eyebrow.

He tries to find a quiet place in his mind and not think about this latest detour. The longer he stews here, the time Theia will have to go to ground. Again. Realization that when he returns Aric will have healed from the wounds he'd inflicted, makes any hope for a calm demeanor; a long shot.

After casting a withering glance at the closed doors just ahead, Riordan spins on his heel and approaches the receptionist with a flaccid smile. "Let them know I was here and that I'll be back when they can see me."

Almond-shaped eyes widen. Under the stark white lights, her creamy complexion pales. "I'm s-sorry, S-sir." Lips tremble as her she braces herself against her desktop. "They instructed me to keep you here until they're ready for you."

"Keep. Me. Here?" Towering across the hip-high desk, Riordan stops just before he bumps into her perfect nose. "You and whose army?"

"Mine."

Withdrawing a smidge, Riordan's eyes close as Michael's voice comes from over his shoulder. Fingers grip the marble top hard enough for cracks to grow in the immaculate surface. Counting to ten allows Riordan to contain the inferno bubbling in his stomach. "This is ridiculous," he begins, stepping away from Michael's looming figure. "The longer I stay here the harder they'll be to find again."

"They?"

"Aric and his Nephilim," he answers through a clenched jaw.

"Ah." Arms fold across Michael's broad chest while clear blue eyes pin Riordan with a cool stare. "Correct me if I'm wrong, but your orders are for the Nephilim. Not Aric."

"I consider bringing him in a bonus."

"Rounding up renegade seraph's is no longer part of your job description. Or have you forgotten?"

Riordan's scowl slips free before he can call it back. While Michael phrases it as a question, there's no doubt he already knows the answer. "I haven't forgotten."

"Perfect. So you'll leave bringing Aric before the Council to your betters," Michael adds silkily. "I think you'll find my methods differ from yours."

"I've been doing this for hundred's of years!"

Michael's easy smile twists. "So have I. The difference is in the number I bring in alive compared to the ones you retrieve dead."

Riordan scoffs just as the massive door swings open to reveal Councilor Gregory on the other side.

Adjusting the fold of his robes over a robust figure, he steps aside and ushers Riordan forward. "We're ready for you."

'*Bout damn time!* Reigning in his initial reaction, Riordan bows his head. Once inside, his teeth grind and his fingers clench at his sides.

A grand room with floor to ceiling windows, the conference hall offers a stunning view of majestic snow-capped mountains and regal spruce trees. Each step echoes off marble floors and bare walls as he stalks between the aisles full of his fellow Seraph's. The combined weight of their silent judgement settles across his shoulders.

At the front of the room, the Council members sit behind a raised platform. Reclaiming his seat, Councilor Gregory motions with a quick bob of his head to the time keeper. Catching the ripple in his double chin turns Riordan's stomach.

Clearing her throat, Councilor Rebecca draws his hostile gaze. While not the head of the committee, she commands respect with a monarch-like bearing and a stiff posture. "Please take a seat," she instructs while reading over the papers strewn in front of her.

"I'll stand." Riordan widens his stance amidst the gasps behind him and folds his hands tightly behind his back. "This won't take long."

Lavender eyes flash in a heart-shaped face. "That isn't for you to say," she responds icily, her hand sweeping to a solitary chair on his right. "Sit."

The atmosphere is tense and thick with the scent of power and authority. Trapping his tongue between his teeth, Riordan carefully sits in the designated chair. The slight narrowing in Rebecca's eyes alerts him to her knowledge of his most recent injury so despite the pain, he holds his spine straight.

"Do you know why we summoned you?" Councilor Gregory asks, his tone neutral.

"No," Riordan mutters, "but the timing couldn't be worse."

Despite the red flush staining bulbous cheeks, Councilor Gregory continues. "We understand you've had some difficulty with this particular Nephilim."

Snorting loudly, Riordan gives his head a shake. "That's putting it mildly."

"Is there a reason this one is posing such a challenge?" He prods.

"You mean aside from the fact that she's the offspring of a Seraph?" Riordan's eyes sweep across each councilor before he settles his attention on Rebecca. "Or that she's getting help from one of us?"

Extending a finger, Councilor Samuel raises his hand. "Have we confirmed the parentage?"

Stepping forward from the just out of view, Michael dips his head in acknowledgement before answering. "There's been no sighting of Julian anywhere near the Nephilim."

"I don't need confirmation," Riordan sneers. "I know who the father is."

"Unfortunately, we don't operate on what you know. We operate on facts." Councilor Rebecca cuts in, clasping her hands tight in front of her. "Facts, I might add that are piling up against you."

"Like what," he challenges.

"Your blatant disregard of exposing yourself to humans. Behavior that leads us to believe you've no intention of bringing the Nephilim before us, alive." When she peers over the bridge of her nose at him, a shiver skips up Riordan's spine. "Not to mention your vicious attack on a brother at arms."

"Aric stopped being a brother when he allowed a Nephilim to grow into her powers," Riordan defends tightly.

Councilor Gregory coughs. "If that's true, our researchers will find it."

"What Aric allowed to happen holds no bearing on this meeting." Councilor Samuel declares, sitting back in his chair. "You hold no authority to bring him in."

Riordan pulls another breath and meets their cold-hearted expressions with a steely smile. Squaring his shoulders, he removes any trace of weakness infecting his bones before making another attempt. "He's betrayed us."

"So you've tasked yourself with bringing him to justice?" Councilor Rebecca quirks an eyebrow, her eyes scrutinizing him. "Do you also mean to be his judge, jury and executioner?"

"I'll find him and I'll bring him before you for a fair trial," Riordan answers with a confident nod.

"For that, you'll need to bring him in alive." Councilor Samuel challenges, his timid voice missing anything that resembles intimidation.

"I understand that," Riordan replies in measured tones. "I believe I'm the best equipped given my experience with him."

"Your experience has been less than satisfactory," Councilor Rebecca interjects. "According to our reports you've made no significant progress in apprehending the Nephilim."

Riordan's jaw tightens at the barb. "I assure you, I'm doing everything in my power to bring it-"

"And yet," Councilor Rebecca interrupts, her tone icy. "it remains at large and at full strength."

"I do what needs to be done." Riordan's heart rate echoes in his ears as he struggles to remain seated under their accusations. The weight of their displeasure covers him like a shroud. "Aric's interference could cost us everything."

"Perhaps." Lifting a hand to silence any further argument, Councilor Gregory eyes him shrewdly. "What you're failing to understand is that your own actions are becoming reckless and dangerous."

How dare they accuse him of losing control! Riordan bristles as the full brunt of the implication sits in his chest. "I am a Seraph. I've always acted in the best interest of our kind."

"It is not the existence of our kind that worries me, Riordan." Councilor Rebecca states when it seems she's found her emotionless demeanor. "It's the existence of everything else. This Nephilim could wreak havoc and chaos in every world. Not just ours."

Councilor Gregory thumps his fist on the table, turning all eyes on him. "Precisely! We must judge it for danger. And stop it if needed."

"It's not in full control of it's emotions yet," Riordan points out. "There is still a chink in the armor I can exploit."

"Alright, Riordan," Councilor Rebecca purrs, her eyes hard flints, devoid of color. "You'll have another chance at bringing this situation to a satisfactory resolution. Should you fail, however, you'll join your brothers and sisters in the ether."

Icy dread swarms through his body unchecked. Breathing becomes a chore while his skin breaks out in a cold sweat. Perching on the edge of his seat, he attempts to silence the trembling in his legs.

Part of him wants to argue the ultimatum is hasty. The only thing keeping his mouth shut is the hard resolve in the faces before him. Only a successful mission will earn him a reprieve. The possibility of it going the other way, squeezes his heart under bands of wrought iron.

Swallowing thickly, Riordan's eyes dart from one member of the council to the other. "I won't fail," he squeaks out but the soft tremor in his voice leaves much room for doubt.

"See that you don't," Councilor Samuel warns before dismissing Riordan with a wave of his boney hand.

Standing from his chair, Riordan blinks repeatedly to bring the room into focus. As he strides out, the eyes of his fellow Seraph's track his progress, some with pity and others with obvious contempt. *I don't have time for their judgement and doubt.* Tipping his chin and straightening his shoulders, Riordan focus his attention to the task at hand.

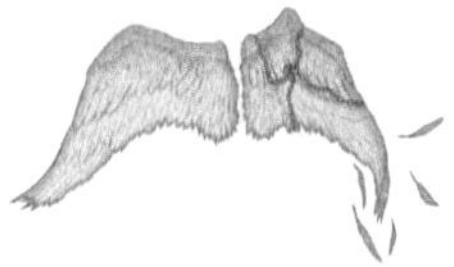

When the fog of sleep between her ears lifts, Theia registers she's in bed alone. The sheet Aric pulled over them earlier is damp with a chill. Sitting up, she presses one end of the scratchy material to her bare chest and searches the dark room.

While she slept, the inky black blanket of night replaced the soft rays of the sun that struggled to peek through thick rain clouds. Not even the moon adds a measure of light to the room, forcing Theia to squint as she scans every corner.

He's left? Despite telling herself she's a big girl and can more than handle a little heartbreak, Theia senses a coiling snake in the pit of her stomach. With whispered words in the farthest corner of her mind, it tries to feed off raw emotions. Scrunching the sheet in one fist, she wraps the thin material around her and shimmies out of bed. He wouldn't just leave. Not after everything that's happened. *Right?*

Shoving at the heavy mass of hair shrouding her face, Theia perches on the edge of the bed with a wince. Everything hurts. Muscles she never knew she possessed until now, launch a complaint with every movement.

Unlike the ache of training or running for her life, however, this is a sweet ache. A gentle reminder of their time together. Theia recalls the wildfire in his hazel-green eyes as he showcased restraint and loved her with a need she never knew existed. "He wouldn't just leave," Theia confirms aloud just as the shower cuts off in the bathroom.

With his damp hair pulled into a ponytail, Aric steps out of the bathroom with a towel wrapped around his hips and another trailing from his neck. A soft, satisfied grunt slips past his lips the second they lock eyes. Muscles across his chest heave with every breath as he pads barefoot deeper into the room.

"Good evening, sleepyhead," Aric grins and tosses one damp towel on the matching bed standing against the far wall. "How are you feeling?"

"Fine. Just, uh, cold." Theia folds her hands in her lap and fiddles with the hem of the sheet. "I didn't hear you get up."

Her breath hitches as she tracks his movements and the towel that rides above the swell of his ass, leaving nothing to the imagination. Pressing a hand to her aching torso, she squeezes her eyes shut to calm the heavy beat of her heart. Visions of him and the things he did to make her squirm run through her mind. Instantly, her muscles hum with the need to experience it all over again.

"I didn't want to wake you." Fastening one hand on the folds of his towel, Aric takes a seat next to her on the bed "I thought you could use more sleep."

Hiding her smile behind a soft curtain of hair, Theia nudges him with a shoulder. "How long were you in there? Did you save me any hot water?"

"Long enough to get myself under control. And yes, there's plenty of hot water."

"Control, huh?"

"Mmhmm. If I laid there any longer, you wouldn't have been able to sleep in." The deep, husky growl of his voice brings her eyes back to his. "We needed the rest. I know I was beyond exhausted," he adds as he pulls her close with an arm around her shoulders.

Theia laughs. "I didn't think you were capable of exhaustion."

"You have no idea how capable I can be, Theia."

The soft grumble of his words and the heat in his eyes send a fresh stab of desire through her body. Despite her best intentions, the fluttering of her heart grows until it pounds in her ears.

She meant to explain he didn't owe her anything. That she wouldn't expect anything from him. Now all she can think about is the warmth of his body and the intoxicating scent of his skin.

Closing her eyes, she shifts away to clear her mind. The quick jolt of pain that answers sends her hips jerking with a hiss.

"What's wrong?" No sooner are the words leaving his lips before a large hand smooths up her spine.

"Just a little sore."

Shadows flicker across his face, his jaw hardening instantly. "From me?"

"No." Heat floods her cheeks, warming the tips of her ears. "Well, yes, but not that kind of sore. I think this is from when the truck crashed yesterday."

"Anything I can do to help?" Aric's fingers move in small circles across her back as he leans down to press his lips against the nape of her neck.

His light, teasing touch sends a shockwave of lust through her veins until her muscles tense and quiver with anticipation. Her skin burns under the slightest caress. With a slight wriggle, she worms closer, craving for more with an intensity that leaves her breathless.

Reading the desire on her face, Aric pulls back. "Riordan is still out there."

"Yes, he is." Theia nods, pushing herself to her feet. Twirling on the ball of one foot, she faces Aric and holds the tattered ends of her nerves together. The tremors in her voice give him a peek at the emotions rolling just under the surface of her skin as she lets the sheet pool on the floor at her feet. "I don't really care at the moment. Do you?"

Her hand trembles as it hesitates over her shoulder, reluctant to unveil the image hiding behind her thick hair. Butterflies swim through her veins as she lifts the curtain to toss it over her back, exposing her flawed figure.

Fuller than she'd prefer, Theia's all too aware of each imperfection. Toes curl into the coarse carpet as she awaits his judgement, her heart pounding a furious tempo. Every tick of her pulse stretches like foggy whispers of hunger the longer he sits there without moving.

Reaching for her, his fingers wrap around her wrist. After a gentle tug, she's standing less than a foot in front of him. His eyes scan slowly across every inch of her from head to toe as if seeing her for the first time. The whisper light finger he drags across her hip drags a strangled gasp from her lips.

"You're beautiful."

Butterflies dissolve as heat floods her, painting her skin red. Murmuring the words again, Aric presses his lips to hers, snaking the breath from her lungs. The heat of his palm gliding over the flare of her hip sends her senses into overload.

Pulling her down, Aric lays her across the width of the bed as he continues to explore every inch of her mouth with his tongue. A husky moan shakes her voice when his fingers skim up and down the flare of her ribcage.

Theia melts into the mattress beneath her, surrendering to the heat of his body and the gentle touch of his lips. Every sensation takes her a step further from reality until all that remains is the thundering of his heart under her hand. Slamming against his chest, it beats like an ancient drum loud enough to erase the entire world.

"More," she breathes against the line of his jaw.

Happy to comply, Aric trails kisses over the curve of her neck as his fingers dance along the underside of one breast. "You can have it all," he responds thickly, his words a strained growl that unleashes a fresh wave of hunger in her stomach. With a whimper, Theia tucks her face into the crook of his neck as her hands glide over the wide expanse of his back.

Fingers tangle in her hair, pulling her head back to face him. "Don't hide from me."

Leaning upward, Theia captures his lips with a hungry growl of her own. "I'm right here." When he rolls his fingers over one hardened nipple, light explodes behind her eyes sharp enough to make her moan.

"You're beautiful."

A smile tilts her lips. "You said that already."

"I mean it," Aric insists, his voice thick with need. "You take my breath away," he whispers, giving her a glimpse of the same desperation and need riding hard on her muscles.

Soft pants fall from her lips as her fingers glide across the thick cords of his neck before dragging her blunt nails over the swell of muscles in his back. With a low hiss of appreciation, Aric tortures and teases each hard nub until Theia is ready to fly off the bed.

Gasping for air, she arches against him. "More, Aric. I need more."

Hovering above her, he tightens his grip on her hair and dips his head to swipe and swirl his tongue over the sensitive tip of each nipple. While Theia struggles with the constant pressure at her core, her muscles beg for release,

"Are you wet for me?" His husky voice is a breathless rumble against her skin. Clenching her thighs tight, Theia attempts to find some measure of control over the liquid heat scorching her skin.

"Yes," she groans. Fear of coming apart at the seams has her latching onto one of his shoulders.

"What do you want?"

"You."

With her heart hammering against her ribs, Theia lifts her hips to find any sort of relief. Chuckling, Aric continues his torture until his lips and fingers dance fire across her skin, driving her mad. His tantalizing touch trails slowly over the curve of her hip before dipping down to brush across her center.

"Aric," she pleads breathlessly, her hands clawing at his shoulders. Theia's fingers slide down his spine and trace the firm curve of his ass. The slow drag of his teeth across the other hardened tip causes her body to shudder. When a moan rumbles in her throat, the hand in her hair jerks her head back so he can scrape his teeth against her jaw.

"Do you know what you do to me?" he asks, voice thick with a lusty growl in her ear.

"Show me."

Raising his head, he pulls her toward him and captures her lips in a long kiss. Her mind fogs with the need to feel him between her legs. It mutes the hunger in her belly only for a moment before it gnaws at her insides again, demanding attention. "You're mine." The words come out like a growl. "What do you want?" He repeats the question with a slow stroke against her heated skin, sending a flurry of shivers along her spine.

"More," she begs.

"What do you want?" He repeats the question with a slow stroke against her heated skin, sending a flurry of shivers along her spine.

Theia's voice cracks. "You already know."

"Say it, Theia." Aric's lips seal over hers as his fingers slide inside of her, stretching and filling her. Shuddering, Theia's body responds to the gentle caress.

"Aric," she whimpers.

A groan rumbles in Aric's chest and Theia's muscles clench around him in reaction to his restrained desire. "Fucking hell," he mutters against her neck, his voice gruff. "You're so tight."

His words send another wave of heat washing over her skin, her cheeks burning bright red as a low moan falls from her lips. Nibbling softly at her jawline, he teases his fingers to go deeper before sliding out almost completely.

With a firm thrust, his fingers slide deep again, making the throbbing at her core come alive. Her muscles clench down hard as an explosive orgasm rocks her body, stealing the strength from her bones. Groaning, he cups the back of her head and guides her lips back to his. "Say it for me." Lazily trailing his tongue over her lip, Aric growls. "Say it."

"I want you."

Growling low in his throat, Aric pulls away. Rising on his knees, he settles between her legs and drops into the cradle of her thighs. She tries to respond, but her words lack the control of forming a coherent sentence. Theia's breath hitches as he slides into her in one smooth stroke. His teeth sink into her shoulder as he grinds against her, filling her to the hilt. Tightening around him, she cries out.

"Not yet," he growls.

Theia's vision blurs with the sudden explosion of heat. Her muscles prime and twitch with restraint as her mouth falls open, a low, desperate moan rattling in her chest as Theia arches her hips off the bed. Grinding against him, she draws a deep groan from him before he leans over to drag his teeth across the soft swell of her shoulder.

Rocking, her hips sends a tremor through his arms as he throws his head back with a roar, venting his pleasure into the air. Unwilling to relinquish his control, Aric tugs her down with one hand while the other settles on her thigh.

A rush of heat pools between her thighs, causing her muscles to burn with the need to be touched. A deep groan vibrates against her lips as Aric rolls his hips against hers, easing her slowly over the edge of lust. Gasping, they kiss, her body craving the rush of adrenaline streaking through her bloodstream.

Once she cannot bottle her desire any longer, and releases the dam of pleasure that had held her back. It explodes through her body like a wildfire, and burns through her veins until even the tips of her toes tingle with sensation. Aric's triumphant roar follows. Their combined bliss sending reverberations shattering against every wall of their room.

"Aric," she whispers against his chest, her body relaxing as it comes down slowly and her arms wrap around his neck.

"Mmm..." Resting his head against her shoulder, Aric groans. His body is slick with sweat and his heavy breaths fall against the curve of her neck. When his muscles relax, a low moan escapes his lips as he lifts her to lie silently against him. "You're amazing. I didn't hurt you, did I?" His question is a husky growl against the skin of her throat.

"No," she shakes her head. Her muscles are still twitching and pulsing, unable to find relief from the ache in her core.

Aric's fingers slide over her flushed skin as he leans back to meet her eyes. "How do you feel?"

Biting her lower lip, Theia exhales a deep breath and gives him a half-smile. "Like I could run a marathon."

The hard rap on the door of their motel room douses them both under a deluge of icy water.

CHAPTER 22

After sharing a worried glance with Theia, Aric recovers his discarded jeans from the floor. Smoothing a hand through his hair, he tightens the elastic that holds it in place and approaches the door. The instant he peers out the peephole, the bottom drops out of his stomach.

A peek over his shoulder shows Theia scurrying to retrieve her clothes, her plump backside swinging back and forth. Tearing his eyes away with a strangled groan, Aric's jaw tightens when another knock rattles the door in its frame.

"Go to the bathroom and get dressed."

Theia stops mid-motion. Sensing the urgency in his voice, her brow furrows. "Who is it?"

"Your father," he replies tightly. "You need to get dressed."

For a moment, shock ripples across her face, then confusion followed by sheer panic. Scooping up an armload of clothes, Theia scrambles to the bathroom and shuts the door behind her. Once Aric registers the tumbler sliding into place, he opens the still rattling door.

"Julian," he breathes, his eyes widening in what he hopes passes for complete surprise.

"Can I come in?"

"Of course. Sorry." Stepping aside, Aric holds the door open for his friend then locks it behind him.

"I hope I'm not interrupting anything."

"Not at all," Aric says, rubbing a hand across the back of his neck.

Julian's eyes flit over Aric's shoulder to the rumpled covers on the bed. "Theia with you?"

Aric forces a smile. *He's going to kill me. Hell, I'd kill me!* "Of course," he hedges and gestures toward the closed bathroom door.

"Everything okay?" Even as Julian phrases the question innocently, Aric notes the small tic pulsing in his left cheek.

Shit. "Why wouldn't it be?"

Instead of answering, Julian stalks deeper into the room and turns on the television. Staring straight into the camera, the news anchor reports on a multi-car collision on Interstate 35. *While they have reported no fatalities, they list several in critical condition.*

"Shit." Scrubbing a hand over his face, Aric drops onto the foot of the bed.

"What are you doing?"

Dragging his eyes from the young reporter's face, Aric flinches under Julian's dark glare. "She didn't mean it."

"Well, that's a plus. Better than her doing it on purpose," Julian roars, motioning wildly towards the bathroom with his hands. "You're supposed to be training her Aric."

"I am training her." Surging to his feet, Aric stands between Julian and the bathroom.

"If that's control, I'd hate to see her unhinged."

"Fuck off," Aric growls dangerously.

"Yeah, you seem to do that too!"

Aric's chest tightens until his heart feels like it's making an escape plan. Desperately fighting for control, he recites the German alphabet, seeking solace in the mundane repetition. However, when he speaks, a quake of emotions takes a joyride on the words he spits through his teeth. "Why are you here?"

"You're supposed to keep her safe. Teaching her how to control these emotions."

"She's learning. You and I both know it's not as easy as it sounds and we're not *half-human*."

Shrugging him off with a fling of his arm, Julian paces a short distance. When he turns towards Aric, fear glitters brilliantly in his eyes. "At this rate she'll kill someone before she finds the same neighborhood as control. If that happens, they'll stop trying to capture her. He turns towards Aric with heat brilliantly glittering in his eyes. "At this rate, she'll kill someone before finding the same neighborhood as control. If that happens, they'll stop trying to capture her, and instead, mark her for death, Aric."

The sound of a muffled gasp behind him brings Aric face to face with Theia. Her complexion lacking any color, her features twisting cruelly. Before he can reach for her, she scrambles past the both of them, bolting out into the moonless night.

"Awesome," Aric snarls. Before he runs after her, he jabs a finger in Julian's direction. "Stay here."

"If you think-"

"Julian, just because I like you doesn't mean I won't snap your legs," Aric warns quietly. "I'll find her and bring her back, but you have to stop running your mouth."

"She's all I have left. I'm not going to just sit back and-"

"What happened to not running your mouth?"

"She's *my* daughter," Julian rages, shoving past Aric and marching towards the door.

The pressure Aric battles with spills over into his stomach. Gripping Julian's arm, he spins the man around, meeting his shock with cold, hard facts. "She doesn't know you." The pain pinching his friend's forehead leaves Aric kicking himself. Forcing a level of calm into his tone, he tries again. "Just wait here. Please." Once Julian manages an imperceptible nod of his dark head, Aric runs outside.

The second he's out the door, Aric opens his mind, searching frantically until it zeroes in on hers. The pain she's struggling with blasts into his head with enough force to knock him off balance. Theia's mind-numbing fear flourishes between his ears, anger snapping at its heels. Red hot and bitter. Gasping against the agony clawing at his skull, Aric covers the distance quickly.

"Theia." His wrenched plea catches on the wind. Just ahead, he hears someone stumble. Boots slap wildly against the pavement as he barrels across the street to the small park on the other side.

Using the large tree beside her for support, she let each sob rip itself from her body. Sharp heat tortures his heart, twisting it into mush as the full force of her emotions assault the link he'd opened. With a grit of his teeth, Aric severs their connection as he moves slowly to rest a hand on her shoulder.

"Please don't cry."

"I'm a monster!"

"No, you're not." Aric caresses her back, helping her to relax until she can take deep breaths without hiccups. Squeezing his eyes tight, he looks away for the time it takes to smother each raw chord until he can breathe without the stitch in his side.

"I can't do this," Theia explains, her voice a barely audible whisper. "I'm going to get someone killed."

"That's not true. Your father is just scared."

"He should be!" Whirling around to confront him, Aric's head tilts at the wild spark in her dark blue eyes. Her fingers tangle in the hem of her shirt in a gesture he's familiar with. "All I do is destroy things."

"That's because your fear controls you." Bridging the gap between them, he rubs hands along her bare arms to ward off the chill in the air. "You need to let the fear go."

"I don't know how."

Overhead, the wind whistles and pops, sending a shiver down his spine. "The first step is to admit that there's nothing wrong with having fear."

"You're not afraid of anything."

"I'm afraid of everything," Aric argues, dipping a finger under her jaw to tip her eyes up toward his. "I'm terrified of making the wrong choice. I've locked myself away from everyone and anyone for years to keep from having regrets. Mostly, I'm scared shitless to go back in there and explain to my oldest friend that I'm in love with his daughter!"

Red, puffy eyes round in her face as the true weight of his confession finally registers. Aric stares at the ground as his confession hangs heavy in the air, an anvil over his heart. When his lungs begin to burn and stutter, he remembers to exhale. To him, years pass by as time ticks on happily, mindless of the torment he's under. In reality, it's probably closer to seconds.

"You're in love with me?"

Aric winces at the pinched tension in her voice. "I'm sorry. It just sort've happened."

"When?"

"Truthfully?" Theia nods, her teeth chewing anxiously over her lower lip. "I think I fell in love with you from the moment you appeared in my driveway." Aric takes a step forward, reaching out to touch her but stopping just short of making contact. His heart races as he waits for her response, for any sign of how she might react. She looks up at him, her eyes searching his face for answers.

Finally, she speaks, her voice soft and trembling. "Why didn't you tell me sooner?" she asks, wonder adding a soft thread to her words.

"I didn't know how."

Stepping into his arms, Theia's holds onto him for dear life. Pressing her cheek against his chest she mumbles the words he's waited centuries to hear. "I love you too, Aric."

Five small words strike Aric like lightning, overturning his world and leaving it spinning out of control. In desperation, he buries his face in her hair. Inhaling deeply of her sweet aroma, it seeps into his essence, an eternal torture that both tantalizes and tortures him.

"You're terrified of my father?"

Aric stiffens as the question leaves her lips. The warmth of her smile seeps through him to tug at his heartstrings. He answers honestly, his voice rough and heavy, like molten lava. "He never fights fair." When a peal of laughter jumps off her tongue and fills the air, Aric's chest swells with joy as he surrenders to the beauty of her laugh; a sound designed just for him. "You ready to meet him?"

Theia tenses in his arms and stutters a nod. "Now or never."

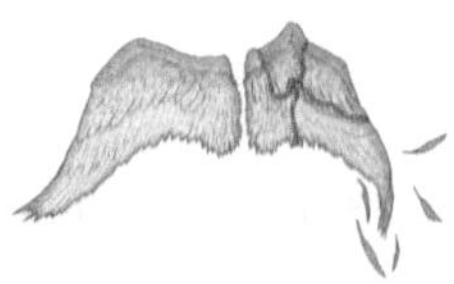

With a squeeze of his hand, Aric leads her back towards the motel. The closer they get, the harder the rhythm of her heart pounds against the walls of her chest. Her fingers tighten almost painfully on Aric's hand as they step inside and she registers Julian's looming presence. Silently, she stares at the stranger, desperately searching for any familiarity.

Only an inch taller than Aric, her father stands proud, with wide-set shoulders and incredibly long legs. Dark brown hair similar to hers brushes the back of his neck, just shy of the t-shirt collar. His eyes resemble a clear blue summer sky as he stares back at her. The expression on his granite-like jaw is unreadable until a measure of softness creeps in around the edges.

"Theia," he murmurs softly, his eyes glistening with unshed tears. "You're so...grown up."

Beside her, Aric becomes her one lifeline in a turbulent sea of raw emotions. At first, inflating her lungs with so many other things filling her chest is impossible. But when she squeaks in enough oxygen to inflate them a little, some of that pressure eases to allow for a deeper breath.

Fingernails pick over the pad of her thumb as she searches her mind for something to say. For thirty years, she's been racking up the questions, not daring to hope for such a meeting. Now that it's here, she's having difficulty settling on just one.

"Are you really-"

"Your father?" Julian finishes with a wry twitch of his lips. After jamming his hands into his pockets, he shuffles from foot to foot. "Not that I have any right to the title, but yes, Theia."

A scent of lemon and lavender wafts through the air. Each breath reignites her memory of love and regret, driving home the questions she's been pushing away for years. *Where did he go? Why did he leave her behind? Who is this man that crushed her mother's heart so completely?*

As a child she'd lay awake in bed, dreaming of meeting his mystery figure while Granny seethed with barely suppressed anger for him. Yet, no matter how Theia begged for answers, she refused to say what happened. When she finally learned that he'd died, it was like a shard of ice had ripped through her heart. That one moment left a deep ache in her chest as it shattered all her childhood fantasies.

"I thought you were dead," Theia croaks, inwardly wincing at the flicker of pain that flashes in his clear eyes.

"I'm sorry," Julian whispers. "So sorry for what I put you through." He takes a step towards her, his arms outstretched and Theia flinches. Her reaction leaves a hitch in his step, his smile fragile as his arms drop to his side. Forcing herself to inhale and exhale, she studies the tattoo gracing the inside of his right forearm.

Large petals identical to the moon flowers Granny grows for her mother's memory spans from wrist to elbow. The sharp contrast of color and shading gives the impression they'd rustle in a warm breeze. So realistic, Theia gets the feeling that if she were to inhale deep enough, their calming and familiar scent would engulf her.

"I know I screwed up Theia. I just want to make things right," Julian chokes.

Her eyes flicker to Aric, who stands resolute by her side. He hasn't moved since they entered the room, offering sanctuary without a uttering a sound. Sensing her gaze, he regards her quietly before offering a small nod of encouragement.

Releasing his hand, she takes three steps forward and allows her father to embrace her in a deep hug. *Okay, this isn't awkward at all.* Theia grapples with what to do with her arms before eventually she wraps them around his waist and allows herself to relax into the hug. Sensing her acceptance, Julian's arms tighten around her with a broken gasp.

When she pulls away, Theia recognizes regret in his eyes as he stares down into her face. It's obvious he carries the weight of his decisions like an anchor around his very essence. A lump grows in her throat, but Theia chokes it down. "Why did you leave me?"

Julian studies the floor with a newfound interest. "I knew they'd never stop hunting me. I hoped your grandmother would give you a better life than the one I could."

Her voice trips over her words with a soft flare of heat in her chest. "She told me you were dead."

"I know," he admits woodenly. "We both thought it was for the best."

The searing inferno that explodes within her is so absolute it sends her back a step. Teeth clench and grind so hard that she prepares herself for the sound of cracking. With a shake of her head, she retreats another step, drawing Aric's concern.

Hands ball into fists so tight, her short fingernails draw blood against her palms. *She lied.* The one person who preached and lectured *honesty*. How lying was a lazy way out. The person she'd loved and trusted her entire life had lied! The realization is a poison coursing through her veins until her body is a walking, talking wildfire.

"Better for who?" While her voice is dangerously quiet, Julian seems oblivious.

Aric on the other hand, takes a step forward, reaching out with an upturned palm. "*Theia.*"

Her eyes close as the sound of his rich voice soothes across frayed nerves. It'd be so easy to just latch onto the emotions he stirs inside her. To let the warm, fuzzy cocoon smother the fire unleashing in her chest until hot steam bathes her skin. Lifting her lashes, Julian's face fills her vision. The confusion wrinkling his brow adds a steady stream of fuel to her emotions until sparks dance across her fingertips.

"You need to calm down."

The thought of her father speaking with such an air of authority has her chuckling softly. "What makes you think you have any right to tell me what to do?" Theia spits out, venom lacing her words. She takes another step back, putting distance between them.

"You're out of control," Julian snaps tightly.

"Whose fault is that?" Theia challenges hotly. "You could've stuck around and helped me. But you didn't. And now, you show up and ridicule Aric for teaching me what little control I've found?"

Julian's face falls, a deep sadness creeping into his expression before it hardens. "Seems like if he spent more time on training and less on taking advantage, you wouldn't be a mess of emotions right now."

"Julian," Aric cuts in, his voice flat. "You're not helping."

"Taking advantage?" Despite the scent of Aric's calming fragrance inches from her face, Theia's vision narrows until all she can focus on is Julian. Twenty-eight years of abandonment issues. Keeping herself so tightly contained, she feared sneezing too hard; infects her body.

The sparks across her fingertips erupt into violent bursts of magenta and azure as a cyclone of power swirls around her. Snagging her loose hair, the wind whips it wildly against her face as it reaches a fever pitch. Walls tremble and quake, bowing to the might of the tempest, as if nothing can contain it. Once the pressure builds to the height of its peak, the window shatters. In the center of it all, Julian stands frozen as flames leap and dance around his feet like wild beasts ready to consume him.

As quickly as it begins, it ends. Inhaling a shaky breath, Theia closes her eyes and searches for that island of calm Aric keeps nagging about. Once she finds it in her mind's eye, she plays his voice over and over in her head until the sense of security he offers douses her raw emotions with a violent hiss.

Only after she's confident she can look at her father without wanting to obliterate him does Theia open her eyes. Shock and something else taints his strong features, his mouth opening and closing.

With a glare at her father, Theia speaks slowly, her words overburdened with menace. "If I was out of control," she hisses, "you wouldn't be standing here right now."

Turning, she gazes up into Aric's face to find his eyes shining with pride and unbridled love. Warmth radiates outward from her chest. This man hadn't lied to her. He accepted her for all of her strengths and weaknesses. With a pained smile, she reaches up to brush the pad of her thumb along his stubbled jaw. "I just need some air," she whispers. "Don't worry, I'll stay where you can see me."

Aric nods, his eyes never wavering from hers as she steps outside. After her display of control, a slight breeze remains, carrying the scent of fresh rain with it. *Anything's better than the stifling judgement in there*, Theia muses and climbs on the picnic tabletop with a sigh. From her perch, she stares out at the city sprawled before her, its bright lights flickering like manmade stars.

Lost in thought, Theia sits there as the cool night air washes over her exposed nerves. By the time she senses Aric's presence, the last trickle of heat subsides.

With a heavy sigh, he sits down beside her, wrapping an arm around her to pull her close. His warmth leaks through their layers of clothes to incite a soft exhale from her. "Are you okay?"

Theia tips her head back to meet his gaze, smoothing a finger over the wrinkles etched into his handsome features. "I will be."

"Good." He jerks a nod with his chin as his hand runs soothingly along her bare arm. "But if not, you can still go back in there and kick his ass."

Theia laughs and although his lazy smile does weird and amazing things to her stomach, she gives him a soft nudge with her shoulder. "You're supposed to be a good influence on me."

"Damn. Does that mean no more sex?"

The intense heat of his gaze sends a bolt of electricity through her. Theia's laughter cascades like waves in an ocean, and the tension that winds tightly around her heart unravels entirely. Her body relaxes, the weight in her limbs lifting.

Leaning in, she captures his lips in a heated kiss that ignites a flame of another kind in her belly. His arm tightens around her as he pulls her flush against the wall of his body. When they break apart, Theia rests her forehead against his chest and centers herself on his slow breaths. The passion burning between them is palpable, a current that singes every nerve ending in Theia's body. She feels alive, more alive than she's ever felt before.

Turning in his arms, she sits with her back to his chest and stares up into the night sky. *How will my story end?* In most of the romance novels she's read, they'd get a happily ever after. The reality she fears won't play by those rules and the closer she gets to the end of this chapter, the bigger her dread becomes. She thought about all the prayers Granny sent up to the Heavens and can't help but wonder if she sent one up now, if anyone would hear her. *Would they even care?*

CHAPTER 23

"So, what are our options?"

Aric scrubs a hand across the side of his face. Despite asking the same question three times previously, he still doesn't have a suitable answer for Julian. When Aric remains silent, the same as every other time he'd asked, Julian resorts to pacing back and forth within the motel room. The tension in the room is heavy with both Julian and Theia, refusing to even look at the other.

A quick knock on the door ramps it up several degrees. Ushering Julian back and sparing Theia a warning glance, Aric peeks through the peephole. When he's met with Colin's familiar scowl, his shoulders relax as he inches the door open.

"Any problems?" Aric asks, his tone clipped.

Colin plows a hand through his hair as he enters the room. His curious gaze sweeps over Julian and Theia before he zeroes in on Aric. "No problems. I satisfied the owner with the compensation you offered."

"I'll bet," Aric replies wryly. "Probably more than the entire building is worth."

Colin chuckles. "Personally, I think what Theia did was an improvement on an already festering shithole. But you said compensate him," shoulders shrug nonchalantly. "It's *your* money."

"This isn't a joke," Julian chimes in. "How is she going to face Riordan?"

One dark brow climbs high on Colin's forehead. "Is that the plan?"

Julian scowls at Aric before answering. "We're still trying to figure that out."

"Well, the clock is ticking. So, we better come up with something."

"We know that Colin," Aric grinds through his teeth, pinching the bridge of his nose with his thumb and forefinger.

Theia, sitting cross-legged on the double bed, finally speaks up. "Maybe we need to go back to the beginning."

"Where will that get us?" Julian challenges in a tight voice. "We already know what happened."

"Well," Theia's head cocks to one side, her smile sickly sweet. "Some of us do." Across from him, Julian visibly stiffens. "What I mean is, how did Riordan find me in the first place?"

Aric's gaze darts from Theia to Julian, his brow furrowing. "That's a good point. I just assumed he sensed your power?"

Theia gives her head a quick shake. "Not possible."

"Seeing how you can't control your emotions, it's entirely possible," Julian grumbles.

The anguish twisting Theia's tight mouth unleashes a heavy dose of adrenaline within him. His skin flushes hotly as his control snaps like a fragile twig. Whirling on his old friend, he places himself between him and Theia like the walls of Jericho. "You're not helping," he grits through clenched teeth, his body thrumming.

"And for your information, she's right. When Colin brought her to me, the drugs her grandmother had been giving her for years were just out of her system. Hence the meltdowns. *After,* Riordan attacked."

Julian nods though Aric spots the tic in his cheek. "If you didn't tap into your gifts, how did he know where to find you?"

"Wait," Colin raises his hand before slipping between Aric and Julian. "Why would your grandmother put you on medication?" Spinning to confront Julian, his brows pinch. "Did you tell the woman what to expect?"

"I thought it best not to. It devastated her when Damara died," Julian explains quietly, forcing a quick look at his daughter.

"That was my fault," Theia confesses. While her voice is soft, it commands all three of them to turn and pin her with curiosity. With a sigh heavy enough to power a wind turbine for years, she quietly retells a tale of school bullies and the first accidental unleash of her gifts. By the time it's over, her voice is near non-existent, and her hands tremble in her lap.

Crouching in front of her, Aric covers her hands with his. "What happened after that?"

"A man came. He pulled something out of Mercedes and told me to go home. Later, he showed up to tell Granny we had to leave." Lifting her deep blue eyes from the bedspread beneath her, she pins Julian with a withering stare. "He was the first one that had been completely honest with me."

Sharing a look over his shoulder with Julian and Colin, Aric muses aloud. "A demon?"

"He called it Aamon."

Julian's eyes widen as he staggers back a step. "Are you sure?" When Theia merely bobs her head quickly, he sucks air in through his teeth. "That could be a problem."

Aric stands, leaving one hand curled around Theia's. "If this Aamon remembered her scent, he could easily track her again. We need to talk to him."

"That's the problem," Julian gripes. "He attacked Melchom. No way there's enough left to ask him anything."

When Colin digs around in his pocket to pull out a pack of cigarettes, Aric's tight growl has him stuffing it back where he found it. "Where would a low demon get the power needed to take on Melchom?" Colin muses aloud.

"Riordan," Aric supplies. "It makes sense. The demon knew how to find her, but he wouldn't do something for nothing."

"No way the Council would approve that."

"And if the Council isn't aware Julian? How many things did we get by them the centuries they pulled our leashes?" Aric counters. "Childs' play."

"Specially with none of my Guardians reporting on any suspicious activity," Colin adds.

"What's a Guardian?" Theia asks, her tone lighter for the first time since meeting her father.

Aric and Julian share a strained expression while Colin simply smiles. Instead of his usual shit-eating grin, though, this one carries a tightness at the corners. "That's a story for another day. I think you'd enjoy getting to know Nora, though."

"Later," Julian clips. "If Riordan is making deals with demons, the Council will strip him of his title."

Aric nods. "So the question is, how do we get word to them without getting smoked in the process?"

"I still don't like it," Theia says on a rush of exhale. "What's stopping him from killing you?"

Beneath her cheek, Aric's chest expands. While the finger he uses to draw lazy circles across her hip doesn't falter, she can sense the tension in his muscles. "We have a code. To betray that code will also betray the virtues given to us."

"Okay, tell me about this code?"

"After Colin's regiment fell from Heaven, the Council implemented a code of sorts to keep Seraph's from straying off track."

"Why?"

Aric heaves a sigh big enough to fill the room. After several moments of silence, Theia jumps when he suddenly answers. "They meant the Guardians to watch over humans, learn from them, and hopefully help the rest of us understand them as well. When that backfired, the Council took precautions to insure it didn't happen again."

"They're solution was the code?"

"It's not much different from what soldiers in your militaries live by. Loyalty, duty, and so on."

Theia wrinkles her nose. "Loyalty to whom, though?"

"What do you mean?"

"I mean, Colin is your friend, right?" Without giving him time to confirm what she already knows to be a fact, Theia trudges ahead. "If loyalty to him contradicts loyalty to this council, how do you choose?"

"Loyalty to the Council, and my duties should always come first."

"But, why? Is it breaking the code to choose loyalty for a friend above a committee? And wouldn't choosing not to be loyal to Colin break your code, anyway?"

Aric chuckles and places a finger against her rambling lips. "I've never thought of it that way before. It's questions like these that the Council deems humans to be dangerous to angels."

"I'm sure." Theia huffs softly and clamps her lips on the acerbic reply bubbling up from her chest. "So, you believe Riordan still follows the code?"

"He may not observe all of it, but if I request a meeting with the Council, to refuse would earn him their judgement as well. I can't see him risking their wrath."

"Wrath meaning what, precisely?"

"At best, banished from Heaven. They would send the worst to the ether."

Theia tenses in Aric's arms and tips her head back slightly to search his face. The hardening in his jaw adds a layer of apprehension to the term. "What is the ether?"

"No one really knows. I only know of one angel to return from the ether and he's not really the chatty kind."

"You think Riordan has enough self-preservation to ensure you get the meeting you'll request."

"He wouldn't risk the ether for a personal vendetta."

"I wouldn't put it past him." Her breathing quickens and her chest compresses as she contemplates the consequences of Aric's trust in Riordan's honor. The dread tightens its noose around her lungs like a vice with each gasp of air until her heart is ready to burst from the pressure. What seems impossible, now looms ominously on the horizon and while she's eager to bring an end to this chapter, the potential outcome tightens every fiber of her being.

Aric presses a kiss to the crown of her head. "I won't let anything happen to you."

"It's not me I'm worried about."

"Oh?" Tipping her face toward his, Aric offers a playful smile. "Growing on you, am I?"

"I'd just hate to break in a new trainer, is all."

His face a mask of mock pain, Aric's head falls back to the pillow, his free hand grasping at his chest. "Brutal."

"Hmm, just like your training methods."

With a chuckle, Aric's hands leaves her hip to dig a finger into the sensitive spot in her side. Even with her lips compressed, laughter bubbles forward until tears prick at her eyes. Rolling and wriggling out his grip, Theia struggles to escape from the playful torture with a squeal.

A fierce struggle ensues as Aric and Theia grapple for dominance. Her fingers scrabble and search every bare inch for the one spot that will render him helpless. When she finally finds it, a ferocious cackle rips from him like thunder, reverberating off the walls. Struggling to pull away, Aric teeters on the edge of the bed as his laughter ebbs. Eyeing Theia with a sharp intensity, his hazel-green eyes alight with a brilliant sparkle as he offers a lazy smile. "I yield."

Adjusting himself back near the center of the bed, he hooks an arm around her waist and pulls her flush against him. After a deep breath, Theia rests her cheek against the crook of his shoulder, her body loose in his embrace. "Be careful," she whispers, her voice scratchy within a tight throat.

"You have my word, little bird."

Raising up on her elbow, Theia meets his curiosity with a savage expression. "I need you to be careful, Aric. Just because you live with honor doesn't mean Riordan does." Grazing her palm across his cheek, she draws it along his jaw to grip his chin. "If anything were to happen to you, I will burn this whole goddamn world to the ground."

Aric's hand tenderly glides up the arch of her back. His fingers curl in her hair as he roughly pulls her into him, pressing his lips to hers with a gentleness that leaves her aching and breathless. He whispers a promise against her lips, as his thumb brushes away the single tear on her cheek.

Melting into him, her arms wrap around his neck to deepen their kiss. Once the full weight of their situation dissolves around them, they lose themselves in each other.

With a groan against her lips, Aric's hands roam her body, his touch igniting a fire her body fights to contain. As if sensing her need, Aric flips her onto her back and trails his lips down to her neck. The brush of them across her pulse point racks her body with a shiver. His teeth nipping lightly at the sensitive skin elicits a tight gasp from her lips.

Arching into him, her hands grasp at his back, pulling him closer. Theia's heart stammers out of control as her fingers tangle in the golden curtain of his hair. The cool air in the room raises goosebumps across her flesh but the heat of his body pressing against hers is enough to chase it away.

Aric growls deep in his throat, his hand moving to the flare of her hip while his lips trail lower. Along the slope of her breast, his breath fans hot against her skin making her arch into him with a desperate plea. The brush of his tongue hardens her nipples into small peaks as her body becomes a live wire.

Sparking and crackling with electricity, Theia revels in the feel of his skin beneath her hands, tracing every muscle and curve with a possessive touch. Blind pleasure courses through Theia's veins, her moans echoing in the room as Aric's mouth works magic on her skin

Their passion builds in a frenzy of heat and urgency as they cling to each other, seeking solace from the chaos that surrounds them. Aric's lips find hers again, his tongue sweeping into her mouth as they taste each other deeply. With a deep moan, her body arches up to meet his as desire coils tightly within her.

She's still fighting for breath when he raises above her, his eyes meeting hers. "You're mine," he growls hungrily.

"And you mine," Theia replies with equal intensity before kissing him soundly. "Aric," she pants, tearing her mouth from his. "I need you."

"I'm right here little bird," Aric presses a kiss to the crook where shoulder meets neck, his hands sliding up to cup her breasts. When thumbs graze sensitive nubs, she squirms restlessly from the heat pooling inside her stomach.

"Please," she whimpers, her hips shifting in slow, undulating motions.

Theia's hands glide up the muscled expanse of his back as he lowers himself between her thighs. Her hips rise to meet him as they both groan at the welcome feel of his skin against hers. She moans his name as he enters her, his body filling hers, every inch of her being vibrating in their union.

Aric moves with a fierce intensity, his hands gripping her hips as he thrusts into her, each movement taking them closer to the edge of ecstasy. Theia matches him thrust for thrust, her body writhing beneath him as she climbs higher and higher, her breathing ragged and uneven.

Her lungs forget how to function while his touch sends shivers through her system, each one more passionate than the last. Aric becomes rougher. His thrusts pushing her body deeper into the bed. The wooden frame creaks as the headboard slams against the thin wall.

Theia's hands grip the sheets beside her head, knuckles white as she struggles to remain a part of her body. Her grip tightens even further when her body threatens to break free of his grip. When the first flickers of her climax spark and burst, legs shake and muscles clench around Aric. Curling her toes from the heat, she cries out his name, her body shuddering beneath him as she comes apart in his arms.

With a few sharp thrusts, Aric's release chases hers over the edge before they collapse in a sweaty, tangled heap. With a satisfied growl that always unleashes butterflies in her stomach, Aric gathers her against him, the heat of his skin soothing against hers.

They lay there for a long moment, their breathing gradually returning to normal as they bask in the afterglow of their lovemaking. Aric brushes a strand of hair from Theia's face. "Try to get some rest. We're going to need it."

Sleep doesn't come easy, her mind replaying the last few days repeatedly. The paths they've taken have been far from similar, but they both have a darkness to face. If they can find the strength to fight it, perhaps the light they have for each other will be enough to beat the shadows.

A soft kiss brushes her neck. "Don't give up on me," he whispers against her skin.

"Never," she replies.

Aric's warm, heavy arm rests across her stomach. His breath tickles her ear as it evens out, sleep taking him. He'll be gone in a few hours. While there's no reason for her to believe this will be the last time she sees him, she can't shake the heavy weight in her chest.

Lashes droop as she bathes in his scent. When she considers every ending that could play out, one minor fact offers comfort from the brewing storm. As long as they're both alive, they'll continue to look for each other within the chaos of this world.

If he leaves her to wrestle with cold reality alone, Theia will feel sorry for the innocents caught in the crossfire. As sure as she's laying there, as certain as she is of her own name, Theia knows without a smidge of doubt the world will burn. And the next. And the next. Until she's spent and meeting her Maker. Without Aric, her fury will be a reckoning for all things angelic.

No matter what garbage Riordan spews, what beliefs he or the Council clings to, she refuses to accept that she's an abomination. A mistake on mankind. If she exists, it's because God willed it, isn't it? Following that train of thought, it suggests he orchestrated Aric's presence in her life. There will be no escape from Theia's wrath if he knowingly caused heartache.

She lay there unmoving for so long that the faint traces of dawn slinking against the dark sky surprises her. As if awakened by his internal alarm clock, Aric shifts in his sleep, pulling her closer with a soft sigh of content.

"Did you sleep?"

His voice, thick and rough, draws a shiver across her skin. "M-hmm."

Chuckling, Aric places a kiss on her forehead. "Liar." Suddenly, he stiffens beneath her, his voice tight. "It's time."

"I know."

The two of them spend the next few minutes dressing. When they each run out of things to stall over, Aric gives her hand a soft tug. Stepping into his arms, Theia's eyes lock onto Aric's. In this moment, she recognizes the burn of confidence hiding his dark traces of fear. Suddenly, the prospect of him not returning from this mission smothers her with sorrow. She's never been one to depend on anyone, but Aric has become her rock, her refuge in a world of noise.

"Come back to me," she whispers, her voice barely audible.

"I will," Aric replies, his voice firm. "I promise."

With one last kiss, Aric yanks on his black combat-style boots. Wrapping her arms around herself, Theia watches him with a mixture of pride and fear, knowing that he is walking into danger for the sake of her kind.

As he reaches the door, Aric turns back to her, a small smile on his lips. "I love you, little bird."

"I love you too," she replies, her voice thick with emotion.

His lazy smile is all too brief. The sparkle in his eyes is short-lived. Stepping over the threshold, Aric strides across the near empty parking lot, never once glancing back in her direction. She tells herself to trust him, but her mind rants and rages that this is a very grave mistake.

CHAPTER 24

The soft morning sun banishes what remains of the night's shadows by the time Aric settles on a meeting place. In a city this big, there's a church on almost every corner, but the first two were closer to slumbering neighborhoods than he'd like. It isn't until he takes an impulsive right through the rundown part of the city that he stumbles on the humble house of worship.

Though small compared to the magnificent buildings deeper within the city, the weathered limestone and wooden beams look like they've sustained a couple centuries and will absorb many more. Stopping just outside the heavy mahogany doors, Aric wrestles with uncertainty. He'd be lying if he said some of Theia's doubts hadn't crept into his head. Priding himself on his level head and calm nature, Aric isn't sure what to do with the trembling in his hands.

Could Theia be right? Am I being foolish?

"It's a solid plan," he argues aloud but his words ring hollow in his ears. "Well, standing out here isn't helping," he mutters. Inhaling beyond the slight pang in his chest, he tugs open the doors.

The atmosphere from the previous day's morning service still lingers in the air, with Aric inhaling the distinct aroma of wood polish and wax. Maple floors groan beneath his feet, carrying soft scuffs and signs of wear against the narrow runner the color of poppies stretching between the two rows of pews. Though worn and old, intricately carved designs within the wood evoke a feeling of serenity as Aric passes by. Narrow racks built into the back of each pew contain stacks of hymn books and the occasional bible.

Brilliant sunshine floods through wide bay windows on either side, erasing the morning gloom while glowing stained glass designs cast soft colorful rays across the polished floor leading to the solid wooden altar at the far end of the church. Adorned with a simple crucifix, statues meant to depict Michael and Gabriel flank the altar on either side.

As he ventures deeper into the church, Aric can't help but process a sense of wonder. Some people view these buildings as a reason for persecution, while others see them as a safe harbor from their personal storms. Brushing a reverent finger along the first pew, he continues towards the back, stopping at the only closed door. Knocking softly, Aric counts to ten before poking his head into the room.

As simple as his church, the office is small. A place where the pastor can work in peace, but also visit with the members of the flock. Bookshelves line one wall, glaring at Aric as if to say, "*What are you doing in here?*"

Each picture and knick-knack shines brightly after someone dusts and polishes them. The leather sofa bears the signs of many meetings, as they wore it smooth in several places. The air itself carries a hint of pipe smoke. While it's not a scent that bothers Aric, he can't help but smile when he thinks of all the sneezing Theia would do if she'd spent any time in here.

The office itself is pristine, everything in its place. The desk is another matter entirely, with papers, pens and notebooks cover one end of the desk to the other. Occasionally, Aric finds old paper coffee cups with dried remains of froth around the lip.

Just on the other side, an elderly man glances up in surprise at Aric's entrance. Pushing back his rickety wooden chair, he stands and offers a smile, kindness twinkling in his eyes as they hide behind thin wire-framed glasses. "Can I help you?"

"I hope so," Aric begins, claiming one chair opposite him. "I find myself in need of sanctuary, Pastor..."

"Benjamin, but most people call me Benji. And you are?"

"Aric."

"Pleasure to meet you, Aric," Pastor Benji says with another smile, reaching across his desk to shake Aric's hand. Once he resettles in the creaky chair, he eyes Aric curiously. "I have to admit, I've never had a request for sanctuary. Not in all the years I've been here."

"I suspect that's true for many places of worship these days."

"May I ask your crime?"

"I think it's more dereliction of duty than criminal."

"I see." Pastor Benji sits back in his chair, the wood giving a sharp creak of protest. "You're a soldier? Gone AWOL?"

A faint smile tips the corner of Aric's mouth. "Something like that."

"You realize the legal effect sanctuary carries has diminished since its birth, correct?"

"I do. Although I'm not expecting anyone to actually challenge my claim."

While the pastor grows quiet, Aric can hear every thought pin balling around his head. Still, he never voices them. As he weighs Aric's request, his gentle face remains impassive. Once he reaches a decision, he sits forward with another squeak of his chair and withdraws a leather-bound ledger from a draw in his desk. Poising with pen to paper, he peeks over the rim of his glasses at Aric. "Name?"

"Just Aric."

"No last name?"

"I'm afraid not."

Pastor Benji rubs a hand over his narrow jaw before he scribbles the traditional spelling of Aric's name within the ledger.

His business complete, Aric stands and gestures towards the door. "I think it's best if you treat yourself to breakfast. Away from the church."

"You're telling me to leave?" The weight of his question relieves his face of any remaining kindness, replacing it with an indignation that pinches the corner of his eyes.

"More, suggesting."

"Dress a pig in a fancy dress and it's still a pig."

Aric chuckles lightly. "I suppose so."

"Perhaps it'll help if you explain why you want me to leave my church."

"Until I conclude my meeting, I cannot guarantee your safety." Aric answers as honestly as he can. While the pastor may welcome an angelic visit, the ones hunting Aric may instill more fear and less awe.

"What *are* you, son?"

The question, so softly spoken, takes Aric by surprise. Swinging his gaze back to the pastor, Aric squirms like a bug under a microscope. "How do you mean?"

Pastor Benji gives his head a shake. "I can't explain it, but there's a light surrounding you. It's soothing. Comforting." Pinching the bridge of his nose with his thumb and forefinger, he sits quietly for a minute before shoving himself to his feet.

"There's a small diner just around the corner," he remarks, picking up a stack of folders and placing them under one arm. "You have one hour," he says and leaves the office, but not before giving Aric a stern look.

Once the door closes behind the pastor, Aric slumps back into his chair, eyes closing as thoughts race. A large piece of him kicks himself for dragging the pastor into this mess. While his head reasons, its still a solid plan, his body disagrees whole-heartedly.

After a deep breath, Aric stands and makes his way back out into the main sanctuary. Taking a seat in the first pew, he leans back and releases another sigh. Finally admitting he can't guarantee this plan to be successful, Aric's done all he can to tip the odds into his favor. All that's left is to arrange the meeting.

The hustle and bustle of the city is a cacophony of noise that creates a dizzying sensory overload. It's as if he's drowning in an ocean of voices and faces with no life raft in sight. His heart hammers and sweat trickles down his face as he works tirelessly to find Riordan's location, straining to latch onto and usable information before the trail goes cold. Once he's able to pinpoint Riordan's general whereabouts, he forms the connection.

"Riordan."

"Aric?" Shock graces Riordan's slow response.

"I'm done hiding. We need to meet."

"Absolutely. Just tell me where you are."

"I've claimed sanctuary within a small church in the city."

Riordan scoffs. "I thought you said you were done hiding."

"I'm requesting a meeting with the Council."

A long second passes before Riordan's voice snaps across the link. "You have no right."

"I have every right. I'm still a Seraph."

"Not for long."

"That's not for you to decide."

"Where's the Nephilim?"

Aric's breath creeps from his chest as he struggles to keep his heart rate even. "I don't know."

"You're lying." Riordan growls. "You want a meeting. I want it's head. Seems were at an impasse, you and I."

"I've formally requested a meeting, do you refuse?"

There's a cold silence on the other end of the connection, and Aric fears he's pushed too hard. But then, Riordan speaks, his voice low and measured.

"I accept. But I don't see how it changes anything."

"That's between me and the Council."

"Fine. Tell me where you are."

Aric gives Riordan the address and ends the connection. Resting his head in his hands, he takes deep breaths. While he's one step closer to ensuring Theia's safety, Aric can't shake the gnawing pit in his stomach. As the hour ticks by, he spends that time in quiet contemplation. He's risking everything for this meeting, but the Council needs to know what Riordan has been doing and with whom. The sound of a dozen footsteps on the hardwood floors is a signal that his time is up.

Just let me make it back to Theia, he prays silently before pushing to his feet and splaying his arms out wide. "I'm unarmed," he declares calmly.

Stopping a few feet shy of Aric, Riordan gestures his men forward. "Secure him," he orders, his voice tight.

Aric struggles with the urge to fight back as a half dozen angels descend on top of him. Before a burst of light and a flash of pain erupts within his skull, he registers Riordan's triumphant smirk.

Darkness washes over Aric's senses until his eyelids are too heavy to keep open. Bile rises in his throat as rough hands grab him with a bruising force, only to drag him towards the door. *Theia, I'm sorry.* Shadows wrap around him like a veil until Aric can no longer keep his eyes open, and all that's left is a heaviness in his chest.

Theia seethes in silence as she strides the width of the small motel room. Her mind spins with frantic thoughts. Aric should've contacted her by now. *Something isn't right*, she rages, increasing the tension in her shoulders. The ticking of the clock on the wall behind her drags on endlessly, each tick landing like a physical blow until her heart pounds away at her chest like a drum.

"Colin's been gone awhile. How long are we supposed to wait?" She snaps as she whirls on Julian's resolute figure at the window. Fingernails dig into her palms before she forces herself to take a deep breath.

"He should be back any minute."

"He left over an hour ago."

"Colin knows what he's doing, Theia. If there's information to be found, he'll find it." His eyes never stray from the window but the soft chiding tone in his voice frays at what remains of her nerves. *What an asshole*. Grinding her teeth against her impulsive response, she resumes pacing.

The soft crunch of the worn carpet beneath her feet only drops her heart closer to her stomach. *Never should've let him go alone.* Despite his fears and objections, she should've insisted she'd gone with him. The not knowing what happened to him, or if Riordan upheld the code, Aric regards so highly builds until it saps the warmth from her hands.

After another glance at the clock, Theia's certain it's broken. Have the hands moved at all? As her stomach churns away, she swallows against the sour taste it leaves on her tongue. The longer it takes Colin to get back here, the longer Aric is at Riordan's mercy. That prospect alone snaps a decision into place.

Theia whips around, her breath coming out in short bursts as she quickly laces up her tennis shoes. Her movements jerky, she gathers up her hair and twists it into a messy bun at the back of her head, fingers shaking with determination. "I'm done waiting," she declares and strides purposefully for the door.

"Theia, Aric would want-"

Without a flicker of hesitation, she holds up a hand to silence her father's argument. Lifting her chin defiantly, she hisses around the clench of her jaw. "He could be in trouble." The air thickens between them as Julian turns. Recognizing the pinch that twists his strong features forces her to pause. "Riordan could've killed him by now."

"Killing Aric before the Council reaches a judgement would be risky for Riordan."

Theia's head spins as she considers his words. Reluctantly, she can see the reason for his argument, but it does nothing to stop the hard twist of her heart. "I can't take that chance," she whispers. "I have to know he's okay."

"We should wait for Colin. It's too dangerous for you to be out there alone."

"I can take care of myself now." Theia's tone is hard enough to give Julian a moment's pause.

"You can't charge in there blindly. You need a plan."

"I have a plan. Find Riordan and make him squeal like a stuck pig," Theia retorts, her eyes narrowing. "I need to know Aric is safe." Brushing past her father, she marches towards the door.

"You love him." More statement than question, Julian's eyebrows furrow.

Her shoulders heave with a long breath. "I do."

"I'll come with you."

For twenty-eight years, Theia's held her own despite the ache of an absent father. Now that he's within reach, she's terrified by the thought of losing him again. With a slight hitch in her breathing, she throws herself at him, wrapping her arms around his neck. After a quick gasp of surprise, he pulls her close and squeezes until she fears she might break.

"Thank you," she murmurs against his chest after several minutes, pulling away to flash a tremulous smile.

The sight of Colin striding into the room, his face contorted, drops her heart around her knees. Judging by the way the door slams behind him, he doesn't bring good news. "What happened?" She demands, her voice quaking in her chest.

"My contact can't narrow down Aric's location," Colin grinds, his hands forming tight fists at his sides.

Theia can feel the blood drain from her face as she staggers backward into her father's hands. "What are we going to do?"

Digging the pack of cigarettes out of one pocket, Colin dips his head long enough to light it and inhale a deep breath of smoke. When the stench reaches her, Theia's nose twitches with the first of several sneezes. Flashing an apologetic smile, Colin opens the door and stands in the threshold to allow most of the smoke to billow out into the night. "We're going to get him back," he seethes aloud before drawing another lungful of smoke. "We need a plan."

"Theia has a pretty good one," Julian says with a smile resembling pride on his face. Theia's head tips lightly once she experiences a small flutter in her chest.

"Okay. Let's hear it."

"Simple," she says with a grin. "Find Riordan and make him squeal like the bitch he is."

White tendrils escape with Colin's dark chuckle. "While I do so love the idea. He's going to be hiding somewhere until he figures out what to do with Aric." With a snarl that curls his full lips, he gives his head a shake. "No way you're going to get close enough."

Without skipping a beat, Theia plants hands on her hips. "So, how do I get close enough?"

Colin takes a long drag on his cigarette, the tip glowing orange in the darkness. Smoke curls up around his stubbled jaw as he considers the question "We wait for him to make a move," he replies before flicking ash from his cigarette. "He won't keep Aric hidden forever. He'll want to use him as leverage, or worse, dispose of him. When he makes his move, we'll be ready."

"No way," Theia spits. "One, there's no telling how long that will take, but two, who knows what he'll do to Aric in the process."

"Aric knew the risks, sweetie," Julian replies softly, resting a gentle hand on her shoulder.

"Fuck that," she seethes.

"Colin's right," he continues. "You can't ascend. Our only other option is to draw Riordan out of his hole."

"You mean use yourself as bait," Theia accuses, eyes narrowing. "I'm not exchanging one man in my life for the other."

"This is how we get Aric back."

"We're not doing it. You didn't see the hatred in Riordan's eyes when he asked where you were hiding," Theia snaps. "He'd give himself a gold star for killing you."

"We can't just sit here and wait, Theia. We need to act fast before it's too late." His voice is low, but firm contradicts the softening around his mouth.

"That doesn't mean this isn't a horribly, awful, nail your ass to the wall idea!"

"I can handle myself. I've dealt with worse in my time."

Theia's eyes flicker with doubt, but Colin speaks up before she can protest. "Who says she can't ascend?"

"What?" Theia and her father answer in unison, wearing similar expressions of confusion.

Colin's smirk is quick as he crushes out his cigarette on the sole of his boot. "Who says she can't ascend?"

"You have to be an angel, Colin. I know it's been a few years, but certainly you remember that part."

"Yes, thank you Julian, you dick," Colin growls. "What I mean is, she's half angel. Maybe there's a way."

"And maybe we can find a golden lamp with three magical wishes."

Elbowing her father in the side, Theia arches a brow. "This is why no one likes you."

Julian blinks, his brow wrinkling. "What makes you think no one likes me?"

"A lucky guess," she murmurs and turns her attention back to Colin. "Where would we even start?"

"Your dad gave me an idea. Not a genie per se, but maybe a book."

CHAPTER 25

When they appear outside a sleepy little street tucked away in a small suburb, Theia resists the urge to be sick all over the ground. Pressing for time, Colin insisted they shift instead of any normal means of transportation. The queasy sensation in her stomach leaves Theia wishing she'd pushed harder for driving.

Her struggle must be obvious because Colin reaches out and touches her elbow, his amber eyes sparkling with concern. "You good?"

"Good? No." Theia gulps in huge lungfuls of air, bracing her hands on her knees until the ground stops spinning. "Not good."

"You'll get used to it."

"I'd rather you poke me in the eye with a sharp stick than do that again."

Appearing behind them, Julian rushes forward, laying a hand against her back. "Focus on breathing," he instructs calmly. "It'll pass." He shoots a glare in Colin's general direction as his jaw hardens. "Are you sure about this?"

"It'll be fine." Directing his attention down the street bathed in warm orange hues from the streetlights, Colin nods again for good measure. "Just wait here."

Don't have to tell me twice, Theia grumbles inwardly. When she opens her eyes again, the ground beneath her feet seems more solid. A maddening flip-flop fills her stomach, threatening to empty the contents of her stomach all over the sidewalk. An unsteady breath sends a shudder through her legs, overcoming her body with deep tremors. She swallows hard when bile rises in her throat sharp enough to make her eyes water. Pressing a shaky hand to her forehead, she sighs with the cool touch against burning skin.

As her body steadies, Theia looks up to see Colin approaching in his familiar long-legged lope. "It's fine. Come with me," he says quietly and heads back the way he'd come without ever checking to see if Theia and her father follow.

The three of them continue in silence, only to stop outside a simple two-story home complete with bright yellow shutters against soft gray siding. On a quiet, tree-filled street, the house is more charming than any home Theia has ever seen on television. The mammoth wrap-around porch spans the entire front of the house with an extra-large porch swing at one end. Bright flowers decorate the railings, with red, purple and white blossoms.

Theia's steps falter as the giant man appears from within the house to block the entrance. An immovable fortress as a wall of muscle and menacing aura that radiates from his dark eyes, he stands silent.

Theia steps closer, her heart thudding against her ribcage as she senses the apprehension in his gaze. Thick forearms flex in a stance of intimidation while his face remains impassive, unfathomable. With a fortitude she never knew she had, Theia wills her heart to steady until it finds a more tolerable pace.

"Theia, this is Kegan. Kegan, Theia."

"Nice to meet you," she murmurs while attempting a small smile.

Instead of returning her cordial greeting, he simply arches a dark brow. "That remains to be seen."

Just then, a whirlwind of activity behind him produces a petite red-head with a swollen stomach, a charming smile and kind eyes. "Don't mind him," she gushes happily before giving the giant a quick glare of disapproval. "My husband's etiquette is still a little rusty." Bracing her stomach with one hand, she climbs down the porch steps. "You don't look well lovie."

Flashing a shaky smile, Theia presses a hand to her still churning stomach. "Colin sent us here. Apparently, he has an aversion to driving."

"Ah, yeah, I've noticed that too." The woman says with an imp-like grin. "I'm Nora by the way."

"Theia."

"Ooh. I hope you don't mind if I add that to my growing list of baby names."

"Nora," the giant behind her growls softly. While the sound frays what's left of Theia's nerves, his wife simply meets his dark glare with one of her own.

"Come on inside, I'll get Kegan to put on some tea." Nora offers before hooking her arm through Theia's and pulling her up the porch into a quaint living room.

Walls in a warm pumpkin tone compliment the cream-colored over-stuffed couch spanning the entire length of one wall. The fireplace on one end flaunts pretty ceramic tiles on either side with several photos of Nora and her husband scattered across its smooth mantle. The coffee table in front groans under the weight of baby books, nursery guides and a large orange tabby cat with golden eyes.

Hovering just inside the room, Nora offers another smile that reaches her eyes. "Please, make yourselves comfortable."

The low rumble of Kegan's voice carries a hint of exasperation to fill the room. "You're supposed to stay off your feet, *mo chridhe*." Without giving her a second to argue, he guides Nora gently but firmly to a thick-cushioned recliner heavy with blankets and pillows.

Crouching down in front of her, Kegan tucks a thin lap blanket in around her before resting his large hand against the swell of her stomach. With a soft expression, he caresses gently, as if to remind her to take extra care now. "You sit, I'll make tea."

Frozen, Theia struggles to equate the gruffness of the man she'd met outside to the tender one in Nora's presence. His rough, deep baritone sends shivers down her spine, and yet its tendrils wrap around his wife in a gentle caress. The passion they have for one another leaves no room for doubt; their love an unyielding force.

Like an intruder, she takes in the sight, realizing she's stumbled upon a real-life happily ever after.

As if sensing her unease, Nora pats the arm of the couch next to her. "Come sit," she offers gently, her eyes bright. "We get little for company outside of Colin and a few friends."

"You're saying I'm not a friend," Colin questions with a scowl while Theia sinks into the cushion closest to Nora.

"No," she answers with a sweet grin. "You're family."

Theia sits in fascination as Colin's face transforms, his serious features softening with wonderment at Nora's words. After a long moment, his lips pull back into a wild grin that exposes white-even teeth. Light glitters in his whiskey eyes, resembling something in the neighborhood of pure adoration. While Nora's words linger in the air, a simple whisper escapes him. "Thank you."

"Yeah, the one who always shows up to the family reunion with a stripper on each arm," Kegan chimes in as he returns with two steaming mugs of tea.

"I have never brought strippers," Colin defends, his scowl once again in full force.

"Only because you never show up," Kegan points out with a grin as he passes one mug to Theia. The other, he carefully tucks into Nora's hands before taking up a position behind her.

The moment her icy hands wrap around the warm cup, Theia shivers in response. Tilting her head a bit, she studies Kegan, who radiates enough danger and intensity to make anyone wary. When he gazes into his wife's face, however, the steel in his face melts away under a layer of tenderness.

"Okay you two," Nora brings an end to the friendly banter, "why don't you tell us what brings you here?"

Since she aims the question in her direction, Theia fights the urge to squirm. "Colin thinks you might help me," she answers after taking a sip of her tea. The mixture of warmth and its aroma works in tandem to ease a bit of the tension in her shoulders.

Her words inspire one dark eyebrow to climb Kegan's forehead. "Help you with what, exactly?"

Colin's short answer brings a stunned silence to the room. "Theia needs to ascend."

The couple eye each other quietly with Kegan recovering first. "You're a Nephilim," he points out in a deadpan voice. "You can't ascend."

"Why not?" Leaving her tea next to a thick stack of books about baby names, Theia's spine straightens. "Just because no one's ever done it?"

Kegan never falters under her blunt determination, earning a small smidge of her respect. "Because you're not an angel. You have no business even trying."

Beside Theia, her father visibly stiffens. "You don't need to talk to her like that."

The tension in the room rises as if someone cranked up the dial. Fingers pick over the side of her thumb as she struggles for a way to diffuse the situation. While Kegan's words hit her hard, she can't fault him for his honesty. What he says next, adds another chill within her bones, her eyes widening in a suddenly pale face.

"She's hunted. They will track her to the ends of the earth, and you both brought her to our doorstep." Kegan accuses hotly, his intense eyes jumping from Julian to Colin. "I have a family to protect."

While his stature remains relaxed, Colin cuts in with a soft air of warning. "If you'll let me explain-"

"Is it worth putting my unborn child, your goddaughter at risk?"

While Kegan speaks in a dangerous tone, Nora's voice lends a sense of calm to the room. "Why don't you men go somewhere else and let me talk with Theia?"

"I'm not leaving you alone with her."

Her father bristles, Colin sighs, Nora just smiles and brushes her hand along the inside of Kegan's arm. "I think the kitchen is close enough should she sprout a second head or start breathing fire."

Unconvinced, Kegan looks ready to mount another argument, but compresses his lips into a thin line instead. "Fine."

Nora and Theia sit in silence while the three men trudge unwillingly into the next room. Once they're alone, she regards Theia quietly, framing her first question with a soft voice. "Why do you want to ascend?"

Pausing, Theia casts a glance around their living room. Indecision increases inside her skull until it squeezes with a vice-like grip. *Will this knowledge put them in danger? If Riordan came here looking for me, would he spare Kegan and his family?* She has no way of knowing the answers, but in the end, the comfort in Nora's gentle voice tells Theia it's the only option left. "They have someone that belongs to me," she answers shakily, finally meeting Nora's probing gaze.

"Who do they have?"

"Aric. He's a Seraph that's been teaching me control," Theia feels a little too alive when she says his name, like every fiber of her being is suddenly alight with the sparks of a million memories. Her stomach tightens as if to hold onto the warmth and her heart clenches in desperate longing for him. "I need to get him back." Her answer inspires Nora's silent eyes to study her. When she looks up from her tightly folded hands, the soft glow of sympathy she finds there gives Theia a bit of hope.

"I understand the importance of rescuing someone you care about, more than you know. You should know it almost never works out the way you plan."

"I have to try."

"And if it hurts him in the process?"

"Anything has to be better than what they're doing to him right now."

Nora nods, hiding her face behind the mug in her hands while she sorts through her thoughts. "Have you considered you'll be giving them exactly what they want? You?"

Theia swallows around the lump in her throat, her stomach rolling with the weight of her decision. "I have, but I can't just leave him there. Either they'll kill him or-" her voice trails off unable to continue.

"They'll exile him to the ether," Nora supplies.

Theia draws in a sharp breath and stares at the tiny woman. "You know about the ether?" A spark of hope ignites deep inside her chest. The fierce flame soars higher and higher, threatening to consume her, drowning out all other thoughts except the thunderous beat of her heart.

"Kegan spent some time there. It was the longest few months of my life," Nora explains, her hand spanning protectively against her belly. "He refuses to talk about it, but I know he still carries it with him."

"I won't let Aric end up there."

"You love him?"

He's my lifeline, the voice that grounds me. Aric keeps me alive, his touch fueling each breath I take every morning like a match to a flame. When Theia can't trust her voice to speak those words aloud without breaking, she simply stutters a hard, jerking nod.

"Love," Nora calls towards the kitchen, smiling when her husband appears in the threshold. "Prepare the guest room for Theia. She needs to rest."

"No," Theia sputters, "I need to get to Aric."

"We will do our best lovie," Nora explains, placing a warm hand over Theia's. "You're dead on your feet and there's no telling the toll the book will take on you. It's best if you rest first."

"Nora's right," Colin chimes in. "I have no idea how you'll react, but if it's anything like how we do, you're going to need to be at full strength and at the peak of your control."

Theia nods reluctantly. "Okay," she grumbles. "But please, I need to get Aric away from them as quickly as possible."

"We'll do everything we can," Kegan promises. His change in tone and demeanor is no doubt the effect of Colin's rundown of the situation.

"I understand."

Nora squeezes her hand and offers a small smile of encouragement. "Rest now. We'll figure it all out in the morning."

With a heavy heart, Theia climbs the stairs to the second floor behind Kegan. While he remains quiet, she notices he no longer regards her as a bug to be squashed. When he leads her to the first door on their left, Theia doesn't bother with a light switch. She simply collapses onto the bed and allows exhaustion to take over.

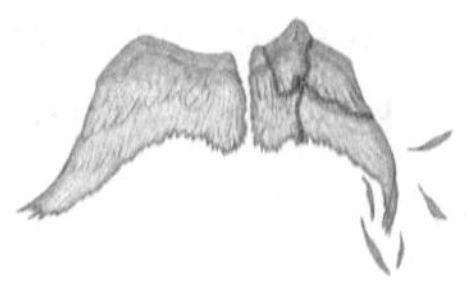

As Aric rouses with a moan, his surroundings reek of body waste and blood. Smothering his gag with the back of one hand, he tries to determine just where Riordan had dumped him. Unfortunately, thanks to the pitch-black interior, all he can make out are grimy walls and a stout metal door with a short row of bars to serve as a window.

Unable to draw a full breath, he rolls across the uneven stone floor onto his side. The one simple movement brings a stab of pain with it, his body stiff and sore from being beaten and tossed away for who knows how long. His pain indicates his injuries are severe if sleep hasn't healed them. With the help of his hands, he pushes himself off the cold floor and stumbles groggily towards the door.

While he'd prepared himself for the worse, Aric's shoulders deflate when his attempt to open the door produces nothing but a harsh whine of metal. Beyond the door, he picks up the muffled screams and sounds of a scuffle before they eventually fade away into silence.

Bracing his weight against the wall, he tries to calm the racing in his mind. When the stone walls press unmercifully against tender spots left on his body, Aric swallows his wince. After the one eye he can still open adjusts to the darkness, he spies a rusted bucket hiding amongst the shadows.

Shuffling towards it, his dry mouth aches at the promise of water. Wrapping his fingers around the handle, he raises it a few inches before dropping it back down with disgust. The pungent odor of excrement and urine crinkles his nose.

How long have I been here? Days? Weeks? Without a light source, Aric can't even determine the time of day, let alone his location. *What about Theia? Is she safe?* Silently, he sends up a prayer that she's stayed out of sight and that she does nothing foolish. "Not like they're going to answer me," his voice scratches aloud.

The sound of keys rattling outside his door jar him from his thoughts. Despite the agony flooding his brain, he takes up a defensive stance, ready to lash out at whoever comes in.

Unable to make out the form amongst even more darkness, Aric retreats until his back hits a wall. Seconds tick away in strained silence as his jailor attempts to determine his position. Either it's too risky or he's too lazy to enter himself, so he ushers his soldiers into the cell.

While Aric can't make out much with his sight, his ears pick up the hurried scuffle belonging to four sets of feet. The one on his right gasps at the rank filth of his cell, drawing Aric's focus to a position less than five feet away.

Teeth set, Aric's fists clench for a moment before he launches himself toward the sound. Hunching his shoulders, he slams into the hard plate of armor a second before they both crash into the floor. The deafening crash rattles the cell. Seizing the opportunity, Aric delivers a swift kick to his head before turning his attention to the others.

Sprinting forward, he lands a blow on the nearest guard's jaw. As he stumbles back, Aric swings his legs in a wide arc, sweeping the guard's legs out from under him. Ignoring the pounding in his head and the swift stabs of pain in his side, Aric uses a well-placed boot to strike the guard unconscious.

Alarmed by the scuffle, the other two guards react. The hiss of metal unsheathing alerts Aric to their drawn swords.

Ducking the first blind swing, Aric plows his fist into the guard's stomach. Ears perk with the subtle scuff over his shoulder, pulling his attention to the one behind him. Crouching low, he slows his breathing and waits for the advance.

When the guard stabs at the surrounding darkness, Aric latches onto his arm, twisting it behind him with enough force to loosen his grip on his weapon.

Any other time, the guard's shriek of pain would give Aric a moment's pause. This time, however, he can't locate the mercy required to care as he delivers a sharp blow to the back of the guard's head. With a deep grunt, the guard drops in a crumpled heap, his breathing slow and steady.

Panting, Aric presses an arm to the stitch in his side as he returns to the first guard. Still on the ground, he rouses himself with a strained curse, allowing him to pinpoint the location once more. Knocking him back to the floor with a shove of his boot, Aric places it across the guard's chest, applying enough pressure to keep him from getting back up.

"Where's Riordan?" Aric growls, his voice hoarse.

"I-I don't know," the guard sputters around his gasps for air.

"Bullshit," Aric snaps, adjusting himself to apply more weight to the chest beneath his boot.

Air gurgles up from his throat as his hands scrabble desperately to remove Aric's foot from his chest. "I sw-swear!"

"Where am I?"

Before the guard can offer a clue as to his whereabouts, light explodes against his skull. Like a fireworks finale, Aric winces as his skull vibrates from the impact. Before he can react, something considerable slams into him from behind, knocking him to the floor.

Aric grunts over a fresh wave of torment, his body trembling with the exertion it requires to not succumb to the hurt. When he attempts to push himself upright, firm hands clamp down on his shoulders and pin him to the ground. Gritting his teeth, he struggles against the hold but his previous injuries sap his strength, leaving him too weak to mount any kind of resistance.

The soldier on his back releases a laugh as his hands tighten around his arms to drag Aric to his feet. After a shove towards the open door, Aric stumbles forward, his head pounding from this last blow.

They march him in silence through the dark, winding corridors before stopping outside a set of doors at the end of the hall. Not wasting any time, one guard rushes forward to swing the doors open. When the bright lights of the room wash over him, Aric flinches and digs his heels in.

With a soft mutter behind him, the angel behind him increases the pressure of his grip to cause searing pain throughout Aric's body. Gasping aloud, he squints and ducks his head as he's shoved from behind.

Falling to his knees on the white floor, Aric's head reels with each pulse of agony riddling his body.

"Get him up." Aric swallows the torment long enough to turn his head in the direction of Riordan's deadpan tone.

Once again, brutal fingers grip his arms to haul Aric to his feet. He sways side to side as another guard fastens cold metal around Aric's wrists.

Several seconds pass before Aric creaks one eye open just enough to absorb the light in small doses until he can finally open it fully.

In the middle of the large room, Aric teeters precariously, attached to an anchor within the floor. Since his cuffs are already draining what's left of his strength, Aric doesn't bother testing their durability. Instead, he centers his focus on surveying his surroundings.

Long, bright white lights radiate from the sterile lamps in the ceiling, bathing the room in artificial daylight. The air is heavy with antiseptic that coats his mouth with a bitter taste. Cold creeps across the floor, cutting through the thin fabric of his shirt with ease. Instantly, goosebumps rise on his skin, marching with an innocent cruelty up his arms and across his chest.

A long metal table on the far wall serves as the only piece of furniture. From one end to the other, tools of torture spread across its surface. Racks, blades, snips and vises carry a promise to cut, puncture and break him forcing Aric to straighten his spine. The sight of bloody rags spilling over the garbage bins carries more apprehension than the dozens of sigils smeared across otherwise pristine walls.

"Leave us," Riordan orders.

Aric peers through his one good eye as indecision wars over Titus' face. In the end, a smooth transition of hardened resignation smothers any flare of hope Aric might have felt igniting in his chest. Without a word, his once comrade follows the others from the room and slams the door shut behind him.

"You've broken your code, Riordan," Aric wheezes.

"You're one to talk. How many oaths did you break the night you left that thing alive?"

"Only one."

The sound of feet shuffling across the floor signals Aric's brain just as Riordan circles around to his front. His jaw locked, Aric lifts his chin and stares defiantly at the angel he'd fought alongside for centuries. Confusion and disbelief twist his narrow features until wrinkles appear in his otherwise smooth brow. "Only one? How do you figure?"

"The only oath I broke that night was the one of duty. Can you say the same? Even before all this?" Aric gestures around the room as much as the chain attached to his cuffs will allow. "How many have you broken just getting to this point?"

Riordan's face remains stoic, his eyes flat as he regards Aric. "You think you're so righteous, so pure in your intentions? You're nothing more than a traitor, a deserter who abandoned his post."

While Aric makes no effort to dispute Riordan's words, his hand clench into tight fists. "And you? What cause are you fighting for?" Each word is a scrape against the raw flesh in his throat.

"I fight for the greater good."

"What kind of twisted logic is that?"

"The kind that allows us to rid the world of its impurities," Riordan's eyes narrow as he creeps toward the long metal table. "The logic that'll ensure victory in the war to come."

"What war? We haven't been at war for thousands of years."

"The war against demons. The war that will decide the fate of humanity. I *will* protect us."

Aric snorts, his eye flickering to the table on his right. "So, you'll torture your own kind?

With a roar, Riordan rushes forward and backhands Aric across the face. "You betrayed us!"

As Aric's head snaps to the side, white-hot pain shoots through his neck and down into his spine. Gritting his teeth, he ignores the searing ache long enough to fix Riordan with a steady glare. "I betrayed no one."

"You betrayed us the moment you let it grow up."

"Unlike you, I never had the taste of killing the innocent."

Riordan's face twists in anger, his wings fluttering behind him with a sharp rustle. "I have never killed an innocent."

"Damara." Aric's voice is barely audible as he utters her name, yet the impact it has on Riordan is a shockwave of emotions.

All at once his face flushes, with red splotches as his hands shake violently at his sides. Nostrils flare and eyes narrow as his shoulders quake as if he's preventing himself from bursting into a thousand pieces. The tension between the two of them is almost palpable as Riordan's wrath intensifies. "She wasn't innocent."

"Bullshit," Aric hisses. "I was there, remember?"

"She lost any chance of claiming innocence the moment she tainted herself with that abomination."

"Theia," Aric grinds out. "*Her* name is *Theia*."

With a harsh sigh, Riordan retrieves a short-handled machete from the table. "Speaking of that. Where is it?"

"I don't know."

Wings flex as Riordan turns to face him, his lips curled into a hard sneer. "You will tell me. One way or another."

CHAPTER 26

When Theia's dream shifts, she finds herself in her favorite childhood home. Unshed tears prick at her eyes as her first inhale carries the familiar aroma of yeast and peppermint. She spends a long minute willing her feet forward before they comply enough to bring her toward the kitchen.

Lips tremble as she steps inside, half-expecting to find Granny at the table or in front of the stove. Instead of the soothing melodies of Country Classics from the old radio on the counter, only an eerie silence remains to greet her.

Fingernails pick over the inside of her thumb as she turns in place. Funny, in her memories, this room is bigger. Now, it's simply average compared to the others they'd shared.

Perhaps it's the time they spent here, or the warmth of her memories, but Theia always thought of this place as a magical island. A place where fears and doubts can't touch you. Their every attempt to sneak over the threshold to torment her, denied.

"I've been waiting for you."

Theia's sharp gasp explodes from her chest as she whirls around to confront the stranger sitting casually at the table. The first thing she notices is how comical he looks, tucking his gigantic frame into one of Granny's small kitchen chairs. Short, disheveled blonde hair falls across a prominent brow and around a pair of striking blue eyes. Half-turned in his chair, he offers her a smile that takes years from his face.

"Who are you? How did you get into my dream?"

"A friend, Theia," he answers in a rich baritone before gesturing to the chair across from him.

"How do you know my name?"

Full lips twitch with a ghost of a smile as his head cocks to one side. "I imagine there aren't many angels who don't know your name by now."

As Theia weighs the outcome of her situation, a deep dread presses against her chest. Except for Aric, her experience with angels has been more terror and less the divine intervention one learns in Sunday school. Peeking over her shoulder towards the only exit, Theia calculates her chances of escaping before this one can react.

From where he sits, the stranger follows her gaze and chuckles lightly. "No need to be afraid, Theia. I'm not here to harm you."

Turning her attention to where he continues to dwarf the table and chairs tucked in the far corner, her eyes narrow as she wraps her arms around herself. "And I should just believe you?"

"If I wanted to harm you, I've had a thousand chances to do so. Long before this mess ever began."

Air tingles at the base of her neck, but she inches closer to the table. "What do you want from me?"

Leaning forward, the stranger clasps his hands together before resting them on the table's surface. "I want to help you. You and Aric."

Just the mention of Aric's name sends a jolt through her body. Every fiber of her being begs her to believe him, to cling to the hope he offers so casually.

Her experience with Riordan nags her to err on the side of caution. "Who are you?"

"I am Michael," he declares, his voice carrying the massive weight of authority.

"You're the one that's been visiting with Granny," Theia mumbles softly, taking another step closer to the chair across from him. The mention of her grandmother adds a twinkle to his blue eyes and a dimple in his smile.

"I find her refreshing." Once more, he gestures to a chair, "Please sit. We have much to discuss, you and I."

Despite the warmth in his voice, a shiver skips along her spine as Theia sinks into the chair farthest from him. While he arches a brow over her choice of seating, he doesn't comment on it. Instead, he leans closer, his gaze intense. "I know you're searching for a way to rescue Aric. I also know Riordan will not make that easy."

"Riordan doesn't scare me anymore." Even while the words fall from her lips, she's surprised to find how accurate they are. When she stopped being afraid of him, she can't say. After their first meeting, all she could think about was never doing it again. Now, the prospect of having Riordan in front of her ignites the fire within her blood.

As if sensing the truth of her statement, Michael falls back in his chair with a soft smile. "Good. You've found your strength."

"I don't know if it I'd call it that."

"There's more to being strong than physical capability, Theia. You can call it whatever you like, but Aric is going to need it when you find him."

The implication of his statement has her heart hammering against her chest wall. "What is he doing to him?"

"It might be better if you don't know the specifics," Michael answers quietly, wrinkles growing in the corner of his eyes. "Riordan wants your location. He won't stop so long as he believes Aric has any knowledge of it."

A cold pit opens up in Theia's stomach as the weight of Michael's words settle over her. "The Council is allowing this to happen?"

"The Council doesn't know. Riordan has missed his last two check-ins."

Snapping her spine into place, Theia lifts her chin to meet his eyes. "The Council doesn't know, but you do. I hope you know how suspicious that sounds."

Although the tension in the air creeps up between them, Michael eyes her with the patience of a mother and a toddler. "Members of the Council haven't left their chambers in centuries. They rely on their seraphs to gather intel and bring it to their attention. With the rumor of Aric's betrayal, Riordan has the support of many in his corner."

"What betrayal?" Theia gives her head a fast shake and stills her fingers from fidgeting. "Aric would betray no one," she snaps tightly, leaving little room for argument.

Regret flickers across Michael's strong features to wrinkle his brow. When he speaks, his thin voice causes her to strain to catch every word. "Twenty-nine years ago, Aric was given an order. When he made the choice not to follow it through, he fooled many into believing otherwise. Unfortunately, his fellow Seraphs view his actions as treason."

"What was the order?"

Michael's shoulders drop, as if the weight of his answer is too much to bear. His gaze lowered, Theia shudders at the raw pain that accompanies his reply. "His order was to kill a child, a baby really. Not more than a few months old. He couldn't do it."

Theia's heart sinks as she digests his answer, her heart twisting at the thought of Aric having to make such a choice. "Why would they ask him to do such a thing?"

"The baby is a Nephilim, Theia. A child thought to bring about a significant change in the balance of power amongst the humans. Since the father was Aric's best friend, our Council thought it fitting for Aric to be the one wielding the sword."

Theia's throat constricts as her lips stumble over the words. "His..." she trails off, the truth sinking into her like a frigid winter storm. Me. They sent him to kill me! *The terrifying thought ricochets around her head like a hammer smashing glass. Her entire body locks up as the reality of her situation hits. Silently, a deadly whisper weaves its way through her veins and bones until she's shivering like a leaf in the wind.*

"I'm sorry," *Michael murmurs.* "I know this is a lot to take in."

"Why would they even consider killing a small baby?" *Theia chokes out.*

"It isn't a decision anyone takes lightly. The Council believes the Nephilim will bring chaos and destruction to the human realm," *he explains, his voice gentle.* "By eliminating every child like it, they believe they're protecting mankind."

"But Aric refused to kill me."

"He couldn't bring himself to harm an innocent child. So, he allowed your parents to escape with you while he staged a bit of theatrics to convince everyone else you were dead."

"And because of that, he's branded a traitor." *Unlike moments before, Theia's voice doesn't tremble. When she speaks, her words are quick and concise and full of a white-hot rage that billows within her chest.*

Yesterday, she didn't believe it was possible to love him more than she already does. Today, she's near bursting with it. Instead of finding a measure of calm in the knowledge, her determination to rescue him increases a hundred times over. Forcing Michael to meet her hardened stare, she allows the question to fall from her lips unhindered.

"How do I get to him?"

"No way!" Julian roars at a volume that rattles the windows in their frames.

Theia winces slightly, tightening her arms around her stomach as her pulse quickens. His reaction to her plan sends a flutter of concern over Nora's face before she steps closer to Theia's side. She can't blame him for his reaction to her news. His dealings with anything angelic have been tenuous over the last few decades. The hand Nora lies on her forearm works to bolster Theia's nerve long enough to form a steel-like grip on her decision.

"It's the only way," Theia injects a token of calm into her voice even while she simmers underneath.

"The hell it is," Julian snarls, planting his hands on his hips as if he's scolding a child. "You can't trust them, Theia."

"If Michael wanted to kill me, he could've done it a long time ago," she argues softly.

As the tension mounts, Kegan steps from behind Julian to lay a hand across the small of his wife's back. "You need to take a breath and calm down," he instructs Julian in a tone that sounds more warning than suggestion.

"Fuck you, Kegan. This is my daughter. I won't just hand her over."

Kegan's lips curve into a smile lacking any semblance of warmth. "And this is my daughter," he snaps quietly resting a hand over Nora's round belly. "You know the danger you've put her in, and yet you're still here. Take it down a notch."

Theia's gaze flits between the two men, her teeth chewing along the corner of her mouth. Casting a pleading look in Colin's direction has the angel heaving a deep sigh before stepping between the towering giants.

"Let's all take a breath," he says simply, his smooth Irish lilt applying another layer of serenity along with the tension Julian creates. When Julian simply throws his hands up in frustration, Colin turns his amber eyes to Theia. "Why do you believe you can trust him?"

"Because he didn't have to tell me anything. He could've chosen to let Riordan torture Aric to death and left in the ether," Theia explains.

"Stupid child, this could all be part of his plan for you turning yourself over to the council."

Fire sparks to life in Theia's gut at the condescension she picks up in her father's voice. Narrowing her eyes on him over Colin's shoulder, she takes a slow breath. "If you ever call me stupid again, we're going to have a problem. You and me." The dangerous note in her voice as Julian rocking back on his heels.

"I'm sorry," he mumbles softly. "But this is an enormous risk, and you're seriously asking me to stand back and allow it."

"I'm not asking you to allow anything," Theia grinds through her teeth. "I'm an adult. You missed the chance of controlling my actions by about eleven years. Give or take."

When sparks of heat appear in Julian's eyes, Kegan steps in front of his wife. "I think you two should discuss this outside."

Theia jerks a quick nod of her head. "I agree." After giving Nora's hand a quick squeeze she marches out the door and into the backyard.

Exhaling loudly, she tips her face up to the morning sun. Warmth ripples through her as she anchors herself on an island of calm.

Large and open, a tall privacy fence separates this backyard from the neighbors. In one corner, the drooping branches from a massive weeping willow offer cover and shade from the morning sun. She inhales and smiles at the sweet fragrance of freshly cut grass wafting on the wind. On one side, the distinct rumble of a lawnmower grows and fades from the other side of the fence. On her right, the sound of children squealing and laughing trickles in from the opposite yard.

As she stands there, basking in the noise and sunlight, the full weight of her decision sticks with her. Her father has said nothing, she hasn't already told herself. This plan is incredibly risky, but it's also her only chance to save Aric.

Closing her eyes, she takes a deep breath and focuses on her heart. Slowly, she forgets about everything else and just exists in the present. When she opens her eyes, Julian is there, his face a war of emotions.

"Are you sure about this?" He asks quietly while he searches her face.

"No," she answers honestly before giving him a small smile. "If you have another option, I'm all ears."

The hard lines in Julian's face soften as he reaches out to tuck a strand of hair behind her ear. "I don't," he admits, his thumb tracing the line of her jaw. "I just don't want to lose you."

Understanding his fear, Theia leans into him, resting her forehead against his chest. "I won't let anything happen to me," she promises, her voice muffled by his shirt.

"You're too much like your mother," he declares with a strangled voice, wrapping his arms around her shoulders. "I couldn't tell her no either."

"I'll be careful."

"I'm not about to let you face them alone."

Drawing back, Theia can't ignore the spine-chilling reaction she has to his words. "If you go there, they *will* kill you."

"Maybe," he hedges, his eyes looking everywhere but at her.

"No maybe. They've been hunting you for years. There's no way they'll let you walk out of there."

"It's a risk worth taking." Dropping his head, he inhales shakily. "I love you too much to let you do this alone," he mumbles into her hair.

"I love you too," she whispers thickly, tears gathering in the corner of her eyes. Theia bites her lip, willing herself not to cry. Pulling away from her father, she swipes at her eyes with the back of her hand. "Which is why you can't come with me."

"Theia-"

"Michael promised no one will harm me."

Julian scowls, his fists clenching and unclenching. "His word means nothing to me."

"I have to do this. For Aric. For me."

Julian releases a heavy sigh, his broad shoulders sagging with defeat. "Fine," he growls, his voice gruff. "But I'm not letting you out of my sight until you leave."

A tiny smile tugs at the corner of Theia's lips as she reaches out to clasp her father's hand in hers. "Thank you," she whispers, her voice thick.

Fear crinkles the corners of Julian's eyes until it pinches the corners of his mouth. "Just promise me you'll be careful," he asks, dragging his knuckle along the curve of her cheek.

"I promise," she replies.

"Are we in agreement, then?"

Theia knows without turning who she'll find behind her. Aside from the now familiar rich voice, it's her father's reaction to it that prepares her for the sight of Michael under the large weeping willow.

"Yes," she answers. Turning to face Michael, she stands beside her father. "I'll do it." Theia's voice is clear, unwavering even with the burn of her father's gaze on her, begging her to reconsider.

Michael nods, his expression unreadable. "Very well. We begin now."

"I should warn you, the last time Colin transported me, I felt queasy afterwards." Theia mutters quickly. "Just in case your boots suffer from collateral damage."

Even as one thin brow climbs up his forehead, an amused smile twitches across Michael's lips. "You misunderstand. I won't be transporting you."

"But-"

Michael lifts a hand to halt the protest on her lips. "You'll be transporting yourself. If you still end up queasy, I will take a step back."

Theia's brow furrows softly. "They told me Nephilim's can't ascend."

"Strictly speaking, they can't," Michael explains in a voice oozing patience. "Unless they unlock the ability to do so. This is where I come in."

After laying a hand on her shoulder, Julian steps forward. "And you're doing this out of the goodness of your angelic heart?"

"I mean your daughter no harm."

"So, she said. Still, I can't help but wonder what's in it for you."

Michael's eyes hold Julian's in a steady gaze. "Let's just say that Theia's existence aligns with some of my own interests."

A silence falls between the two men, each studying the other. It's Theia who breaks the tension. "I trust him."

Julian's eyes skip to hers and back to Michaels. "I'm sure you do. I don't."

"I understand," Michael replies in a soothing voice. "I swear on my essence that I only wish to help your daughter. Should the threat of harm occur, I will return her safely to you."

There's a moment of hesitation while her father digests Michael's vow. After what seems like ages, he gives him a curt nod. "If anything happens to her-"

"It won't," Theia cuts in. Crossing the lawn, her heart hammers away as she draws closer to Michael. Once she's within arm's reach, she braces herself. "What do I need to do?"

"Find that place within yourself that connects you to Aric."

Scrunching her eyes tight, Theia searches for the pull. At first, there's nothing. Her heart drops a little before she recalls the moment Aric's eyes met hers. The thrill that shot through her veins and ignited her soul.

"Do you feel it?"

Shutting out the world, she zeroes in on Aric's face. It's a memory she's held so tight the last few days, conjuring it is second nature. His hazel eyes, the curve of his lips, the way his hair falls through her fingers.

"I have it," she whispers, opening her eyes to find Michael watching her intently.

"Good," he murmurs, his hand coming to rest on her shoulder. "Now take a deep breath, and let it out slowly."

Theia does as he says, inhaling deep then exhaling. For a second, nothing happens. Then there's a tug, like being sucked through a tunnel. Michael's grip tightens just as a rumble of thunder rattles her insides.

The heat that follows is so intense, Theia doubles over on a muted scream. Every nerve ending cauterizes at the assault before her brain can fully process the pain. When it does, her scream rips free from her throat.

Nails dig into her palms, as her arms fling out to either side. When the shudders barrel up from her toes, she's thankful for Michael's grip keeping her upright.

"Breathe, Theia." Although he stands beside her, his voice is miles away.

She struggles to do as he instructs, but every inhale is a shard of glass scraping her throat. Locking her jaw tight, Theia braces against the wave after wave of pure agony. The only thing that keeps her from crying mercy, is her memories of Aric. After a sharp hiss of air, she clings to the promise of his embrace when this is all over.

"Don't stop."

The ground beneath her feet trembles, shaking Theia to her core. The relentless assault pulls Theia in different directions. Her body and mind struggling to hold on as a dominant force overtakes her. Just as she fears she's about to shatter into a million pieces, the pain fades.

Slowly, the sensations lessen until Theia's screams turn to whimpers. Michael's hand is still on her shoulder, his other arm wrapping around her waist until she steadies herself. As the last of the pain recedes, she's left with a sharp ringing in her ears.

"Open your eyes."

Prying her lids open, Theia gasps at the sight sprawling out before her. Like nothing she's ever seen, she stares in wonder at the vast open space. A billion stars glitter among an inky blackness as galaxies swirl like ribbons in a breeze. Weightless, Theia figures she could float away into the wide expanse of the universe if she's not careful.

Beside her, Theia can feel Michael's gaze on her as she takes in the spectacle. "Where are we?" she asks, her voice barely louder than a whisper.

"Somewhere you've never been," he replies, a smile tugging at his lips. "Welcome to the celestial realm."

As they ascend, an ethereal energy surrounds her. Its vibrant hues of pink, blue and purple radiate across an otherwise black background. Emitting a heady pulse, it encompasses her as if the universe itself is alive and trying to pull her into its embrace.

All too quickly, it's over and Theia gapes at the stark white building in front a startling landscape. Built in the basin of a grand mountain, the buildings stretch high into the heavens as fat snowflakes float down around them. Instead of the chill she's expecting, the warm air hums over her arms, easing the tightness her muscles still carry.

"Queasy?"

Theia blinks and takes a moment to assess the state of her stomach. Unlike the last time, there's no flopping around like a landlocked fish, no dizziness to pitch the ground back and forth. Nothing. When she gives her head a soft shake, she half expects for the nausea to slam home, but again, nothing.

"Good." With a hand on the small of her back, Michael guides her towards the tallest building. Once she steps inside, the serenity in the air is so thick, it leaves Theia on edge.

Strange creatures line the long, narrow hallway. Tall and lithe, with skin that gleams like polished marble, each one stands erect and at attention. Eyes and hair as different as the next, sparkle brightly. Wings fully extended, shimmer with intensity to rival the brightest star.

At their arrival, one steps forward, his face stern and his eyes narrowed. "Why have you brought it here?"

"I made a promise," Michael replies, gesturing towards Theia. "She's here to see the Council."

Sapphire eyes flick to Theia. While his upper lip curls in disgust, he says nothing more before stepping back into line with the others.

"Are they angels as well?" Theia asks after they scurry past the last one.

"They are Goulidair. Our version of what you call Gargoyle," Michael explains quietly. "They serve as protectors of the Council."

"Oh." As they continue on in silence, Theia can't help but consider she's made a mistake trusting Michael. Should he betray her, getting back out won't be as easy as getting in. Unfortunately, she's come too far to turn back now.

CHAPTER 27

By the time Aric is aware of the severe pounding in his head, everything hurts. While his left eye still refuses to work, he pries the right one open with a little extra effort.

After countless hours under bright lights, he releases a soft sigh to find only darkness waiting for him. Judging by the unforgiving stones beneath him, he's back in one of their cells. This room reeks worse than the last, but if he's being honest, it probably has more to do with him than the room.

Massaging stiff fingers around his temples, Aric fights to clear his mind. Instantly, an image of Theia flashes behind his eyes to suck the breath from his lungs. The moment he grabs onto it like a lifeline, Aric finds his center.

Once his focus is sharp, he's immediately reminded of the throb in his head and the ache in his body. A surge of heat and pain hinder his first attempt to push himself upright. He doesn't need a light source to know that bruises, cuts and many other injuries decorate his skin.

Breath held, he makes another attempt to sit up. Groaning when his limbs protest the movement, he bites down on his lip and shoves beyond the pain.

"When did I pass out this time," Aric wonders aloud, his voice a useless brush of air. Sorting through his most recent memories, he searches for any clue regarding his latest session with Riordan.

Like every time before, he pressed Aric for answers. Unrelenting in his demand, Riordan's voice reverberates around the room like an iron fist banging on a steel door. *Where is Theia?* Since any answer Aric will spit at him would do little to change his situation, Aric clamps his jaw tight and endures the abuse. The interrogation will continue until Riordan gets a location from him. Aric's only hope is to outlast Riordan's madness.

Unfortunately, at this moment Riordan's instability and fury are the only things Aric is sure of. Where he is, leaves too many possibilities. How long he's been here is a joke to consider. A rubber band twisted out of shape one time too many, the minutes he spends here stretch and warp out of place.

Once he brushes the cobwebs off his brain function, the only thing Aric can recall from his last session with Riordan is Theia's blood-curdling scream. The torment filling his chest over such a sound, rivals anything Riordan tries to inflict on him. He remembers genuine shock exploding across Riordan's face before everything goes dark.

Heavy footfalls just beyond the door jerks Aric from his thoughts. Stumbling unsteadily to his feet, he braces his shoulder against the far wall. The creak and protest of rusty hinges release a banshee-like screech as they swung the door outward. With a flinch, Aric lifts a hand against the stab of light that replaces it.

"If you're awake, then I have orders to bring you to Riordan."

Titus.

Aric's heart sinks at the once friendly voice. He'd rather swallow razor blades than have another meeting with Riordan, but any sign of weakness is blood in the water. Setting his jaw hard enough to crack teeth, Aric jerks a nod.

Keeping one hand up to block out the light, Aric limps towards the door. Once he's close enough for Titus to catalog the damage Riordan already inflicted, his voice softens. "I'm sorry."

"Bite me."

Instead of the flare of Titus' quick temper, Aric spots a flicker of shadows in his familiar face. "I wish there was another way."

"Save your pity, lieutenant," Aric scoffs while giving Titus his back. "I don't need it."

"I hope I'd say the same thing if I were you," Titus mumbles. "Still, I am sorry."

Without warning, he jerks Aric's arms behind him, stretching joints and tearing at fresh wounds. Aric struggles, but the extent of his wounds are more severe than he originally hoped. *Sleep isn't healing me anymore.*

"Why don't you just tell him what he wants to know?"

"Last I checked, I don't answer to Riordan," Aric rasps.

With his wrists secure in shackles, Titus marches him along the narrow corridor. Some of the doors they pass are silent as the grave. Others either carry cries for mercy or foul curses.

As they walk, Aric can sense Titus' gaze, scrutinizing every detail. His determination to keep his head up and his shoulders square adds another layer of agony until a cold sweat coats his skin.

"You really care about it?" Titus asks suddenly, breaking the silence.

"Theia," Aric spits. "She has a name. Use it."

"I don't understand. Has she bewitched you?"

"You're right Titus. You don't understand." Directing a withering glare over his shoulder, Aric continues in a quiet growl. "I pray someday you will."

The two continue in silence, drawing closer to the white room. The door looms before him and Aric's heart wrenches at the sight of it.

He's lost track of the visits he's paid to Riordan there, but each time he emerges with more wounds.

"I've never seen him so obsessed."

"What do you mean?" Aric croaks, his voice hushed.

"He's not himself. When he's not with you or out looking for *Theia*, he's in his chamber here."

Aric's eyes narrow at the comment. "Does the Council know I turned myself in?"

Titus tenses, "No."

His world shatters as the single word drops like a blade from the guillotine. In an instant, it rips his hope away, leaving an ache in his chest too vast to comprehend. Suddenly, he realizes what it truly means to be hopeless. With an unbearable pain, his lungs struggle for air and his heart strains against the iron bands tightening around it.

This is my last visit, Aric muses to himself. Cracking his neck from side to side, he places each step carefully. Fingers ball into enormous fists behind him as he prepares to push Riordan over the edge.

"What is the meaning of this?"

Frozen, Theia chases the tremor from her hands as the woman at the far end of the long table surges to her feet. Long, white-blonde hair frames her heart-shaped face. Even from where Theia stops, the power rolling off this angel is enough to knock her knees together. While the two men exchange a look of confusion, the woman continues to stare at Theia with a mixture of confusion and suspicion.

Once she gathers the use of her legs again, Theia advances with her head held high. *I'm an idiot. This is the stupidest thing I've ever done*, she vents internally before stopping near the middle of the room. "Forgive my intrusion," Theia contains a small smirk when her words come out clear and steady.

The robust angel in the middle clears his throat. "Who are you?" The nasally pitch of his voice ruins any chance he has at intimidation.

"My name is Theia St. James," she declares. Swallowing hard, she locks eyes with the woman. "I believe you're looking for me."

"You dare bring a Nephilim into our private council room?"

While she directs the question at Michael, Theia is the first to respond. "I've come to make a deal."

The heavier-set angel huffs hard enough to shake the bulk of his weight. "We don't make deals with," he stops to cover his nose and mouth with part of his silk robe. Taking a breath under cover, he peeks out with a curl of his lip. "Your kind."

Just like that, a flare of heat steadies her racing heart. When she meets his obvious disgust, her stomach tightens. "So you'll make deals with demons. But you draw the line at my kind," she questions, her voice flat.

"How dare you-"

Still standing, the woman holds up one dainty hand. "What makes you think we've done any deals with demons?"

Theia flings a quick look over her shoulder at Michael. When he simply responds with a nod, she plows forward with her plan. "Riordan made a deal with a demon named Aamon. My location, in exchange for the power to unseat Melchom." Her eyes skip to the man protecting his delicate sense of smell. Theia's voice becomes sickly sweet as she continues. "Was that not on your orders?"

The woman's eyes narrow before she bends to share a whispered conversation with the other two members of the council. Theia's heart squeezes. *Did I overplay my hand?*

"How do we know you're telling the truth?"

After a slight scoff, Theia lifts her chin. "I know you have ways of confirming what I've just told you."

For the first time since she arrived, the angel on her left stands. Gesturing toward someone out of view, he tips a curt nod. "Summon Damien."

Less than thirty seconds later, the large doors swing open. The tall man striding through dresses impeccable in a dark blue pinstripe suit that accents the iciness in his eyes. He wears his black hair neat, not a strand out of place. Long fingers curl tight around the leather-bound book in his arms. After passing Theia with barely a passing glance, he stops just before the council.

"You summoned me?" He asks in a rich tenor, his back straight enough to use for measurement.

"This," the middle one begins, removing the material covering the lower half of his face to points a stubby finger in her direction. "Thing, claims a demon challenged Melchom for his seat."

"Yes, Councilor Gregory. My sources tell me a demon by the name of Aamon," the newcomer answers in an emotionless voice. "Though how *it* would know that, I cannot say."

Theia sucks in a sharp inhale. *Thing. It. My kind.* Instead of allowing every derogatory remark to chip away at her self-confidence, Theia uses them as the mortar needed to shore up the cracks.

The angel she can now refer to as Gregory sputters in an unflattering manner. "How did this demon get the power needed to do such a thing?"

"I couldn't say," the newcomer states smoothly.

"What can you say?" Rather than retake her empty seat, the woman simply rests her hands on her hips.

"Aamon made a challenge. And lost, Councilor Rebecca. Anything else would be pure speculation on my part."

Rebecca nods her head. "That'll be all Damien. Thank you."

With a deep bow, the newcomer adjusts his suit and retreats from the room, his eyes straight ahead.

"That still doesn't mean-"

"Forgive me, Gregory, but I believe it does." Theia snaps.

After another sputter that vibrates in his double chin, he pins her with a sneer. "That's Councilor Gregory to you."

Theia's soft chuckle earns her another deep scowl from Gregory and a soft shake of Michael's head from over her shoulder. "You're not my council. You've all made that perfectly clear." Clasping her hands together to still the shake, she notes each one of their gaping expressions. "Aamon failed. But that doesn't change the fact Riordan bartered with him. If he's willing to deal with demons, how long before he's striking deals with this Melchom character?"

"True," Rebecca concedes quietly. "That doesn't explain why you've come to us."

Now or never! Closing her eyes, Theia uses a long breath to steady her nerves. When she opens them again, she meets Rebecca's hard stare. "I would like to make a trade. Me for Aric."

"Aric?" Shadows flicker in Rebecca's eyes before she turns them on her fellow council members. When both men respond with a look of confusion, she turns back to Theia with a frown marring her impeccable features. "What makes you think he's here?"

Her question causes Theia's stomach to plummet. When her mouth waters, she resorts to breathing in and out through her nose until she's certain she won't be sick all over their pristine marble floor.

Sensing her distress, Michael steps forward. "Aric turned himself over to Riordan days ago, in return for an audience with you."

Obvious confusion slowly gives way to different degrees of horror. While the thin man on the left looks about as nauseous as Theia feels, Rebecca's expression shifts from fear to one of rage.

Theia's voice shakes, her throat tight as she grinds out the words. "You're saying he's not here?" Her fingers tremble as she tips her head back to choke back a rising wave of bile. Squeezing her eyes tight against the threat of fresh tears, she sucks in a ragged breath, the burn traveling all the way to her toes.

"I'm afraid not."

Rebecca's tight reply bathes Theia's skin in ice water. Inside, she's a boiling pit of unchecked fury. The heat bubbling within her stomach slowly spills over into her arms and legs. Sparks skip across her fingertips, forcing Theia to bury them into tight fists. Her vision narrows until all she can focus on are the self-righteous angels sitting straight ahead. As if sensing her rampant emotions, each one eyes her warily. "I want him back," she grinds around through the clench of her teeth.

Gregory's eyes narrow. "You'll give yourself up? Willingly?"

"For Aric? I would give everything." Theia's eyes shift toward Rebecca. Absently, she notes the tightness pinching the angel's features. "Either I get him back," she swallows until steel replaces the tremble in her voice. "Or I will burn it all to the ground."

"You'd take innocent lives?" Wrinkles appear on Rebecca's forehead. "Human lives?"

"I said nothing about humans," Theia clarifies.

"Forgive me, Councilors," Michael chimes in, "she means us."

Gregory thumps the table with one meaty hand. "You can't possibly think to take on Heaven. You'd lose!"

"Perhaps. But how many would I take with me?" Theia questions, arching an eyebrow. Her lips curve into a slow smile. "Trust me when I say I'll start here. I may be new at this, but Aric trained me. It would be foolish to underestimate me."

Instead of answering her, Rebecca pins a frosty glare at Gregory. "Summon him."

Gregory gives his head an uneven shake. "We shouldn't give in to her demands."

"I want Aric brought here now!" Though dainty, Rebecca's hands produce cracks in the table.

"We don't even know that Riordan has him. If he does, why wouldn't he bring him to us for sentencing?"

"Because Aric planned to tell you the same thing I did," Theia snaps. "I told him it was a bad idea. I warned Aric not to trust Riordan." As her heart ticks off each beat, she quietly counts to ten, holding the tattered remains of her control together by mere threads.

The angel on her left speaks up. "Summon him. Now." The hard command of his voice is at odds with his slight stature.

Gregory throws up his hands in defeat and roars in a voice they can hear several worlds away. "Riordan!"

In an instant, the Seraph appears between Theia and the Council. His sudden arrival causes her to blink rapidly, but the state of his appearance adds fuel to the heat brewing in her chest.

Disheveled, his blonde hair stands at odd angles around his narrow face. Covered in sweat, his rumpled clothes sport enormous blood stains. While some splotches are dark from being exposed to the air too long, others are still a bright red. With a wild look in his muddy brown eyes, he drops the lethal blade to the floor with a loud clatter. The droplets of blood it leaves behind rips more of Theia's control from her grip.

Riordan gives his head a quick shake before snapping his body to attention. Shoulders back, spine straight, he folds his still bloody hands behind his back. "Councilors."

"We've had some troubling accusations leveled against you, Riordan," Rebecca purrs cooly. Her face is a hard, unreadable mask. "Judging by the state of you, I fear they may be true."

From where she stands, Theia spots a tremor of apprehension skip along his back. Surprisingly, his voice never wavers. "I've been scouring every back alley I can find trying to track the Nephilim."

One finely sculpted brow climbs upward on Rebecca's face. "Is that so?"

"Of course, Councilor." Riordan dips his head slightly.

Theia isn't sure if the Council members experience emotions like the rest of them, but Riordan's reply inspires a faint smirk to grace Rebecca's lips. "Perhaps you should look there."

Riordan whirls around in response to Rebecca's command, and Theia's lips curl into a triumphant smirk at the fear that washes over him. His chin quivers with shock as she savors the moment of power with each passing second.

As he turns back to face the Council, Riordan's eyes narrow dangerously. "Michael captured her? Alive?"

"Theia turned herself in," Gregory snaps, "in exchange for Aric."

Riordan's lips twist into an ugly sneer. "You choose to believe her lies." He spits the accusation out as if it's coated in ash.

"Fortunately, we don't have to take anyone's word for it." Rebecca adds, her voice falling like silk. "Michael?"

Spinning on the ball of her foot, Theia notes Michael's blank expression. His head tips as if he struggles to hear something too faint to make out properly. When his eyes suddenly flash with an incandescent light, a shiver trickles over Theia's arms. The air around them crackles with strained energy and she realizes with a jump that he's searching for Aric. His head swivels from side to side, his eyes scanning the room as if searching for a hidden object. Any hope of breath leaves her when she notes his grim expression.

The longer time ticks by, the more restless Riordan becomes. Shifting from foot to foot, he casts a frantic look at the double doors behind him. Theia braces herself. Before he can decide if he should run or not, Michael's voice shatters the silence.

"I've found him. He's too weak to travel on his own."

Rebecca nods, her eyes dancing with a dangerous glint. "Bring him to us."

Michael disappears in a flash of blue light, then reappears with a man in tow.

It takes Theia a minute to recognize the man in front of her, but when she does, her heart attempts to leap out through her throat. "Aric!" she cries, rushing to his side, catching him before he falls to the ground. "Aric," she whimpers and lowers them both to the floor, cradling his head in her lap.

Theia gasps in shock, tears streaming down her face as she takes in the broken man before her. His once-handsome face is now unrecognizable with cuts and bruises and congealed blood covering his skin. Pressure squeezes her chest so tight that all she can muster is a whispered plea: "What have they done to you?" She presses a soft kiss to his forehead to soothe his pain.

He's barely conscious, his body shaking with fever and pain. Someone cut his hair. crudely. Nicking the scalp underneath in various places. Theia discovers countless wounds covering his body, the blood seeping through his torn clothes. Sitting there on the cold marble floor rips what little remains of her control slips from her fingers. Choking back her sob, she pins a deadly glare where Riordan shifts anxiously.

Rebecca approaches them, her expression softening ever so slightly. "We'll get you help, Aric," she says, her voice surprisingly gentle.

"None of you are touching him," Theia snarls, her hands clutching him tighter.

Taken aback by the venom in her voice, Rebecca hesitates. "We have healers that can help him."

"We don't need your healers!" She shouts defiantly, her hands already pressing against his chest, sending her powers into him. Aric had always told her destruction was easy. Now she silently prays her attempts at something else will be just as effective.

Theia grits her teeth as she melds her hands together, coaxing out a brilliant white heat. Her veins light up with energy as she takes on his pain and suffering, the violence of it crashing over her body with searing hot intensity. Her heart races as she pushes every ounce of power she has into him, willing him to survive. She pushes deeper than before, battling through the agony that radiates across her entire being.

Aric's body spasms, and his eyes snap open, shooting daggers of pain into Theia. His lips twist, forming a rasping whisper that pierces her soul like an icy spear. She can't move, transfixed by the sound of her name laced with his agony. Every sound carries a raw emotion until all she wants to do is cradle him in her arms and make it all go away.

Finally, after what seems like hours, Aric's shaking stops, and his eyes flutter open. "Theia," he whispers, his voice a rough croak.

CHAPTER 28

The sound of his voice and the sight of his lips moving adds a stutter to her pulse. Since her hands still press to his chest, the thrum of his heartbeat returning to normal leaves a tingle in her skin. Locking her eyes onto his, she leans in and brushes her lips gingerly across his. "I'm here," she whispers.

Aric's eyes search hers, the pain in them slowly fading. "Thank you," his voice scrapes as he drags a finger along the curve of her cheek. Reaching up, he runs his fingers through a thick lock of her once dark curls. Under the bright lights of the council's chamber, the strands shine with a muted silver color. "You used too much power."

With a shrug, Theia tucks it behind one ear. "I don't care."

"You were supposed to wait for me."

Theia laughs and pins her teeth against her lip. "A girl could grow old waiting for you."

"Just as long as you're growing old with me."

"Deal." Brushing her fingers gently through what remains of his hair, Theia fights back a fresh stab of tears. "Can you stand?"

Aric lays quiet for a moment as if to assess his physical ability. After a quick nod, Theia scoots back while he climbs to his feet, her lips twitching over a ghost of a smile when he extends a hand to help her up.

Just then, Rebecca steps forward to remind Theia where they are. "I've never seen anything like that before."

"You never should've allowed this to happen to him," Theia hisses.

Rebecca doesn't flinch away from the venom in Theia's words, offering a solemn nod instead. "You're right. And we're truly sorry for what you've had to endure, Aric."

Theia slips her hand into Aric's as he gives Rebecca a stiff nod. "There are others he's keeping prisoner down there."

Even as Rebecca's face remains in passive, Theia recognizes a flicker of shame in her eyes before it's gone. "Michael?"

"Right away, Councilor." His proximity inspires Theia's gaze in time to catch his warm smile. "Knew you could do it." Before Theia can ask what *it* means, he's gone.

"Please understand, Aric. We were unaware of Riordan's actions against you," Rebecca mumbles quietly.

"That's no excuse!" Theia seethes, her eyes blazing. Her words hit the air like a thunderclap, as Aric's firm grip on her hand reminds her to take a deep breath. Once she exhales, the fire simmering in her stomach slowly ebbs away, allowing her to continue. "If you consider yourselves as the authority, then ignorance is not an excuse. You should've made yourselves aware of the situation every step of the way."

"You're right," Gregory concedes from where he still sits behind the table. "He will face judgement."

Aric squeezes her hand, his eyes sparkling with a newfound determination. "I would like to be part of that judgement," he rasps, his voice still rough from the entire ordeal. "I want to make sure he pays for what he's done."

Rebecca nods, her expression grave. "You will have your chance, Aric. But first, we need to decide what to do with Theia."

Rushing forward, Riordan's face twists into a deep scowl. "It needs to be executed! You've all seen the power it wields. How long before it's turning on the humans?"

"Not everyone who has a bit of power is a raging psychopath," Theia argues, her eyes shooting daggers in Riordan's direction. "You have a fraction and look at all the damage you cause!"

Riordan gives his head an uneven shake, his eyes skipping over her towards the council. "I am well within my rights as a seraph to question any prisoner for the location of valuable targets."

"Question?" Theia growls darkly. Aric's hand tightens around hers. "You beat him. Tortured him. Cut his fucking hair!"

Riordan's face contorts as his eyes narrow and his lips curl. "He brought shame upon himself!" he roars, making the walls tremble with fury. Every syllable ricochets off the walls like a gunshot, reverberating with condemnation.

"Enough!" Rebecca roars, stepping between Theia and Riordan. "He's baiting you. And you're playing right into it."

Although her stomach still bubbles with a liquid heat, she steps neatly into Aric's arms. The light caress of his hand on her back wrangles her emotions into a more manageable storm. When she's sure her voice remains steady, she faces the council once more. "What are you going to do with me?"

Rebecca studies her for a moment before speaking. "We can't just let you go, Theia."

"I understand," Theia says. "I'll honor our deal," she whispers, her voice shaking and straining to break free from the tight grip of her throat.

The arm Aric wraps around her waist tenses. Nudging her chin with a finger, he brushes the pad of his thumb over her lower lip. "What did you do?"

When her lips tremble, Theia draws in a breath. "Nothing you wouldn't have done first."

Gregory rises from his seat. "For the time being, you'll be under armed guard until we can decide what's being done with you."

The dozen Goulidair storming into the room cuts off any further debate. Three veer off to drag Riordan out kicking and screaming. Four surround Theia, hands on their weapons, while two more pry her from Aric's grip.

Theia imagines their grip is like being encased in cement, wincing when their fingers clamp around her upper arms. Unwilling to relinquish his hold, Aric's arms tighten in steel bands. Between their determination to pull her away and Aric's desperation to keep her close, pain floods her system. Radiating in her arms and across her midsection, the pain unfurls forward until drawing breath becomes difficult.

"Aric," Rebecca chastises gently, "you must let her go."

"Yeah, that's not happening," Aric snarls. When a third one steps forward and grabs Theia's wrist hard enough to make her cry out, Aric reacts with a quick fist. Staggering on his feet, the Goulidair scrubs a hand across his jaw, eyes wide with shock.

Aric's eyes blaze with a fierce intensity that sends shivers down her spine. In that moment, she realizes no one has ever fought so fiercely for her before. With a soft sigh, she wraps herself in his embrace, her only refuge.

Stretching on the tips of her toes, despite her long legs, Theia claims his lips. Arms struggle against her captors to wind around his neck in order to pull him closer. His soft moan of approval ignites a familiar spark within her core. When his hands come up to frame her face, Theia's heart twists a second before she steps away from him.

With a violent heave, the Goulidair rips her from Aric's grasp. His agonizing cry tearing through her soul like a tornado, leaving in its wake a desolate wasteland of despair and anguish.

As they drag her towards the doors, she fights back her own strangled sobs as a thick blanket of thorns clings to her soul.

Every minute Theia spends in this cell ticks by at an agonizing pace. Except for an occasional scowl, the Goulidair standing guard remains silent and vigilant.

Strange marking decorate three of the four surrounding walls. Thick, iron bars that reach from floor to ceiling make up a fourth. Warm to the touch, they give off a slight vibration from the shimmering light spanning each gap.

On her left, carved from the wall, stands a narrow bed. The thin mattress and threadbare blanket would do little to guard her against the trickle of cold air slinking through a small rectangle window.

Balancing on a three-legged chair, Theia uses the short bars in the window to pull herself up high enough to peek through the opening. Her first close-up view of stunning mountains causes her to gasp sharply.

Under an ethereal light, jagged peaks glisten like gemstones as sharp and deadly as daggers. Just below, a blanket of white coats the peaks and valleys as far as she can see.

Everywhere she looks, snow falls gently. A blanket of white noise amongst the silence. A howl of the wind drowns Theia with in as much peace as a death row inmate on the eve of execution.

Crisp air invigorates her senses with a breath of pine, spruce and the barest hint of fresh water nearby. Although the cold pricks her nose and peppers her skin with goosebumps, Theia stares in wonder.

Known as a flat-lander most of her life, Theia can't help but allow the beauty to distract. Soon, the scuffling of her footsteps echo off the walls once again to fill the room with a maddening decibel.

"Will you please stop that?"

She freezes as Riordan's snarl cuts through the wall between them. Leveling a glare at the wall on her right, Theia gives her head a rueful shake. "You've got to be fucking kidding me."

"Right?" Riordan scoffs loudly. "Not only am I locked up, but I'm locked up with you."

"Serves you right."

"You can blame me all you like. I was just doing my job."

"Really? And that means making deals with demons?"

"Ah. Well, I do what I must in order to keep humanity safe."

With a roll of her eyes, Theia plops down on the too thin mattress. Just the idea of Riordan less than ten feet away jams her heart into overdrive. His sorry excuses for the things he's done leaving a bitter taste in her mouth. Blowing out a series of quick breaths, she bounces one foot.

Even if she can overlook every attempt he's made to kill her, his torture of Aric adds a tightness to her jaw. "Bastard," she grumbles softly.

"Believe it or not, there was a time when the ends justified the means. Especially with your kind."

Baring her teeth at the wall across from her, Theia resumes pacing to keep from blasting through the wall. "Stop talking to me."

Riordan snorts. "We could sit her for quite a while."

"Personally, I'd rather watch my life wither up and end than listen to anything you have to say."

"Careful," Riordan cautions with a laugh, "that moment is coming up sooner than you think."

"You don't scare me." Even as the words leave her mouth, a flare of pain grows in her chest.

As if aware of her reaction, Riordan continues. "You're not foolish enough to believe you're walking out of here."

"Bite me."

"One of two things is going to happen," Riordan announces, his voice growing louder, as if he stalks closer. "One; they turn you into their own personal weapon. Or two, they separate your head from your shoulders." Silence hangs between them before Riordan finishes with a smile she can hear. "Personally, I'd wager on option two."

"Just as long as you go first."

"You really think they're going to execute me? Next to Aric, I'm the highest-ranking Seraph they have."

"Maybe you were. I doubt that's true anymore," Theia purrs sweetly. "Not since you went and sullied yourself with demons."

With a huff, Riordan retreats from the wall they share. Her smile genuine, Theia continues as if she hasn't a care in the world at this very moment. "Not to mention the torture of a superior officer. Something like that could really ruin your chances at the next raise evaluation."

The crack of something hitting the connecting wall causes lines to spider web outward from its center on her side. "Aric stopped being my superior when he let you live."

"Hm. The Council doesn't seem to see it that way."

"Aric has always been Rebecca's favorite lapdog. She's never been able to see him for what he really is."

"Strong?" Theia challenges. "How 'bout honest? Humble?" After exhaling a dramatic sigh, she calls over her shoulder in a sing-song voice. "You'll let me know when I land on the right one? Yes?"

"Think you know him just because you spread your legs?" Riordan's derisive chuckle answers Theia's sharp gasp. "We've exiled angels for less, you know."

"Fuck you."

"What if I told you Aric isn't as honest as you think he is?"

"I'd call you a liar." Massaging the stiffness in her jaw, she shoots a quick look at her guard.

"So, then he's told you how your mother died?"

As sure as if he'd launched a physical assault, Theia reels from the blow. She opens her mouth to tell him to go to hell, but no sound comes out. Brows fold and her nose crinkles as she studies the wall he hides behind.

"Is that a no?" His voice is almost chipper considering their circumstances. "Aric didn't mention killing your mother while your father ran like the coward he is?"

Theia tugs repeatedly at one earlobe while his words hit home. "I d-don't be-believe you."

"You don't have to take my word for it," Riordan answers easily. "Allow me to show you."

Before Theia can form the words needed to refuse, the connecting wall hums under a soft glow.

"What the-" Theia stumbles backward. Breath stales in her lungs as Riordan paints the wall with the interior of a small bedroom. The sight of Aric, wings spread beside a baby crib, sends a jolt to her brain.

Sheathing his sword, he turns slightly while his lips move soundlessly. As the camera shifts, Theia resists the urge to be sick as her eyes fall on Riordan's shrewd face. While the vision has no sound, she notices the tension in Aric's shoulders increasing.

Suddenly, the image changes to a large cornfield. Overhead, the moon hangs high in a black sky, covering the events below in mysterious shadows.

Just ahead, Theia watches with a tightness in her chest as her father weaves and slips through stalks of corn as high as his shoulders. In one arm, he clutches a small bundle wrapped in yellow fleece while pulling her mother along behind him with the other hand.

"Pay close attention now," Riordan calls, shocking Theia out of her stupor.

"What kind of game are you playing?"

His laugh is low and bitter. "No game. I'm simply showing you what happened that night."

Time drags on as the moon disappears behind a cloud, shrouding the ground below. When her mother stumbles to her hands and knees, Theia covers her gasp with both hands.

His eyes wide, Julian doubles back and scrambles to pull her mother to her feet. The next few seconds, he spends assuring himself she's uninjured before they continue on.

When large shadowy figures surround her parents, her father freezes as her mother searches frantically for another escape route. When he doesn't find one, Julian draws himself up straight, squaring his shoulders before he turns towards the invisible camera. Hazel eyes, more blue than green, narrow as his nostrils flare.

Adjusting the bundle in his arms, he pulls her mother close, wrapping an arm around her waist. Theia's heart twists as he lowers his head to breathe in the scent of her mother's red hair. His expression is full of adoration, his eyes bright with unspoken emotions.

Her mother casts a warm look at the bundle in his arms and then says something that has her father shaking his head furiously.

Tears spill over porcelain cheeks as her mother wrings her hands within his shirt. Dark blue orbs, like the world below the sea's surface, dart left and right. Once more, lips flutter soundlessly between them before his gaze softens. One hand cups her mother's cheek, immediately softening the lines in her forehead.

Standing on her toes, she brushes a kiss to his lips before training tear-filled eyes to the bundle in his arms.

Theia can do nothing but gawk in open-mouthed silence as her mother's features twist into a heart-wrenching look of longing. After brushing a hand over the baby's dark curls, her mother wastes no time sprinting off into the night. Without hesitation, Julian runs after her.

"What do you think he was thinking at that moment?" Riordan asks with a smirk. "Did he worry over his wife as he ran? Perhaps he was more concerned about their baby sleeping soundly in his arms? We both know what choice he made, Theia."

"Shut up!" Theia backpedals until the bed hits her calves, nearly knocking her off balance.

After a dramatic pause, he continues. "He had no clue what would happen next."

The first tear streaks a hot path along Theia's cheek before she realizes she's crying. "No," she whispers hoarsely, her arms wrapping tight around her waist.

"Don't look away," Riordan growls. "Watch what your precious Aric does."

"No," Theia pleads again, her head shaking violently as she presses her palms against her ears. When the image blurs and becomes nothing more than a smudge, she jumps to her feet. "STOP!"

What happens next will haunt Theia's dreams for as long as she has them.

In one moment, her mother stands amongst the trampled corn, her full lips curling with a smirk. Shoulders back, she waits as the angels pursuing them file in around her. Weapons draw, wings spread. Strangely, Theia doesn't spot Aric in the small group of angels surrounding her mother. Lifting her chin, she takes several steps in Riordan's direction, her eyes hard.

Once again, a soundless conversation takes place before the camera spins erratically. The next time it steadies, her mother lay motionless on the cold ground, her blood already pooling out from under her. Kneeling beside her, Aric's strong features twist. With a curl in his upper lip, he scoops her mother's lifeless body off the ground and carries her out of the cornfield. Brows knit, his eyes unfocused; each step covering his armor under thick rivers of blood.

By the time the scene disappears from the wall, Theia is panting in quick gasps, her mind racing. Blinking rapidly to keep the rest of the tears from falling, she struggles to make sense of what she saw. *Really* saw.

Picking over the ridge of her thumb, Theia shuffles to the bars and back. She couldn't deny most of what Riordan showed her appears legit. Except for the lack of sound and the jerky camera movements. Not to mention a complete section missing between her mother's defiance and her death.

Flushing, her skin breaks out in a thin layer of sweat as her internal temperature rages. Wrapping her hands around the iron bars separating her from freedom, she attempts to regulate the heat boiling in her stomach. When she can speak without fire leaping from her tongue, she does so in a measured tone.

"You're lying."

"I just showed you what happened!"

"You showed pieces. With no sound," Theia spits over her shoulder. "That could mean anything."

"These sigils on the wall are to suppress angelic powers. I'm not strong enough to show you the entirety, complete with audio. Do I look like Steven Spielberg to you?"

For a split second, Theia faces a temptation to consider his explanation. Then she recalls every moment she's spent with Aric and gives her head another shake. "You're nothing but a liar," she accuses in a scathing tone. "You could tell me water is wet, and I'd still call you a fucking liar."

"Says the abomina-"

A soft, solemn voice comes from out of nowhere to cut short Riordan's reply. "The Council is ready for her."

Breath held, Theia searches for the source.

Standing before the Goulidair guarding her cell; is an angel with a severe presence. Cut short, her pitch black hair sweeps upward in thick and unruly piles near the back of her head. She styles several longer pieces on either side of her pixie face, adding a softness to her features. Blue eyes Theia compares to Michigan's frozen trees glisten with an air of confidence. The only other color in her appearance are orchid-purple streaks running through her hair. Her arrival flicks a switch in Riordan's demeanor.

After a scramble of movement, Theia watches from the corner of her eye as he plasters himself to iron bars. "Sylvie," he breathes, "get me out of here."

Though she addresses Riordan, Sylvie's eyes never waver from Theia's. "I don't take orders from you anymore," she replies icily. With a gasp, Riordan stumbles backward into his cell as if she physically struck him.

Unfazed, she directs her intimidating glare at the Goulidair once more. "I'm here to bring the Nephilim to the Council. Release her."

"I think you mean it," he corrects in a startling deep voice. When Sylvie merely tips her chin to deliver a frosty stare, her guard produces a key from his uniform and unlocks Theia's door.

Before she can escape to freedom, however, Sylvie is there with an unreadable expression on her face. Shoulders back, arms folded behind her, she speaks without a single flare of emotion.

"The Council tasks me with bringing you before them for judgement. You're not going to make my job harder by running, are you?" She smells of lilac, sweet and musky, mixed with a delicate hint of jasmine.

Theia's lower lip wobbles until she steadies it with the press of her teeth and gives her head a quick shake. "N-no," she whispers, her fingers fidgeting with the hem of her shirt.

"Very well," Sylvie allows a small smile to tip the corners of her mouth, though her eyes remain cold. "If you'll follow me, they're waiting for you."

CHAPTER 29

As they walk in silence, Theia can't help but steal glances at Sylvie. Though she holds herself with a serious, regal posture, Theia wonders how deep that façade goes. Anyone that adds personality to her hairstyle can't be as rigid as they seem. Despite the sense of danger surrounding the angel, Theia's curious to learn more.

Finally, they reach a set of enormous double doors. As they glide open, Theia's knees shake and she offers a quick prayer she doesn't pass out from a lack of breathing.

The room itself boasts serenity and magnificence. Arching ceilings, a prismatic wonder of colors and hues, illuminate the room below. Gilded balconies decorated with Heaven's symbols groan as their occupants all scramble to get their first glimpse of her.

As Sylvie escorts her down to the center of the room, Theia toys with the end of her braid that drapes over one shoulder.

Packed shoulder to shoulder, hundreds of angels fill the many pews on either side. A symphony of shuffling feet, whispered conversations and creaking wood that quiets as she passes by. Her heart races when they finally reach the end of the aisle.

Before her, sitting elevated above the rest in what Theia would describe as a throne, are three empty high-backed chairs.

With a slight touch on her elbow, Sylvie steers her toward the short table on her right. Theia's eyes widen as she stares at the faces already waiting for her.

Michael sits at the far end, his glorious wings folded neatly behind him. At first glance, his handsome face is impassive until it softens with a warm smile of encouragement.

It's the sight of Aric in the middle that rocks the ground beneath her.

At her approach, he stands to his full height, his eyes demanding contact with hers. When her brain computes the slow burn there, her heart leaps into her throat.

Changed into a clean pair of jeans and a t-shirt without rips or bloodstains, he's a sight to behold. Power radiates off him unchecked and for the first time since she's met him, Theia shivers under its full weight. They made him for this power, she realizes, her steps faltering, her mouth dry.

As if sensing her nervousness, Aric rushes forward and folds her stiff hands into his. His touch is enough to send electric shocks through her veins, and Theia wonders if he's aware of the effect he has on her. Gripping her chin between thumb and forefinger, he searches her eyes.

"Are you okay?" he asks, his breath warm against her cheek.

Theia nods, not trusting the strength in her voice. Her only thought is to sink into his embrace and let the outside world fade away. When Sylvie clears her throat behind them, she reluctantly admits now is not the time.

With a nod at her escort, Aric pulls Theia toward the small table and places her in the chair between him and Michael. Not long after, the Council arrives to take their seats as well.

Councilor Gregory begins with a dramatic clearing of his throat. "We are here this morning to decide the fate of a Nephilim. We will not tolerate any outburst." Apparently satisfied that it will all run smoothly, he turns his attention to their table. "Who speaks for this one?"

Michael stands tall, his powerful figure exuding an aura of confidence and tranquility. His wings give a slight tremor as he shifts his shoulders and tucks his hands together in a casual gesture. Theia stares, transfixed at the sight. "I do," Michael states clearly, and the room erupts into a series of sharp gasps.

Obviously, Michael's involvement isn't something they expected. When the brunt of his responsibility settles over her, she meets his gaze with a grateful nod. Taking a deep breath settles the sudden flip in her stomach as Michael steps forward and unfolds his wings.

Councilor Gregory frowns, a red flush creeping into his face. "It's highly unusual for an archangel to involve themselves in these proceedings."

Without hesitation, Michael nods. "But not forbidden," he argues. "I have the right to see you serve justice impartially."

"I don't think-"

"Michael is well within his rights to take part in our judgement," the Councilor to the right of Gregory chimes in, his voice on the verge of boredom.

"Thank you, Councilor Samuel." Michael shifts his stance to address both the council and the spectators filling the room. "Unlike most of those here today, I've spent quite a bit of time observing Theia and her actions. I believe I can offer valuable insight towards a decision."

Rebecca stands as Gregory drops his portly frame into his chair. "Let us begin."

"The Nephilim stands accused of breaking the laws of creation and endangering the balance of our universe." His voice loud enough to reach the angels in the back pews, Gregory pauses for effect. "How does it plead?"

Theia opens her mouth to answer, but Michael beats her to it. "She pleads not guilty." Again, audible shock explodes against the walls containing the mass of spectators. While Theia's teeth chew on the corner of her lip, Michael is a stone. Maintaining an air of serenity, his shoulders relax.

"Are you certain?" Gregory prods, eyebrows high on his forehead.

"I am," Michael states simply.

"Then let us begin with the evidence against it."

Theia braces herself as a Gregory produces a small white orb. Holding it in the palm of his hand, he raises it high for everyone to see. "These are recordings of her actions on earth and the devastation each one caused."

The room falls silent as the ceiling reflects the orb's contents like a giant movie screen to display a girls' school bathroom. The instant Theia catches sight of the familiar green tiles, her face falls into her hands.

One by one, Gregory puts her destructive powers on display. From the burning of her own house to the pileup she caused trying to save Aric. Of course, without the context, to anyone else, it looks as if she's out of control.

The moment her shoulders drop, Aric gives her hands a squeeze. Heat flows from him to warm her chilled skin. The expansion in her chest grows until she lifts her eyes to his. Instead of the disappointment she'd been expecting, Aric's eyes glow.

Releasing her breath, Theia swallows and forces herself to watch the rest of Gregory's evidence without a flinch.

As the videos end, Rebecca commands the room with a hard tone. "Do you deny these actions?"

"Not at all," Michael declares. "But if you'll allow it, I'd like to elaborate on each one."

When she responds with a curt nod, Michael replays each scene in its full entirety, starting with Mercedes merciless assault.

He shows the physical attack on her friend leading up to her destruction. The sight of Adriel pulling a demon from the teenage girl sends a ripple of reaction amongst the observers.

When he moves on to the next events, Michael shows Riordan's actions as the catalyst for them all. His ruthless pursuit to kill rather than capture.

Just when Theia believes Michael is done, the ceiling splits apart and shows the Council's personal meeting room. Her heart plunges to her stomach at the sight of Aric sprawled on the ground, his skin bruised and battered, ashen with death. A guttural scream rips through her throat as she falls to her knees beside him. She watches herself shatter into a thousand pieces before mustering every ounce of power within her to heal him.

As she bathes Aric in a blinding white light, Michael broadcast her actions to save him without a hitch for all to see. Gasps of disbelief ripple through the crowd. After a moment of silence, a thunderous applause ricochets like gunshots against the walls. Unsure if her heart wants to speed up or stop altogether, Theia shifts restlessly in her seat, hands trembling.

"Just as much as she can be destructive, she also has the gift to heal. I think it's about time we stop fearing what the Nephilim can do." Michael says smoothly. "I think it's our responsibility to ensure we're not executing the good along with the bad."

The room falls into a stunned silence as Michael finishes speaking. Theia watches as Councilor Gregory's face turns a deep shade of red. She experiences a sense of admiration for Michael for standing up for her and her kind against the judgment of the council. She looks over to Aric, who is gazing back at her with intensity, and it sends a hum through her body.

Rebecca clears her throat, breaking the silence that had befallen the room. "Councilor Gregory, I believe we have heard enough. It's time to vote."

Gregory, still fuming, nods his head and stands up. "I vote the Nephilim guilty of putting humans at risk with her uncontrollable powers." He pauses for effect, scanning the room with his eyes. "We must restore the balance. The punishment must fit the crime."

Theia's her heart shatters into a million pieces as the harsh reality of her situation overwhelms her. With dread settling heavily in her chest, it is painfully clear that she has no control over their decision.

But then, to her surprise, Aric stands up. The room falls silent as all eyes turn to him. "May I say something?"

The councilors exchange furtive glances while Gregory narrows his eyes. "No," Gregory snaps. "The Nephilim has caused irreparable damage to the balance of our universe. We cannot overlook such actions."

A murmur of agreement ripples through the room, but Aric stands firm. "I beg to differ, councilor. If all she wanted was to destroy the balance, why did none of these events end a human life? You claim she's out of control. The amount of control it takes to contain a maelstrom of emotions from claiming innocent lives is astounding."

Theia feels a lump form in her throat as she watches the proceedings unfold. The weight of her actions and the potential consequences bear down on her. Her fingers tighten against Aric's and her foot bounces uncontrollably under the table. Unsure if she's hot or cold, her body switches between sweating and shivering. But Aric's touch is a reassuring presence, a lifeline that keeps her grounded.

A hush falls over the crowd as all eyes turn to Rebecca. Standing slowly to her feet, she says something to cause a gasp of shock. "I vote Theia innocent. It's clear much like their human halves, the Nephilim's knack for good or evil varies. Capable of creation or destruction."

With bated breath, Theia pins her eyes to the tall man at the end. Without sparing Gregory or Rebecca even a glance, Samuel stands and issues the words that will either condemn or free her.

"I vote Theia innocent," Samuel says, his voice resounding in the chamber. "As Michael pointed out, she has shown a remarkable ability to heal, not just harm. And in every instance presented, she acted in defense of others or out of a desire to save lives. The balance of the universe is important, but so is the preservation of life. The Nephilim are not the enemy here. Riordan is the genuine threat. We should focus on bringing him to justice instead of punishing someone who has done nothing but try to protect those she loves."

Tears prick at the corners of Theia's eyes as the weight of Gregory's accusations lift off her shoulders. She looks over at Michael and Aric, her heart swelling with gratitude and admiration for their unwavering support. They've risked a lot to stand at her side. *I'll never forget it*, she vows silently.

Gregory slams his fist down on the table, his face turning purple with rage. "This is preposterous!"

But Rebecca remains unmoved. "The majority has spoken," she says calmly. "Theia is innocent."

Theia's head snaps back as she pulls in a full breath since entering the room. She can hardly believe what she's hearing, and she looks around the room to see the reactions of the others. To her surprise, there are nods of agreement and quiet murmurings of support.

Then chaos erupts as the councilors argue amongst themselves. Aric's grip on her hand tightens, a show of support that gives her the strength to face whatever comes next.

Finally, after what feels like an eternity, Rebecca speaks up. "Theia, we will allow you to return home. Along with Aric, Sylvie will accompany you both. Should you give her any reason to believe you're a threat to mankind, she *will* report it immediately. Do you understand?"

Theia nods, her throat still tight with emotion. "Yes, I understand."

"Good," Rebecca says with a curt nod. "You are free to go."

Her legs are unsteady, her glances furtive for anyone rushing forward to claim it all a mistake and march her to execution, anyway. As she makes her way out of the room with Aric and Sylvie flanking her, no one runs forward. *Can it be possible?* Despite having just met Sylvie, her presence is comforting as they navigate their way through the Council's chambers and out into the cool night air.

Theia takes a deep breath and looks up at the stars until she can speak without too much difficulty. Laying a hand against her heart, she gives Aric a genuine smile as she fights back a fresh stab of tears. "Thank you," she says softly. "I don't know what I would have done without you."

Aric grabs Theia fiercely, crushing her against his chest as he entangles his fingers in her hair. When his lips find hers a searing heat passes between them as they lock into a passionate kiss. When he finally pulls away, his voice is thick with emotion. "You are my everything," he whispers against her lips. "You have been the love of my life since the day I met you."

Behind them, Sylvie clears her throat. "We should probably get out of here before they change their minds," she says, her voice soft.

Theia buries her face in the crook of Aric's neck. Her body is weak, her muscles limp as she gives in to the relief of surviving. His arms are strong, his presence her sanctuary. Even with the world crumbling around them, he remained her anchor. "Let's go home."

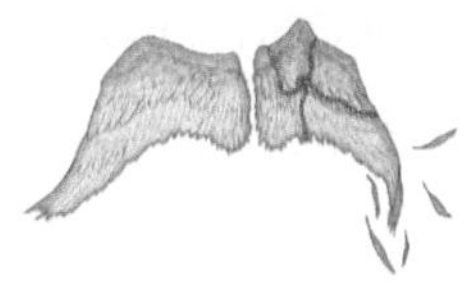

"10,387. 10,388," Riordan mutters with each step he takes in his cell. He can't be sure how much time has passed since they collected Theia, but judging by the wear pattern on the floor, it was some time ago.

Why is this taking so long? Riordan's stomach tightens into a knot as his mind turns to Theia. How hard is it to remove one Nephilim's head? He'd have done it for them if they asked. Gladly.

He closes his eyes as he clenches his fists. Why couldn't they do it? It would take less than a minute to decapitate her. Just pull out a sword and make the cut.

Riordan shakes his head to dispel the image. Theia's hair would tangle. A pool of blood would spread beneath her lifeless body as the rest of her body followed her head to the floor. Soon, the god-awful stench of burned flesh would fill the air. *What I wouldn't give to see that.*

Riordan runs his fingers through his hair, tugging at the sparse strands as he tries to hold on to his sanity. He feels a sense of panic welling up and knows he'll lose his mind if he doesn't act quick.

"They are requesting your presence in the Great Hall."

The familiar voice rounding just out of sight perks Riordan's attention.

His Goulidair guard casts a quick look at him through the bars of his cell, his confusion clear. "But I was told-"

"Don't worry. Another guard is on its way to replace you."

Indecision wars over its strong marble face, his gray eyes bouncing between them. "If that is the order," he mumbles after a moment.

Riordan smirks, knowing that the Goulidair guard has no choice but to obey. He stands up, stretching his arms and legs, feeling the tension in his body ease slightly.

It seems the Council has finally come to their senses. They've realized the error of their ways and are finally going to let him take care of Theia once and for all. He can feel the excitement build up inside him as his guard slips from the room.

"The Council has voted to spare the Nephilim."

Riordan rocks back on his heels, heat flushing his face. "No. This is a joke."

"We don't joke."

"Even after everything it's done?"

"Yes."

"And what about the Seraph? Aric? Is he getting a free pass too?"

"Both the Nephilim and Aric will remain under our protection."

Riordan throws his head back, a low growl rising in his throat as he feels the anger unleash itself. "They're protecting it?"

Riordan glares at his accomplice. Their relationship is an odd one, but lately, it's been more like a partnership than a master-servant relationship. "They can't release it."

"It's true. It will go back to Earth. Sylvie will be returning with it to keep the Council appraised of any further threats it poses."

Riordan clenches his fists and whips around to face him, their faces almost touching as he opens his mouth to protest, but his captor holds up a hand to silence him.

"If you're going to act. You'll need to move fast. It won't take them long to figure out where you're heading."

As he pulls a key from the depths of his robe, Riordan's eyes glitter dangerously.

Snatching the key from his accomplice's hand, Riordan unlocks the door to his cell, his heart beating fast with anticipation. He has a plan, and it's one that will finally put an end to Theia and Aric's existence. They may have been spared by the council, but that doesn't mean they're safe.

"I'm going to need soldiers," Riordan whispers.

"You'll have them."

The tension in the air is palpable as Riordan dons his armor, feeling the rush of adrenaline coursing through his veins. He's going to finish what he started, no matter what the cost. The thought of Theia's painful screams is almost too much to bear.

CHAPTER 30

As Theia busies herself with setting up the guest room for Sylvie, Aric finds himself contemplating the last couple of days.

From hunted, to tortured and then standing before the Council, Aric's fairly sure the entire ordeal has taken a few hundred years from his life.

Soon, the poisoned memories will curl its way around his heart like a snake squeezing tighter and tighter every day. Already, the infection festers within him, threatening to consume and ruin all that he loves. Unless he takes action soon, the only option left will be to cut out the darkness once and for all. He refuses to let it get that far.

Striding to the kitchen, Aric fills a glass with water and drinks it in a few frenzied gulps. Theia deserves better, he muses. *Get a handle on it.* His brain reminds him, though his hands still continue to shake.

Trading the water for bourbon, he pours himself a shot and dumps it down his throat. The rich liquid is smooth as it burns a path towards his stomach. Refilling the glass, he savors the lingering burn on his tongue as it soothes the stiffness in his body. He's vaguely aware of of someone entering the room before Sylvie speaks.

"Might want to check on your Nephilim."

"Theia," Aric grinds out, his voice brittle. "And what's wrong?"

Sylvie's head tips, dropping bright purple locks across her brow and over one eye. "The council spared her, but you'd be a fool to believe Riordan is going to let this go."

Aric's stomach lurches at the mention of Riordan's name. Just the thought of him coming for Theia clouds his judgement. "Riordan's in a cell," he says aloud to remind himself as much as Sylvie.

"For now."

"What does this have to do with Theia?"

"If he comes for her, she won't be ready," Sylvie insists, her voice thick with something Aric can't quite put his finger on. "She needs to be resting, not changing out already clean bedding."

"I'll talk to her." Aric nods and makes his way toward the guest bedroom.

Despite the tension between them, Sylvie and Theia have been civil towards each other since their arrival. He knows Theia is still distrustful of Heaven's intentions and perhaps rightly so, but at least they're working on it.

He glances at Theia from the corner of his eye as she rummages through a chest of drawers. Unbound, her long dark hair flows down her back, the large patch of silver catching his eye. The voice in the back of his head reminds him to watch her over the next few days. While her hair will never return to normal, she'll need plenty of rest to keep from burning out the rest of her essence.

She's lost a little weight since the last time he saw her, but she's still so beautiful it almost hurts.

He studies her from the door of his bedroom as Theia turns to face him. Eyes the color of some of Earth's deepest oceans, Aric happily drowns in their depths, regard him quietly. Her mouth set in an unread-able expression.

"Everything okay?"

Theia's eyes dart for a second to the side, the muscles in her face tensing. "Yeah. Just trying to find pillowcases that match."

"Uh-huh."

Eyes narrow as her chin notches. "What?"

"Nothing. Pillowcases are important."

"Don't patronize me, Aric."

After taking a deep breath, he crosses to the bed beside her. "Then tell me what's eating at you."

"The Council has voted to spare me."

"And?"

"And I'd be lying if I said that it should matter," she clips. "Why do they get decide if I should die or not?"

Snatching one of her hands, Aric holds it between both of his. "They don't." *Wow, she's warm,* he muses. Pressing his hands tighter together, the heat rolling off her skin trips an alarm. "Are you okay?"

"I'm just tired."

Aric stands and brushes her hair back from her forehead. When the heat emanating from her skin singes his fingertips, Aric resists the im-pulse to pull away. With a sharp hiss, he scoops her off her feet amidst a shower of weak protests and carries her to the master bedroom.

"Aric," she mumbles, her eyes glassy and unfocused. "I'm capable of walking."

I'm an idiot! The weight of the past few days has been crushing her into submission, and he hasn't even noticed. Her lungs are struggling for breath as she pushes her exhausted body ever onward, determined to carry on despite her exhaustion.

"And you do it so well, I can't help but enjoy the sight," Aric mur-murs.

Setting her down gently on the bed, he pulls the covers to her chin and tucks her in. Letting his hands linger for a second, he brushes a whisper soft kiss across her lips.

The fire of desire roars to life inside Aric's gut, electrifying his veins with anticipation. Lustful images of Theia prance through his mind; her long hair splayed across the sheets, her body inviting and ready to be taken. With a will of its own, his body aches to obey the call, but she needs sleep more than anything else. He takes a few steps back, determinedly ripping away from temptation.

Just then, her hand shoots out to latch onto his arm. "Stay with me."

Aric's heart skips a beat as Theia's fingers curl around his arm. He turns to look at her, and in the dim light of the room, he can see the exhaustion etched into her features. He can feel the heat emanating from her body, the scent of her skin filling his senses. It's not just desire that pulses through him now, but a deep, overwhelming need to protect her from the world.

"Of course," he says, his voice low and gentle. "I'll stay with you."

Climbing into the bed beside her, he pulls Theia into his arms, holding her tightly against him. She snuggles in closer, her head resting on his chest, as he runs a hand through her hair. The room is silent except for the sound of their breathing, mixed with the soft patter of rain against the window.

"Aric?"

"Hmm?"

"I need to ask you something."

The hand he runs along the slope of her back stills momentarily with the somber tone of her voice. "Anything."

She shifts slightly, tucking herself even closer into him. When he peeks down, he can see her teeth abusing the corner of her mouth. The familiar trait acts like an elephant on his chest. "What is it, little bird?"

"When I was waiting in that cell, Riordan said something."

"I'm sure he said a lot of things."

"True," she succumbs to a yawn that swallows half her face before nuzzling back against his chest with a sleepy sigh. "He showed me the night my mother died."

Aric's grip on Theia tightens at the mention of her mother's death. He remembers the day vividly. "What did he show you?" he asks, his voice gentle.

Theia takes a deep breath, her body shivering. "He showed me who killed her. You."

Aric's heart sinks at the revelation. He had suspected as much, but hearing it confirmed only makes it worse. His heart clenches in his chest as Theia's words sink in.

"But there was something about it that felt off," she continues, her finger drawing a lazy circle near the column of his neck. "Like a video that people doctor, and blast to show their version of events."

"I don't know what he showed you, love. I failed her, yes. But I promise you, your mother did not lose her life by my hand."

"How did you fail her?"

"I couldn't get there in time to stop the fanatical monster that lives in Riordan's head." Kissing the top of her head, Aric inhales the scent of her hair. "For that, I am sorry."

Theia is silent for a moment before speaking again. "I believe you," she says, her voice barely a whisper. "But why did he show me that? What's his game?"

"He's a conniving snake who will stop at nothing to have his way!" Aric seethes, heart pounding furiously as he considers Riordan's merciless machinations. "He knows you are my world, and he is trying to poison our bond with lies."

"This isn't some silly storybook full of cheesy fairytales, Aric." After another yawn, she drags a finger across the corner of her eye. "Just because someone says it doesn't make it true."

"Thank you for believing in me," Aric whispers and tightens his arms around her. "Now, get some sleep, little bird."

Minutes later, her breathing evens out as she finds the rest her body sorely needs. Aric lay there, his mind reeling as he considers what their future holds.

He watches her for a few more moments, his heart heavy with guilt and regret, before closing his own eyes and letting sleep claim him as well.

In his dreams, he sees her mother's face, twisted in agony as she takes her final breath. He sees himself, too late to save her, and Riordan standing over her body, a twisted smile on his lips.

He wakes up with a start, his heart racing. Glancing down at Theia, he relaxes to see she's still asleep in his arms. Unfortunately, the soft knock on the bedroom door makes further sleep for him impossible.

When the door inches open just enough to allow Sylvie's head to peek through the crack, he exhales loudly.

After another glance at Theia, he gently extricates himself and slips from the room. "What is it?"

"It's Riordan," she says, her voice low and ominous. "He's escaped."

Ushering her away from the bedroom door, Aric stops when they reach the living room. "What do you mean he's escaped?" He demands, his voice rough with concern.

"He's gone, Aric," Sylvie says, her eyes flickering with an eerie glow. "And he's coming for you and Theia.

"How in the hell did that happen? There are sigils in place to keep this very thing from happening?"

"He didn't break out, Aric. Someone let him out."

Aric's heart sinks at the news. Riordan is dangerous but that someone would help him escape creates a bigger problem. To bypass the Gouldair, it'd have to be someone with a lot of power.

"We need to go after him." Sylvie says, her tone resolute.

"No need," Theia says from the doorway, her voice thick from sleep. "He'll come for me. We just need to decide where that will be."

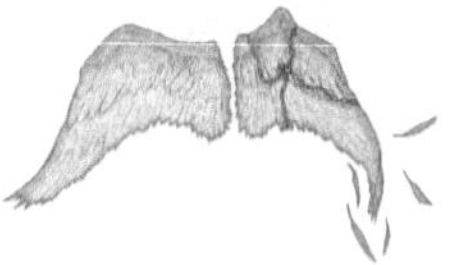

"Can I just say again for the cheap seats how amazingly stupid this is?" Colin mutters while digging a misshapen pack of cigarettes from his pocket.

Theia rolls her eyes as Colin's words echo off the thin metal walls of the abandoned warehouse. "We have no choice," she says, her tone clipped. "We have to be ready for him."

"You know I'm all for taking down Riordan, but this is insane," Colin grumbles before he lights his cigarette and takes a drag. Smoke curls around his face like a noxious cloud. Theia wrinkles her nose as the first of several sneezes threatens to escape.

Aric steps forward, his eyes flashing with determination. "Riordan has to be stopped," he says.

Julian nods in agreement. "Riordan is a threat we can't ignore."

"He's going to come for me," Theia adds in a lighter tone. "We'll be ready for him when he does."

Colin arches a brow. "What's to stop him from showing up right now and slaughtering us all like cattle?"

"Sylvie raised a protection spell on the warehouse," Aric explains, his lips twitching with a crooked smile.

The group falls into a tense silence, each lost in their own thoughts. Theia can feel the weight of their gazes on her, the pressure of their expectations weighing heavily on her shoulders. She can't shake a nagging feeling itching just under her skin. *This will be the battle I lose.*

Aric's gaze locks with hers, and his hand tightens possessively around hers. His grip tightens and surges with electricity, igniting a warmth that courses through her veins like a wildfire. Instantly, it creates a warmth that radiates from the depths of her soul.

Giving Sylvie an abrupt nod, she says the words that fall like lead between them. "Drop the spell."

Sylvie hesitates for a moment before nodding her agreement. Theia feels the heavy weight of the spell being lifted and the cold rush of air that fills the warehouse. She shivers as the sounds of the night filter in, the rustling of leaves and the distant sounds of traffic filling the space.

The group stands in tense silence, waiting for Riordan to appear. Theia's heart races in her chest, her palms slick with sweat. She can feel Aric's hand trembling slightly in hers, his own nerves betraying him.

Minutes tick by, but there is no sign of Riordan. A creeping sense of unease travels up her spine, a sense that something is horribly wrong. Just as she is about to voice her doubts, a dark shadow moves in the corner of her vision.

"He's here," she whispers, tightening her grip on Aric's hand.

The group falls into a defensive formation, weapons drawn and ready. Colin takes another drag from his cigarette, his eyes flickering back and forth between the two of them before crushing it out under the sole of his boot.

Closing her eyes, Theia takes a deep breath and lets the power inside her stir. It's there just beneath the surface; steadfast and sturdy, coursing through her veins like liquid fire. She has had the power inside her all along, waiting for this precise moment to be fully unleashed.

With a slow exhale, Theia opens her eyes and fixes her gaze on the shadowy figure emerging from the darkness.

Riordan steps into the light, a wicked grin playing at the corners of his lips. "You thought you could hide from me?" he taunts, his voice echoing off the metal walls of the warehouse.

Aric laughs. It's a humorless sound, but it still draws goosebumps over Theia's bare arms. "Who says we're hiding?"

"That's good," Riordan prattles softly. "It makes our job so much easier."

A deafening rumble erupts from within the walls as he summons nearly a hundred warriors into battle. Group by group, angelic figures spill out into the room, marching like a tidal wave of divine retribution that imprisons her friends in its center. The clanging of armor and pounding of feet fill the air with an unbridled ferocity.

Theia sets her jaw, readying herself for what's to come. She can feel Aric beside her, his own power sparking and crackling in the air. There is a moment of pure stillness, a moment where everything seems to freeze in place, before the battle begins in earnest.

Aric moves first, his blade flashing in the dim light as he charges towards Riordan. Theia follows close behind, her own sword glinting in the moonlight streaming in through the tall windows. Colin and Julian flank them, their weapons at the ready as they face down the horde of angels that have descended upon them.

The sound of clashing swords and the screams of the dying fill the warehouse as the group fights for their lives against Riordan's army of angels.

Theia's heart races with adrenaline as she fights for her life. Her powers surge within her, a never-ending well of energy that she draws upon to defend herself and those she loves.

The screams of the warriors fill the air with a primal fury, matched only by the fierce determination in Theia's heart. She moves with fluid grace, her body a deadly weapon as she battles against Riordan.

Shielding her back from anyone hoping to seize a victory, Aric battles the onslaught. His own power flares to life in a burst of lightning that crackles through the air like a whip.

Theia ducks and weaves, her sword moving in a deadly dance as she deflects blow after blow. She can feel the heat of Aric's presence behind her, his own blade striking true as he cuts down angel after angel.

Colin is a blur of motion, his knives flashing in a surge of power as he takes down warrior after warrior. Julian's own skill is a thing of beauty, a shimmering force field that deflects the blows of his attackers with ease.

The battle rages on, the group fighting with a fierce determination that leaves them drenched in sweat and blood. The air is thick with the scent of iron and the sound of metal biting against metal. Theia's arms ache with the effort of keeping her sword aloft, but she refuses to give in. She's aware that surrendering will cause the loss of everything.

Riordan is a blur of motion, his sword flashing as he uses his strength to overpower her. Their swords clang together in a shower of sparks that dance across the air like fireflies.

When he falters, Theia sees an opening and takes it, her sword slicing through the air as she charges towards Riordan. "You can't defeat me," he taunts, pushing against her with his own blade. Theia grits her teeth, her arms straining as she drives him back.

Just then, something shifts within her. A sudden surge of power that swims through her veins, filling her with a strength she never knew she had. Theia pushes back against Riordan with all her might, and he stumbles backward with a surprised grunt.

Pressing her advantage, she lunges forward with her sword. Riordan tries to dodge, but her reflexes are quicker.

Theia's face twists into a mask of blind rage as her blade finds its mark, sinking deep into his chest. A look of disbelief crosses Riordan's face before he crumples to the ground. Blood flows freely from under his hand, falling in thick red rivers across the stained concrete.

Instantly, the sound of battle swords fades. Without a word, angels return to Heaven one by one.

Theia stands there, her chest heaving with exertion, her sword still held tightly in her hand. The weight of what she has done settles heavily on her heart as she watches the last of the angels disappear. The silence in the warehouse is palpable, broken only by the sound of their ragged breathing.

Aric's hand reaches out to touch her shoulder, and it's only then that she realizes she's shaking. She turns to face him, seeing the concern etched into his features. "Are you okay?" he asks softly.

"Yes," she mumbles. Pinning her burning eyes on Riordan, she watches him battle for each breath. "No."

"Y-you think you've w-won?" Riordan rasps between breaths.

"I think that's what it means when it's your blood painting the floor," Theia challenges. "Not mine." She looks up to see Julian and Colin standing a few feet away, their weapons still at the ready. They exchange a wordless nod of understanding before sheathing their weapons and moving to join Aric and Sylvie a few feet away.

Theia stands there, panting and covered in sweat and blood, counting every breath Riordan wrangles. *Won't be long now.* The weight of the sword in her hand hangs from her fingers like an anchor. A weapon now stained with the blood of her enemy.

Riordan's eyes begin to darken and glitter, his lips twisted into a cruel sneer as power skitters across the floor. Too late, Theia recognizes his last stand for what it is. Murder-suicide.

Panic flows freely as she realizes what Riordan is about to do. "No!" she screams, lunging towards her friends. The energy from Riordan's last act explodes in a fiery blast that engulfs him and everyone else in the vicinity. The force of the blast tears across the room at her friends and family, giving Theia no other option but to react.

Gripping her fists tightly, she throws out both arms with all her might. With a harsh scream, she channels every bit of power into a wall of energy to stand between them and the fiery mass barreling toward them. The heat radiates off the flames and swirls around their bodies like an inferno, ravenous for destruction. Every second counts as the crackling sound of fire reaches its crescendo.

Theia grits her teeth and focuses all of her power into the shield, willing it to hold as the flames lick and claw. Despite the heat burning her skin, Theia persists. Dropping to her knees, she digs deeper.

She can hear the muffled sounds of her friends' cries of pain and fury behind her, reach her ears, but she can't afford to turn around. Holding the wall in place falls to her.

Suddenly, there's a surge of power within her, a force that she can't quite control. It pushes through her, filling her with a strength that she's never felt before. Theia grits her teeth as she applies it to the wall. Growing stronger and brighter with each passing second, Theia resorts to looking away.

When she drops her eyes to her hands, she blinks to find Aric's large hands covering hers. His light blazes, enveloping her like a cocoon and strengthening her own power tenfold. His essence surges through her veins like a raging river, pushing her own strength to its limits until she feels as if she might burst from the intensity of it.

With a last burst of energy, the wall holds strong against the fiery onslaught. When the flames sputter and eventually die out it leaves them all battered and singed, but alive.

Theia collapses to her knees, the weight of what just happened crashing down on her. Tears stream down her face as she looks around at the destruction wrought by the battle. The warehouse is in shambles, the bodies of the fallen littering the floor like burned and broken dolls.

Aric's arms wrap around her, pulling her close as they both take in the devastation before them. "You did it," he whispers, his voice trembling with emotion. "You saved us."

Theia nods, her throat tight with unshed tears. "But at what cost?" she asks, her voice barely above a whisper. The moment carries a sense of finality, as if they've reached the end of something that cannot be undone. Beside her, her sword rests on the ground, stained with blood. "So many died. And for what?"

Aric brushes his thumb over her damp cheek, his eyes filled with a fierce love. "That isn't your fault."

Once the adrenaline fades, Theia's body aches with a pain that goes deeper than just the physical. She's lost so much since this all started, and there's no going back to the way things were before.

"Theia," Aric calls, framing her face with his hands. "Do you hear me?"

Theia nods, her heart aching with grief. "I just wish there was another way," she mumbles.

"I know," Aric murmurs, pulling her into a tight embrace. "But sometimes, there isn't. Sometimes, you have to fight for what you believe in, no matter the cost."

Pressing her face against his chest, Theia drowns herself in his scent. "Let's go home."

EPILOGUE

Aric stops in the doorway as Theia rinses the plate under a steady stream of water. Setting it in the rack with the rest, she moves on to the pots and pans.

It's been months since Theia and her grandmother moved in and he still marvels at the sight of her so relaxed in his home.

With a soft hum, she dances lightly on the balls of her bare feet, drawing his attention to the pale pink painted toenails. Her jeans hug in all the right places. Their faded denim is a tribute to the countless washes. The tails of her lilac purple racer back fall just below her belly button, allowing small strips of skin to tease him. Each muscle in her back quivers and twitches with such a mundane task.

While he'd been gone, she gathered the length of her hair into one of those messy piles he loves so much. He recalls her dismay when, a day or two after facing Riordan, her chocolate curls changed to a dark silver. She's spent months using one brand of dye or another to restore her hair to its natural color.

Stepping up behind her, Aric wraps his arms around her waist. Her sharp gasp brings a smile to his lips as he trails them across one bare shoulder. "You're stunning."

"Perhaps you're biased," Theia answers with a soft chuckle before she turns off the water and leans into the wall of his chest.

"Found this under the sink," Aric begins, setting a full box of the latest brand of hair dye next to the dish rack. Under his hands, Theia tenses slightly. A peek over her shoulder confirms she's chewing her lip silently.

Turning her gently in his arms, Aric traps her between him and the sink as he eases her lip from between her teeth. "As much as I love to watch you do that, I wish you wouldn't abuse your lips." Dipping his head, he brushes a kiss to the slightly swollen corner her teeth leave behind.

The instant she melts into his touch, Aric pulls back with a groan. *Can't fall off track.* Theia has become an expert at distracting him with a touch, and this conversation is long overdue. "I love you."

"I love you too," she whispers thickly, her voice rough with desire.

Aric gives his head a shake. "No, no. I love all of you. Even your hair, little bird." The moment she figures out where this conversation is heading, her eyes darken. "You could color it green and I'd still love you."

"I know."

"So why are you still wasting your money on hair color?"

Theia bristles. "Believe it or not, most women don't buy beauty products, so men will love them."

"That's fair. Why then?"

"I hate looking at it."

"Why?"

One shoulder shrugs as she twists a finger in the soft flare of her shirt. "All it does is remind me of that night. Sylvie said that much power should've killed me."

"But it didn't," Aric argues. Using a finger, he tips her chin up to force her eyes to meet his. "Instead of letting it remind you of the bad, let it remind you of incredible strength. Because when I see it, all I remember is your bravery and determination to save the people you care about."

"Really?"

Aric's heart squeezes at the soft sound of insecurity in her voice. Dropping his head once more, he places another kiss on her lips. "Absolutely."

"Sorry to interrupt." Aric sighs at the familiar voice in the doorway. Peeking over his shoulder, he gives Maria a warm smile. "I settled Ellie for the night, so I'm going to take off."

Squirming out of his embrace, Theia dries her hand on a small towel and gives their in-home nurse a bright smile. "Thanks, Maria. We'll see you on Monday." Her grin grows mischievous as she turns back toward the sink. "I'm going to check on Granny. I believe it's your turn to dry."

"What did I miss?" Balancing the bowl of popcorn in one hand, Aric takes a seat beside her on the couch.

Theia peeks under the fringe of her lashes, a small smile playing at the corners of her lips. "Not much," she says, reaching for a handful of popcorn. "Just the beginning of the movie."

Aric nods, his eyes flickering to the screen as the opening credits roll. But his attention is only half on the movie. He's too distracted by the warmth of Theia beside him, the way her body seems to fit perfectly against his.

His fingers curl into fists so tight that his nails bite into his palms, leaving crescent-shaped marks on his skin. The urge to yank her hair free from its carelessly arranged confines grips him with a fierce intensity. He can imagine each strand cascading around them like a liquid metal, igniting every nerve in his body with a searing passion that borders on obsession.

Taking a breath, he lifts a shaky hand to brush a strand of hair from her face, his fingers lingering against her cheek. "Damn it hurts to look at you," he murmurs, his voice low and husky.

Sitting so close, Aric catches her breath hitching in her chest a moment before her eyes darken slowly. "Don't use that voice on me," she laughs before shoving a handful of popcorn into her mouth. "You're the one that wanted to watch this."

"I did," Aric grins. "Now I want to watch something else."

Before he can press the matter, her nose crinkles softly. "This needs salt."

After popping a kernel or two in his mouth, Aric chuckles. "It's fine."

Theia raises an eyebrow, a mischievous glint in her eyes. "Are you sure?" she asks, leaning closer until their faces are just inches apart. "Because I have a feeling that I can make it taste even better."

Aric's heart hammers in his chest as he watches her lick her lips, her gaze never leaving his. Between the heat radiating off her body and the sweet scent of her skin mingling with the buttery aroma of the popcorn, he's lost. It takes all of his willpower not to grab her and kiss her senseless.

Instead, he leans even closer, his lips brushing against her ear. "Show me."

With a knowing smile, Theia closes the gap until their lips barely brush. A quick inhale of breath sneaks between them before she jumps off the couch with a laugh. "Salt." Spinning on one foot, she runs to the kitchen.

"You're a horrible person," he growls. Aric's heart skips a beat as he stares into the opening scene, not comprehending a word of it. He snatches for the remote to hit rewind when an unseen force ricochets around the living room.

Every nerve in his body stiffens as he frantically scans for the source of power. His stomach flips over and over until a piercing scream comes from Theia, halting the search.

"Aric!"

Jumping over the arm of the couch, he runs towards the kitchen, dreading what awaits him.

In all her regal glory, Councilor Rebecca stands in their kitchen, her eyes swimming with tears. Rushing forward, Aric wraps a protective arm around Theia's shoulders as she clutches the salt shaker tightly in an iron grip.

"Forgive my intrusion," Rebecca says, her voice heavy with urgency. "This couldn't wait."

"What's happened?" he demands, his voice straining.

Rebecca's gaze flickers to Theia before returning to him. "We've determined Gregory is the one behind Riordan's escape."

As Theia's face pales, Aric's grip on her shoulder tightens. "Are you certain?"

"I'm afraid so."

After exchanging a glance with Aric, Theia gives her head a shake. "Why?"

"We don't know for sure," Rebecca admits. "Something is brewing. I can feel it."

"What do you need us to do?" Aric asks, his voice steady despite the rolling emotions inside him.

"We need you both to be ready."

Theia looks up at Aric. Eyes darken in gradual degrees before her jaws tighten. "We've been ready since the day you voted to spare my life," she says, her voice firm.

Aric nods, his jaw clenching as he thinks of the danger he's putting Theia in. Again.

As Rebecca disappears from the kitchen, a sense of dread settles in the pit of his stomach. Gregory is a formidable opponent. That he was behind Riordan's escape only confirms his worst fears.

"I need to call my dad."

Aric pulls Theia closer to him, holding her tight against him as he breathes in the calming scent of her skin. "We'll do whatever it takes to bring an end to this."

Theia nods, her eyes shining with an unspoken understanding. "Together," she says, her voice unwavering.

But even as he holds her close, his mind races with thoughts of the impending danger. Gregory is cunning, powerful, and vengeful. He won't stop until he gets what he wants.

They have to be ready. They have to be prepared for anything that comes their way. Because this time, they might not come out unscathed.

ABOUT THE AUTHOR

Sarah is a Michigan native, living in Northern Iowa. A mother of four, she still copes with the idea her youngest is in college. Married seventeen years, Sarah and her husband learned quickly that communication, laughter, and resisting the impulse to maim makes their marriage work. He continues to be one of her most energetic cheerleaders.

Writing had been a secret passion of hers since high school, after an English teacher knocked the dust off. While being the typical stay at home mom, she took classes and workshops to refine her skills. After a lot of anxiety, and a bout of self-doubt, she's excited to introduce the characters that live in her head to the world.

When she's not writing, she's a grandmother of four granddaughters and a soon to be grandson, as different as the seasons. Between the rambunctious nature of children and the neurotic nature of her three Great Danes, life is interesting. If asked, she'll tell you she loves every minute of it. Even if some of those minutes result in ice cream, buckets of coffee and a little solitary confinement.

www.ingramcontent.com/pod-product-compliance
Lightning Source LLC
Chambersburg PA
CBHW030920300726
48970CB00001B/248